"*A Midnight Dance* is an immersive read set in the glittering world of the Victorian ballet, where nothing is as it seems and even the familiar echoes with secrets. With an ability to create characters who twirl right into our hearts, Politano has written a story that is at once deeply atmospheric, yet grounded in the universal ache to belong and be loved. A gently charming romance seamlessly weaves through Ella's quest to unravel the mystery of her past. And underscoring it all is a hymn of praise to the One who spins beauty and art with a wave of his hand. A book I plan on reading again and again."

Kimberly Duffy, author of *A Mosaic of Wings*
and *A Tapestry of Light*

Praise for *The Love Note*

"Politano returns with a lovely Victorian saga of love lost and found. Wholesome characters pining for true love and winsome twists keep the mystery unresolved until the very end. Fans of Victorian inspirationals will love this charming effort."

Publishers Weekly

"Politano presents a well-crafted story about the healing power of words and genuine love in this satisfying, inspirational love story."

Booklist

"*The Love Note* is a passionate, faith-driven novel that incorporates a beguiling tale of loss and redemption."

Foreword Reviews

A Midnight Dance

Other books by Joanna Davidson Politano

Lady Jayne Disappears
A Rumored Fortune
Finding Lady Enderly
The Love Note

A Midnight Dance

JOANNA DAVIDSON
POLITANO

Revell

a division of Baker Publishing Group
Grand Rapids, Michigan

© 2021 by Joanna Davidson Politano

Published by Revell
a division of Baker Publishing Group
PO Box 6287, Grand Rapids, MI 49516-6287
www.revellbooks.com

Printed in the United States of America

Library of Congress Cataloging-in-Publication Data
Names: Politano, Joanna Davidson, 1982– author.
Title: A midnight dance / Joanna Davidson Politano.
Description: Grand Rapids, Michigan : Revell, a division of Baker Publishing Group, [2021]
Identifiers: LCCN 2021006659 | ISBN 9780800736903 (paperback) | ISBN 9780800740566 (casebound) | ISBN 9781493431816 (ebook)
Subjects: GSAFD: Christian fiction.
Classification: LCC PS3616.O56753 M53 2021 | DDC 813/.6—dc23
LC record available at https://lccn.loc.gov/2021006659

Scripture used in this book, whether quoted or paraphrased by the characters, is taken from the King James Version of the Bible.

Baker Publishing Group publications use paper produced from sustainable forestry practices and post-consumer waste whenever possible.

21 22 23 24 25 26 27   7 6 5 4 3 2 1

To my sweet daughter,
the little ballerina who dances with her whole heart
and often to her own rhythm.

The most beautiful moments of any ballet are the unscripted ones, yet we often waste these fleeting experiences by resenting their intrusion.

~Delphine Bessette, Craven Street Theatre

1

*H*e was so very *blue*. That was all my scattered mind could gather as he sailed past the window of Craven Street Theatre. Blue and sparkling under the glow of streetlamps that shone down the alley. I ended my three-point pirouette in demi-pointe with a soft landing in the quiet of the old abandoned room of the theater and stared again out the window, but he had vanished. Curiosity drove me to abandon my solitary practice as the second act carried on below, and I ran to the window for a better look.

Breeze from the broken window cooled my skin, rolling in pleasant waves over my too-warm body as I stepped out onto the balcony and looked down upon him, straining to see. He was a shining streak in the night, halfway down the alley, gauzy cape billowing behind him. A dancer, in full costume. How curious!

As the muffled music crescendoed below, several colossal ogres of men barreled around the corner of the Lamb and Flag Pub, jeers trailing them in the night. They cornered him with harsh, echoing laughter that vibrated off the walls. They meant to rob the man. I crouched out of sight behind the doorframe, hardly breathing. A man with one suspender holding up his dirty trousers smashed a gin bottle on the brick, advancing with playful thrusts like a sword. I shivered, anticipating the plunge of glass into flesh, but I could not look away.

Run!

But that dancer was trapped as a cornered pig, poor fool.

Why wasn't anyone coming? Another dancer, a passerby, a confounded bobby, for pity's sake? But everyone around was safely cocooned in the theater, and there was only me, way up here. The Almighty possessed a sense of humor, he did. Ella Blythe was not one for high places—especially approaching their edges.

I stepped out onto the balcony and forced myself to look down as I clung to the rail, my breath coming in thin gasps, prickly panic climbing my skin. I yanked off one beloved scarlet ballet slipper that had been my entire reason for sneaking in here tonight and held it up, but the men were too far away. Climbing upon the low brick railing, I poised myself and focused on the stair landing a little to the left and a few feet lower. One glance down and my vision blurred at the sides, the familiar panic cinching my ribs. Moisture tickled my skin.

Fear be hanged—it had to be done. I sprang and crouched into a soft landing, still gripping the precious red slipper.

I rose, and with a final goodbye squeeze, I whipped the shoe at them, satin ribbons rippling behind it. It struck the face of a pursuer and crumpled in the street. The sloshed assailant stumbled back, bracing for an unseen attacker in the darkness beyond the streetlamp's reach, then lurched off. The others hesitated, and in that brief uncertainty, the blue wraith slipped into the safety of the shadows.

I sank hard onto the stair landing and exhaled, trembling as I shoved hair off my face. Drunk as they were, it hadn't taken much to scare them off—just one of the enchanted red shoes. I slipped the other one off and clutched it close, then stole back inside to the forgotten old materials room, where I could be alone until I'd collected myself.

I pressed my face to the window glass, half afraid to see, but no one moved about in the alley. Only the strains of the *Nymphes des Bois* sounded from the ballet performance in the main auditorium, all the familiar sights and creaks of the old theater surrounding me, and my tension began to unspool.

The rest of London may have forgotten about this old room hidden away in the theater's side wing, with its dust-laden crystal chandeliers lying on their sides and silk faille draped over painted wooden clouds, but to me it was a sanctuary. A haven for my own private dances.

But there were footsteps in the corridor, echoing over hard flooring outside the room. Heart fluttering like a million trapped butterflies, I leaped behind a silk-draped ladder and crouched, barely daring to breathe. The door squealed open and there he was, filling the doorway, filling the room, his crepe de chine cape fluttering against his solid frame.

I didn't know anything about men. I seldom spoke to them. His presence here in my private sanctuary was unsettling.

He strode in like a lion, glancing about for his prey. Awed at my close proximity to him, I looked into his magnificent face from the shadows, the sculpted and dimpled features highlighted in the dim light. The grease paint tried to cover the ruddy glow of his skin, disguise the deep vibrancy of his expression, but it could only do so much. He moved on, then turned back, his roving gaze resting on me cowering like a little fool behind that ladder. I hadn't any idea what one was supposed to do with oneself in such a moment. Should I go to him? Smile and make introductions? How vulgar.

Well, I *was* in a theater just now. The rules were a bit different here.

He moved the silk aside like a curtain and smiled down at me. I wasn't prepared for the glorious sunshine that radiated from his masculine features. I rose, eyes still on him. Merciful heavens.

"Ah, here's my gallant rescuer." Rugged and warm at the same time, the man stood before me, my rescued shoe close against his chest.

My poor heart. It thrummed like a drum about to pop.

"I wanted to come up and thank you . . . and perhaps defend my masculinity." But his deep voice proved it aplenty. "I was in desperate need of a small drink before my part comes back in the third act, you see, and the theater's supply sprang a leak this morning. I hated to run into the pub this way, but there is nothing for it when one is dying of thirst and every spare hand is needed. Not unless I cared to scrape up what's leaked onto the cellar floor, which I didn't."

I worked my jaw as his voice echoed about the room, but my head was a scatter of random letters that refused to form words.

"That, of course, left me in the rather awkward position of dashing to the pub in costume during my off time in the second act, falling in with a pair of men deep in their cups, and thus being rescued by a . . ."

"Girl."

"Ah, you *can* speak." He folded his arms and looked intently into my face, his presence softened by dark, glossy hair that all fell over his forehead in one boyish twist. "So tell me, dear rescuer, what brings you so boldly into this haunted part of the theater? And how ever did you learn to spring and land like a cat?"

"I'm a dancer."

He raised his eyebrows in a way that somehow wasn't mocking, bless him. "Are you, now? That explains this." He held up my rescued shoe—that precious red slipper I desperately needed back. My hand itched to snatch it close. "I might have known it with a mere look, though. You wear dignity like a royal cape, even when you're afraid and hiding. Like an exotic wild animal, perhaps."

I had no answer for such a response. No one had ever looked at me and labeled what they saw as *dignity*.

"Which company do you dance with? Who is your manager?"

I stiffened. "N-no company. No manager." So many questions. I hated questions.

"You're a *petit ra*—forgive me, a member of the *corps*."

Miserable, I shook my head again. I was not even one of the lesser dancers onstage.

"I'm curious, then, what makes you call yourself a dancer?"

I looked at him solemnly, chin edging up. "Is art only validated by the presence of an audience?"

His eyebrows shot up, eyes flashing, and I knew I'd won his admiration—and that I was in trouble. One good look into his compelling eyes, I couldn't stop staring, couldn't keep my composure. They were magnets at the soul level. He moved closer, as if drawn, and I backed to the wall.

He slowed his approach. "Forgive me, but I simply don't know what to make of you. I've never heard of anyone willing to take on the label of a dancer without any of the spoils of the trade."

"I've never admitted it before."

"But you practice."

"Every day."

"Hmm." He shifted down onto his right knee, gaze still holding mine. "May I?"

I nodded, and he slipped the shoe onto my foot. Butterflies—oh, the butterflies. How beautifully that red slipper fit. It struck me again as his solid hands wound the laces, the small kindness wrapping itself around me.

I looked away. "Why must you stare? Haven't you seen enough?"

"It's just that . . . well, these do resemble a rather famous pair of slippers. One might wonder how you came to have them."

"Oh?" I focused my gaze on the floor beside him. He knew these shoes, of course. He had to. They were legendary.

"I'm speaking of the missing ballet shoes of the extraordinary Delphine Besseau." He watched my face.

"Oh." I tried to act properly astonished, but he'd gotten it wrong. It was *Bessette*.

He looked at me as if I'd stolen them, which I hadn't, thank you very much. Not exactly. Three weeks of extra wash I had done for the pleasure of having her slippers, my hands rubbed raw just so they could hold the gleaming satin shoes at last.

Mrs. Boffin, Craven's laundress, had scrunched up her face as she handed them to me only an hour ago, jamming a hair cloth back over her wiry wisps. "What do you want these for, anyway?"

I paid the woman my extra wages to filch them from that old underground dressing room long since abandoned, since everyone seemed to have forgotten about them, so that made them more mine than anyone's.

"Ain't none of my nevermind, but you ain't no dancer, Ella Blythe," she'd declared. "You're a regular churchgoer. A good girl, you are."

Good, indeed.

Supremely *good* was precisely how I felt as I slipped my foot into that other shoe, heart beating the rhythm as if it was already inside me, tapping away. Was dancing truly so divorced from God that they could not both be woven tightly into the fabric of the same girl? Something inside me resonated so deeply with the immensity, the vibrant beauty, of both. I had quite a weakness for beauty. Such as this man—the sight of him pulled at the core of me.

He tied off the slipper and rose, gaze still searching. "Did you know, she died in a tragic gaslight fire in this very room, a dozen years ago or so."

I knew.

"The room has been gutted and rebuilt, of course, but it used to be her private practice room, and was the place where she died. It's where people have claimed to see her ghostly figure, which is why you'll seldom find anyone in it."

I shuddered. "How awful." I knew the story, of course, but it still affected me with every telling. All but the brick shell had been pulled down and rebuilt throughout the entire theater, yet I could still sense the uniqueness that remained in this room. I always had.

"It's said she's looking for her famous red satin ballet shoes . . . and for poor Marcus de Silva."

"Marcus *who*?"

"De Silva. The man who supposedly killed her, of course."

My heart skittered, mind turning that name over. "How do you know all this?"

He laughed. "How do you not? Everyone in the ballet world, especially at Craven, has stories about being haunted by poor Delphine's ghost. She is known for her tragic end, and for her red slippers." He sobered, something odd flickering over his features.

He went back to studying me again in that terribly unnerving way. "Ones that look exactly like these." His gaze dropped toward the shoes, then at me, head tilted in question. Our gazes tangled and held, and I couldn't breathe. He lifted one hand as if to poke me. "I've never seen her, though. That is, until . . ." His fingertips brushed across my face, a whisper-soft movement.

I shivered again, then ducked away, flustered and speechless.

"Very well then, you're not a ghost." He continued to watch me, a sparkle of wonder dancing on the shiny blue surface of his face. "Care to try the shoes? I hear they're special—the secret to her legendary success."

Normally I'd refuse, but moonlight softened my reasoning. It cast an intoxicating glow over this man who saw the ballerina in me, melting my insecurities. He moved so close, his breath warm on my cheek, and I felt suddenly, for the first time, that I could not fail.

The evening's encounter with this stranger was brief but significant, sinking deep into my memories to remain forever bottled there—a most precious experience that would never quite seem real once we left this place. "All right, then." I took his hand and we moved toward an open space. He pulled me directly toward his solid frame, hands resting on my waist, and with a thrill I finally understood why the finer set of London declared dancing immoral.

I could smell whatever made his glossy black hair wave so perfectly across his forehead and feel his breath across the part on my scalp. I felt his heart beneath his shirt. The moment was dreamlike, separate from my fruitless days in the washhouse, and I could not turn away from the gentle frame of his arms, the promise of my first *pas de deux*—a partner dance that, for once in my life, included a partner.

Yet the minute we stepped into the muffled rhythm, moving through the familiar paces—*relevé, attitude* leg lift, *cambré* to the right—my defenses melted in the cool moonlight. This was not carnal—it was art, and it was sacred. My feet arched easily into tiny *pas de bourreé* steps forward, propelling me into a spin with foreign hands bracing my waist. He was self-assured but in an easy, gentle way. I became aware of my every curve in a manner that made me feel more alive, more comely, than I ever had before.

We danced through discarded scarves, thick cobwebs, and broken chairs, then he spun me with a lavish release, and the distant music of the second act twirled me up in its magic. I arched my back and glided into the familiar precision of ballet, feeling that glorious stretch again in my calves. I lifted the warm air with my arms, and I was off, spinning and gliding, my patched skirt flipping against my legs.

I twirled over and over, the world fading easily away around the face that held my focus with each turn. As the music below crescendoed and faded in its finale, I finished with a small spring, folded down, and rose with a gentle curved back, chest high, arms overhead. When my vision centered on his painted face, the astonishment there was absolute.

And utterly gratifying.

His clap split the silence as I caught my breath. A giant smile broke over his face and he stepped toward me, glancing at the shoes. "Perhaps they *are* enchanted."

I pushed stray hair away from my eyes. "As I told you, sir, I am a dancer."

That gaze was back on my face, studying. Assessing. "Indeed." His reply sank into the silence.

I sat to remove the slippers and replaced them with my well-worn work boots, wondering how I could possibly return to the washhouse at five the next morning.

He crouched before me, face vivid as if wanting to say more but not possessing the right words. I wasn't about to offer any information—he'd already gotten more out of me than most anyone ever had.

"You're quite blue." I nodded toward his costume, desperate to divert the focus.

"As the North Wind should be. Come to think of it, they'll be expecting me onstage with the third act, so I should take my leave. Such is the life of a dancer. It's a terrible flurry of—"

"Of wonderfulness." The words slipped out on a breath.

He paused, eyeing me. "Would you care to see it?"

My mouth hung open. "The *ballet*?"

"Come." Grabbing my hand, he pulled me out the door, into the dark corridor, then up narrow steps that led high into the rafters. "The third act will begin presently." He stopped me in a narrow passage and pushed open a tiny peep that looked down over the lavish royal-blue and ivory auditorium glinting with gold trim and muted gaslights, over the upswept hair and top hats and smartly glittering jewels in the audience.

I'd never seen it this way, so full and alive. "It's magnificent."

"I used to watch from up here at times. Just keep quiet and no one will know. And watch out for Delphine's ghost." He winked.

"*North Wind!* Get your sorry hide in here." The harsh whisper jolted through our quiet moment and the dancer sprang up. I cringed at the way the manager spoke to the stranger who'd been so kind to me, even though this level of rudeness was far too common in theater.

He paused and cocked a half smile, seeming to sense the longing he'd magnified in me. "How's about this? I'll put in a word, and we'll see where it gets you. One day we'll be dancing together on that stage. I vow it. Keep that focal point as you spin through your days, and don't stop dancing." With a salute, he spun in a whirl of sheer organza and crepe but quickly turned back, grabbing the doorframe. "Oh, and keep those shoes close, love. Wouldn't want anyone else knowing you have 'em."

Then he was gone, lighting like a gazelle down the stairs.

I stared down at the red shoes in my hands, fingering the perfect stitching along the soles. *Enchanted*, he'd called them. But as I flexed the tingling hand he'd squeezed, I wondered if maybe it wasn't the shoes.

Settling noises sounded throughout the auditorium as the intermission melted away, musicians cuing up, then the orchestra eased gently into the third act. Two callboys parted the heavy blue curtain, and I plastered my face against that little peep, my nose pressed into the rough pine-scented wood around it. The music thrummed and so did my heart, matching beat for beat, then the dancers leaped onto the stage from both sides, two by two, trailing flowered ribbons and spinning pirouettes. Color. Beauty. Artistry. Symmetry and grace. My heart unfurled as a blossom in spring.

The lead ballerina in bright red twirled into the center, her skirts whirling into a filigree flower around her. Amalia Brugnoli, favorite of the great choreographer Armand Vestris, had captivated my imagination since I'd glimpsed her through a window one day in the rehearsal room. Now here she was, dancing before me with acrobatic bursts and the most complex footwork I'd ever seen. I squinted at her tiny slippers—how was she doing this?

Everything about her was strength and perfection, from her smooth chestnut hair to her paces. Astonishment and jealousy wound in equal parts through my veins, thick with angst. With desire. When she landed in an *arabesque* and tilted to the right, the music rose to dizzying crescendos, and suddenly *there he was*—leaping with bold precision onto the stage, springing forth and spinning in the air, his powerful legs propelling him across the stage again and again.

His legs scissored above the other dancers, and he landed with a double spin on one knee, arms overhead, and swept back into the air with an effortless leap. I sucked in my breath. If ever I'd imagined that ballet damaged a man's masculinity, he disproved that notion in three beats of my heart. He was all muscle and control, skill and artistry—and such *power*. It oozed from him as he overtook the entire stage, the other dancers merely a background to his stunning performance.

And to think, I'd been in his presence—dancing alongside him.

I withered to the floor when the curtain shut, siphoning off my view of the most magical sight I'd ever witnessed, its intensity still sitting hard against my chest. Ballet was so much more real, more stirring and magnificent, than I'd ever realized. I was alight with more happiness than any devout member of St. Luke's Church had any right to feel inside a theater, but I couldn't help it. I straddled two worlds, my heart evenly divided.

I danced my way home through Covent Garden's crowded

streets and up the Strand, clutching the soggy program I'd managed to rescue from the gutter outside Craven. When I reached our home on dirty old St. Giles, I paused amidst distant shouts and banging doors to look through the paper for the name I desperately had to know.

North Wind ...... principal dancer, **Mr. Philippe Rousseau**

I gasped, cold fingers over my mouth, and read it over and over. Principal dancer. I had danced with the *principal dancer*.

I looked up at the tiny square window with its four panes of greenish glass, the wealth of moss slicking the walls of our building in this little Covent Garden side street that clung by a thread to respectability. A single errant flower dared to grow between the building's stones, and I plucked it, spinning that rare show of color between my fingers—beauty amidst poverty. *"One day we'll be dancing together on that stage. I vow it."*

Impossible as it seemed, I ached with a crushing desire for that promise to be true.

When I climbed the stairs, barely remembering to skip the broken one, dear Mum's warm smile greeted me, then Lily's sisterly scowl.

Poor Lily was a pretty, dimpled thing two years older than I, who'd been built for a life of pleasure and amusement, but fate had stolen her real mum years ago and left her stuffed with us in this little flat, a life that snuffed her dreams of men and gowns and coquetry. Her mum, a longtime costume designer who'd worked in the theater when mine was dancing there, had once dressed her daughter in fine leftover ribbons and paraded her about London. I was seven when her mother died, and Lily nine. Now here she was with us, stirring her specialty—*soup de scraps*—in a pot over the fire, charging me with her look for every minute of work she'd had to do in my absence.

I pinched back a grin as I clutched the precious shoes and program under my cloak. I met Lily's stare with a smile and spun her around with my free arm before bending to kiss Mama. "Happiest of birthdays, Mama. I'll finish that cake, I promise. But first, a gift for you."

Grinning so hard my cheeks hurt, I knelt before this gentle woman and placed the sacred shoes in her lap, ribbons spilling down over her knees. Weeks of extra work and secrecy . . . all for this.

And it was worth it. She blinked, mouth falling open and hands framing her face as tears swelled in her eyes. She dabbed them with the corner of her apron and lifted the slippers as if they'd been the crown jewels. "Oh, Ella. Child. Are they . . . ?"

"The very ones."

"Oh, but how—why . . ."

I shrugged with a little smile. "Merely returning them to their rightful owner."

2

She cradled them in her scarred hands, face radiant. "Heavens, child. Where did you find them?"

"You've told me a million times in a thousand stories where you kept them after every performance. Those underground dressing rooms are almost all that's left of the old theater, and there they were, just waiting to be enjoyed again."

The burn-scarred skin stretched tight over her cheekbones in a soft smile as she seemed to sink back into her memories—the theater, the stories, the telling of them to her girls in tender bedtime moments.

I laid my head on her lap, tracing the folds of her apron. "Won't you dance again, Mum? It would be so good for you."

Her hand rested on my hair. "I dance only for my precious girls now. Delphine Bessette is dead, my love."

Yet I felt Delphine Bessette's warm hand on my head. It caressed my scalp and communicated her deep love with every stroke. It hurt my heart to call Delphine dead, but in a way she was. A dancer is a rare artist, I've been told, because her art vanishes the moment she leaves the stage.

She hadn't even set foot outside in years, afraid someone

would know that the great *prima ballerina* of the London stage had survived the fire. Or perhaps, I now realized, it was a person she feared. "Who was Marcus de Silva?"

Her hand paused, fingers curling a little against my scalp. "Another dancer. Wherever did you hear that name?"

I felt her shift and knew her other hand would be creeping up her neck, absently feeling for that little birthmark near her shoulder. With all the strife we'd had in our life, she never did anything to reveal her worry to her girls . . . except that. I rose and took her fingertips off the worry mark, as we called it, and kissed them. "Was he jealous of you? Did you quarrel?"

"Let's not ruin this night speaking of such things. I mean to enjoy and savor your beautiful gift."

When we'd finished eating, she put on the slippers and danced around the mismatched furniture, my little fairy-mother spinning like the dancer in her music box. I opened the broken box and wound it with a hairpin, watching them both twirl. How could I help but love ballet? It was impossible not to be swept up in Mum's romantic charm as she danced about our dreary flat, our gray lives, and gave us a small taste of loveliness that was larger than our little home. It made the chipping plaster seem artistic, the close quarters cozy, the empty larder unimportant.

The flush of delight remained on her features through dessert, the pathetic little cake I was too excited to attend properly, and later followed her toward the curtained-off mattress where Lily and I slept. She bent to kiss each of us, even though we were fairly well grown, and her hand lingered on my face, that webbed burn scar on her palm smooth against my cheek. "Precious daughter. Thank you for a most perfect gift."

Lily rolled away from us and was soon breathing deeply. I sat up, the quilt scrunched over my knees, and dared to quietly voice the thought that had hovered all night, pleasantly glowing like a star through the smog. "Mum, I'm ready to join the theater. Next time they hold auditions for the corps, perhaps." I was fifteen already, far older than most beginning members of the *corps de ballet*, but I'd start anywhere just to be near the ballet.

Her pained shock halted my flow of excitement, and it melted in the face of her stony silence. She shook her head, loose wisps of hair dusting her pale cheeks.

"Whyever not?" Practice consumed me, the dire need to perfect and to polish, and she herself had trained me. Yet we'd never spoken of what would come of it.

She looked as though she'd cry as she fingered the loose strands of my hair. "No daughter of mine will be lost to the theater." She touched my cheek, her fingertips cold against my now-heated face. "We are so similar, you and I. Yet I want nothing more than for your story to be wonderfully different than mine."

I looked away from the softness of her gaze. We *were* different—she, with her gentle meekness that was both a strength and a downfall. Things happened *to* her. Me, I was just as quiet, but made of stronger stuff.

"It was one thing when you were a little girl, so excited about the world I'd come from. It was a joy to do it together, to teach you everything, but now that you're grown . . ."

"I love it even more. Love it enough to practice every day. Surely you see that. Even while I'm working at the laundry, I am strengthening my feet. Preparing. I'm ready to try, Mum."

She took hold of my shoulders, her glassy gaze holding mine. "I will not let the theater ruin you as it did me."

"I won't dance near a flame, I promise. It's—"

Her squeeze tightened. "It was not merely my skin that was ruined that night, my love."

I looked at this delicate woman and tried to picture her dancing before Princess Charlotte with flowers in her hair. I could see it, with her eternal grace and elegance, music in bodily form.

Yet now, no one but us were witnesses to it. Dancers who were not onstage were forgotten. What of the ones who never reached it?

"My story will be different." I spoke with conviction as I rubbed her arm. There was simply something at my core that was drawn to the beauty, the symmetry of ballet, and I felt compelled to be a part of it—to bring that loveliness and order to a world that seemed to have forgotten its value.

"Naught but God is strong enough to handle the burden of fame and praise."

"Well and good, because I want no part of that. I'm not one for spotlights anyway. Just to be in the midst of it all . . ." I considered her as my words faded. "They're creating all sorts of legends about you, you know. The great dancer, whose spirit still flits about the theater in search of her lost slippers."

She smiled and hugged the shoes I'd given her. "Well, then plain and tired Mary Blythe can sleep in peace tonight, no?"

I gave a wan smile. She had so many surnames—her true and legal married name, her maiden name, her stage name . . . yet she only used the assumed one we now all wore like a cloak to hide us: Blythe. We had for as long as I could remember. Yet I so desperately wanted something about me to be authentic and fully on display before the world. Especially if doing so would earn me enough money to bring her a comfortable life. "Won't you let me at least try, Mum? Just to be part of the corps would thrill me to no end."

Her smile disintegrated, and she rose without answering, disappearing through the curtain that surrounded our bed. I shifted, burying my face between the two pillows and centering my soul on the only father I seemed to have. *Please . . . Please . . .* was all I could get out in my prayer. He knew what I meant, for we'd had endless conversations about it already.

Soon I could hear Mama speaking to God at the table, those indecipherable utterances that always seemed to carry so much weight with the Almighty. Was she flat-out asking him for my failure? My stomach twisted. Never in my life had Mama and I prayed for opposite outcomes. I'd for sure be on the losing end of that match.

Yet Philippe Rousseau's promise lay awake in me, vivid and pulsing with life. It couldn't possibly come to pass without a true miracle, but I could not snuff the thing from my heart. The very notion had taken up residence there and lit a warm, glowing fire on a cold night.

In the morning, Mama hovered by the hearth as if she hadn't slept. When she saw me unplaiting my hair on the end of the bed, she opened her arms and welcomed me close, kissed my hair with trembling lips. Her presence was warm, always embracing with a look even before her arms came around me.

I buried my face in the honeyed scent of her arm. "You needn't worry so, Mama. Aunt Luce made certain we were raised in the church, and the theater can never make me what I am not." Lucy Kimball—Aunt Luce, as we called her—was someone from Mama's past, and the only other person besides Lily's mother whom she trusted. Aunt Luce had been our door to the outside world, coming to fetch us to market and to church every week.

"It isn't you I worry about, love." She combed her fingers along the hair trailing down my back, and I felt the ripple of her burned skin, the angry marks ballet had gifted to her. "Do you know why I never found out who set the fire all those years ago? Because there were so many people it might have been. I've found threatening letters, had my costumes mysteriously destroyed . . . You have no idea how many secret enemies a woman can have in the ballet if she's any good. Even among her supposed friends."

"That solves it, then. I shan't be any good, Mama. I vow it. Merely good enough to remain."

Another kiss to my hair as she held me close. "In the end, I don't think you'd be able to help it, love." She held me at arm's length. "No one would be able to miss your talent."

I shifted back, looking into her face to watch the play of tender emotions that always lived just below the surface. "Was it Marcus de Silva who did these things?"

She paled, those rosy lips the only bloom of color on her face. Carts rumbled by outside, feet pounding through the street as costermongers and drunken men called out as they stumbled home. "No. No, I don't think so," she said at last, but her pause was not lost on me.

"Was he a very important dancer? A thwarted suitor?"

A long, shuddering sigh. "He was your father."

A powerful weakness swept through my middle at that word, thoughts instantly fracturing. The lack of that particular person in my life had wound through my being with a taut thread of insecurity that left me anxious, always with something to prove.

"You see why you cannot be in the theater, Ella." She grasped my hand. "Life there is so complicated, so ugly. No one can be trusted, for they all want something—and they all know how to play a part."

"But you just said he *didn't*—"

"I said I didn't *think* so." She fiddled with the hem of her sleeve. "We ran away to be married, and we kept it secret. That's how much we loved each other. So I cannot imagine . . . But things between us were not so simple. Especially at the end."

"Perhaps I can find out if he did." For her as much as myself. She had silently tortured herself over this, it seemed—the unknown—for all this time. Closure would be a gift. "I've never met him, after all, so he wouldn't know me."

She straightened, giving a glimpse of the regal dancer she'd once been. "You will go nowhere near Marcus de Silva, Ella. He must never have a chance to find out who you are."

"Why ever not, Mama? You once gave up a great deal to marry the man, so I cannot understand why you will have nothing to do with him."

She laid a slender hand over mine. "This is how it must be. Will you do that for me?"

There was to be no father, no answers . . . no theater. I hesitated, but with the wan look on her face, I nodded. Of course I understood. I didn't *need* my father. Truly, I didn't. I was an independent soul. Fathers, for girls like me, were optional.

Truly.

But it came about that one day a miracle did occur and I returned to ballet, to Philippe Rousseau, and to Craven Street Theatre.

As a dancer.

3

*T*he silent question swept through the air in that pillared greenroom like the breath of Delphine Bessette's ghost—*Who is she?*

Perhaps returning to Craven had been a mistake. I couldn't dance with the special scarlet slippers here, for they'd surely be recognized. I glanced at my worn carpetbag against the wall, seeing the lump of them within—perhaps it was a bad idea to bring them back here too.

"Torso stacked. Body long." Signore Bellini, our formidable instructor, swept his arms up with dramatic arcs, as if to will our legs higher and straighter. "*Lift* from the legs and *explode* through the torso."

In neat rows we lifted and arched, leaning forward to brush the floor with our fingertips and rise as one. It was a beautiful, synchronized picture—and at last I was part of it.

"She certainly has poise," one whispered as we moved into *pliés* at the barre. I dared not turn to look.

"If that's what you call it," said another. "Where did she even come from? Look at her nose in the air."

I gripped the velvet-covered barre and focused, chin lifted. A hard ball of fear existed behind the poise—did they know that? Not one second of that day went by when I was not fully aware of the many years of formal training these dancers had over me, and that I was here by a mere fluke. An odd series of events. God's grace.

Sheer good luck.

The barre held my focused attention and I continued deep pliés, brushing the floor with my fingertips over and over, until the sun dropped low behind London and Signore Bellini released us from training.

The man took a cloud of tension with him when he left, and the room unwound, the air ringing with feminine chatter as dancers draped themselves across chaise lounges and discarded sashes, chitchatting and laughing amidst the after-dance stretches. Tulle and satin billowed everywhere, giving the room a celestial feel.

I leaned my lower back against the barre and glanced around at the coveted greenroom rich with dignity—its tall, papered walls; gilded mirrors on the east side; and marble columns rising to the ornately carved ceiling in the center. So much light and color, more than I'd imagined.

No, this wasn't a mistake. I'd been given one chance and I *needed* to be here. I felt the ache of it in my bones, ever since I'd received word of the scholarship. I'd had to give up the flat with Lily, leaving her behind in a rooming house with a job at a textile place, but this place felt like home. Dancing in this theater was a final link to my mother, now three years gone, and a chance to maybe—just maybe—catch the eye of my mysterious disappearing father. I'd promised not to find him, but I couldn't help it if he found *me*, now could I?

Then the double doors burst open and the gentlemen invaded, tall and swarthy *abonnés*, as they were called in Paris, with generous swaggers and a highly agreeable air as they looked us over, judging who was fit to be set up in a discreet flat in Westminster. I dropped my gaze to the scored floor as I continued to stretch, trying not to think about the men's wives—women bustling in earnest about their homes, maintaining warm sanctuaries and an efficient household, sadly believing their husbands belonged only to them.

I knelt before my worn carpetbag, digging aimlessly through the contents simply to dissuade the men from approaching. My fingertips found the satin of Mama's scarlet ballet slippers and I paused, caressing them and drawing them to the surface of my bag for a look. How I missed home, and Mama and Lily. I hadn't yet seen my adopted sister since returning from training in Paris.

I stiffened, feeling a presence behind me, someone's eyes on my back. I turned, and my gaze met that of a bent, aged woman collecting the shoes. Her face was gray with shock, gnarled hands trembling. I rose, dropping the red slipper back into the shadows of my bag and shoving it closed with my foot. With a small, strangled cry, she dropped her basket of slippers, satin laces tumbling across the floor. The room quieted and several others glanced her way.

The wrung-out old woman, clutching a slipper from the basket, stepped closer to me. Her head came only to my chin, but she stared up at me. "It's you." Her glassy eyes seemed to look everywhere and nowhere on my face.

I straightened, firm in the knowledge that I looked very little like my fair-haired mother. "You must have mistaken me for someone. I've only just arrived." She couldn't have seen the slippers. They hadn't even come all the way out of my bag. I attempted to comfort myself with that notion.

She inched closer, wonder on her bright little face, as if she hadn't heard a word. She reached gnarled fingers that shook with a sort of palsy and touched Mama's starfish pendant hanging from a black ribbon at my throat, her nails clinking against the metal jewelry. "I told them you were a survivor. No one ever listens to Maymie Dobbs now, do they?"

I held perfectly still, breathing in the scent of lye and talcum on her hands as my insides quaked. I had the sensation of approaching the mouth of a mysterious cave, and I had only to wait and blink as my eyes adjusted to see what lay in the gloomy dark. "Who are you?"

Then a man stepped near with the slick air of polished boot leather, positioning himself between me and the old woman. "A new one, are you?" He was playful and silky, his voice low. The older woman crouched out of the way, collecting her basket of slippers and hurrying away. I nearly reached out to touch her shoulder, but she was quick.

The man before me tipped his head toward me with interest. "Care for a—"

"I'm not for sale." I met his stare. I would not be brought to some discreet flat and made to belong to some stranger just for the sake of favorable standing in the ballet.

One eyebrow jerked up. "Just a friendly welcome. Perhaps you'd care for a small token of my admiration." He dug in his pockets, but I didn't wait to see what would emerge.

"What part of no wasn't clear?" I lowered my voice, pushing past him to run through the doors. I glanced about the gaslit corridor for the woman, old Maymie Dobbs, but she had vanished.

Returning to the greenroom with a pounding heart, I stood at the barre, back stiffly to the others. A golden-haired dancer who had been watching from her chaise lounge untangled herself from her companion and approached. She arched one arm overhead and stretched her heel to the barre, evaluating me thoroughly. "That was quite the performance."

"I didn't care for his behavior."

She cocked an eyebrow in a way that made me feel utterly found out. "Where on earth have you come from? Haven't you ever danced in a theater before?"

"I trained in Paris."

"Certainly our men are not as base as the French."

"Men are men in every theater. That doesn't mean I enjoy it."

"Why ever not? Doesn't it flatter you just a bit?"

"I'm not one for the attention of strange men."

"They're only strange until you let them close." She winked. Somehow she reminded me of Lily, which made me like her and fear her at the same time. "Oh come, don't look at me that way. I've formed an attachment with a count and I merely keep civil with the others. Attracting more bees with honey and all." She watched me with stunning blue eyes that refused to be ignored, her mouth pert. "I'm Minna Frank, by the way. How did you come to Craven? You seemed to appear out of nowhere. The others are mad with curiosity."

"I'm Ella Blythe. And . . . I'm here by sheer good fortune." I edged my chin up and returned to pliés, hands crossed over my pounding heart.

Her smirk was knowing. "Which gentleman came to your aid?"

"None." Well, not in *that* way.

"With whom did you train, then?"

"Coulon."

Her rosy lips parted. "Of the Paris Opera House?" She looked me up and down. "How ever did you manage that?"

It was a stroke of bad fortune for Craven that had led to a stroke of very good fortune for me, in the form of a scholarship. A free pass into some of the best training on the continent, followed by a promised contract to dance as a soloist, a member of the *sujet*, for Craven and no other theater. I still didn't completely understand how it had all come about. I'd never had anything free in my life. Even though I'd worked harder than anyone to keep up in Paris, I'd felt like a guilty cheat.

I opened my mouth to offer some vague answer, but a familiar figure crystalized in my distant vision. The breath left my lungs—*there he was*. Philippe Rousseau's easy manner set him apart from the lecherous men around, and it flooded my being with a cool mix of relief and pleasure to know he was as I remembered him. If only he'd come closer.

"Well, look at you, blushing like a girl in the schoolroom." She examined me with amusement sparkling in her eyes, now that she'd at last gotten the upper hand. For a moment, anyway. I couldn't tell yet if she had pegged me friend or rival. Perhaps a mix of both. "Where did they keep you in Paris—a priory? Why, you've barely begun to live, it would seem."

"I live every time I dance onstage." I leveled a weighty glance. "I'd hate for anything to ruin that." There was a clause in my contract, one that had implanted itself upon my mind. If I was associated with the least bit of impropriety, I would be dismissed from the contract with no help in the future, no place in the theater world.

Her lips pinched, one eyebrow arching. "Indeed." By the look on her face, I was a riddle to solve, and one she wouldn't let rest.

Yet it didn't matter, because he was coming. Philippe Rousseau was striding toward us with those powerful legs that had carried him in unforgettable arcs across the stage that night so many years ago. No doubt they still did. Butterfly wings tickled my chest.

He flashed a warm smile at my companion as he neared and bent to kiss her fingertips. "Minna. You've made a fine recovery, it seems." His voice was low and weighted with calm. "You're prepared to dance again?"

She shrugged with a wry smile. "What else would I do with myself?"

Then Philippe Rousseau turned that soul-deep gaze on me. "You're new?" He smiled and offered a little nod of welcome.

Breathe. Steady. Keep breathing.

"I've not seen you before."

Tell him. Just *tell* him! I opened my mouth, but no sound came.

He shifted, smoldering eyes intense, as if prepared to hang on my every word. "I assume you're dancing at Craven this season."

"Ahemafle—" My tongue caught. Words halted. Mind froze.

His smile flickered. "Well, then. Welcome to our little family." With another nod of his dark head, he swept past and hailed an older man coming in.

I gushed out a sigh, blowing hair off my face, and leaned my back into the barre. Of course he wouldn't know me. I had been a mere fifteen when we'd danced in that creaky old room in the theater wing. I'd gone from a girl, a washerwoman in patched clothing, to a trained ballerina in full costume. A fine one I turned out to be too. I cringed at the nonsensical syllables that had just come from my lips.

Minna's pinched little smile and sparkling eyes turned on my misery. "Rather agreeable, is he not?"

I steeled against her amusement. "I'm here to dance, not make a match." Yet Philippe Rousseau wasn't just any match. That lovely moment between us years ago had been knit into my beauty-loving heart, and I knew—much as I knew my paces—that he was different. I stole a glance at his back, and after a moment he turned to look at me too—just for a brief second, but I saw it. A fleeting smile, then he turned. Perhaps he *did* know. Insufferable man.

"That's perfect then, because he isn't in the market." She nearly always smiled as she spoke, this Minna creature. I wondered again if I was friend or rival to her.

"Perhaps he simply hasn't found what he's searching for, and he won't settle for less."

He strode among the dancers yet somehow floated above them, too, as if nothing they said or did could truly ruffle him.

"Many have tried, but he's as closed as a stone-hewn wall."

"Except with her." I said it with hushed surprise. He now hovered near the west wall with a most stunning dancer, leaning close for a private conversation. Where had *she* come from? At a distance, the woman's features were not striking or even particularly attractive, but with her aura of exquisite grace, no one could call her anything but beautiful. Not a movement or smile was wasted, and everything contributed to the feeling of art on display.

Minna laughed. "She's not a woman, she's a legend—Annika Friedl, principal ballerina. Besides, they are always together.

One cannot avoid growing close with one's dancing partner, now, can he?"

There was a remarkable intimacy between them. I watched the pair moving in tandem with long strides as they left their corner and wondered just *how* close they'd grown. "One day that'll be me." I gripped the barre—had I said that aloud? I'd only halfway meant it.

Minna's features hardened. "So says the girl who's afraid of men."

Rival. Definitely rival. "Perhaps I simply haven't need of one. Some dancers are fully able to climb on their own merits."

Her mouth pinched. Before she could respond, a bell clanged and a flurry of tulle and satin erupted like a feathery dovecote as the dancers bounded for the door. Had it already reached nine in the evening? I hurried out with them, funneling into the narrow sconce-lit corridor that I felt I knew so well from Mama's descriptions, even though I'd scarcely been in it.

Like a medieval castle, the corridor meandered in a long, shadowy column behind the stage, the greenroom at one end and the enchanted materials room, I knew, at the other. I paced toward that old room, wondering if it was the same. That dance . . . ah, the dance. I would never forget the evening encounter there. In the dimness I glanced up from beneath lowered lashes, looking for the face that had remained in my mind for years. *Please, please let me run into him again. I just need another chance.*

But then the corridor opened into a great palace of an auditorium, a gleaming, gilded openness, and I forgot everything except what my eyes were taking in. I'd never seen it from the stage. Rows of perfect blue-velvet seats and gold trim reached high into the balconies, where everything glistened with fresh oil, reflecting every trace of light. The largeness hit me in the chest, weighing on me with awe. To be surrounded by it, in the very heart of such immensity—I felt small, but part of something grand.

Great chandeliers were held up by cherubs on the balconies, each with no less than twenty ivory candles, and I nearly expected to hear angels singing hallelujah in the rafters. Muted gaslight sconces lay flush against ivory walls, casting soft shadows. It was so perfect, so very—

Oof. A spindly body collided into my side. I felt a tug at my waist, and a sudden release as my sash was loosed. I spun, shocked. Before I could place who had snitched it, the culprit went down, Minna standing over her. "Keep your hands off, you hear?"

Friend *and* rival. Was that even possible?

A little stick of a girl dressed in a dirty tulle practice skirt cowered in the shadows, clutching my rose-colored sash in her grimy hands. Her large dark eyes shone with fear, and the sight melted something crucial within me. They truly were *petits rats*, these little child dancers, desperate and scrambling for crumbs.

I reached for the sash, and she fell back as if I would hit her when I took it, eyes wide. "*Je suis désolé. Je suis désolé.*"

I ignored the apology and crouched before her, fingering the satin from Mama. "Come, let me show you." I twisted and wound the fabric as she watched, her spider arms braced against the floor, ready to propel her away.

She blinked, fear turning to wonder as the satin bunched into lovely, layered rosettes.

"How becoming these would look in your dark hair."

She stared, my words not crossing the language barrier, or perhaps the wall of fear, so I leaned near and held the flower against her grimy hair, then at the shoulder of her once-white gown. "Here, or here. Either place would suit, no?" Finally I tucked it against her cap sleeve and tipped my head with a smile. "*Magnifique.*" The touch of color did wonders.

She blinked, lips parted, then looked at the creation and back at me with a flicker of a smile in return, and that glimmer warmed the hollow places of my heart. I had so little of it myself, but giving love away filled something deep within, where the cracks had become far too large.

When she scurried off with my sash, I rose to catch up with Minna, who frowned at me. "You're inviting trouble. Give in to one, and you'll have ten more running up with their hands out."

Fortunately, sashes were replaceable, and kindness, as Mama had always said, was free. To this new acquaintance, I simply smiled and said, "Thank you. I'll remember."

"Come, you need to meet the others." Minna pulled me along, and we approached the other *sujets*, dancers chattering and spinning in a cluster at the center of the stage, and I backed away, feeling the intruder. Yet my beautiful new friend drew me into the group with an arm about my shoulders and a bold smile. "Ladies, welcome our newest member—and the perfect one to be the angel." Pulled into the flurry of dancers, I felt myself instantly caught up in their delight, and it made me happy, almost to the point of tears. The Paris theater world had been so hard. So foreign, so corrupt, so difficult. But now I was *home.*

Another girl looked me over. "You think she should be the angel?"

"Be gracious, Rosalie. Besides, it's only here, with us, just to see if she'll fit. Then we can suggest her to Fournier. Can't you be the least bit welcoming? Come, let's see if she'll fit."

I blinked. "What do you mean, fit—?"

Minna hustled me toward the back of the stage. "Let's just try it, shall we?"

Before I knew it, I was strung up in a halter around my waist, ropes tied around my wrists and legs. Panic beaded over my skin, but it was too late. I tugged at the halter. How could I admit my deepest, most foolish fear to these girls who'd just begun to accept me? "I thought we were finished for the night."

"Just for fun. We sujet are a chummy little group. If we can help you achieve a wonderful role, we'll do it."

Then Minna gave the word, and the rope went taut, hoisting me up, higher and higher until the air felt too thin. My vision doubled, then refocused as I looked over the auditorium and the scrollwork on the balconies so far away. The lever thunked into a locked position, and I had the dizzying sensation of claustrophobia—yes, even up in the air.

How high it was. How very high. There was no way to control this thing, and a million terrible ways to land. I imagined them all as sweat gathered along every crevice of my body.

Then a burst of laughter sounded below. I strained to see their faces, these beautiful girls in tulle and satin. Minna turned that lovely white face like a Dresden figurine up at me, her voice echoing. "Well now, look who has reached the top on her own adorable merits." She approached, smiling with a tilt of her head as I swung above her. "You are a *dancer*, you know. Just who are you saving your virtue for, anyway?" She laughed and the others skittered away. Then she followed with bouncing little steps, and they were all gone.

There I hung, trembling and alone, the farthest thing from an angelic creature that ever lived. As the echo of their voices faded, silence wrapped itself about the theater, folding me into its chill.

The gaslight shadows were dark fingers climbing the walls with each flicker of flame, and a low moan shuddered through the drafty space. A spark of the sacred Psalms lit through my mind.

LORD *my God, in thee do I put my trust: save me from all them that persecute me, and deliver me.*

I held still enough to feel my heartbeat, my erratic pulse, and simply breathed, a sudden awareness settling heavy on me of all those legends, the story of Delphine Bessette's ghost in this very theater. I could hear Mama's voice in my mind, as if it echoed about the auditorium, warm and alive and almost pleasant despite the eeriness. The ghost of what was. The gilded room seemed to sparkle with the memory of her presence, traces of her elegant beauty all over the grand auditorium. I trembled. *Mama?*

I stopped short of saying it aloud, but I could feel something here, like her essence that had been stripped away the night of the fire had remained, trapped in this massive echoing cavern where she'd once danced. Where they had once danced together. The quiet was intense, the room waiting to see what I'd do.

Nothing, as it turned out. That's all I could do, even while my thoughts ran like wildfire.

A distant *tock-tock* echoed deep within the building and I shuddered. Normal night noises, of course. But then a door banged deep within. The *tock-tock* began again and solidified into confident footfall. Fear spiked, and I swung and kicked, helpless up in the air. I flailed everywhere, tangling wires, ropes, and limbs in one sorry, hanging mess, desperate for escape.

Which is, of course, precisely when God chose to answer my earlier request.

My head snapped up, throbbing with the sudden redirection of blood. Tall and handsome, with arms folded over his chest,

Philippe Rousseau strode up the aisle with a half grin on his solemn face. "Keen for hanging about, are we?"

Horrified, I dropped my head, hair curtaining my face, and groaned.

"Stay put, and I'll get you down." He took the steps in two leaps and ran behind the curtain. A few small jerks brought me lower in increments. Then when I was most of the way down, there was a metallic *thunk*, the ties went slack, and the stage rushed up to meet me. *Oof.* I landed on my side, hip smarting, cheek stinging, but I was down.

And Philippe was there.

4

*M*aymie Dobbs wasn't one for keeping things in close. Not when secrets tasted so juicy on her lips. She pounded on a familiar bright red door in Belgravia only an hour after it happened, having tottered the entire way there by herself. Legs could carry one anywhere, and for free, after all. She liked free.

Face scrunching, she fisted her right hand and banged again. This time, a slender white face under a mobcap appeared in the narrow crack. Maymie squinted, forcing the face into focus, but she didn't recognize it.

The girl's voice was low when she spoke. Nervous. "What is it, then? You really shouldn't be at this entrance, you know."

"The butler won't answer the door to me, is that it?" Too good for Maymie Dobbs, it seemed. Just wait until they heard why she'd come.

"Not this door, I'm afraid. Try at the back, ma'am."

She straightened her stiff back. "I'm here on business with your master, not his staff, if you'd be kind enough to fetch him. It's private." His name . . . what was his name? Something with a *B*. No, it was *C*.

The girl's brow furrowed. "Just go 'round back and they'll give you summat to eat. Don't take it hard, they're very particular about who they let in."

She took a deep inhale and wasted a small taste of her news on the maid. "Very well then, tell him Maymie Dobbs says . . . *she's come back*. You tell him that and see what he does. I'll wait." Maymie clasped the handles of her clutch and braced herself on that stoop.

After a long wait, she was admitted, with some hesitation, into the small front receiving room. She squinted, trying to make out if it was where they accepted calling cards and let the delivering servants warm themselves, or if she was in a proper drawing room. Long curtains blocked most of the light, and bookshelves flanked the small fireplace that glowed with warmth.

A man's voice came from behind her. "What is the meaning of this?"

She turned, squinting at the tall figure who'd come in. Rather pleasant chap, with a voice not terribly unkind. Not much different than he'd always been. "Didn't your maid tell you?"

"Yes. *Who* is back?" He knew, though. The worry stretched across his face told her so. He only needed to be sure, since he didn't want to believe it. And for good reason.

She turned to face him head on, the sweetness of her secret exploding flavor in her mouth. "You know who. *You know*."

He narrowed his eyes. "You cannot possibly mean who I think."

She held up one finger, pointing it at his face. "She couldn't die. She isn't the sort, and you know it."

He paled, down to that stiff collar around his neck. The man stepped closer, leaning down toward her as all traces of cheeriness fell away. "Stop playing games with me, you miserable old crone. She died in the fire, and that's the last of it. There is no more Delphine Bessette."

"Right, then." She shrugged, quite pleased with herself, and spun toward the door. "I suppose them red slippers mean nothing, then."

A hand clamped on her shoulder, spun her clear off her feet, and she was held up only by his grip on her. "You saw someone dancing in them?"

She fidgeted, pulling at the strings of her cape. "Not exactly, but she had them. In her bag, all tucked in with the skirts."

He searched her face, his eyes a little wild. "Who? Who had—that is, where can I find her now?"

Her smile returned, spreading with ease. "At Craven, of course. Where she always belonged."

His face was grim, mouth pressed into a line. "Have you told de Silva yet?"

"If I happened upon him, I would. See him at Craven sometimes, I does. Wouldn't mind shocking him the way I've done you." She laughed. "Jolly fun."

He whipped out his pocketbook. "How much? How much will your silence cost me?"

"Oh, it isn't for sale, Lord Gower." She finally remembered the man's name. "I do like shocking people."

5

I couldn't tell Philippe now, of course. Not like this. My limbs tangled with my layered skirts as I struggled to rise from the floor with at least a scrap of dignity.

He came bounding across the stage, horror streaking his face. "Are you hurt?" He helped me sit, and I shook my head, wriggling free of the harness and ropes. "I suppose I ought to learn what the lever does before I operate it. My humblest apologies—I only meant to help you."

I offered a smile. "Quite all right. Better down than up."

His smile was generous. Relieved. "Quite right. Here, let me help you, and we'll fetch your things." He took my hand and pulled me up in one smooth move, and I stumbled onto my feet, balancing so I didn't fall into him. Our faces close at last, mine looking up into his, he studied me, then looked again. The pull of recognition showed in his features, but he said nothing. Yet.

His hand went protectively behind me as he guided me toward the back room for my cloak. "Won't you tell me what adventures drove you up there?"

I blew the hair off my face, but it fell right back. "The mistaken leap into a new friendship."

"Ah. You've angered one of them. Welcome to the world of ballet."

I sighed, wishing I dared limp to accommodate a throbbing spot on my hip. "Are they always this way?"

He shrugged. "I suppose they sleep at times."

I laughed, then smothered it with my hand. What a child he must think me. But somehow this man had momentarily lightened the secret burden I carried of "not enough."

"They're not horrible. Most are quite helpful and supportive of one another, but a few at the top—they're desperate. Scared." He helped me on with my cloak, then turned me to face him again, those fathomless dark eyes snapping in the chilly air of the empty theater, and once again the butterflies danced in my belly. It was almost more than I could bear. "Where exactly did you come from?"

I blew out a breath, all my secrets piling up behind my lips, and one word escaped as I pulled on my gloves. "Paris."

"I should have known," he mused. "A vibrant city produces a vibrant dancer." He laughed, slipping his fingers around the back of his neck. "Forgive me. What I should ask is, where are you staying?" He lifted my hat down from the hook and held out his arm. After I grabbed my carpetbag, we walked down the short flight of steps and out the stage door into the cold, quiet alley. "Would you allow me to carry your bag?"

Embarrassed at the broken handle, the very shabbiness of it, I held the old thing close. "Thank you, I can manage. It really isn't heavy."

"I assume you haven't far to go, then. You still haven't told me where you stay."

"Soho, just off Haymarket." I pulled my carpetbag into the folds of my wrap and tried not to cringe at the notion of him seeing my dirty little rooming house with its single soot-stained upper window. I hadn't even unpacked my meager trunk yet.

He hesitated as we reached Craven Street, out in front of the theater. Raucous laughter and music from the pub across the way drifted past us. "So far? You'll grow weary of such a journey, on top of dancing all day."

"Decent rooms are not plentiful in Covent Garden. Not for a beginning dancer."

Traps of all sorts rattled by, crunching over rocks and broken bricks. He spoke above the din of London, the passing voices louder and oiled with drink. I didn't relish the late walks home, now that I was standing out here at night.

"There's a place a few streets away that houses dancers. It's safe and clean. Shared rooms, but only five shillings a week. Would that suit?"

"Oh yes, quite." My face heated as my words gushed out, like a desperate woman accepting his invitation to dance.

He merely offered a bow with a most gentlemanly smile and led me along under the gaslights, allowing the snow to gather on his broad shoulders and felt hat.

Icy flakes whipped against my cheeks. "How is it so . . ."

"Modestly priced? It's owned by the theater. The Great Fournier, as he's called around here, likes to manage his ballerinas on *and* off the stage."

Fournier. Craven's owner, if I remembered right. I'd seen that name in a flourish of signatures on all the pages of my contract. "What makes him 'great'?"

He stopped in the snow. "Haven't you met him? You'd certainly know the answer if you had."

"Is he quite terrible?" I dreaded meeting him, dancing before him.

"Don't let him scare you. The secret is to look just past him, never directly in the eyes. That's where his power lies."

I shivered.

He pointed to the east. "Come, I'll deliver you to Mama Jo at the dormitory. She's far more agreeable than those dancers. And Fournier, for that matter."

We crossed onto Bleaker, and I doubled my pace to keep up, neatly dodging a horse and carriage clopping over the cobbled road as my carpetbag bounced against my shins. The odd mix of aromas—beached sewage and rotting food crossed with fine leather and horses—merely demonstrated what a blend of classes London was. The poor living separately, yet so near the rich to better serve them, launder their clothing, and drive their carriages.

I slipped my gloved hand farther into the crook of his arm and resisted the urge to lean into his warm wool coat, drinking in his nearness. The words between us that night were few and simple, but there was a weight to them that lingered, each dropped like a stone in a pond.

"You'll have to send for your things, of course."

"Yes, I'll see to it."

"I do hope you find the room comfortable."

"If it has a roof and a bed, it'll do."

"A roof *and* a bed?" His quiet smile warmed right through the cold of the winter night.

I allowed the conversation to remain on the surface while I studied him. So handsome, so reserved, compared to what he'd once been. The theater had used him up, it seemed, but hadn't Paris done the same to me? Change had settled on both of us these past years, but his both intrigued and worried me. There was a depth, a knowing sadness in his expression that made me want to ask him where he'd been and what he'd done. Or what had been done *to* him. Life had worn down that boyish enthusiasm, paling the sparkle and dimming his eyes considerably.

He caught me staring and smiled. "Feeling better now?"

"Yes." My cheeks were surely pink—from the cold and other things. "Thank you for the rescue and for escorting me."

He gave a gallant bow and stopped before a rough wooden door. "My pleasure. And I'll repeat the gesture whenever you find yourself alone at the theater come nightfall."

I sensed many late-night rehearsals in my future. "Thank you."

"I've done it for many dancers over the years."

My smile froze. He'd gone and cheapened the offer. No matter, he was still the finest gentleman anywhere in the theater world, and it validated my years of infatuation.

Which was quickly hardening into something rock-solid.

The door opened and a dark-haired woman with classic, gently aged beauty looked out from the shadows. "Why, Monsieur Rousseau. A pleasant surprise." Her voice carried the gentle upward clip of a French upbringing.

"My apologies for dropping a boarder on you so late." He flashed a quiet smile. "The girls gave her a bit of a rough time tonight, and she was held up."

I choked on a laugh, scrambled for a smidge of dignity. "Ella Blythe." I curtsied.

"Come in, Miss Blythe." Her wide smile was warm and generous, her nature magnetic. "Thank you, Monsieur Rousseau, and don't be troubled over the hour. I'd much rather a new dancer here safe with me than wandering through London alone."

"Shall I send for your things then, Miss Blythe? I'd rather see to it than have you trying to find a boy on your own at this hour."

I could hardly stand to look at his gentle face—it was so gracious and refined and everything I was not accustomed to. "How kind of you, sir. I would be in your debt." I scribbled my address in Soho, then after a quick bow, Philippe Rousseau was gone from my side.

The woman ushered me into the darkness that was pleasantly warm with the scent of honeyed cinnamon and yeast. "My name is Josefina Herrera, but the dancers, they call me Mama Jo." Her low voice came silky smooth in the dark, skipping over the *j* at times with a *y* sound. "It's my task to keep you reasonably moral and your evenings exceptionally dull. Fournier hates for his dancers to be inflicted with . . . *immorality*." She paused to light an oil lamp on a small table and turn up the wick.

With child is what she meant, of course.

"You've had a taste of life at the ballet tonight, I understand." She led me up the tightly curling steps. "Which of them was it?"

I racked my mind for the name on the edge of my memory. "She has blonde hair and little earbobs, and she always looks as though she's laughing inside at some little secret."

"*Oui*, Minna Frank."

"Yes, that's her. I suppose I said something to offend her."

"Or not." Shadows leaped on either side of us in the narrow stairway. "It is the great paradox of art, *ma petite*. Ballet is all delicacy and grace, yet it brings out the barbaric side of every woman who dances it. They are like starving wild dogs, fighting over the few choice pieces of meat." She turned and inserted a long gold key, the light she held flickering between us, and pushed open a door. "One only has to worry if she is any good."

I shivered at the words, an echo from my past. The woman

ushered me into my new home awash in blue-black dusk, her lamp heightening all the shadows hiding within.

It was a small, square room papered with a floral design and filled with two brass beds, twin wardrobes, and dressing tables. "Everyone wishes to be principal, Miss Blythe, or to lure the wealthiest abonné to sponsor her on the stage and . . . beyond. A sparkling position on the stage and a generous annuity is all they dream of in this life. How else will the dancer survive, once she outgrows her youthful bloom?"

I shrugged, throwing a smile her way. "Become a *Maman* to the younger."

She studied me in the flickering light, her knowing smile proving I'd pegged her accurately. "You will do well at Craven, Miss Blythe. You'll not be in the corps for long."

"Sujet, actually." At her shock, I was struck by my mistake, but I was too late. "Lower tier, of course." As if that fixed it.

Confusion shadowed her smooth face. "You are beginning in the sujet? How long have you trained?"

"Two years."

More surprise, lifting her arched eyebrows. "And where are you from, Miss . . . Blythe, is it?"

"Ella Blythe. From London, ma'am." I ducked from her gaze. "I'm here on scholarship."

But that only deepened her frown, one eyebrow raising. "Scholarship?"

"Yes, through Craven. I'm contracted to dance for them exclusively in exchange for my training."

Her stare seemed to last an eternity. Then it broke with a swish of her blue poplin skirt. "We'd best keep this to ourselves, no? You needn't let the other girls know you've come here for free, for they'll only despise you more."

I laughed. "I'm certain that's not possible."

She turned, standing as a statue with that lamp accentuating her elegant features. "I assure you," she said in measured tones. "It is quite possible."

The air suddenly felt heavy under her stare. The distant clock chimed once, marking the quarter hour. I'd lost all sense of the time.

"You should know that Fournier operates a unique sort of theater." She set the lamp on the table and opened the glass to light a smaller one to leave behind. "You'd best be excellent at memorizing combinations if you hope to stay."

I cringed. Memorizing them was my weakest point as a dancer. Nothing caused me more stumbles and hesitations than forgetting what came next.

"Rather than going to the expense of traveling with his company, the Great Fournier holds all performances right here in the theater, with just weeks of preparation in between each one."

I frowned. "How can the dancers possibly—"

"As I said, you must become exceptional at memorizing combinations. He is a master at rearranging a series of combinations into a completely new dance, telling a fresh story, over and over. That has become Craven's model and it has worked well for many years." Her gaze lingered.

"Thank you for explaining it to me."

"Minna and the others, they shall make it their business to catch you off guard. It's best to arm yourself with as much knowledge and experience as you can, and very quickly. Then . . . do what you can to make friends with them. They are terrible chums, but dangerous enemies."

When Mama Jo left, I spent a few quiet moments shaking

off a sense of doom and looking over the contents of my new roommate's cosmetic table—the bold red lip grease, the pink tin of rice powder, the many stoppered bottles of different colors and sizes. What sort of woman was she? Perhaps she could be a confidante in the way Lily had been.

My curiosity shuddered to a firm halt when I heard a thump outside, then a *scratch-scratch*. It was nearby, somewhere just outside the window. I leaped into bed fully clothed, shucking my boots, and tried to ignore the noises. I had a third-floor room, and it was likely a feral cat or some such nonsense.

Then, a *bang*.

The LORD is my light and my salvation; whom shall I fear? the LORD is the strength of my life; of whom shall I be afraid?

I was trembling by the time the window to my little sanctuary burst open and a pile of skirts and finery tumbled in. Then, a face appeared among the fabric. Minna Frank rose, a white porcelain pillar of disdain, and glared down at me. "What are you doing in my room?"

Her room? I groaned and shrank farther beneath the coverlet. Understanding wrapped its tentacles around me. Of all the devious, underhanded . . . There was no denying it—Mama Jo had once been a dancer.

Minna came toward me, heeled boots stabbing the floor with each step. "Where exactly did you come from?"

I harnessed all my poise. "The boardinghouse was recommended to me. Mama Jo placed me in this room."

"Did she, now?" Her gaze lingered, but she turned, discarding her wrap and allowing me to breathe again.

"The choice was certainly not mine." I caught sight of myself in the long mirror across from the bed as I heard those words leave my mouth, and suddenly I saw *her*. I saw Mama in the lift of my chin and the defensive way I spoke, and it horrified me, as if I'd spotted a ghost in the mirror. *"We are so similar, you and I. Yet I want nothing more than for your story to be wonderfully different than mine."*

And it would be. It would. If I had to bend the future to my will, it would not take the same tragic turn as Delphine Bessette's. I had complete control over what became of me, of my career and my life. Things would only happen that I let happen.

I rolled over on the bed with a creak of springs. I had to prove to them all that she couldn't intimidate me. It was the worst turn of events since coming back to Craven, and in the moment, I couldn't imagine anything more troubling.

Then I met Jack.

6

He was tall and blond with a sparkle of amusement flickering in every feature—and he was mocking Signore Bellini from behind. He mimicked the man's impassioned rant in grand, sweeping gestures as Bellini carried on.

"What sort of circus is this? Your landings are all over the place." Bellini stalked up the rows. "You must move as a unit. Is that truly so hard for you to grasp? Move as *one*."

The blond man offstage stabbed the air with a finger as Bellini carried on. I coughed a laugh into my hand, unable to look away from his audacity. Poor cad would be murdered if Bellini saw him. The man caught me staring and flashed a bold grin that glinted white in the shadows, and a wink. I blinked, officially offended. Privately amused.

Bound in woolen practice stockings and floating tulle, we lunged as one, silently assessing the lines of lifted legs around us. I'd been back in England a whole week, and Signore Bellini's training had tied me up in knots with each passing day. He often singled me out, pushing me harder than most, until I feared a call to the front office to cancel my contract and demand repayment for my training. But now, watching the daring impersonator with a bubble of amusement, I found those knots loosening for the first time all week.

Focus. Just focus.

I stumbled my landing, colliding with a curly haired dancer who fell into another. Bellini threw up his hands and dissolved into a fit of Italian as he stalked toward the stairs. "Practice is *finito* for today. I shall seek to endure you all tomorrow."

"I'm so sorry," I whispered to the other dancer.

"At least you're no threat." She offered a playful half smile.

I laughed, sinking into a comfortable silence with her, but my gaze flicked to the man still out in the empty audience. He smiled and lifted his eyebrows, as if asking something, inviting, and I stiffened.

"You'd best not give him any ideas," whispered the curly haired dancer as she sat beside me. She had a soft voice but a wild, long mane of curls that she now released and a wide, friendly smile that drew a person in.

"Who is he?"

"Jack Dorian, the greatest scoundrel God ever made." Her grin was wry. "He trifles with all the dancers. Especially the new ones."

"I don't trifle." But he seemed to have singled me out for his special attention. When this Jack Dorian's stare deepened, one eyebrow angling up, I looked away. Reputations were such delicate things, and I clung to mine like a cloak against the cold.

"You won't want to make an enemy of him either. He's in charge of the dances—choreographer."

Of course he was. "Well, I don't have to make it easy on him."

She reached down into a stretch, her grin widening. "That'll only make him try harder."

Naturally.

He was the kind of handsome that made one slightly uncomfortable, a quicksand that might suck one under if she came too close. I stared harder, allowing my glance to linger. What was it? His eyes, perhaps. No, his entire face. He looked out on the world with both amusement and indifference, as though everything was merely a game and nothing truly worth his deep concern.

She smiled at my frown. "It's perfectly acceptable to find him attractive. There isn't a woman in this theater who's immune."

Odd. The wider this Jack Dorian smiled, the more immune I felt.

"Just don't be caught alone with him. Even a *hint* of impropriety will give Fournier a reason to cancel your contract. He despises all romantic entanglements among dancers. I'm Tovah, by the way."

"Ella Blythe." I brushed the hair off my moist forehead. "They must have a hard time keeping dancers if they cut so mercilessly."

"They make cuts after every performance, and for hardly any reason at all. They're looking for reasons to sack us these days. Ballet isn't what it once was."

This much I'd known already, but it must be hitting Craven harder than the rest. Ballet had fallen out of favor with the London elite, and many theaters had shifted more to opera and pantomimes to fill their seats. Craven, a small ballet-focused theater that merely rented the establishment to traveling acts when there was no ballet to perform, had to shift things in a different way.

My scholarship, for example. They could no longer afford to bring in foreign dancers from the continent, who sometimes demanded upwards of 10,000 pounds a season, so they turned to hardworking London girls delighted to accept training and a mere 500 a year.

It was Lily who'd seen the advertisement several months after cholera had taken Mama, and she'd nearly pushed me out the door to audition. We had so little and were about to lose the flat as it was. Nothing tied me there, and I couldn't justify saying no. So, just after years of uprisings and unrest in France, I had traveled to Paris to begin my training. Perhaps being here on scholarship made me more immune to those cuts—or far less.

Tovah looked me over. "Just keep your chin up and your eyes forward. Don't make any waves."

I nodded, idly wondering what sort of waves I'd make if someone discovered the red slippers now in the bottom of my wardrobe.

Two quick claps sent the lingering dancers scurrying. It was time now for the principals to practice together, and they strode toward the stage with graceful, paired strides. I stood rooted and held my breath, composing myself as Philippe Rousseau neared.

But when he'd come within mere feet of me, a startling figure sprang up before my face, nearly knocking me backward.

Jack Dorian. With a bold smile, he bowed and kissed each of our hands, mine and the curly haired dancer who seemed to be waiting on me, bless her. That trifler held on to mine, and I glared as I yanked away, but he seemed not to care. "Good day, ladies."

"Well, it *was*," I mumbled as I stole a glance past his shoulder. Philippe had paused, watching from a discreet distance. His brow looked shadowed. Disappointed? He turned toward the stage and took his position with his partner.

"Now then, how is our new dancer getting on?" Jack's smile was glaringly white, his face like a gaudy paste jewel.

"Well enough."

I watched Philippe and Annika dance, drinking in the sight of Philippe's lithe body as if I'd never see it again. He was bending and spinning, his arms easily guiding his partner's waist in that same careful way he'd done with me. I couldn't look away. *"One cannot help but grow close to his dancing partner, now can he?"*

Jack watched me, reading the longing and angst in my face. "Don't concern yourself over Bellini." *Misreading*, as it turned out. "He's all bark. Besides, it's *him* you have to impress."

He jerked his head toward a plume of cigar smoke rising from a single seat in the near-dark auditorium. I turned and blinked, the outline of a man's face appearing behind the smog. It was a wide and aged countenance with a white beard that came to a point atop a rather mountainous body. And he was staring at me directly, eyeing Jack with displeasure and me with suspicion.

I wrinkled my nose. "Who smokes in the presence of ladies— in a theater, no less?"

"Don't you know him?" Tovah blinked her disbelief. "How in heaven did you ever sign on here without meeting the owner? That is *the* Great Fournier."

I cocked an eyebrow at the smoking ogre-like giant staring us down. "As in . . . no one could be *Fournier*-looking than him?"

My new friend spit out a laugh, eyeing me with amusement.

Jack's eyes sparkled in my direction. I did not like it.

"Fournier, as in the French word for *oven*," he said with a smile still about his lips.

The other dancer, Tovah, eyed me, sobering. "As in, don't get near the heat or you'll be burned."

So this was the Great Fournier, the bear of the theater I'd heard so much about. The man rose in a column of enormous dignity, and I stiffened. "Oven, indeed. He certainly smokes like one. Which reminds me." I straightened with a smile. "Luncheon should be set by now."

"Oh, come now, it's only pickled tongue and potatoes. You could fish better food from the Thames."

"And clotted cream on tarts," Tovah added. "We'll be lucky if there's any left by the time we get there." She backed toward the curtain and abandoned me.

Jack approached and I sensed his mysterious aura that charmed so many. I could feel my will beginning to bend as I continued to put off luncheon, as he wished. I was becoming Mama, in all her suppleness, losing my spine. Perhaps it was the theater, perhaps it was because I was her daughter, but the parallel felt entirely inescapable.

I backed away. "I never miss clotted cream." So sweet. Just like freedom. Freedom from this quicksand. Fournier, taller than I imagined, rose from his seat and strode toward the offices with one final glance toward Jack hovering over me. I was holding onto my dreams, my remarkable future, by a very thin thread. *God, please don't let it snap.*

I ran toward the curtain and brushed through it. The past, which had always seemed distant and something to be gently unraveled at will, now seemed most significant and threatening and urgent. Almost a curse I could not escape. I had a sudden need to understand it, shine daylight on it, before it caught up and completely overtook me.

After a quick luncheon, I snuck out toward the front of the theater to see the entire place for myself. I felt an odd kinship with this theater as I moved silently through it toward the offices, a sort of déjà vu, as if it were a previous home that I knew mostly by memory and it welcomed me back. From Mama's stories, I knew the entire layout by heart—the great entrance hall with its thick pillars and sweeping double staircase, the richly appointed auditorium just beyond, the long green corridor in back with the greenroom on one end and the materials room on the other.

I missed Mama with a wringing pain, especially here in the exquisite theater she'd described in such detail. *We are so similar, you and I.* It was my theater too, and my future was here. Every shadowy corridor and closed door drew my attention as if my name had been called, as if the theater was holding on to something of my past and inviting me to discover it.

And I needed to understand it. How powerless I'd felt in the face of that charmer, as weak and controlled as she had been. Only when I fully understood what had happened, shed the light of day on those old mysteries, could I truly be free of its echo in my own life. And the only way I could do that was to act completely opposite of Mama—taking control of my own future rather than waiting for someone else to do it. It was with this thought that I knocked at Fournier's office, hoping to establish a decent working relationship between us, and perhaps find out what he knew about one long-ago dancer.

A small oil lamp flickered inside, but the room lay empty, the door ajar. Papers covered the top of a worn walnut desk and cracked red leather chair off to the side. Light filtered through a high stained-glass window, coloring the room with a prism of dusty sunshine. I stared at the dim space until my gaze rested on a large book opened and facing me on the desk. It was names and addresses—a logbook. And it was simply sitting there, open and waiting.

Curiosity curled inside me. I wanted to know—*deserved* to know, didn't I? Mum had been so secretive, but this theater held countless details she'd refused to reveal. With shaking fingers, I flipped toward the beginning of what turned out to be a pay log, scanning for her name—Delphine Bessette. I found it and followed the line across to her real name: *Jane Fawley, Number 11 Tavistock Place.*

I read the name again, absorbing it fully: Jane Fawley. That was Mum, in her mysterious other life, and oh, how that name fit her better than the ornamental one they'd given her, and everything she'd used since. I memorized the address and flipped back to the page my finger had been holding. I slipped out before I was noticed, equal parts elated and grieving anew, with a small pinch of guilt for snooping.

But if I found something important, it would be worthwhile.

"I'm trying to trace Jane Fawley. Were you acquainted with her?"

The tall liveried servant who opened the door at Number 11 Tavistock Place peered out at me through the narrow opening he'd allowed. It was nearly tea hour in most London homes, and I was certain to be an unwelcome intrusion.

"Only that she's dead, miss. Many years now."

"But she lived here once?" How different it was than our little home, this brick-and-stone-pillared place with perfectly manicured shrubs around an iron gate.

He nodded his head. "She occupied the largest flat on the first floor."

"Any relations? Next of kin?"

He shrugged. "Alone in the world, far as I could tell, miss. She wasn't one to talk to the staff, though. She mostly worked at the theater and stayed out to all hours."

"Did she ever have visitors? Siblings, perhaps, or—"

"I'm sorry, miss. I truly don't know more than that. Good day."

The crack in the door narrowed, and I put my palm firmly on the wood. "Please, sir, it's terribly important. Isn't there anything else you can tell me? I've no one else to ask." Desperation tainted my voice.

He dropped his gaze, fingers still gripping the edge of the door. "She is . . . important to you?"

I nodded, my eyes pleading with him.

"Wait here."

He shut the door, then came back clutching a black box with papier-mâché roses on the lid and little stone pieces embedded on the side. "Exactly *how* important?"

I stared at that unusual box, which was big enough to hold something crucial—something of her life I'd never seen before. "She was my mum."

The man gripped the box and looked at me with wonder. "That one, a *mum*?" He shook his head, as if ridding it of fog. "Well then, I suppose you should . . . you should have this." He extended the box. "Found it behind a bureau when the master went to sell her things. We didn't know what else to do with them, of course. You understand."

"Of course. And thank you for this." I pulled the box close, fingering the scalloped edge of the lid. "If you would, please, don't mention—"

He held up his hands. "I never do. Best of luck to you, miss. Hope you find whatever it is you're looking for."

7

They were love letters—all of them. Some from working-class hopefuls, others from discreet noblemen, all full of passionate adoration of Delphine Bessette. I strained to read them by the glow of a few candle stubs in the materials room after lessons were over for the day. This, of course, was the only place I could freely examine these—and the place I'd need to hide the box. I'd waited until everyone left so that no one would stumble upon them and make them fodder for the press.

It was bittersweet to read all these words of adoration directed at my mother and terribly unsettling to see the sheer number of men from which they came.

To the brightest star of ballet, the incandescent and wholly unforgettable Delphine Bessette. I will ever remember the sight of your lovely white arms sweeping through the glow of theater lights, your beauty perfectly harmonious with the music filling the auditorium, dancing as if only for me. What is it about you that charms me so, charms every man who catches sight of you? No one else brings the world to life as you do from the stage, stirring every molecule of air and infusing it with your glow.

I closed my eyes and I could picture her. How radiant she had always been, how splendid, even in her patched gown in our little flat. All my life I'd been fooled into believing, by watching her dance, that it was effortless. No harder than rising up on one's toes and moving along with the music.

Yet she had something special, as the letter said, and I'd quite forgotten that when I'd set out to have the same career. "It takes much work to appear effortless," she'd once said, and I felt every inch of that in my tired body. Yet for all my straining and rehearsing, I wasn't any closer to what she'd been. This time I did not feel our lives running parallel. I felt only my lack.

After making it through only a third of the letters, I forced back tears and rose to go. This was leading nowhere I wished to be. Why had she saved all these? Surely she couldn't have encouraged this many men. The way she'd spoken of Father . . . No one could be so double-minded. No one.

Shoes clicked through the echoey front hall and I tensed, sensing the presence of Philippe in the theater. I tucked the box away and rose onto demi-pointe and made a slow spin, feeling the perfect line of my body and waiting. For a flash, I imagined Philippe looking at me with the same admiration as that letter writer had felt toward my mother. It made my pulse flutter.

Yet ever since I'd returned to Craven, he'd been so closed off and difficult to read. A little attention thrown my way, then silence.

"There's a secret part of himself he never shares with any-one—at least, not anyone in the ballet world," Annika had told me. I could hear her quiet voice imparting these words, echoing what Minna had said, in a private training session in the morning hours. Bellini had asked Annika to tutor me privately, and I learned from her as the one who had already achieved all my dreams. I also soaked up everything she said about Philippe. "It fuels him . . . and isolates him."

"Why does he do that?" I'd asked. I'd taken advantage of how open she became without the crowds of dancers around, and she'd already noticed how interested Philippe seemed in me.

"There is deep hurt somewhere in his past, something that holds him back from trusting. About certain matters, he will not open up to anyone."

There was always a first.

Philippe's voice rang out in the auditorium, deep and unmistakable, sending a shiver up my spine and drawing me back to the present. He was coming, and there would be another escort home. I swept up to a finito pose and waited. But while those steps clipped over the distant stage, I suddenly became aware of a steady stare already in the mirror. I stiffened. Jack Dorian leaned against the doorframe, a playful look angled directly at my reflection. No telling how long he'd been there.

I had a full view of his well-cut figure, golden hair, and almost divine appearance the others found so intensely attractive. Judging by his manner, he shared their opinion.

"Spin like that for too long and you'll need someone to catch you." His voice was smooth, effortless.

Steel hardened my spine. "I don't fall."

"Everyone falls." He pushed off the doorframe and ambled in. "The question is, what will you do about it?"

Philippe's footsteps still echoed, coming down the hall now, and I stiffened like a child with a pilfered treat. "I'm not like the other dancers. Why don't you leave me—"

"What, to fall alone?" He assessed me, arms still crossed.

I moved to walk past him, but as I neared him, the footsteps stopped at the door.

"Oh." Philippe stood framed there. His look of awkward shock strangled me. "I beg your pardon. I thought you were alone again, Miss Blythe. I saw the light and assumed . . ."

"I was, actually. I—"

"Quite all right, Rousseau." Jack Dorian's bold smile flashed, his commanding words barreling over my own. "I'll escort the lady on my way home."

Philippe hesitated, their gazes sparring for a moment, then the finest gentleman I knew gave a single nod of assent and backed away. "Very well, then."

But it wasn't very well. Not at all. I opened my mouth, but the words were stuck again. Philippe did that to me, nearly every time.

"I'll wish you good day then, Miss Blythe."

Before I could untangle my voice, he was gone, the shadows swallowing his lithe figure. So much for not letting things merely "happen." What had become of me? I was not myself. I was like . . . In an odd moment of vertigo, I felt that I had transposed my life for Mama's, living out her passivity and meekness, trapped by her vices.

Hurtling toward the same end.

I caught my breath, sucking air in quick gasps, and spun on the self-satisfied weasel who still watched me with that maddening grin. "Why in heaven's name do you do that? Why are you always about, leering and flirting as if I'd given you the slightest encouragement?" None of his flashy smiles, the bold stance or invasive charm, held a candle to the solemn, scruffy, deeply poetic face of Philippe Rousseau.

He narrowed his eyes with another of his smiles. "Fancy the man, do you?"

My flesh heated, top to bottom. "More than I fancy you." The words tasted succulent on my lips, but he seemed unmoved by the rejection.

He squinted, hands in his pockets. "Did I ever tell you of the time I wrestled a tiger to save a woman's life? Brawny thing he was, and full of fighting spirit."

"Philippe Rousseau is no tiger."

But he wasn't listening. He swooped down on the invisible animal and pretended to slam it to the floor. "I wrestled that beast down and held him by the throat, yelling at the woman to get away, and she escaped. Barely. Then I was alone with that mongrel and we had it out, and eventually . . . well, I ended up making friends with him." He folded his arms and stepped nearer. "You remind me of that tiger."

I turned away and rolled my eyes. He took to heart Shakespeare's line about all the world being a stage. Yet I couldn't understand how he expected anyone would believe those grandiose tales, let alone feel attraction to the narcissistic flirt who had, unfortunately, attached himself to me like a leech. Did women truly take to him for more than thirty seconds? He was always there, hanging about, ready to siphon my dreams away from me.

He moved toward me, looking me up and down. "What sort of role are you hoping to land with all this practice? I'm arranging the production, you know. I do have some say."

Desires battled within my heart. "So I've heard."

"I could make you into a lovely butterfly in the next production. Or perhaps a bird. Yes, I do like that."

I pressed my lips together—I must play nice, at least, for that was the cost of remaining. Of survival. Mama Jo's words came back to me. *"You needn't let the other girls know you've come here for free."* I sat with a grumble and peeled the slippers off my raw feet. "'Free' indeed."

"What's that, a tree? That can be arranged. You'd make a fine birch, with those long, white arms. How tall are you, anyway—more than five and a half?"

I brushed the slippers aside and wrapped my blistered feet in rags before forcing them into my day shoes and rising to face the man. "I refuse to let you target me this way, simply because I've not come under your spell. Not every woman wishes to fall at your feet."

"I see no circles on you. Thorns perhaps, but no target."

I glared, but he held out his arm to escort me.

"I've a promise to keep, I believe," he said.

I took his arm with reluctance. It struck me as we left that perhaps he was the sort of man an escort should protect me against. I didn't speak again until the frigid night air struck our faces out the side door and we strode down the alley toward Craven Street.

He spoke first. "You remind me of someone, actually."

"Do I, now?" Sarcasm tainted my voice.

"It's remarkable, really."

"Isn't it?" I forced a prim smile.

"You asked why I'd . . . targeted you, as you say. It's because you look like someone I hold in high regard, and I cannot ignore the striking similarity. It's uncanny, really." He stared openly in the night's dimness.

I narrowed my eyes. "Who?"

"No one you'd know, I'm certain. Yet somehow . . ."

Suddenly panicked, I lurched for the door of the rooming

house. "I'm home now, you may go." I didn't want to hear my dear mama's name on his lips.

Yet he only stood there in the dark street, hands jammed in his pockets, golden hair wild about his head as he blocked my way. "It's those remarkable eyes of yours—so brilliant and vivid. I've never seen the like in all the world, except in one other person." He tipped his head, gaze piercing. "Ever hear of the world-famous dancer Marcus de Silva?"

Everything stopped, curtain closed. I stood in the street as if I'd become a statue. I opened my mouth. Pressed it shut. Suddenly I looked at Jack Dorian as more than a threat to my dreams—he was even more dangerous, prying open boxes I'd locked away in my heart. "You're claiming you *know* Marcus de Silva?" It made my heart hammer to say his name, knowing who he was to me, and I could feel the curiosity inflaming against my will. "That's as likely as your tiger story. It seems he's something of a disappearing mystery."

He smiled, looking me over. "I did know him, actually."

"Prove it." I leaned forward, hungry for his answer. I didn't want to, yet somehow I *had* to know more about this man with eyes that looked like mine. What did the rest of him look like? What were the timbre of his voice and the expressions of his face? Was there anything else of him in me? I'd never imagined sharing any similarities with the man, this stranger, yet suddenly I was a part of him. Connected by eyes no one else had.

Jack studied me, seeming to see through my snappish words. "One day you will find him, Miss Blythe, and right under your very nose. And that's all the proving I care to do." Another nod and he was gone, stepping through the night.

My heart hammered with an oddly unsettled fear. I pulled the door open and hurried up the stairs, trying to clear my head of everything I'd discovered, yet I found no safety in my little flat. A breeze lifted the white curtains into my room like two arms out to greet me, and something seemed off. I couldn't shake it. I ran to close the window and that's when I saw it— my wardrobe, with a bit of tulle caught in the closed drawer, a door slightly ajar. I wouldn't have left it that way, costly as those practice skirts were. I knelt and dug through my things at the bottom of the wardrobe, the piles now disturbed, but I had nothing of value. No coin hidden there.

Then it struck me with metallic awareness what was missing, just as the door opened and someone entered.

Minna frowned down at me on the floor. "There was a man here earlier tonight, asking after you. I told him I wasn't your keeper and to check the local priory."

I ignored the jab. "What sort of man?"

"Tall, quiet, well-dressed but rather ill-mannered. He kept to the shadows, mostly, so I didn't see more than that. He took off his ugly green hat—honestly, who wears such a color upon his head?—and insisted on waiting for you. Until I told him you might be gone for hours yet." She unpinned her hat and dropped it on the dressing table.

I stopped myself from asking about his eyes, and if they resembled mine. Then I felt about in the bottom of my wardrobe to be certain of what I expected—yes, they were gone. Those red satin slippers were gone.

I felt their lack intensely, for so many reasons. I had not set out to find my father, but it seemed he had located me. Thanks to Jack Dorian, most likely, for I couldn't imagine how else he might have suddenly known to look for me. I swallowed hard. Did he even realize who I was, exactly? He felt threatened by my reappearance, it seemed, and apparently by the shoes. But why take them? What clue did they hold to that wretched night so long ago?

Yet I didn't really want to know more. Not about him, or whoever it was who had hurt Mama.

"If you've a mind to find a sponsor, Ella Blythe, you'd best let me help you form alliances. It's clear you haven't any idea what you're doing." Minna unleashed her long hair and shook it out before her mirror. "Unless he's simply a hanger-on you've failed to dislodge. Do you plan to see him if he comes again?"

I pressed my lips together, then licked them. "I'm not certain what I should do." I tried not to stare at the empty space in the bottom of my wardrobe, tried not to imagine where those scarlet slippers might be this minute and whose hands might be holding them.

8

*I*n a long papered hall that ran along the west side of the auditorium, I glimpsed my father's face for the first time. It was in a series of paintings in gilded frames that spanned the entire wall, capturing in muted tones Craven's best dancers from years past. My mother's showed her poised in her red slippers at a distance from the artist, lifting into an arabesque, but Marcus de Silva's showed his entire, memorable face at close range. I knew without even looking at the embossed plates which one was him. *"It's those remarkable eyes. I've never seen the like in all the world, except in one other person . . ."*

I'd never expected to feel a connection to this man—it was my mother I wanted to discover more about. Yet the further I pushed, a horrible awareness of my father swept around me like cool air, cutting through my garments and chilling my flesh. I stared at him, and the magnificence of the man utterly captured me, his features so starkly white against dark hair, his prism eyes that held such eerie familiarity blazing right into mine.

I reached up and touched those eyes, that rock-hewn face. I had lost all sense of belonging when Mum had died, but here was the other half of me—the half that had always been missing and was still out there. Perhaps the island might find a link to land after all.

"Handsome, is he not?" The feminine voice, low and controlled, shook me loose from my thoughts.

I turned to look into the knowing face of Mama Jo, who stood several portraits away. I'd come here after a thorough search of my flat for the red slippers, willing them to appear in some cobwebbed corner, but they did not. And my confusion only grew.

She stepped forward, her boots echoing in the emptiness. "It doesn't do any of them justice, believe me. They were never this still, this flat, in real life. Ah, what an extraordinary time that was." Mama Jo inhaled, shoulders straight and elegant as always. "It's too bad you did not know him then. You would have been proud—proud to be connected to him."

I blinked, a little stunned. "You know who I am, don't you?" It felt a bit like airing out a stuffy attic, having someone who already knew about my secret.

A long, lingering look. "I recognized you almost immediately as his. Besides, no one is ready for the sujet after a mere two years in Paris. That is, unless dancing is already in her blood." She came to stand beside me, looking up at the vivid painting. "It's easy to see at once that you belong to him, and to ballet. One has the notion from looking at you that you never walk anywhere. Not when dancing is an option." She winked.

I smiled at her and returned my gaze to the portrait, learning every feature and nuance of the man who had always been naught but a shadow. "What was he like?" It was a vulnerable question, revealing the huge lack in my life, but she took it graciously in stride.

"A gentleman. Refined and genteel, but all fiery passion on the stage. I often wondered if he was a dangerous man behind closed doors."

"Whatever became of him?"

Shock flitted across her features at this admission that I had missed more than his past. "I have no idea. He disappeared. No one's heard from him in years. They say he changed his name after the fire and remained in the shadows, though which ones I could not say."

I stared at him, trying to decode the guarded look on his face. "Was he . . . that is, do *you* believe it's possible he's responsible for the fire?" I nearly asked her if she'd let him into my flat last night, if she knew anything about the missing shoes, but I'd already gone too far.

She studied that portrait, measuring her words. "Yes. I do."

Something delicate shattered within me, as if I'd lost a parent all over again, but I fought to keep my face impassive.

"I've no doubt he had good reason, though. Delphine, she was a difficult partner—demanding and passionate when it came to ballet, which is what made her magnificent."

I blinked in shock. "Demanding?" Yet fire melted things, of course. Melted and softened. It was the first time I'd let myself believe the fire had brought any good to Mama's life.

"Everyone loved Delphine, and she cast a charm over them. Women were drawn to her femininity, men to her seeming need for protection. But when it came to ballet, and Marcus de Silva . . ." She clasped her hands before her. "They complemented one another well onstage, he the gentleman and she a true lady in every way, but they were a constant explosion. She wanted nothing less than perfection in ballet, and he was much more of a free-form artist. Besides all that, she never liked the woman with whom he fell in love. I never heard who she was, but it seems she and Delphine simply could not tolerate one another."

I blinked, mind stretching to accommodate the odd revelations coming one after the other. Another woman? The tortured look on Mama's face haunted me now, with new layers of understanding. Perhaps *this* was the reason he'd kept their marriage a secret. And why she'd never told him she'd survived the fire. He'd found another woman.

"I suppose your mother, whoever she is, came into the picture later—after things blew over with Delphine and this . . . other woman. Or perhaps . . ."

I looked away, unable to fill in the information she sought. No, my mother was *not* this other mystery woman. She was the original woman, my father's true partner and wife, no matter what Mama Jo seemed to believe.

I wanted to cry. And to never search for my father.

No, I wanted to find him so I could give that wretched deserter a piece of my mind.

"You see, it is all a complicated muddle, and it seems your mother knew that if she kept you away from your father for long enough . . ." Her statement was followed by a raised eyebrow, asking a question.

I wasn't sure which question she was asking, but I sidestepped them all. "So this is why you think my father set the fire, because he wanted to be rid of Delphine and her jealousy of this woman?" I nearly choked on the ridiculousness of that notion—a wife being jealous over her own husband.

She turned her shadowed face to me, staring me up and down. "Marcus de Silva kept a great many things to himself. If he ever held affection for Delphine, no one in the theater knew it. Or perhaps it was all a different matter. No dancer is without a certain amount of theatrics in real life. It simply leaks from the stage to the home, no matter how hard one may try to avoid it." She sighed. "Mark my words, ma petite. Every romance that begins in the theater ends with just as much tragedy as the ballets themselves."

I stiffened my spine. "Not *every* ballet is a tragedy." Philippe's face swam through my mind, somehow mingling with the dramatic face of my father.

"You see, this is one reason I never married. When you work as hard as I once did, and the only men you meet are dancers . . ." She shrugged.

When I looked back at the portrait, my father looked down at me from that portrait, and suddenly the oils on canvas were not enough. His face was unreadable, just like Philippe's, and I had a wicked, selfish desire, despite my promise, to know what was behind it. What he would think when he truly looked at me. It was as if, by understanding my father, I could understand that stony, silent Philippe.

I thought of my father quite often in rehearsals that day, as if he were watching. As if he would recognize me across whatever divide separated us and realize, as Jack and Mama Jo already had, that I was his daughter.

My muscles quivered in their hold as the man known as the great furnace came around the side of me and scrutinized the line of my *attitude* leg lift. He frowned, one eye nearly disappearing in the folds of his face.

"Like a flower, not a tree trunk." His voice was low, rumbling from somewhere deep in his chest. He reshaped the circle of my arms, and I felt brittle to his touch—stiff and fragile. "Now, try again."

I swept my arms down and made the turn, forcing poise and grace into my steps, but his grimace did not lighten.

"Again."

I repeated, muscles sore with tension.

"Again, again. Lift from the chest."

His frown had deepened every time I saw it.

"You will stay for extra training again tomorrow night. Find Annika and tell her so."

I was shaking and near tears by the time Signore Bellini dismissed us for luncheon, feeling a little glad that my father *hadn't* just witnessed all that.

Tovah paused to invite me out with them, but I shook my head. "Another time." I couldn't rest these days, couldn't stop pushing myself, without feeling odd pangs of guilt. Time was short, and the distance to my goals long, to be bridged only by hard work, and I would do it. A half hour in the materials room away from Fournier's scrutiny would ease out the kinks, solidify the paces that still felt awkward.

I followed the few remaining dancers to the large prop room behind the stage where luncheon tables were laden with food, but I swallowed only a few bites of bread with cheese and stewed fruit before disappearing down the east hall toward my peaceful haven. A thought had struck me, and though it was unlikely, I wanted to pursue my theory.

I lit a stubby candle and touched it to the others I'd propped about the room until it glowed softly, cozy in its chaotic shambles. I breathed in the familiar scent, thought of Mama, and set about searching every inch of that room for her red shoes.

I'd brought them here to practice a time or two, and though it wouldn't explain the skirts caught in the wardrobe drawer, there was a chance I'd merely left those slippers here. I lifted every bit of silk and tulle, looked in every hiding place I used in that room, but the scarlet shoes were gone, a bit of color missing from my life. I couldn't bear to think of it then—all I'd lost, all that was missing that should be mine.

I jammed a hairpin into Mama's music box, watched it spring to life, then stood in fourth position among the leaping shadows of the room where Mama had supposedly died, where people said her presence still lingered.

And it did—I could sense it. Not in a ghostly way, but in the way a room is familiar and enchanting, rich with important history. For those few moments, with the music from Mama's box plinking through the cool air, I became lost in my passion and fell deeply in love with ballet again, sensing my connection to her even without her magnificent slippers. My spins and paces came perfectly, and I was weightless, poised as a white stag. Around me, rafters creaked and muffled voices carried on, but nothing interrupted my dance.

When I finally stopped to catch my breath, I sat to rub a cramp from my left leg and let my mind wander. But it swirled and focused on a sharp point in the mirror. My fingers froze, digging into the muscle as I stared across the empty room at a craggy face reflected in the mirror beside mine, staring at me from the dark corridor. It was a man, tall with hunched shoulders, his face veiled in shadow except two very set-apart eyes and a green bowler on his head. The chill of the room dug beneath my skin.

I started and blinked, jarring myself from panic, and he'd vanished. My tired brain was playing tricks on me. How many times had I imagined seeing a face in my mirror at home? It had been my recurring nightmare. Ever since Mama had told me that bit of her story from that night, about the face she'd seen in the mirror just before the fire, my paranoid mind had run away with that image and conjured it in nearly every mirror I glimpsed.

Yet there was one thing I saw for sure reflected in that glass— the exhaustion that used to line Mama's face eerily matched on my own. I leaned closer, fingers to my sallow skin, as my heart pounded beneath my dress. It wasn't happening, though. I was a completely different person. Completely. Opposite, in fact. Very little—

A sudden flare of light. The candle—my skirt! I flew toward the drop cloth and rolled, smothering the tiny flame, panting and wrestling it into nothing. I peeled back the cloth to inspect the large burned spot on my skirt, silently berating my carelessness for leaning so close to the flame, for being so afraid of the tiny echo from Mama's life. It hadn't killed me, had it? I'd put it out. Yet I was shaking uncontrollably.

After a blessed eternity, someone stepped loudly down the corridor and the door squeaked farther open. Heart galloping, I looked for that face again, that green bowler—but it was not the same man. I blinked several times, and there was Philippe Rousseau in the shadows of the corridor, with that look of ten thousand unwritten poems battling for release from his troubled mind.

9

*H*and to my chest, I puffed out a breath. "Oh, it's you." The sight of him shattered the haunted sensation and returned me to reality. Lives did not repeat, after all. Not in real life.

I sat and undid the laces of my slippers with trembling fingers and replaced them with day shoes. There was still ten minutes or more before the next session, but I needed to be away from this room and its dark history.

"My apologies for startling you, Miss Blythe. I saw you leave, and I . . ." He blinked, catching sight of the slightly burned skirt layer, then looking at my face. "A mite shaken, are we? What happened?"

"This old theater is full of ghosts. Ghosts and open candles and long skirts." I blew out the rest of the candles and hurried out of the room, closing the door behind us. "I've simply had a rough go of it today." I shrugged. "You know how it is."

"Ah, one of *those* days." His smile was kind. "I've had a few myself. Come, I'll walk you back. I know it's only the theater, but these dark corridors can be treacherous."

He extended his arm, but I did not take it. "I believe I'll walk around a bit before the afternoon session, if it's all the same to you." I had to rid myself of this uneasy tension still tickling my skin before I could face the others.

He looked down, toeing the wood floor. Thick tufts of hair curled over his forehead, that same boyish curl I remembered from that night long ago. It was coming full circle, being here with him. "Waiting on someone else, are you? It seems you and Jack Dorian—"

"No!" My skin warmed at the speed of my reply. I took a breath. "No. I'm not waiting for anyone. Especially not him."

He studied me, those deeply intelligent eyes snapping with interest. "May I offer some company on your walk, then? Mine specifically, that is."

I smiled in the chilly corridor, little explosions of delight detonating in my overwrought heart. "You may."

We strolled down the hall to the stage, then down the center aisle of the quiet auditorium, my knees aching like rusted machinery as we descended the stage steps, but Philippe's presence muffled all pain. I'd pay for it when I climbed into bed that night, but just like the extra practices, it'd be worth it.

As he opened the rear doors for me, I glanced at Philippe's profile from my peripheral vision. One slender curl hung down to brush the side of his well-chiseled cheek, dusting the masculine indent that ran along it. There was a deep divot in his upper lip, and I could imagine it moving with eloquence as he read poetry aloud or smiled in that warm way he had.

He caught me staring and I dropped my gaze, but he only smiled. "Just the gruel of the day, is it? The hard work that's trampled you down? Come now, you can say it."

His kindness punctured my attempts to appear collected and refined. Suddenly I could not hold my mask of dignity so firmly in place. "I was hoping to be further along by now, I suppose. Closer to where the other sujet are." I stepped through to the theater's grand entryway with brass railings and wide steps that spilled down into the three double doors, my plain brown skirt with the burn brushing the thick carpets. "I'm afraid I'll never be good enough to stay." It was vulnerable. Too much.

"Nonsense." He tipped his head, and his reaction balmed my cracked and dry spirit, making my doubts seem overblown. "You dance so wonderfully, quite on par with any of them. Better, in some ways. You've something special about you, something immensely enjoyable to watch. One can tell you deeply love ballet, and you wear that affection brilliantly."

Can I keep you? That was the only thought in my foolish head.

"We are our own worst critics, you know. I suppose you spend all your thoughts analyzing what you've done wrong, and gloss over what you've done well."

I lowered my gaze, gave a little shrug at his on-the-nose summary. "It's Fournier, actually. I cannot seem to please the man, and now he's asked me to do extra training."

"Ah, so that's what's got hold of you. Might I offer a word of advice?" He held the middle doors of the main theater entrance and ushered me out of the gloom and into the sunshine, the cold fresh air of a London winter tipping just a smidge toward spring.

"Of course."

"Don't let him trouble you. The Great Fournier is a man of few compliments but immense discernment. That's what makes *him* stand out in the theater world. Rather than being caught up by flashy smiles and polished poise, Fournier can spot raw ability in the simplest girl and fan it open like peacock feathers. So if he says two words to you, even harsh ones, it means he thinks you're worth teaching, and you are most privileged."

I huffed out a cold breath. "Privileged, indeed." I tried to embrace his words, but there wasn't a compliment big enough to outweigh the massive doubt that nibbled daily on my soul. There were simply too many threats to my future, my position too tenuous. And if I failed, what then? I would leave the theater, and . . . well, everything. My past, my future, a large piece of who I was.

"I'm certain he sees what I see—a most stunning dancer."

Stunning. I shivered at the shock of that word and tucked it away in my heart for later. He noticed my shiver and I ducked my head. "I left without my wrap. I should return for—"

"Take mine." With a gentle swirl, his coat was off, its weight embracing my shoulders. "He was a dancer once too, you know. Fournier understands what he's putting you through, and he knows what he's doing."

I let that statement hang without refuting it, and my mind lingered on the oddness of the great bear of Craven once having been a dancer.

Nearing the Strand, we followed the crush of vendors and pedestrians beneath the colorful hanging signs, and he guided me toward the square, where we stopped before a horse-and-rider statue of King George IV. A carriage veered and clipped close, and I fell against Philippe, but it didn't jar him. Nothing did, it seemed. He was so solid. I needed solid.

He sighed. "Theater is not an easy life. The days are not cushioned with ease or kind words. Perhaps it would be bearable if it weren't so lonely."

My chest tightened at his admission. "Oh?"

He was quiet for a moment. Thoughtful. "Ours is the only

profession, it would seem, that is incompatible with marriage. No matter how much we wish for it, no one will have us in their parlors, or their hearts."

Except other dancers. "Certainly there's a woman out there who—" I bit my lip to stop the foolish words that were about to leave my mouth.

Silence cooled the air between us as we walked on, his hand lifting to swing a butcher's sign overhead. At last he spoke, his voice low and timbered. "There was. Once."

My head jerked up, so shocked I was to receive an answer to something personal. "What?"

"Several years ago, of course. Before I knew how downright wretched women could be—and how foolish, men. Forgive me, for I'm certain you would not trifle with a man." He sighed again. "Serves me right, though. Love seldom ends well for dancers, and I shouldn't have expected to be the exception."

I let his words linger in the air and thought of the great theater love story of the past as I said, "All real love is rare." We approached the Waterloo Bridge and the silvery Thames below, shimmering with the sun's reflection on little shards of ice floating downriver. "You are more than merely a dancer, you know. You are a man like any other." Only better, of course.

Something bobbed in his throat, but I dared not acknowledge this subtle show of emotion. "I've always been who I am. My parents were in theater, and I was born in a dressing room in Munich. I've never known anything else. It's in my blood, like a curse. I knew it then, and I knew it when Florentine left me."

Florentine. Even her name sounded exotic, and I suddenly felt homely. *Ella. Plain Ella Blythe.*

Yet I was here, plain or not—and unlike Florentine, I wasn't leaving. A lump in my throat blocked the words, but I squeezed his arm. Then we turned down a narrow street, quiet with modest brick-front homes, and stopped, Philippe facing me, and it struck me with a pounding heart—this was the perfect moment to tell him. The door was open, and we were alone. With an inhale, I summoned the best of my practiced speeches.

He spoke first. "I'm rather glad it's over. I suppose I should *thank* that Jack Dorian. There's a lot of pressure involved in marriage and . . . well, women. Begging your pardon again, of course. I simply haven't found one I could trust."

I looked up at his clean, handsome profile lit with sunlight, praying my heart was not glowing through my face. *Yes . . . yes you have.* Yet it seemed as if he was warning me. Informing me of the truth about himself and what he'd never be able to give. I waited, afraid to break the tenuous spell that had opened him up. I sensed an ocean of story beneath the murky waves, and I wished to unleash it all. "You never tried to win her back?"

"Well, she married a marquis within the month and is now quite happy in her Berkeley Square home."

"Oh."

"Jack Dorian never keeps anything for long, you know." He looked down at me, taking my hand and holding on to it. That gaze, the one full of warm syrup and poetry, lay heavy on me now. I could not look away. "Beware of the men who hang about the theater. They're all a bit like Jack Dorian underneath, just waiting to take advantage. Some even . . . place bets. I did catch wind of something of this nature afoot. You do understand my meaning, don't you?"

Jack Dorian. I gave a dull nod, for no other part of my face worked. So I was now a game for them all. Including the man who had a say in casting.

But Philippe's thumb traced a path on my open palm, and

at that slight movement, thoughts of Jack melted away. I stared at our hands together. It was a solid step forward, a bridge crossed from feigned ignorance to acknowledging something more existed between us. I could barely manage to keep my head affixed, my arms from trembling. It was all so close, so new. So lovely and full of the scent of soap and comforting wool in the chill of winter's wind.

"Ella, may I . . ." Glass broke somewhere in the distant alley and he straightened, breaking contact. A cat gave a strangled cry. "I beg your pardon. I've forgotten myself. We should return."

I compelled myself back to reality, trying in vain to shrug off the disappointment. We walked back to the side entrance and just inside the door, Philippe bowed in his usual way with a tip of his hat. I forced a smile and took another look at his somber face. It wasn't a thousand unwritten poems weighing him down, but a thousand unspoken sadnesses, and they'd break him as they'd broken Mama. As they threatened to break me. I'd only begun to hear his story, I was certain. *What has happened to you, Philippe?*

"I'd be happy to escort you safely home, if you should find yourself here later than the others some night again."

"I do have a training session with Annika tomorrow evening."

He gave a nod and backed into the shadows. "Tomorrow, then." Spoken like a promise.

"Tomorrow."

Despite the man in the green hat, the small fire in the materials room, the strain of keeping up, I floated through the day on a cloud of blessed hope.

10

"Oh, Miss Blythe, I'm pleased to find you still here."
Mama Jo's low voice sounded in the empty theater
on Thursday as she came around the curtain from
the side.

I shot up like a launched cannonball and crossed the stage
to her. "Has anyone heard from Philippe Rousseau?"

Three days. It had been three days since anyone had seen
him, since our walk, and I came to realize how lonely it was to
trust people. Often, they did not deserve it. Not even Philippe
Rousseau, way up on his pedestal.

I didn't even care that I sounded desperate anymore, that I
might be showing my hand. But then she looked at me with
suspicion in her eyes, and I looked down at my feet. "We cannot
possibly go on with the show if we are missing our principal
dancer, and with no show we shall not be paid." It was a hor-
ribly weak excuse.

"He'll be back, Miss Blythe. You needn't worry."

"Ella, please."

"Very well . . . Ella. He tends to miss a few days of training here or there, but he always appears when it counts. We've never been without our lead for even a single performance."

"Is he well? I feel it's my Christian duty to—"

"I'm afraid I haven't any idea. I've not heard anything."

I blew out a helpless breath and cast a glance out at the empty stage where I'd once seen him dance. Where my mother and father had shone like stars. It was a spectacular place, even between shows, glinting with tragedy and drama and magic.

"I've come looking for you because I have news."

I turned toward the pillar of elegance standing before me. "Not bad news, I hope."

"Not at all." Mamo Jo smiled as she pulled down and folded the tulle from the exhibit that had rented out Craven Theatre the previous week—Madame Tussaud's remarkable wax sculptures. "Bellini is willing to give you a chance, if you work very hard, and let you try a small solo." Her dark eyes glowed in the dimness, and she stooped to sweep up more stray tulle. "This is good. Quite good, for one as new as you."

My chest swelled with dread and anticipation. I felt safest being invisible, but part of me longed to be seen. Especially by the family—cousins, aunts and uncles, maybe even half siblings I had never met. And my *father*.

"It's to be a very colorful Italian ballet about flowers, called *Il Fiore Danzante*, and it speaks loudly to this world's secret desire for the fantastical and romantic. All of Europe has shifted into this new style of art in many forms, except England. How tightly they cling to their classical ideals, their rigid rules, and there is simply no room for romance." She paused to look at me directly. "You, I believe, are quite English."

"Am I?" Rules, without room for romance. How accurate.

"Bellini says you are stiff, and I've never met a stiff *fleur*."

I heaved a sigh, shoulders sagging. "I've no idea how to be precise *and* relaxed. I'm doing the best I can."

"I know, but it isn't enough. You are not competing against dancers, but their abonnés' pocketbooks." She led me with armloads of tulle back into the props area backstage, where she dropped her burden off to the side. "You must have your father's quiet charm and his partner Delphine's liquid grace all in one, for nothing else will surpass what a generous patron's donation can do for the dancer he's advancing."

Looking into her face, realization came with needled precision. "There's never been a truly successful dancer without an abonné, has there?" It was my first glimpse of the mountain I'd set out to climb, an awareness of all I lacked.

But Mama Jo's look, deep and penetrating, did not release me. "I did not say it could not be done, only that it never has." She stepped closer, that lovely, warm smile erasing the chill of fear that gripped me. "And nothing great has ever been accomplished by doing a thing the same way everyone else has, ma petite. You think on that." She walked back out to the stage and I followed her.

"There's certainly no question of my being different from the rest." I said this with a sigh.

"So I've noticed." She arched one eyebrow and began trimming wicks. "They call you the nun, the dancer who will have no man. That alone makes you a rarity—nay, almost an eccentricity in the theater world. In all of England, perhaps."

"I've no desire to become someone's mistress."

"Very good." She smiled her approval. "Though I warn you, Miss Blythe." She stepped back, arms wide and chest lifted. "You are looking at the alternative."

I grinned. "I accept."

Her throaty laugh bounced through her shoulders, lightened her lovely face. "You *are* unusual. In a good way."

"Tell me, then, how can I do it? How will I stand up against that sort of money?"

She rubbed a small section of blue-velvet curtain between her fingers, as if ensuring its thickness, then unhooked the gold braided tieback and released it with a whoosh of heavy fabric. "It's never about how much or how long, but how *well*." She walked along the length of the stage, pulling the released curtain along behind her.

I ran to keep up, admiring her stride.

"Always maintain marvelous posture, even in little things— smaller roles, backstage conversations, darning a pair of shoes—make beauty and elegance a way of life, even in the mundane moments, and they cannot help but notice you shining in your little corner. Give them something stunning to look at in every second. Then go and audition for a leading role and win it." She smiled, her cheeks folding into long dimples. "Now, bring me that chair, if you would."

I considered the woman who lived out her own suggestion quite well, gliding from one task to the next with poise to rival the queen. I carried the wooden chair to Mama Jo. "Who was Delphine Bessette's?"

She blinked at me, fingers curling around the top of the chair I'd brought. "Delphine?"

"Who sponsored her rise to fame?"

"Why, she had several, I believe. There was a marquis for a time and a nobleman from Surrey. I cannot remember all their names. I heard rumors of foreign royalty once too, but I couldn't be certain. I'm sure there were plenty more. She was quite popular."

"What about Marcus de Silva?"

Her eyebrows rose. "Her partner? He hadn't any money to speak of, I'm sure. Not the way all those wealthy patrons did."

"Perhaps he felt a bit jealous, then. They were partners, after all. He might have even felt some affection for her."

"Quite a romantic notion, but nothing could be further from the truth." Her smile was patronizing. "They danced well together upon the stage, but that was all. Besides, he had fallen in love with this other young woman and Delphine had her share of men. She would not be persuaded to settle on any one of them. Even her partner."

I gripped the back of the chair and lifted my chest against the pain twisting inside. "My story, I've decided, will be quite different in many ways."

She leveled a knowing smile toward me. "A fine ideal. I do hope you get your wish."

I'd see that I did.

She turned to go but stopped where the curtain met the brick wall on the side of the stage. "Ella, try not to worry yourself over Philippe Rousseau." She looked at me with compassion. "He does this at times. Disappears without explanation to anyone. Like a cat, he will come back when he needs to, and the ballet will go on."

I couldn't put my finger on what concerned me, but I felt it keenly. Was it a disappearing Philippe or my disappearing father? Perhaps the odd picture that was forming about my mother.

She patted my hand on the back of the chair. "You have a good nature, and you feel deeply. Most ballerinas have forgotten how, especially when they dance. Don't change too much, ma petite." Then she was gone.

I couldn't shake the heaviness and utter confusion as my thoughts swirled. I fetched my wrap and hurried home, where I dropped to the floor and searched every inch of that wardrobe for the red shoes. They had to be here—it was a fanciful notion, thinking he'd stolen them. All of this was in the past, long over.

But at last I had to admit they were gone, one way or another. I sat back on my heels with a sigh. The more I glimpsed my parents' story, the parallel track I was nearly forced onto, the more confusion clouded my way forward. I *had* to pierce it with truth. I left my chilly flat and headed south, my head swirling with thoughts of Philippe, my eyes keenly peeled for a glimpse of him in the dying light.

In a pint-sized flat over a confectionary in the square, Lucy Kimball's withered frame nestled back against her rocking chair until it was almost lost in the cushions. "One must be cautious around such a man."

Time slowed here. She gave the chair tiny shoves with her boot as she gripped the arms and tipped her head back to remember. The fragrant air of the confectionary below billowed around me, wafting all the way up to us from the shop, and I drank in its familiarity.

I looked at the delicate face of the woman who always seemed to know everything. What I knew of faith, the bits of common sense gathered in my head, all came from this tiny frame with the delicate features and faded strawberry-blonde hair. She'd once been my mother's governess, and though Mum had grown and both of them had quit her parents' house, Aunt Luce, as we called her, had never completely abandoned her post. Then she had become, in a way, *my* governess.

"He was a dark horse, that 'un. Always disappearing, never letting anyone know what went on in that mind of his. Never could abide questions. That's the sort who always has something to hide, eh?"

In a quick moment of disconnect, I couldn't remember if she was discussing my father or Philippe Rousseau. But of course, she didn't know Philippe, and I had asked her about Marcus.

"Have a hot drink, lass?" She rose and grabbed for the little side table, then limped toward the kitchen.

"Have you hurt yourself?"

She waved it off. "More of the same."

"Sakes, Aunt Luce. Haven't you gotten those corns off by now?" I jumped up and helped her back to her chair.

"You'll see when you age, lass, a body cannot always bend as it once did. I cannot fix what I cannot reach, now can I?"

I blew out a breath and walked to her tiny kitchen, rummaging for a large pot. "Where's your soap? We'll see to it now."

"In the larder, love."

I warmed the water over her fire, then brought it and the soap over, settling on the floor in front of her. "Give them here."

She hesitated. "You want my feet?"

"How else will those corns come off?"

She readjusted in her chair, pushing up on the arms.

"Come on, then." Steeling myself, I plunged one hand toward her stockingless right foot and pulled it out, settling it into the warm water. Her reluctance softened and her foot sank in. I stared at it, white and misshapen by age, knobbier than her hands and thick with calluses around the edges. Raised red bumps adorned several odd crevices of her toes.

Yet it was simply so very *Aunt Luce*, all aged and interesting and well-used. She lifted the other one in beside it, and I ran my hand over the bumps and calluses, trying not to flinch. This was the woman who had raised Mum, shaping her into the beauty she'd always been, as if Aunt Luce's very nature had overflowed out onto her. I couldn't think her anything less than lovely.

I looked up at her as I worked the cloth over her calluses, letting the corns soak. "He isn't all bad, is he? My father, I mean."

She tipped her head to the side. "Your father, Ella Blythe, is an unknowable, untamable man, and he always will be. Your mother had a rough go of it when she married 'im, and she cried many a tear into this here apron." She shook out the tattered thing that probably was as old as Mum.

I rose and dried my hands, allowing her feet to soak. "I want to hear their story, Aunt Luce. The real one."

"I've told it to you, lass, in little pieces when you were a wee 'un." Her soft Irish voice wrapped around me as I sat on the footstool again, along with the familiar smells of the sugar and yeast below, carrying me back to childhood visits here.

"Tell me all of it—from one grown woman to another. Please."

A long sigh, a pause in the creaking rocker as she moved her feet about in the pan, then she tipped back in her chair and started. She told me of the secret love that had become too much for either of them to set aside. "He were drawn to my lass, the nectar of her spirit, as hungry as a wandering panhandler in the dry season. I was scared for her at first, wee lamb, but she did something to that man. Melted him, she did, turning that walled-up stranger of a man into a fine gentleman who ran to do her every bidding. Ahhh, but they loved each other, those two."

Yes. Yes, this is the way I'd remembered hearing it. Yet it bothered me how the pieces still didn't fit, even with this version. "Why keep the marriage a secret then? Was it simply because they were partners in the theater?"

Her eyes remained closed. "You should have seen the way they danced together on that stage, love. Pure poetry, it were, and then they twirled off the stage and kept right on dancing. A gentle waltz, both so lost on th' other I thought me poor lass would never come up for air." She heaved a sigh that deflated her chest. "They couldn't bear for London society to know, though. Couldn't abide the gossips and the press in their private lives, so they kept it quiet, from the public and the theater folk alike. She was a humble one, my lass, a private woman. Stuck to the background rather than the spotlights, even though they say she was the star."

"That does sound like Mama." At last. Precious little I'd heard of her lately had.

"There was the trouble with her parents too, of course. They were against the match, so they kept it a secret from them, until they eloped and ran off. Never told a soul that weren't family about the marriage, even after it were done."

"How did they ever spend true quality time together to fall in love in the first place?"

She opened starry eyes and pinched her lips into a smile of equal parts delight and mischief. "Aunt Luce made herself quite useful in those days, she did. Still lived with the family of course, up until the elopement when your mother left with him and I moved here to the shop with my Helen's family."

"That's why it was you she came to after the fire."

"Who else? I loved her like me own, didn't I?"

I sat closer and wrapped her wrinkled old hands in mine. "Did they truly love each other? Really and truly? Or was it just an illusion?"

Those gentle eyes folded into crescents of delight. "Aye, lass, 'twas real. You could feel it in the air between them, the way they melted into one another without a single word. He was utterly enchanted with his little ballerina, and she adored her fine man as if he was king, right up to the end."

I clutched the cloth in my hand. "What happened, then? Why did she not go to him after the fire?" I wondered if Aunt Luce knew the other woman's name.

She shook her head. "Couldn't say, couldn't say."

More like, *wouldn't*.

"There was someone else, wasn't there? Someone came between them."

She blinked at me. "That I canna say, love. She didn't tell me the whole of it." She shook her head. "It was a wretched time for us all. Her heart was broken into pieces, that's all I know."

Tears pricked at my eyes. I dabbed at them with my skirt, then fetched the pumice stone from her shelf and knelt beside the basin. I lifted the left foot first and went to work on the largest of the corns. It was a stubborn old thing. After several minutes, I switched to the other. Aunt Lucy scrunched up her face as I worked but didn't say a word until I dropped the stone in the bucket and sat back with a sigh. "You shouldn't let them get so bad. I don't see how you were even able to walk."

"And what am I to do about them?" She bent at the waist, as if to show me she couldn't go more than a few inches toward her misshapen feet.

I hauled the bucket to the window, trying not to look at its grayish water, and dumped it out the back.

I found a cloth in her closet and knelt to pat her feet dry. "Where is he? How can I find him?" His was the final angle to this story that I didn't have, the last piece to put into the puzzle. The only one alive who knew what had happened that night. "It isn't as if she's in any danger from him now, and he deserves to know what happened to her." Part of me wished to know if he believed he'd killed her.

"Now, child, didn't you promise your mother?"

"Yes, but—"

"You aren't one to go and break your word, Ella Blythe." She shook her head.

"You don't think I should find him? Learn the truth?"

"There's nothing you can do to fix the past, lass. It's over and done. As you said, no one's chasing after your poor mum now."

"No, but I can speak with him, find out—"

"You did promise, lass." Her rocking slowed, chair creaking over the floor. "It was your mother's wish."

I narrowed my eyes, scrutinizing right past her placid smile. "What aren't you telling me? What aren't you saying about my father?"

She sat back, rocking again. "Naught but reminding a good and loyal daughter of her promise. She was a good 'un, your mum. Plenty good to you, even all by herself, wasn't she?"

"The finest." I stared at the familiar contours of her face, the loose skin at her throat, the frizzy hair that had somehow managed to remain a fine faded red. "I know when you're hiding something, Aunt Lucy. Please—tell me what it is."

There was a loud fumble at the door, then someone stumbled

in, arms laden with parcels. "I *refuse* to shop in the square again. What a crowd of animals, the lot of them." She closed the door with her foot and dropped the parcels on the bed, then caught sight of me and froze.

"Lily!" I sprang to my sister and wrapped her in a hug. "Oh, how wonderful to see you. You're staying here?" I pushed back to look her over.

"We're keeping each other company," Aunt Lucy said.

This was the "fine place" she'd promised me she'd secured. At least, I countered with myself, she was safe.

"It's only temporary. I've been taking in fine sewing work from Mrs. McCullum, and I have prospects."

I raised an eyebrow. "What sort?"

She flashed that charming, dimpled smile that could thaw a glacier. So like her real mother she was. "Nothing too terrible. A girl must have her romances, you know." With a flippant shrug, she turned to her parcels and began unwrapping them.

My gaze bored into the slender back of the sister of my heart who, despite my efforts, had still not grown up. "You know how that's gone in the past."

She waved it off with a pretty pout. "That was so many years ago, and it's nothing to me anymore. No harm done."

I clutched the edges of the little footstool I sat upon as I thought about a bleak night many years ago that I'd landed in a place called Seven Dials, a district of dubious reputation, facing the most impossible choice of my life because of her *nothing*. She didn't know, of course. She had no idea how much harm *had* been done. I'd hidden it from her all this time.

Temptation niggled at me to reveal that old secret now, to say it aloud and to utterly shock some sense into her as she seemed ready to dive headlong back into the same entanglements. It wasn't resentment that bore down on me, but a strong sense of my own foolishness for once again thinking I could fix everything. I was simply not sister enough for that.

But Aunt Lucy knew what I'd done that night, how I was torturing myself now even while my sister danced blissfully through life. She was staring at me, head tilted to the side as if to say, *See? Some secrets truly are better left in the dark.*

11

"Are you Protestant or Anglican?"

I looked up at Minna's reflection in the mirror, her question tearing my mind away from the "Lily problem." It was Sunday, and apparently Minna was attending church this week. The fact that she was up before ten was a miracle in itself.

I'd been buried under layers of moss-green muslin and voile that would soon be my costume, lost in the minute stitches taking shape. "I've not been in a while." I'd been rejected from my lifelong congregation upon accepting the scholarship, a life of theater, and I hadn't decided what should become of my Sunday ritual. Was I still a Methodist if the church would not have me?

Minna pursed her untinted lips and looked at me in the mirror. "The nun, without a church?" She smiled as she brushed the lightest mask of rice powder over her skin. "You know it's all in good fun, don't you?"

I didn't.

"You're not still cross about the first night, are you? I've already apologized."

She hadn't.

Minna tipped her head, face sobering in the mirror. "Come now, toughen up." She looked me over as an older sister would assess the injuries of her younger sister. "You're soft as an egg without its shell. You really think mine are the harshest words you'll hear in the theater? Someone needs to prepare you."

I pivoted the conversation. "Where will you attend services?"

She allowed her look to linger for another few seconds. "St. Paul's, of course. Where else is there, for one of us?"

St. Paul's—I'd seen the place. Simple and boxy like a barn, the church just off the Strand was known as the actors' church, welcoming those considered unsuitable by polite society.

"Philippe Rousseau attends." She eyed me in the mirror as she unscrewed another jar.

I masked my surprise. Looked away. Why shouldn't he, though? He was a dancer, much as the rest of them. I must stop elevating him to something different than he was. "How nice for him." I could feel my cheeks heating and I despised them for it.

"Even when he's feeling poorly, he seldom misses a week."

"Is that where he's been, recovering from some illness?" I should have thought to ask the other dancers.

Minna dipped her finger in the jar, then twisted a tendril of hair, laying it neatly against her forehead and pressing it flat, then moving on to others. "You've not fallen in love, have you?"

I jumped as the needle stabbed my fingertip. "Haven't dancers a right to fall in love, either?"

She swiveled to face me, half her forehead plastered with ringlets. "Of course we do. I've let it happen to myself a number of times. But never with another dancer."

I blew out a breath, dropping my sewing onto my lap. "Why ever not? It isn't as if anyone else will have us."

"Plenty will, just not as wives." She reached for a jewel-crusted box and opened it tenderly, holding out the blinking, sparkling contents for me to see. "This is from my count, the *Comte de Chillion*. I treasure these baubles, and the affection that goes along with them, mind you, but I'm not above selling the gems to keep myself fed and off the street someday."

I hardened inside at the sight of them, wondering if his wife realized he was gifting such things to another woman.

"Men grow tired of women, whether they are married to them or not." Her gaze was steady, eyes searching mine. "Better to flit about unattached than be tied in marriage to another dancer who can offer you nothing. That's a doomed existence. Have you ever known a pair from the theater to make a go of it?"

Hot and cold passed over my flesh. My gaze shot to the little gold band I'd placed on my table—Mama's ring, worn on a chain around her neck when she danced, then on her finger my entire life. Never a man to go with it, however. "Not *every* theater match is doomed, I'm sure." I stabbed the material with my needle.

She merely raised an eyebrow with a wicked grin.

"It isn't a curse, being in the theater."

She set down her box and picked up a pot of grease, swirling her finger in it. "If two dancers marry, what will become of them when they advance in years? I've never seen a dancer last past five and thirty, even if she's careful. They'd be forced to separate simply to survive, for a dancer's only way of survival off the stage . . . is marriage."

My heart thudded into my throat and I swallowed. I felt I was on the cusp of discovering the truth about my parents' past as my eyes finally adjusted to the darkness that had always shadowed their story, and I began to glimpse small pieces of it.

She rose and took my hand, our faces mere inches apart. "Do whatever it takes to avoid falling in love with a dancer. Even a principal will dry up one day, and they will be forced to choose survival over love."

It was a wretched end to the story that had bandied about in my heart all these years—a terrible reason they should be apart. Yet it seemed inescapable. I myself had felt the weight of the need for survival.

Minna went back to sticking curls to her forehead. "You should join us. St. Paul's is a lovely congregation full of understanding people, and you'll feel right at home." She rose, straightening skirts that hugged her hips. "It's where all the actors wind up in the end."

Where they all wind up.

In the end.

Suddenly, I knew the answer. I knew what must have truly happened to keep them apart. It was what Aunt Lucy refused to say, and the reason my father hadn't ever come forward for us. Disappeared, Mama Jo had said, and "right under your nose" was Jack Dorian's cryptic clue, and there was only one answer that fit both of those.

We had a half day on Monday, and I should have rehearsed *battements* to strengthen muscle control, but by late afternoon when we were released, I was dragging my aching body toward the infamous actor's church instead, in search of closure. There was an angst alive inside of me, an unfinished thread in my tapestry, and it would forever haunt me—*he* would forever haunt me—until I knew. Part of me grieved the possibility while the other felt a tired sort of relief at the realization that my father may not have rejected me after all.

St. Paul's. I would see for myself.

I set out the moment we were dismissed for the heart of Covent Garden, but my aching feet, tight with pain, took me only as far as Lion's Head Inn on the corner of Middle Temple before they seized up. Wincing, I curled into a bench tucked in the shadows of the building to peel off my boots and expose my raw feet to the open air. It was daring among the great throng of people, but I was desperate.

I gifted myself a few precious moments of rest on the fringes of the activity as my feet throbbed behind my skirt hem, watching people and carriages hurry through the square, voices raised and laughter echoing off stone walls. The smell of sausages from a cart on the next block mingled with the dust and fog, making my stomach clench. It was only a few more streets to the church. Seven or eight at most.

I'd last, if I could keep my feet bare and out of view. Rotten traitors.

Then a shadow was there, hovering over me as I poked at the raw flesh with a fingertip. I looked up into the roguishly playful face of Jack Dorian. He watched me, arms behind his back. "Running over the coals now, are we?"

I grimaced. "It's terrible, how unforgiving a wood floor can be." Then heat poured over my skin as I realized my indecency and drew my feet back under my hem.

"Especially with the hours you put in."

"I hold myself to high standards."

"Are you finding your dancing much improved for all this?"

I pressed my lips closed and merely looked at him.

"Give them here." He knelt before me on the walk and pulled one foot toward him before I could object, and inspected it.

Face warm, I felt every inch of my status as a theater girl. "I appreciate the effort, but I'll be quite all right."

He raised an eyebrow. "All that practice will be wasted unless you do something for those feet now." He released them, allowing me to tuck them out of sight again. "You know, the least intelligent choice I ever made was to ignore my swordfighting wounds after a particularly hard battle. Well, no, the *worst* choice was challenging a giant to a swordfight in the first place."

I bit my lip against a retort and tried—really tried—not to roll my eyes.

He stood and looked at me pointedly, arms crossed. "I have lanolin ointment at my flat, if you'd care to brave it. It'll help."

I flushed at the notion. In his flat, alone with him? "That isn't necessary."

"Very well then, a hand, perhaps. You've somewhere to be, do you not? Come, I'll help you get there."

Warning signals flared. I bent forward and shoved ankle boots onto my stockingless feet. "Really, Mr. Dorian. I can take care of myself." All I could think in that moment was *high moral character* and *above reproach*—lines in my contract—and all the eyes on us now. Well, and the fact that I couldn't seem to shake the man loose.

"Why, when you don't have to? Wherever you need to be, let me take you." He stepped close, gaze holding steady but tinged with a smile. "Remember, I know some of your secrets more thoroughly than you do." His voice was low and private yet inviting. Gentle. "You may find me quite valuable for more than a mere walking stick. And for the record, the name's Jack. Just plain Jack. And I'm only offering to help."

I steeled myself against his attempt to win me over. The bet. Of course, it was all about the bet. I tensed with the awareness that he, at some point, was going to attempt to kiss me. Every shield was in place. Yet when I looked at him, I felt the echo of curiosity clang through my being. What knowledge did this man have of my father? What might he tell me that could change everything? "Very well, then. *Mr. Dorian.* You're kind to offer your help."

He bowed as if I were a lady, a comical grin on his face, and it was troubling how much I wanted to laugh. "I promise to be on my very best behavior. I also promise you won't get very far in whatever you're doing without my help."

Within minutes, the man had handed me into a hackney cab and climbed in after me. He had a convincing way about him, that Jack Dorian, and I was not easily convinced. At least, I didn't use to be.

I looked him over from across the dark vehicle. "You must have other places to be."

He shrugged. "No place I wish to be. A most disagreeable engagement that I don't mind missing, if the truth be known."

I stared at this man across from me, openly judging his fickle nature.

"Where to?"

"Just to St. Paul's on Bedford Street. Truly, a cab isn't necessary for so short a trip. You're kind to offer, but it must be less than a mile."

He eyed me. "Did you plan to limp the entire mile, then? Those poor feet. It's a wonder they don't apply for new ownership."

A smile twitched my lips in spite of myself. He was amusing, at least. We drove through city streets in silence and pulled to stop beside tall, stylish buildings with clean squares of glass and colorful merchandise on display. Streetlamps extended from every building out over the paved walk to keep the bustling street alive after dark.

When he handed me down from the carriage, he looked me over as if evaluating my fitness. Apparently, I failed the exam. "I hope you'll allow me to continue with you."

I sighed, my feet throbbing now that they were back in use, and looked down the hectic block where the church sat. "Have I a choice?"

With a keen eye for weakness in others, the man managed to get his way more often than not. He smiled. "Come now, you've made me late to my engagement, so we might as well finish the deal. And please, you'll be rescuing me. I beg you."

I scrutinized him, aware that my only alternative was a warm foot bath and another night of mental anguish. It would be a week before I could get away again during daylight hours. I resented his intrusion even while thanking God he'd come along when he did.

"Very well, but you must promise not to ask a single question." I wasn't about to let the man charm a jot of information out of me. He'd already gotten enough for one day. "Not one."

He flashed his signature smile. "You have my word as a gentleman. Shall we go in?"

We moved up the generous walk to the gate and passed under the arch, entering the churchyard bordered on either side of us by a short black iron fence. There was an instant thrum of peace amidst the muffled chaos, and I thought how fitting that was. Despite its reputation, this place felt sacred. "We're not allowed past. Those are the rules." I pointed at the sign nailed to the gate.

He gave a boyish shrug and hopped the short fence. "Mere suggestions. We aren't ruffians throwing stones now, are we?" He rattled the rusted gate and opened it for me from the inside, ushering me in.

Incorrigible. With a deep breath, I grasped his arm and limped into the narrow churchyard protected on both sides by tall brick buildings and in the rear by the barn-style church.

With shadows from the sinking sun long and gray before us, I steeled myself for the shock of seeing his name, this man who had begun to haunt me against my will. Moss-covered headstones brought back rolling memories of theater legends, all the stories Mama had told me, and I paused to study a few. *Ballet is the only art form that never outlives the artist. A dancer is only alive for as long as she can dance, then the world forgets.*

"Have you someone in mind?"

I ignored his flagrant disregard for my one and only request. He couldn't help himself, it seemed.

"You're looking for de Silva, I suppose. I've made you curious."

"Mr. Dorian. My rules."

"Hang the rules, it wasn't a question!"

"I don't care for people who intrude."

"You won't find Marcus de Silva here. At least, not yet."

I strained to see another stone in the settling dark. "Where is he?"

"Now *that's* a question."

"That rule only applies to you, Mr. Dorian."

"Of course." He crossed his arms over his chest. "And for pity's sake, call me Jack."

"Do you plan to answer me, Mr. Dorian?"

"*Jack.*"

"Is he still involved in the theater?"

My companion quieted, his arm tensing under my hand. "In a manner. Though, not as a dancer. He's too old for such things."

"It should be easy to find him, then. If I wanted to, of course."

"Not as easy as you believe. He had to change his name. No one knows he used to be called Marcus de Silva, except those of us who knew him before."

"And why should I believe you?"

"Have you any alternative?"

I looked up into his face, his daring eyes.

"Right, right. A question. Strike the last comment." He shuffled forward, free hand in his pocket. "I won't give him up so easily, though. Not to just anyone."

I watched his profile, and there glimmered on his countenance the briefest crack in his cheeky nature. "He means a lot to you, doesn't he?"

Silence. "Aye." That single word carried a great deal of weight. He'd sobered as fast as a stone plummeting in a riverbed. He turned me gently to face him. "Look, I'm weary of dancing about. I know you can help me free him, that you know something, and it won't cost you a thing to say it."

Oh, but it would, Mr. Dorian. If only you knew just how much it would cost me. "I wasn't aware that he was imprisoned."

"Only by his own self. He's a shell of a human. He ceased to live the night of the fire, and I need to know—for his sake—what happened. I need answers you obviously have."

"Mr. Dorian, I value my privacy. If he truly is innocent, there must be other ways to clear his name. I will not give up the one thing that is solely mine."

"I should think you'd want his freedom as much as I do. Isn't the man your father?"

I bristled. "I will not answer such private questions."

"That was all the answer I needed, love." He kicked a loose pebble.

"How can you possibly assume such a relationship from mere similarity of the eyes?"

He looked right at me. "You gave away more than you know. There were other things. What I don't know is why you won't claim the man, even to me."

I straightened. "You would presume to know all about my life, all my reasons?"

His eyes were a storm of colors. "That would trouble you, wouldn't it? Having someone see past the lifelong cloak of secrecy you were raised to wear, past the safety of your secrets and shields to the big, looming fear that's underneath. Fear of those around you—whose opinions have become like oxygen—fear of your own doubts and faults, fear that your smooth white eggshell exterior will crack, and the truth will come oozing out at everyone's feet."

I couldn't stop trembling. My legs first, beneath my skirts, but then my arms, all the way down to my fingertips. I wanted to stop him, but I was so stunned by this mirror held up to my soul.

"You do not belong—that's what you believe, isn't it? Because you've only trained two years when the lot of them worked ten years or more. Because you aren't certain who you are, or to whom you belong. Well, let me assure you, Ella Blythe, you *do* belong. You have a gem of a father who's aching for the missing pieces of his life, for forgiveness, for freedom I believe only you can provide. Think of what you both could mean to each other."

I gripped a mossy headstone and recoiled from the sliminess. The trembles passed like lightning through my body. Think about it, he'd said. In truth, I couldn't *stop* thinking about it.

"You value your privacy like a bank box to hold your valuables. Yet I wonder—who are you protecting? Someone you love? Or perhaps yourself, who isn't always as invincible as she pretends to be?"

My voice came out low and soft. "Why do you do this to me?"

"I won't give up on him. Too many already have."

But why? I stared at him, searching for resemblance to the man in the portrait—to me. "Who are you, exactly?"

"How long have you?" His expression glittered with quiet mischief, then he fell silent.

How was it that I'd come here for answers, for closure, but found myself two steps back on both counts? Curiosity rippled through me, and a sense of rejection that my father would be known by this man but not his daughter. It wasn't fair, of course, feeling that way, but my heart could be like that at times.

I breathed in, the gap widening in my fatherless soul. "Very well then, what is it exactly you want me to do, Mr. Dorian?"

He took my hands with overflowing earnestness and held them to his chest. "I have to know—please tell me—how are you connected with Delphine Bessette? What do you know of her death?"

I withdrew my hands, taking a step back. "What makes you think I am?"

"The red slippers. I know you have them. I want to know how—and why."

Heat poured down my face and through my neck. "That

is the one thing I cannot tell you." Whatever had happened between them, whatever love or tragedy, she deserved the protection I'd promised her years ago. "Besides, I no longer have them. They were stolen."

At the shock on his face, at least I knew he hadn't been the thief.

"By whom?"

I dropped my gaze and shrugged, but he saw the guess on my face.

"It wouldn't have been him. He'd have announced himself, spoken to you as a gentleman should."

"You have a high opinion of the man." I walked a few more paces. "Who else would even want them? Or know what they were?"

"I suppose anyone at Craven might have known and had access. What about Mama Jo? How well do you trust the woman?"

I shook my head. "The skirts were shut in the wardrobe door when the thief left. No dancer would have been so careless."

Another question was forming in his expression, but then we rounded a corner and the first grave on the east side of the cemetery stopped me cold. With a pain that shuddered through my chest, I glimpsed a crooked marker adorned with fresh red roses, her favorite, and the engraved name that slammed into my vision and heart—Delphine Bessette.

I had to remind myself there was no one actually buried there. Perhaps they'd collected some ashes from the fire that night so they'd have something to memorialize. Some way to pay tribute.

My legs trembled as I looked at that name, the dates that marked her life before the fire. Not even a mention of her real name—as if all she'd been was a ballerina. I knelt and touched the fading petals of the red flowers, and the dead ones of many former offerings that had dried flat into the ground. Someone grieved her still. Regularly.

"You look pale." Jack knelt to help me rise. His demeanor was utterly different now, melted like snow. "Come, I'll take you home."

Weak, torn, heart raw and vulnerable, I pulled my hand back. "Why do you poke at me so with your questions? What are you up to, besides antagonizing me at every turn?"

Those prism blue eyes centered on my face. "Do you ever grow tired? Of swinging that cumbersome sword around that's too heavy for you? Yes, there's more to my 'why' concerning Marcus de Silva, but as you've already made up your mind about things, I see no reason to tell you."

"You will eventually, whether you mean to or not."

He studied me. "You know, you have a way of saying things that makes me believe nearly anything that comes out of your mouth. And that's dangerous."

We moved slowly past the other stones, but I saw none of them. In fact, the first thing my gaze focused on after that upheaval of my soul was a lone figure in a dark greatcoat out on Bedford Street just outside the churchyard, poised with his gaze affixed on us.

He turned, and as he loped away, I recognized the unmistakable gait that often accompanied me home. It was Philippe.

12

*B*ack in my flat, I soaked my feet until they were numb, then applied salve and wrapped them in rags. Somehow I'd have to dance on them come morning. Then the performance would be upon us in three days' time, and I had a solo. A moment out in front. I could do this—I *would*. Even if I had to practice ten times harder than anyone else, I was capable of dancing and doing it well.

I turned as the window groaned open. I watched Minna descend into the room and close the sash.

"You're home early. The count was tired today, I take it."

"Yes, well. There's nothing for it when his daughter suddenly has need of him."

I cringed.

"A grown woman, and she cannot do without *Papa* to fix her little problems." She plunked herself before the mirror, poked at the skin under her eyes. In *Il Fiore Danzante*, she had earned the part of the maiden's friend, who joins the lead for several appearances and performs a stunning *divertissement* when she warns her mistress against falling in love with a wicked man. A stark contrast from her real life.

"The performance is soon." It seemed almost silly, the way

things were on the continent, the way real life was, to be flitting about onstage as a host of flowers, but Fournier had insisted that the riots had worn everyone down and the audience needed a reprieve for at least one show. A bit of beauty with no politics attached. "Perhaps you should forget about the count and focus on practice."

She eyed me cooly. "And what, become like you?" Her gaze dropped to my wrapped feet as I busied myself with pinning the costume on my body to measure for adjustments. "Good heavens, what have you done to them this time?" She selected a small jar from her table and tossed it to me. "Here. This should help." She folded her arms. "But so would a little rest."

I wanted rest. Oh, how I wanted it. But that notion always came with an odd pang of guilt. I'd gripped the ladder to pull myself up rung by rung, and I simply could not stop. Not unless I wanted to fall off. I pinned like mad along the right seam, ignoring the throb in my feet.

I shifted and felt a sickening *rip*, my costume instantly going slack on the left. I fumbled for the tear with my fingertips, praying it was nothing. It had, however, frayed the costume. My head already swam with exhaustion, and now it would take hours more to repair this.

My passion had ebbed, I realized then, receding like the tide with each day that passed. I worked harder than most. And for what? How did spinning and leaping about have anything to do with God? Or with anything that mattered?

"Don't fixate on it. Don't fixate." Those words from Mama echoed through my aching head as I pulled the calico gaiters

on backstage to warm my legs before the performance. The familiar knots hardened in my belly, churning up everything I'd dared eat that day.

Dear Father God, please help me through this. The quick prayer nudged my heart back into movement on rusty tracks. It had been a while. But now I needed all the help I could find.

"Best of luck to you," Tovah said as she rushed by to take her place, and I followed close behind.

I had all but forgotten about the heat of the overhead lights, the tight pull of my pinned hair, the eyes—oh, the *eyes*—hundreds of audience members turned their attention to the curtain spreading in front of our poised company, then there was applause. Pulse-pounding. Thrilling. Terrifying.

I crouched in position on the stage, and when the curtain parted, flooding the dimness with the glow of golden chandeliers, I fixed my gaze upon my focal point, the little peep above the audience, and fancied I saw a face there. A young girl, starstruck and in love with ballet.

All sound beyond the stage dimmed for one time-stopping moment, the whole place holding its breath. Then the music rolled out from the pit, and I felt the largeness of the ballet again, the full-bodied orchestra resounding in my chest, thudding against my ribs. We rose, slowly animating before the audience and sweeping into the opening of *Il Fiore Danzante* as flowers unfurling their color.

Annika Friedl was stunning as the maiden, so torn over love. I watched her between my dances. Precise and lithe, at home in her body, natural as a silk scarf waving in the breeze. She was a mesmerizing storyteller. Watching her, something akin to envy curled through me. I nearly forgot to sway with the other flowers.

"Focus on where you want to go." Mama had said that, years ago. *"Your eyes are always the first to latch onto something, and they'll guide the rest of you there."* From now on, I would focus on Annika. Beautiful, controlled Annika, who had earned the privilege of dancing every performance with Philippe Rousseau.

I spun with a breathless flourish as the music climbed into a crescendo, signaling Philippe's entrance. He'd done another disappearing act, and I hadn't seen him since the cemetery. We all held our breath in that final moment before his planned entrance, breaking concentration for a moment to look at each other. Would he appear?

I waited, poised. My heart pounded. Then he leaped out with a cymbal crash and spun in center stage, twirling at blinding speed. Mighty leaps carried him around the rear of the stage and back to Annika, whom he swept up in a dramatic embrace. Thus joined, they danced a most perfect pas de deux, an almost intimate portrayal of lovers who moved as one.

Philippe was the glow of that performance, the outpouring of those thousands of unwritten poems pressurized inside him, now spilling out on the stage. What in heaven's name had he done with himself in that absence? He was magnificent, his body in perfect rhythm with the dramatic music, his dance following the push and pull of the song as if it were part of his being.

He whipped past me in an acrobatic spin, sucking the breath from my lungs and splaying cool air across my face. All fell silent, the whole world frozen in time to watch this masterful artist display his strength, to soak up the emotion exuding from his being. It was then I realized just how depleted he'd become, up until now. His technique was always impeccable, but now there was so much life in his dance that I could scarcely take my eyes from him.

Yet this was the man who'd written off love. I watched him and knew—I *knew*—the inner man was capable of feeling what he conveyed on the stage.

He spun one last time and tossed something small into the audience—a rosebud. A delighted sound arose, and one woman stood to catch it. I strained to see who, but something else caught my gaze past the stage. Something green. I blinked, but it was not a hat—only a scarf hanging over the back of a chair near the front. I scanned further, hardly able to see past the first rows, but then . . . I saw *him*.

He sat tall and refined in his seat just off to the side of the stage, dressed in all black save for his silver hair, and those deep prism eyes. I could hardly breathe. *"One day you will find him, Miss Blythe, right under your very nose."*

My muscles suddenly tried to liquefy as I lifted into an arabesque, my heart a thunderstorm within. Suddenly my impending solo took on far more meaning. Two and a half minutes and my father, the stranger-man who looked so much like me, would be focused on my dance. On me.

The flowers rose and circled Annika, then spun off, and it was my turn—my variation. Focused, strong, I lifted into my turns and pulled my arms in tight. Around and around I moved, head buzzing with tiredness, legs trembling, vision snapping back over and over to the peep high above.

I swept into a landing just a little off center and held my position. Another lift of my arms and it was *finito*. The two lines of other flowers were sweeping across center stage, and I fell in with them. Soon the thick curtain blessedly swept across, separating us from the heat of the gaslights. We'd been a success. It was over, and I hadn't fallen on my face. I collapsed against the wall backstage with heavy breaths, then I peeled back a few inches of the heavy drapes, peering out at that man, but the lights blinded me from this angle.

When the final piece came to a close, the callboy moved me aside to pull the ropes and open the curtains again, and the heat, the noise of applause, swarmed us. Pasting smiles, forcing poise into our tired bodies, we floated in two lines across the stage, clasped hands, and curtsied to the sound of praise.

I lifted my head and squinted against the lights as we pas de bourreéd backward toward the shadows. All I could see was a deep, nearly iridescent red ribbon around his hat to match his cravat, making him stand out in a sea of darker colors—red, the same color as Mum's slippers. Unless my fanciful mind was making all this up. If I could only see his face better.

The curtains swept closed again and I nearly spun into Tovah. "You were magnificent," she breathed.

"You as well."

I heard them leaving. Hushed voices, scuffing footsteps up the aisle. Soon he'd be gone, vanishing back into the shadows. I grabbed her shoulders. "I'll be back."

Tovah frowned, but I bolted toward the stairs, applause still popping in my ears. What a little fool I was. Yet I couldn't imagine the berating I'd give myself when I was alone for the night, staring up at the ceiling, knowing I'd done nothing.

I hadn't seen Jack Dorian all night, but somewhere in the backstage area, the man was likely smiling darkly as he watched me fly off the stage and down toward the side entrance in pursuit of the once-famous Marcus de Silva.

13

I often act foolishly and call it impetuous. This was one of those times. I whirled my cloak around my shoulders and hurried out the side door, into the night crisply spiced with the last of winter.

Peering around the east corner of the building like a common snoop, I waited for him, watching throngs of people pour from the doors to be handed into the carriages and cabs that snaked up and down the street for blocks. Snow had begun to fall in large, wet drops that seeped through fabric and chilled the skin, slicking the walks and roads. I spotted that scarlet band bobbing through the growing chaos, through the falling snow clumping on my eyelashes. I fought through the surging crowds, heedless of the looks and grumbles, until I stood a mere horse's length from him. How fine and tall he was, with a shiny top hat over silvered hair. And yes—it was him. The man from the portrait. *Him.* "Pardon, sir. A word, please." My voice was soft, but he heard.

He turned with slow grace, and to my horror, so did a lady on his arm. She was far younger than him, her pale skin flawless and pure, yet they were undoubtedly a couple—her satin dress matched his cravat, and that scarlet ribbon. She challenged me with a lovely blue-eyed stare, laying out the difference in our social rank with a look.

"You are . . ." Not Marcus de Silva. Not anymore. "You are a theater man, are you not?"

"He'll have nothing to do with your kind." The slender woman beside him straightened, cinching his arm against her side. "He's a respectable man and devoted to his wife."

I felt myself blushing at the insinuation, then one word locked into my awareness. *Wife?* But of course. What had I expected? I steeled myself against the sense of betrayal, the questions flooding my being, and met his gaze. "I believe I am acquainted with . . . your daughter."

At this, the man went dark and the woman's gaze flickered, a long-standing ache dulling her features. She knew about us, it seemed, and was ashamed.

He wrapped a protective arm around the small woman beside him, then I heard my father's voice, smooth and silvery, for the first time: "I'm sorry, I believe you're mistaken. It is our distinct disappointment that we have not been blessed with children."

"*Yet.*" The woman's sharp whisper was almost inaudible. The feather in her hat trembled.

My spirit crumbled at the gaping loss on her face, and I could not hurt her further with the truth of who I was. "Please, could you just tell me—"

He held up his hand with a frown, his eyes dull and distant. "I can do nothing to advance your career, no matter the connection you believe you have. I'm sorry. I bid you good night, *mademoiselle.*"

"Wait." I touched his arm and he turned, slight offense

streaking his handsome face. If only he knew who I was . . .
"Perhaps you will remember my mother. She was known for
her red shoes." I lifted my eyes with as much dignity as I could,
hoping they did not resemble a desperate puppy with all the
hope and angst and waiting bottled up inside.

His gaze hardened, which wasn't what I'd expected. He
breathed in slowly, his coat stretching against his chest, then
let it out with a gusty sigh and narrowing eyes. "Delphine's.
You are Delphine's child."

"Yes." I breathed out the word.

His breath swirled out before my face, but he said nothing—
only studied me.

The woman tugged on his arm. "Come, Peter."

"No, no. This woman will know the truth." He turned to
me, steel in his eyes, his voice low. "I'm even less inclined to
help you, knowing you are *her* offspring. No good can come
from Delphine Bessette, and I don't mind saying it. Now if
you'll excuse me."

He turned and left, that man from the portrait, leading his
pretty wife by the arm. I stood alone on that sidewalk, clutching my arms about me, all my shame replaced with disbelief
and a slow-burning bitterness. The chill of the night suddenly
snaked through me.

Crushing. That's what this was. Unexpectedly so. I hadn't
ever needed a father, had I? Yet he'd always been a question
mark. An unfinished scene.

Now I knew. Scene closed.

The moment shattered around me as I watched them go, my
much-anticipated meeting with my father over and done. *"He's
a shell of a human. He ceased to live that night."*

I studied the man handing his much-younger wife into their

126

carriage, and my gaze burned into his back. He was doing an awful lot of living for a dead thing. I turned and felt my cheeks flame on the walk back to the stage door, a sullen sense of rejection hanging about me. This is how the world was—especially in theater. There was always drama and conflict, tragedy and secrets. Otherwise it didn't belong onstage, did it?

I paused to throw one more look over my shoulder, watching him grasp the handles on either side of the carriage door and swing his tall frame up, and then it happened. It was so quick I almost wasn't sure, but he glanced back at me from inside. For a flash, our eyes held.

Then he slammed the door and rode away.

In the morning, the reviews were all over the table at Mama Jo's. They praised Annika for her "perfect execution" and the *Morning Chronicle* claimed she "exercised a singular power over every muscle of her slender frame." The *Post* called her "exquisite beyond compare." All the girls at Mama Jo's gathered 'round the prints to greedily skim for their names, eager for a small taste of honeyed praise on their tongues. Nothing was said of my little spotlight, but I'd already had the most unshakable rejection I could imagine.

Nothing had changed in my life. Not truly. I'd never had a father to begin with.

When the run finally came to a close after two weeks of performances, I began saying yes. I said yes to Annika when she offered more private lessons, yes to Tovah when she invited me out on our day off. That second found me experiencing a public bathhouse for the first time.

The water shimmered in my own private copper tub, clean and inviting.

"It wasn't all bad, you know. Especially for your first performance." Tovah's lively voice carried over the half wall separating us as we undressed in our stalls. Somehow, its timbre matched her thick, spiraling hair full of springy joy. "You should be glad."

"That it's over? Oh, I am." I peeled my chemise off and slipped into the tepid water, closing my eyes as I sank to my neck. Yes, this had been a wise use of our day, even though it cost sixpence apiece.

The run had been hard. Fournier had sought me out for special criticism again, and I wore his words around my neck, along with the memory of my father's turned back.

"Something's been bothering you for weeks, hasn't it? More than the performance. Since the first night, you weren't yourself onstage."

I sank lower in the tub. "I happened upon my long-lost father on opening night. He was in the audience."

Water swished in the next stall, then her face appeared. "Truly? You never said a word. Well then, what did you think of the man?"

I lifted one foot from the water, studying my ugly, calloused toes. "He's wed to another woman."

"Is he, now?"

"It's hard to feel much affection toward the man, knowing that."

Silence ticked by for a few seconds, except water dripping on her side as she lifted out a limb. "Is he not a widower?"

Well . . . yes. *Now* anyway. Likely not when he married. "I still cannot forgive him." I shivered in my bathwater, mentally chiding myself for having told Tovah too much. I'd nearly collapsed in the corridor on the anniversary of Mum's passing, and I'd been forced to give her the reason. She was quick to swoop in and look after me, and I was growing accustomed to it. At least I hadn't mentioned names.

"Give the man a chance. What widower wants to be alone his whole life? It is a sorry matter that he never came looking for you, though." She sank back into her tub. "Or perhaps he simply didn't know where to find you. London's a large place, you know."

"What if he's like Jack Dorian? Or all those married men who keep dancers in flats outside Covent Garden? He seemed very flippant about the past. His new wife didn't seem to know my mother had ever existed . . . or me." I closed my eyes, wondering if he'd have given me a different answer about Mum if his wife hadn't been standing beside him. I'd likely obliterated any chance of finding out.

She sighed. "It was wretched of him, not telling her about you, but he's no Jack Dorian. Besides, Jack only runs after dancers and prostitutes from Seven Dials—the only ones who'd give him a moment of their time. Your mother was in a respectable trade, now, wasn't she?"

My chest constricted. "She took in sewing all my life." My skin crawled with the omission of truth, but I didn't correct it. *For you, precious Mum.* I'd spent my life taking care of her, and keeping her secret was all I could offer now.

"There, you see? It's a completely different situation. I'm certain he's a fine gent who'll be pleased to acknowledge his daughter, once he has a moment to think it over."

I laid my head back on the metal rim. Two weeks. It had been two weeks, and he knew exactly where to find me. Of all the men who marched through that greenroom door, he'd never been one of them. A cold, metallic acceptance settled deep within me as I rose and toweled dry. I felt another string tying me down to this earth loosen, my heart longing once again for heaven and the comfort of the rescuing Father who'd always been there. Even when I had not.

Thwip. Fabric hit my face and I stumbled. It was a clean dress, lobbed over the wall from Tovah's side. "You'll want something clean, now that you are."

I fumbled with the fabric, shaking out a lovely woolen dress of dark blue. I hadn't even thought to bring another set.

"Philippe Rousseau has been asking after you."

My heart climbed into my throat. "Has he?" I hadn't allowed myself to think of him lately, especially after encountering my father. I could feel the hurt and uncertainty that had weighed Mama down settling on me as well, every time Philippe vanished again. My heart was not built for such back-and-forth.

Philippe had been present for every performance in those two weeks, and I for one had been intensely curious, but no one had said a word about his absences. There had been no walks home, for rehearsals had gone late for all of us and we had mostly dragged ourselves home together every night.

Yet he had been asking after me. "What exactly did he ask?"

"Oh, how you'd been getting on, if Jack had been bothering you, that sort of thing." There was a click and a snap from her side. "He seems to think you're attached to Jack. Many of them do."

"I hope you set them straight. There are rumors, you know—a bet. Whether or not he can kiss me."

"Jack may not let you alone so easily, then, if there's something in it for him."

I fastened my stays, hooked my garter, and changed the topic. "I'm beginning to believe in the healing qualities of these places after all. Every inch of me feels fresh and tingly." I slipped into the lovely blue dress and let it fall over my cinched frame.

"It's about time you listened to me." She threw back the curtain and entered to help me button the thing. I tied my hair up high as she fastened my dress. Her fingers slowed. "It's more than kindness, isn't it? With Philippe, I mean. You've broken through. You've gotten him to open up, haven't you?"

I opened my mouth, straightened. "We're . . . friends. I think." I grimaced at the memory of him in the distance, watching me lean on Jack Dorian.

She turned to let me button her and lifted those laughing green eyes to mine. "If he's told you his secrets—any of them—you're more friends with him than any of the rest of us are." Her eyebrows lifted. "Perhaps more than friends."

The clang of rejection still echoed through my hollow chest. I didn't care to feel it again from another man with a tendency to disappear. "I don't know if I could bear to walk any deeper into the shadows around that man. I may not like what I find."

"Or you may find yourself in the middle of the grandest love story this side of the curtain."

Second grandest. I turned with an exhale. "Let's not talk of it anymore. I've had enough of men for one day."

She looped her arm through mine, those twin emeralds of eyes still gleaming at me. "Very well, but you mustn't wait too long to untangle this one. Tomorrow is the cuts, and if you remain, we'll have a new performance to prepare. And if not . . . well, time may be short."

That word *if* echoed in my head, tying me in knots as we walked through town. They cut regularly, and for hardly any reason at all. Every ballet company was struggling, and Craven was no large-scale theater. How many would they cut tomorrow? Delight and heady fear rippled through me as we walked together before the shops, my change in fortune only a day before me.

I'd begun to realize that I belonged nowhere but here, to no one but these people. After working as a dancer, no one else would have me. I suddenly had the sensation of grabbing onto the pieces of my life as they fell away from me.

14

The Great Fournier's cigar came out with a trail of smoke. "You. And you." Two dancers, one who'd had an extended illness and another afraid of her own shadow, released their stance and left the line.

The rest of us held our breath. He consulted his papers, frowned, and took three more steps. "You." Another dancer peeled away. I held my breath as he paused at Tovah, looking her up and down, gaze landing on her wild curls. "Do something with that hair."

"Yes, *monsieur*." She melted back with a curtsy but remained in the line.

Two more strides and his gaze was roving over me from above, inspecting me for flaws. A chill overtook me as I stood waiting, breathing in the odor of his sticky-sweet cigar. I was positive his gaze deepened upon my face and I heard a low, guttural growl. Part bear?

"Put a little romance into your dance—a little warmth, yes? Ballet is not stiff, Miss Blythe." His voice was surprisingly elegant and controlled, all growling aside.

I drew in a breath and closed my eyes, then he was gone with a *whoosh* of cool air, gliding down the line. I opened my eyes and looked about the greenroom where I still belonged. For now.

Romance, though. How did one dance alone . . . *romantically?*

Bellini stood in front of the room, raising his arms to draw a close to the chittering conversations. When the room went silent, he bestowed his news upon us. "The next production will be the fairy tale *Cannatella.* A king and his highly selective daughter, a magician who schemes to gain her hand, and the disastrous consequences."

He paced along the stage, gaze lifted to the ceiling. "Revenge never ends well, a truth this world sorely needs to hear just now. And it's up to you to convey it powerfully." At the hush in the room, we all felt the weight of his words. Apparently he had his way over Fournier this time, and the ballet was to be a political statement rather than an escape.

"The magician, who is in fact the mortal enemy of the king, has married his daughter only to lock her up and taunt her with all the things she cannot have. The princess role will need to portray the depth of longing she feels when she is in want for the first time. Then as the captor begins to fall in love with her, I want every heart swelling with the pain of his unrequited affection.

"Of course the princess escapes, and when the magician comes to get her, I want the audience gasping as the king strikes him down for his crimes. Revenge turned back on the avenger." He stalked harder across the stage. "Our audience must see France's Louis Philippe in the fairy-tale king, and with the magician, *feel* every inch of the righteous anger that flooded Paris. The absolute need to stand up and revolt. Tension is on the rise again in Paris, and so we in theater will do what all art does—

deliver truth dressed in beautiful movement and magnificent storytelling."

Murmurs resumed. Philippe, across the stage from me, stood straight and unreadable near the open curtain. France was his ancestors' birthplace, the Parisians his people. What must he think of this project?

"I'll have partial choreography to give you all by Wednesday. Audition and placements begin next week. Including for the lead female role." That news brought total silence. "Regretfully, we've had to release our beloved principal due to a . . . well, a sore knee."

We all looked at each other. Of all things, a "sore knee"—Annika, with child? She'd never spoken of any romance, any man who might be the baby's father.

"We'll host an audition, as usual."

But this time the stakes were higher, the opportunities more significant.

"Come fully prepared to amaze us. It'll be the finest ballet this side of Covent Garden, and we expect to make headlines. I need it to be sensational, dramatic, and despite the tragic ending, *exceedingly romantic*." He raised pinched fingers to emphasize the last point.

Romantic, of course. The one thing I, apparently, was not.

"It's a retelling adapted, as usual, by our very own Jack Dorian."

Jack, standing just behind the man, pinched the seams of his trousers and dipped in a mock curtsy, drawing feminine giggles. I steeled my jaw.

Perhaps I should study romance from Jack Dorian. He had it in spades.

No, there was one other option I'd try first.

"So about that little romance of yours." I looked my sister over carefully, noting the healthy glow in her eyes. "I suppose I should hear the rest. As your sister, of course."

Lily cut her haddock at a little table in the Blackgate Inn, a place that kept late hours to serve those from the theater. If anyone had insight on being romantic and falling in love, it was Lily. She did it once or twice a week.

Her smile pinked her cheeks, heightening her loveliness. It was easy to see how men had such trouble turning a blind eye to her. One glance and any man would be pudding at her feet. She leveled her playful gaze at me, leaning close. "There's a man who takes walks through the square at luncheon to watch the construction. He's bought me strawberry tartlets from the vendors and hot chocolate sometimes too."

Summer *and* winter treats? "This has been going on for quite some time."

"It's been most unusual, and I have not managed to look at another man since."

"He must be a prince."

"Captain. Of something. Gold tassels, medals, a sash across his chest . . ." She settled in with a crooked little smile.

I raised my eyebrows. She was like a magnet, drawing them to her. I could never be that. I stiffened as Philippe Rousseau's recognizable form entered the café, brushing light snow from his greatcoat. I'd spent so long chasing men away that I hadn't any idea how to invite a good one near. Not even for pretend, onstage.

I blew the hair off my face. "So you just . . . happened to bump into a man at the park and what, you started talking?" I couldn't wrap my head around the way these romances of hers occurred. I attempted to start one, and five years later it was finally showing signs of beginning.

"It's never mere chance, you know. Men only talk to you if they're offered a little . . . warmth."

Philippe spoke to the man at the counter and shoved his hands in his pockets, shoulders hunched against the lingering cold.

"How does one go about showing . . . warmth?"

Lily blotted her mouth and watched me with mirthful eyes. "My dear sister, are you asking for my advice on men?"

"You seem shocked." I heated through to my scalp. "It isn't rare to exchange advice on love between sisters."

"It's never been a two-way exchange."

I pressed my lips together.

"Right, then." She straightened in her chair and leaned forward, voice low. "It's quite easy, and you needn't even open your mouth. Not at first. All you need to do is glance at the man as if you know some secret you can barely hold in, then look down and smile because you're not going to give it away."

"What's the secret I know?"

"Just pretend there's one. And I always imagine the man in his knickers."

My lungs inflated. "Lily!"

"Do you want advice or spinsterhood?"

"Well, I'd blush if I thought of *that*."

"All the better." Her smile was playful. "Only, don't try this with simply *any* man. Merely a few choice ones, or you'll be known as a flirt. You can always tell if he's worth your while by looking at his socks."

I blinked. "His socks?"

"Men never fuss over their socks, so if he's poor, that's the first thing he'll be cheap about. Nice socks mark a well-appointed gentleman fit to offer a fine living."

I spooned stew into my mouth, letting the ample meat dish settle my belly, and looked out the paned window just past my right shoulder. Shops were closed up tight all along the street, and people hurried home to get out of the cold. "How does the conversation work?"

"Work?" She smiled around a bite of carrots. "Well, men never like a woman who talks back, so don't do it. You mustn't ever seem smarter than him."

"What if I am?"

Her wide eyes sparkled. "That's the art of the thing, sister. You must paint yourself as he wishes you to be, not as you are."

I frowned. Philippe had moved to a small table near the back, draped in shadows. What did he wish me to be? Should I even attempt to be that?

Perhaps romance and love were simply not for me.

The next morning, with Lily's advice still ringing in my mind, I openly stared at Jack Dorian. He moved toward a *quadrille* dancer with such simple movements, but his every gesture held fluid strength and ease. I watched him for more than a quarter of an hour as he glided about the room with the poise of a lion, yet his easy manner warmed people whenever he drew near. *Yes, that's it.* I couldn't lay my finger on what it was, this combination of confidence and charm, but I knew I needed it in my dancing.

I didn't have the courage to approach him until everyone

had gone for the night. Then I found him in the auditorium at the end of the empty aisle, speaking in earnest with the Great Fournier. When he caught sight of me up on the stage, Fournier nodded good night to his companion, and Jack stood there watching me, arms folded.

Why did this have to be so awkward? If only Lily could lend me a touch of her charm as easily as I lent her some of my coin. I fidgeted with my skirt, looked down at the steps. "I suppose you may walk me home. Just this once."

"How kind of me." His voice echoed across the empty auditorium as he strode up the aisle. "I didn't know I'd offered."

I turned hot. "No one's forcing you."

He bounded up the steps and extended his arm. "I have a feeling this is something I shouldn't miss."

I laid my fingertips on the crook of his arm, not giving him an inch of room to misunderstand. He allowed me exactly three and a half minutes of silence through the streets of London, up Craven and along the Strand, before he poked at me again. "You might as well come out with it. Something about de Silva, is it?"

The name hit me anew in the chest. "Not at all."

"Then please, do tell what led you to allow me to escort you home after so many sound rejections."

"*That*." I waved a finger at his chest. "How do you do . . . that?"

A pause. "I must admit, now I'm even more curious. I haven't the faintest idea what you mean."

I tucked my chin into my cloak and felt the heat through my layers. What a rotten idea this was. "All the . . . grace. Confidence." I waved my hand around vaguely. "All I can manage is stiffness and—"

"Ah, your dancing. You want advice on your performances."

"Fournier says I need a spark of romance."

"So you've come to me." There was amusement in his voice.

"Well, you are the expert." Heavens, this was unsettling.

His eyebrows shot up. "Am I, now?"

"I've yet to see you without an utterly charmed woman by your side and a smile on that silly face of yours. I suppose that's what I need to do to audiences—charm them the way you charm women."

He fell silent and paced on for two and a half blocks, during which time I worried through more than a hundred different ways he could have taken my words.

Finally his voice, soft but firm, came out with puffs of steam in the cold. "You care too much."

My gaze shot to his.

"Drop the extra practices. You're not perfect, so why waste time trying to be?"

This was headed in the wrong direction. "You've never been a ballet dancer. You couldn't understand." I'd heard it too many times—the *relax your standards* speech, and it only rankled. Everything rested on the precision of each dancer onstage. "Ballet is a show of collective perfection."

"No, listen." He crossed his arms, pausing on the walk. "Perfection is an illusion, and you'll never reach it. It's an utter waste of time to attempt it."

I rolled my eyes with a sigh.

"Scoff if you want, but you'll only send yourself into an early grave trying to impress a roomful of people who don't care about you."

I lifted one brow. "What are you suggesting I do instead?"

His smile widened. "Relax. Enjoy life a little. Don't take things so seriously. Go about and have a little fun now and again. I can assist with that too." He punctuated this with a wink.

I spun and kept walking. "This was a terrible idea."

He touched my arm and I pivoted back. The soft streetlight overhead accentuated his fresh, clear-cut features. His face was nearly boyish. Hopeful. "Come. Let me show you something. Won't take but a moment."

His delight was infectious. Magnetic. Those eyes, so vivid . . . Alarms sounded again in my head and I pulled back. "I should go home."

The light in his face dimmed. "Right, then. I'll take you." He bowed and extended his arm, and everything inside me churned. We paused before the door of the rooming house, and he leaned on the frame, hands in his pockets. "Offer remains, if you change your mind."

I forced a smile. "Thank you, I won't."

As I closed the door between us, looking out the window at the retreating triangle of his back, I recalled another thing Mama always taught me—never speak in absolutes.

15

*E*veryone who's left, you'll be the willow chorus." Bellini's statement left no room for argument.

I blinked, looking from the six chosen soloists to the long line of dancers—myself included—who had not yet received assignments.

That is, until now.

Willow chorus? The dancing trees who flitted in circles, waving tulle-wrapped arms around the dancers with actual parts?

It was a precautionary measure, they said. A decision to have fewer soloists to pay, more small parts in groups. I'd never heard of such a thing—a sujet dancing in a group of trees like a quadrille or even a corps dancer.

Minna's eyes blazed with pride from where she stood with the other chosen dancers. Bellini had given her the role of the advising angel, because the theater was rich with irony, and this had her face glowing with delight.

And I was to be a tree. I steeled myself against tears and tried to summon the merits of willows. Perhaps a reviewer would spot my dancing and call me elegant and refined, legendary with a—

No. Perhaps nothing. No one noticed the willows. They were props. Glorified *props,* for heaven's sake.

A bewitching Italian girl named Giuseppina Esposito was hired on contract to dance the lead, likely in hopes that her recognizable name would bring in enough ticket sales to balance out her fees. "None of the dancers at Craven are ready for the responsibility . . . yet." Bellini's voice carried more warning than hope when he announced this, but we all hung on the meaning. All eight sujet in that greenroom looked at him with lifted chins and gleaming eyes, seeing the possibilities for our futures.

There was a hushed, expectant silence among us as we shuffled to the wings to watch the soloists try out their new parts in the first act.

"They make a fine pair, do they not?" Tovah slid up beside me and sat down. The principals, Philippe and the spirited Giuseppina, filled the floor with their pas de deux.

A thick swirl of disappointment sickened me. Even on my best day I could not dance with such poise and conviction. Philippe kept his eyes on her with a stunned sort of admiration as she spun circles around him, using him on occasion to turn beneath his arm or to leap higher. His gaze followed her everywhere, and even though it was supposed to, it felt different. I turned away as my heart twisted in my chest.

I could hear Mama Jo's words, pulsing through my miserable mind: *she never liked the woman with whom he fell in love.* I closed my eyes. No, it was ridiculous. Absolutely absurd to see Mama's story in every turn of my own. It simply wasn't reality.

"There's always next show," Tovah said with a hand on my arm.

Next show. Yes, there would be more chances. But that buoy hardly managed to get off the floor of my heart.

I danced my part through six and a half weeks of rehearsals and two weeks of performances, but it was the final night while watching Philippe and Giuseppina romancing each other with their eyes, seeing Minna dance in all her glory, finding another man in the seat my father had occupied before, that reality settled heavy on my chest. My dreams were slipping from my grasp and I could not clench my fist tightly enough.

I went through the motions on that final night, pasting on my smile and focusing on precision, my pointed toes, my balance. The line of willow trees danced out and formed a circle around a poised Minna the angel, all those long tulle willow fronds rippling down from my arms. I lifted them higher, but still the fronds dragged on the ground. Round and round we went, twirling and flapping our branch arms.

Then my foot caught, something pulled, and—*rrrrip*. I stumbled, feet tangling. I yanked my arm higher and my feet went up, backside hitting the stage.

I groaned. Willow felled.

The other trees danced around and over me, continuing the dizzying circle. I rolled out of the way and sprang up to rejoin the line, forcing myself between two other willows and resuming the paces even while I trembled. I was so tightly bound after all these years, the external narrative of my demanding trainers somehow becoming internal. That's what happened when you worked so hard, wanted something so badly. You took every criticism deeply to heart and let it live there, echoing back every time you performed.

Ballet had become the worst part of my life, I realized with a start—a source of anxiousness and fear, a huge brick wall between me and God. I'd barely thought of God since coming here, and that wasn't like me. Not at all. Theater had eclipsed most everything—and I couldn't even remember why it was so all-important. I was empty.

God . . . where are you? Where have you gone?

I felt the cool release of nerves as I leaped behind the curtain with the others and gave myself over to heated exhaustion, collapsing against a beam. I stood heaving for breath as perspiration pattered on the floor and my body vibrated to the thump of my heart. Jack Dorian strutted about among the wilted dancers, his white smile visible even in the dimness. His gaze settled on me as I looked away, standing straighter, poise intact.

For a moment, at least.

He ambled over, offering a crooked smile meant to charm me. "Not to worry, I once landed clean on my backside as well. I'd been forced to leap through a raging fire, clearing the flames by no more than an inch, and I was very fortunate indeed." His arrogant voice rattled my sensitive nerves. "Only, my coattails caught the flame just before I landed on them, and . . . well, I couldn't sit right for a week."

"At least you managed to save the little child from the burning building." My voice was saucy. I couldn't help it.

"What child?"

"Isn't that what comes next in your sensational escape story? Some gallant rescue?" Heavens, I was irritable.

He eyed me.

"Not every dancer swallows your tall tales, you know."

"I'm hurt." He put a hand to his chest. "*Hurt*."

"Good." I spun and stepped quickly into the shadows. I closed my eyes and focused on taking long, calming breaths to solidify my jittery limbs that were cool with drying perspiration. One more act to go in this wretched night.

Another breath, and the air became charged with the presence of another person, the scent of something strong and familiar. I turned, heart pounding, to face the chest of the towering man who decided my fate. "Signore Fournier."

His steady gaze passed over me for endless minutes while I waited for him to speak. The cigar aroma lingered, even on the rare occasion that the vile contraption was missing.

"It won't happen again. It was a terrible mistake and I'll never—"

"Indeed." He squinted. "Miss Blythe, to what have you given your heart?"

"I beg your pardon?"

"Who or what owns your heart? What do you love to distraction?"

Why was he asking this? "I love to dance."

God. I should have answered, "God." But I hadn't, and the reply had been an honest one.

Fournier's steady gaze remained, as if digging past my layers of poise to the truth.

"Please, sir. I've worked harder than anyone, spent every spare minute on my paces. Truly, I do love the ballet, and I've poured everything into it." I'd often worked past the point of what I thought was exhaustion, but I'd fallen further instead of climbing.

"Then it should not be so hard. True love never leaves you this way." Fournier shook my arms gently to limber them, and

I wondered what other decent profession allowed a man to put his hands on a woman whenever he wished. Perhaps they were right, what they all said about the ballet, about dancers. A sweeping sense of *I don't belong here* washed over me.

"Real love makes you like *that*." He turned me so I could see Philippe and Giuseppina just past the curtain, bodies delicately twining, dancing a romance under the lighted chandeliers.

With that, the Great Fournier turned back into the shadows and down the steps, leaving me to stare at the magnificent dancers who were just beyond my reach. I breathed slowly even as the pieces of my heart shattered around my slippered feet.

I would never be enough.

Before the curtain opened again for the final act, I knew I had two options. I could find the enchanted scarlet shoes and show the world how gloriously I could dance in them, or . . .

Jack.

The image of his smiling face followed me home that night where I lay in my bed, trying to snuff the glow of lights, the pounding music in my head. In the morning, I couldn't bear to see the reviews. But when I emerged in the dining room, there was not one review lying on the table. With a frown, I hurried over and peeked on the seats, beneath the table.

Then I saw Minna, tending the rather large fire. Blackened newsprint curled in the hearth, then crumbled with a few jabs from her poker. "What are you doing?"

She frowned. "Reading reviews is terrible for the constitution."

"Unless they're positive." Hers had been outlandishly so since she'd danced this role. Surely today's were no different.

She scrunched her nose. "Those are worse than the bad ones.

Praise is a quicksand, you know. The more you get, the more you need."

"How . . . how true."

"Go on, take your tea. There's nothing here to see." Then she turned her back on me, poking at all the lovely words they'd said about her—and the likely wretched ones written about me. I laid a hand on her arm. "Thank you, Minna."

She sniffed.

I had promised myself I wouldn't look, but I would have.

After a hasty breakfast, I asked a stagehand cleaning the theater for directions and slipped out with a veil over my face toward Jack Dorian's Winchester address. It was a stately three-story brick affair with bright green doors and tall, showy windows. I should expect no less of Jack Dorian. Yet when I knocked at the front door, the manservant blinked in confusion and pointed me toward a narrow stair running up the side of the building to the third floor. Obediently I climbed, my heavy skirts and wraps leaving me huffing by the end, and I rapped on the little door. I had no speech prepared, no shield for his barbs, no perfectly worded explanation.

As it turned out, I didn't need them. He stood framed in his narrow doorway in shirtsleeves and suspenders, wiping his hands on a white linen towel as he considered me. "About time." He tossed the rag into the room, grabbed a key and jacket from a hook, and slammed the door behind him. "Come along."

Then his arm was about me and we were hurrying headlong down the steep stairs toward who knew what. I pulled the veil more firmly over my face.

"I assume this means you intend to hire me after all."

I tensed. Hire? "Perhaps we should discuss the exact payment you require."

"Later." He propelled me forward with his very nature. "And you needn't worry, it won't be coin I request of you."

I *did* worry, but I still went. What choice did I have?

Only once I'd boarded a stagecoach alone with the man did I realize what he likely had in mind for his reward. Either a letting go of my sacred privacy, or . . .

"Some even . . . place bets. You do understand my meaning, don't you?"

16

"You're so tense." Jack Dorian lounged against the rear-facing seat of the nearly empty stagecoach, arms propped against the buttoned seat back. The heavy jangling of the matched pairs pulling the coach nearly drowned out his voice.

"I'm not accustomed to riding alone with a man." Truth be told, I felt trapped inside this coach with his extraordinary presence taking up all the space. How alive he was, with that dark blond hair, playful eyes, and nostrils that flared with the least provocation. His quick smile carved dimples on either side of his mouth, and suddenly I didn't know where to look. I was sorry I'd removed my veil and hat, so he could see the unease on my face.

"You seem tense so often, though."

I forced my gaze to the door handle beside me. "Always around you, come to think of it." The man did make me brazen.

He leaned forward into my space, his knees nearly bumping mine as he narrowed his bright eyes. "Make you nervous, do I?"

I could see the smooth curve of his lips, the dark golden

eyebrows that made a statement with every twitch. "Uneasy, I would say."

His grin widened, as if this amused him.

My shields rose higher and firmer. He planned to wheedle a kiss from me, and I couldn't forget it. This was one bet he'd lose.

"You needn't worry, I'm a gentleman in every manner of speaking. Why, my mother—a fine silk heiress from Chelsea, mind you—would turn up her nose at the very idea of my doing anything untoward."

"You can stop that, you know. You aren't impressing anyone."

"Aren't I?" He flashed that knowing smile. The coach bumped and jostled as it left the bricked streets of London and lurched onto a rutted rural road. I clung to the handle by the door as if I were careening over the edge of a waterfall to unknown depths below, but he took it all in stride, his legs braced against the sides of the coach. He must have made this trip plenty of times before.

"Where are you taking us? Have you some brilliant ballet master hidden away out here in this wasteland?"

His mouth twitched up. "Still sore about the tumble last night, are you?"

I straightened against the leather seat until I felt it in the arch of my back. "I've never done such a thing before. I shouldn't have let it happen." Why must he poke at me?

"And no doubt you're determined it'll never happen again. More practice, more late nights, more striving, more exacting rules to follow."

"Or as you call them, 'guidelines.'"

"Precisely. Rules are a worthy fence to keep you driving on

the road, but as a destination, perfection is unreachable. Why tire yourself so?"

I closed my eyes. "'The law of the LORD is perfect, restoring the soul: the testimony of the LORD is sure, making wise the simple.' Psalm 19:7.'" Even stating those words aloud balmed my soul. It had been so long. "That's why." They were something to which I could cling, no matter what men like Jack thought of me, or what became of my dancing. "I refuse to lower my standards—in any matter." When all else failed, God would not.

His eyes danced. "I'm not asking you to lower them, love. Just change them a bit. Go from Charde to Devonnier."

"Who?"

He sighed. "Very well, how about Proverbs to the Psalms? Rules to raw emotion."

I frowned. "*You* know the Bible?"

"As I do many other over-read ancient texts. Begging your pardon, being one of its most ardent devotees."

My stomach soured. "I assume you do not—"

"Put much stock in religion? No. Sorry to disappoint the resident nun."

"Well, then. I suppose that explains your disdain for rules." And why I could disregard most of his advice.

"I follow rules—at least, ones with a bit of sense to them. The church has a frighteningly small number of those. There, see? I'd never be much good at religion, now would I?"

"There's more to God than his rules."

"Such as?"

"Freedom. Freedom from our iniquities." I breathed deep and recited a memorized Psalm. "And I will walk at liberty: for I seek thy precepts.'"

He cocked one eyebrow. "Why yes, of course, you do live as one utterly set free."

I cringed. Oh, how terrible was the corner in which I found myself. But how could he possibly understand the complex nature of my heart these days? If I had to explain at this moment what my relationship with God might be, I'd have to say "sparse." Yet I'd tasted that freedom once, years ago in my lowest moment, in an alley outside the wretched Seven Dials district, and no honey had been sweeter on my tongue.

Like a kaleidoscope that had unexpectedly shifted, I suddenly realized I'd lost sight of so much. God's silence these days—possibly by my own doing—left a bitter taste that mixed with the invasive dust of the road. I turned away with a frown. As it turned out, the trouble was not that Jack Dorian was wrong—it was that he was terribly right.

When we stopped, the sun lay evenly across a field of tall grass, and sunshine had warmed the air with the promise of spring. It was an unusually placid March day, despite the gray clouds overhead threatening rain. Last year's cattails waved stiffly in the breeze as Jack handed me down from the coach, and I couldn't rid myself of the sensation of drowning, of utter despair, as I looked across the empty field stretched before two gray, peeling barns—and little else. What had I gotten myself into?

"Come on." He pulled me along, leaping like a stag across the field. The man who always sparked with color had connected to his life source, and now, with wind whipping his hair about his boyish face, he shone brighter than the sun. "You needn't be scared. There was a ten-foot yeti living here once, but I bested him and made him leave long ago." He winked.

I hefted my skirts higher and trudged after him with a heavy sigh and a slight eye roll. "What is this place?"

"My childhood home. Well, one of them."

When we reached the double doors of the largest barn, a four-story monstrosity with rotting wood curling its edges along the bottom and the earthy smell of livestock and hay, he grabbed my hand and spun me. I had barely caught my balance when he unlatched and flung the doors wide, and everything overpowered my senses. Light, smell, noise, color.

"Welcome, my lady, to the grandest place on earth."

I staggered and gaped, chills climbing my skin. It was a circus—quite literally. Lanterns hanging on every post set the massive place ablaze with light, showing people scurrying about on every level, animals moving about below. An awful roaring came from the west end of the building. I spun with a cry to see an elephant—an *elephant*—saluting me with his trunk from a straw-filled stall.

I grabbed for Jack's arm, and he looked down on me with a blazing smile. Then he raised his arms. "Look alive, old friends, see who's home!"

Like a tidal wave, all the attention turned toward us, and I felt very small beside elephants and loud voices and enough color to knock a man down.

"Ah, if it isn't little Jackie Dorian." A barrel-chested man with a voice to match pounded him on the back as the two embraced. "Welcome back to the fold."

"I'm afraid it's just a visit this time, Doc."

"With company, it would seem." He folded his beefy arms and shined that magnificent smile on me. "What's a sweet little thing doing with the likes of Jackie Dorian?"

"We're working—"

"Hello, Jackie." A sultry feminine voice came from behind, smoothing right through my awkward words. It was a slender woman with flowing blonde hair, her face solemn and snapping with emotion as she sized me up, then turned back to Jack. "You've come back." Every inch of her seemed soft and hopeful, almost like a daisy unfurling soft white petals just for him. How many women waited in various towns across England for dear old "Jackie" Dorian?

"Lizzie, there you are." He swept up her hand and kissed her knuckles. Her lashes fluttered at his touch, but she said nothing. "Would you mind terribly if we borrowed your bar? I've a few tricks to teach a new pupil of mine."

Her gaze flicked over my face. No approval registered. "I suppose."

"Grateful, old chum." With a quick pat that sent her stumbling forward, Jack marched toward the loft and motioned for me to follow.

Poor Lizzie looked on with wide eyes, her far-from-chummy heart upon her white face.

I forced my attention back on where we were going and tried to come to terms with exactly what this unusual man's past was. "This is the circus. You are . . . from the circus?"

He skipped up the loft steps to the third level. "It's the heart of the circus, all holed up in this barn between shows. There's a big white tent folded up there." He pointed to the topmost level above us. "This barn is for keeping warm, practicing, and . . . you know, training reluctant ballerinas." He lifted his eyebrows and handed me up onto the landing with him.

I handled the increasing height perfectly well . . . until I stopped and looked down. My vision doubled and came back together, blurring at the edges. I saw people like tiny crickets below, funneling out the door with jolly shouts of goodbye until only a few were left. I swallowed and shivered with the chill of sudden perspiration along my skin. I backed toward the wall, and Jack folded his arms.

"This doesn't bode well for what I have in mind," he said.

"I prefer to stay on solid ground."

"All the more reason to leave it a time or two." He stepped forward and took me by the shoulders, his eager face pleading along with his words. "Trust me, won't you?"

I stiffened against his touch. "Why should I?"

"Because when a lady asks for my help, I aim to give it properly." Keeping his gaze on me, he unhooked a wooden bar hanging on long ropes and tossed it over. "Now, let's start, shall we?" His look was challenging.

I gripped the bar and tugged. "You don't truly expect me to swing through the air on this contraption, do you? How will that help me dance?"

"What you've done isn't working, is it? I aim to give you new experiences, push you off a few of your precious safety ledges. Now hold on."

"But I'm afraid of—"

"I said, *hold on.*"

. . . *heights.*

A gentle shove against my back and I was hurtling through open space, high over the straw-covered floors. I clutched that awful bar for dear life, digging my fingernails into the wood. I squeezed my eyes shut as I sailed through the air, then I forced one eyelid open. Another platform rose up to meet me, and I scrambled to get my feet onto it, but as my shoes touched wood, my weight pulled me back down. I trembled on the swing back, until I felt solid hands around my waist.

Jack hauled me onto the loft and steadied me. "Now you know what it feels like to fly."

"I could have lived without the knowledge." I had become pudding.

"Lived, yes, but not danced. Not well, at least. You're so stiff, so grounded. Every good dancer should know what it is to be weightless."

"I've no desire to perform dangerous stunts."

"A bit of circus advice for you." He leaned on a pole. "The only way you'll go far is to leap big. You may fly or you may fall, but either way, everyone will be looking at you."

I folded my arms over my chest and glared at him. "I have no interest in making leaps of any sort. You and your fanciful—"

Palms out, he gave me a light shove. I wasn't holding the bar. I flailed, tilted, and plummeted straight down with a cry, my long hair curtaining everything from view. How very long it took to fall. Hundreds of fears had time to surface as I plummeted through empty air, heart pounding double time with the passing seconds.

Thwack. I landed on a deep pile of straw and tumbled legs over head down its side, gasping for breath. My heart still hammered as I stood, brushing the itchy straw from my clothes, my hair. The elephant shuffled in his stall down the way and gave a small trumpet, as if laughing at me. Panic turned to surging anger as I straightened and looked up at Jack, who watched with hands on his hips. "There now, was that so terrible?"

I grasped the rail and marched all the way back up those steps and across the loft. "What on earth was that for?"

"Shall we try the trapeze again?"

"Are you mad? I've already had a spill. I wouldn't go near—"

Oomph. Another shove, and I was sailing over the edge, arms flailing. Again I struck the straw, rump first, and tucked my limbs for the roll down the hill that was becoming far too familiar. Sprawled on the barn floor, I glared up at him. Words evaporated off the surface of my burning anger.

I'd have lain there far longer, firmly on that solid ground, except for a female giggle nearby that jolted my senses. Lizzie watched me from the shadows under the lower loft where she lounged in the straw, sewing a glittery costume. Her smile snapped with a vindictive flavor of glee, and I shot up, unwilling to let her see me downed for a moment longer. Once again I marched up those loft steps to have it out with my foolish trainer in private, to demand he return me to London, but when I reached the top, he grabbed me by the shoulders.

"That was marvelous. First-rate work."

"You truly are mad."

"No, no, the way you fell. It was splendid."

I eyed him with a bit of confusion.

"There was far more grace involved in that little spill, as you call it, than the first one."

"Thanks to you, I had a bit of practice."

His grin stretched his face. "A dancer can fall with as much grace as she dances, if she learns how."

"I'd rather concentrate on *not* falling."

"Well now, that simply isn't an option." He gripped the trapeze again, urging me to take it. "As I told you before, everyone falls. It only matters what you do about it. Now, take the bar again. We'll see if you've improved."

"By rolling through straw? Hardly." I crossed my arms.

"Give her a try. For me."

"You think I'd do anything for you? You have quite the swelled head, Mr. Dorian."

He stepped closer, challenge lighting his eyes, extended one palm, and shoved me again.

With a cry I grabbed for something to hold, but tumbled over the edge again, landing on my back in the straw. I lay there and frowned up at him, blowing hair off my face. "And what was that one for?"

He looked down at me with a shrug. "Just making room for my big head up here."

I climbed again and stood before him, arms crossed. "I've had enough of this madness. What's next?"

He pulled the trapeze close, folded my hands over the bar, and turned to face me, his earnest face mere inches from mine. "What is it you want most? Your dream as a dancer. Something distinct that does not include the word 'perfect.'"

I blanked under the intensity of his gaze.

He softened, as if coaxing a wild animal out of hiding. "Come now, I need to know the shape of that hole in your heart if I've any hope of filling it." He leaned closer, eyeing the details of my face. I half expected to feel the brush of a kiss. The light in his eyes had turned tender. Intimate.

My throat tightened. *Breathe.*

So this was how women fell for such men. How Mum had likely fallen for Father.

"Well?" His eyes danced.

I gripped the bar. "Philippe." The word came hurtling from the depths of my heart in the face of Jack's nearness, wrested out by a combination of deep utter longing and a sense of loyalty to the man who'd been betrayed before. "I wish to dance opposite Philippe Rousseau."

His eyes narrowed, the gold flecks bright. What he saw when that stare bore into my face, with my heart on full display, I'll never know. Perhaps it was best that way, for I'd just revealed a great deal.

"Very well, then. Philippe it is."

I turned away from his gaze, focused on the bar.

"Whenever you're ready."

I steeled my arms and stepped into nothing, with my eyes closed. Cool air washed over me, and my chest felt strong, only lightly sprinkled with fear. I blinked and looked down as I swept across the barn to the other side. With a kick against the other platform, I sailed back and relished the feel of free-falling, of truly soaring. The curtain of fear had been drawn back, and it was both frightening and exhilarating.

This time when Jack pulled me toward him, I fell back against his chest, breathless with wonder and almost eager to do it again. I turned in his arms and his wide grin told me he'd read my thoughts. "There now, you see? Quite different, isn't it?" His breath felt warm and pleasant on my face. "It only takes a few falls to realize falling isn't so bad."

I laughed. It was like a release, a delicious freedom. There was a liberating delight in that swing, in flying through the air that wasn't so far off the ground, as it turned out.

"Come, shall we try again? This time I want you to move your legs, point your toes, pretend you are onstage."

With a slow inhale, I once again held the trapeze and released my firm footing. I allowed myself to glide halfway across before daring to arch my back into position and lift my right leg a little behind me. I was sore from the tension and the carriage ride, and the stretch felt delicious through my muscles. I pushed off the opposite platform and sailed back like a swan skimming the surface of a pond, moving my legs and pointing my toes.

I reached Jack and, with a bold smile, kicked off his platform as well and sailed back, delighting in the weightless dance performed in the air. On the next swing, Jack caught my jittery body up in his arms and spun me around with a delighted laugh.

"I knew you could do it." He twirled me again and bowed as if we'd just waltzed, then lifted that devilish smile. "What magnificence has been trapped in you all this time. It's a wonder they didn't completely train it out of you."

Distant claps sounded below, and I looked down to see a small gathering of remaining circus entertainers, watching the performance. I swept up my straw-covered skirts and bobbed a silly curtsy, earning a smattering of laughter and even more clapping.

If only every audience was as easy to please as this one.

As I climbed down the ladder, a flash of moving stripes caught my attention. I paused two steps from the bottom and blinked toward the cage in the dark corner. "Is that . . ."

"An oversized cat? Why yes, it is. He even catches mice for us."

A tiger. "The one you wrestled?" No snideness curled through my question this time.

He shrugged, that grin always on his face. "We've had our differences. As I've said, we've worked them out. Care to meet him?"

A tremble quaked through me and I jumped down to avoid falling. How did one *meet* a tiger? Wrapping myself in the façade of indifference I normally wore around Jack Dorian, I gave a brief nod. "Why not?"

Jack's eyes sparkled as if he saw through to my fear, and I

flashed a bright smile to prove him wrong. Yet as we approached the cat of immense proportions pacing in his cage, which seemed far too flimsy for my liking, I had to tuck my trembling fingers into the folds of my skirt to hide them.

I paused several feet from the thing and stared openly at this wild creature stolen from the jungles. Golden eyes watched me from a face of exotic stripes that spidered out from his nose and eyes. There was no welcome in his wild eyes, but a sort of bright, burning anger. Bitterness that seemed directed at me. A low rumble sounded in his throat as he advanced, gaze trained on me. *Stay calm. He's caged. Caged.*

I swallowed.

"*Rawr!*"

I jumped. But Jack's playfully crooked smile gave him away, and I dissolved into relieved laughter. Somehow he always managed to do that—drum up all the tension in the world, then pop it like a bubble. His smile widened, a huge, crinkly eyed grin that sparkled with good humor and merriment. I had to admit, I rather liked being around the man. He'd make a terrible suitor, but nothing was to say we couldn't be friends.

"Now let's return to our work, shall we?" He guided me back to the steps, where we ran through paces in the loft. Over and over, I moved through the combinations as he called them out from his lounging position against the wall. Then he rose and stopped me, hands on my shoulders. His nearness, all that bottled energy, unsettled me. "I've conquered your fear of heights and taken a chunk out of your tiger phobia. I've removed your audience. What other qualms might I wrestle to the ground for my lady?"

"Nothing comes to mind."

"Then you should be dancing with all the confidence of the

Queen of Sheba, yes? Not this hesitant, nearly apologetic show I see now."

I huffed out a breath and sank to the straw. "I simply need to practice more. It takes time to become confident."

"Horsefeathers." In one acrobatic move, he dropped cross-legged in the straw, facing me with an unrelenting look. "Whatever you're afraid of happens to be holding you back, so you might as well have it out. I cannot cure a problem you refuse to name."

"I simply can't remember all the combinations. Especially with people watching, noticing everything. There's far too much happening at once to—"

"Psalms."

"Pardon?"

"You've no trouble memorizing those, as I became victim—er, witness to, on the way here."

"I've known those since I was a child." For years I'd feasted on the words. Especially in times of darkness, I drank long sips from those pages, gulping down the passionate words of a young shepherd crying out to God in anger and in praise. So often my heart's vague cries found a clear echo in David's poetry.

"Perfect." He smiled. "Simply pair your combinations to Psalms and see if you don't sail through them when next you try."

I blinked. Psalms. Yes, the *Psalms*. At last, I would mix God and ballet. My smile grew. "Mr. Dorian, I might just have to call you brilliant."

"I accept."

The challenges he gave in the hours that rushed on exhilarated me, yet they were nothing compared to the moment Jack threw wide those barn doors at the end of the day, and I caught my first glimpse of the silky night sky studded with stars and a glowing moon set like a diamond centerpiece.

"Now we'll show you how circus folk spend their evenings."

It gaped so big and wide, that fathomless sky, that my soul finally had a glimpse of the great God I attempted to serve.

It struck me briefly as the others clambered into the backs of two straw-filled wagons that I wouldn't be returning to London that night, and my absence might be missed, but suddenly it didn't matter. With a smile, I placed my hand in Jack's and allowed him to pull me up behind him in the wagon.

"You wouldn't care to work at the circus now, would you, lass?" The boisterous man called Doc bounced along beside me, his good-natured voice booming over the clatter of wheels and cart horses.

"I've a contract with the theater, actually."

"Ah, 'tis a shame. You've a fine strength about you."

"All I did was hold on, really." My hands still ached from gripping that absurd wooden trapeze bar. I'd likely have blisters to match the ones I'd had on my feet.

His mustache curved up over his smile. "Wasn't speaking of your arms, lassie." He threw his head back to drink in the night air, arms behind his head. "You're quite a spitfire, but you'd have to be, putting up with the likes of Jack Dorian. Just like my Gretchen here." He jostled the slender woman beside him.

"You are a regular ogre, you are." The woman narrowed her eyes with a wry smile, then turned that bright gaze on me. "I do believe it takes more strength to live with a strong person than to be one, aye?"

"Indeed."

Rural fun turned out to be an exuberant dance around a fire in the open field, with cider spilling out as lavishly as the songs on our lips, and I threw myself into it. Arms linked, we danced in a circle with high kicks and laughter and loud voices as the fire warmed our faces and smoke saturated our clothing. I was hardly the same girl who danced ballet with such precision upon the London stage, and for a single night, it felt grand. My heart was parched for joy and eagerly grabbed at little droplets of it.

For weeks Jack Dorian had attempted to shake up my calm, as a hand descending to loosen the pins of carefully coiffed hair, and I'd finally let him. The result was not my undoing, as I'd feared, but an odd sort of freedom. Beauty. So many things that normally mattered to me a great deal simply didn't just now. Perhaps it was necessary, at times, to surrender to happiness, no matter how fleeting.

I watched Jack's face across the flames and smoke, its features highlighted by shadows and seeming even more alive. Unlike Philippe, handsomely weighted with deep thoughts, Jack was brimming with contagious delight and energy. I could see why women—everyone, really—were drawn to his flame like plain brown moths looking to absorb his warmth and light.

The music swelled and Lizzie sprang up onto the wide stone fence, skirts splaying with great bursts of rhythm as she danced with every inch of her willowy figure. Jack's eyes glowed his appreciation as her feet kicked and her body whirled in a lively Celtic dance. I swayed and clapped with the others until Lizzie stuck out a hand to me, a challenge in her eyes, and my heart dropped to my stomach.

"Give it a whirl?"

"Of course." Jaw set, I grabbed hold and leaped onto those

stones and onto the toes of my boots. My arms swept overhead and I sailed into a dance to match the rhythm of the music. With the voices blaring, the fire popping, darkness comfortably cloaking all my flaws, I kicked off into a quick spin, plié, and leap. The clapping increased and so did my heart and my feet, beating a delirious rhythm as I spun and lifted, faster and higher, arched, and landed to the sound of cheers.

I brandished a curtsy, then stood back and watched Lizzie dance, acrobatic little leaps and kicks that drew applause. Then I twirled into a full allegro combination right there on that fence, dancing from one side to the other and ending with a double twist that surprised even me. I landed in second position, boots planted on the stones, and delighted in the hearty applause and whistles. Alive with delight, I dipped in another curtsy and leaped down. My, how I'd missed this. I'd forgotten, in all my practices, how to simply dance. Only then did I notice how my legs trembled from the sheer force of balancing.

The little group came around me then and drew me toward the fire with chatter and laughter. I joined their merriment, talking easily of amusing things, and for once I felt as though I belonged. When my strength ebbed, I stepped back from the circle. I observed Jack dancing with Lizzie from a fallen tree where I sat, still breathless as I clung to the rough bark.

Jack Dorian was a restless soul brimming with life that needed constant release, and it seemed that's the way his heart was too. From one girl to the next, he could not remain in one place too long. I wondered why, my heart shifting from distaste to a maternal sort of concern.

"You've settled in nicely." I turned at the sound of a woman's voice, and it was Doc's wife smiling from the shadows. She edged forward, arms tucked around herself under her wool shawl. "For a bit I thought you might turn tail and run from us."

"I'm not used to much outside of London. It's a change, this part of England, and I hadn't any idea what to expect. Jack didn't tell me where we were going."

Her smile widened. "He keeps everything in close, our Jackie. How long did it take until he told you his story?"

I looked at her, suddenly feeling as though I came up short. "He hasn't, actually. Not a bit of it."

Her eyebrows arched. "Well, then. You're in for quite a treat. If he deems you worthy. And I think he will—in time. He's lived ten lifetimes, that boy, and he's bound to live a hundred more if his wild stunts don't kill him." She laughed from somewhere deep in her lovely soul.

I looked at the lively figure now at the center of attention, relaying some tale with vivid animation. As he looked at me beyond the bright orange tips of the flames, meeting my gaze with a sudden flash of a smile, I returned it with a shy one of my own.

Then I wondered what one must do to earn the rest of his story.

17

"Were you truly once a nun?" He asked this out of the blue as we all returned to the barn for the night. We lay on our backs beside one another on the bouncing bed of the second wagon, with the others riding in the first. We were alone at last, enough to converse in private at least, and somehow he was the one asking all the questions. Every word of his story still lay bottled up in him.

I laughed. "A nun, me? I don't believe the theater would have taken me on."

"I doubt that. It's easier to fall down than up."

I pondered this. "There is no place low enough that the Almighty does not go with me. Including the theater." Although even as I said the words, and logically knew them to be true, I wished I felt them.

He angled his head, frowning at me. "What do you love so much about ballet, anyway?" As if a woman of spiritual convictions should not enjoy the theater as I did. Perhaps I was reading my own guilt into his question.

I closed my eyes for a moment and inhaled, trying to compile the elusive words to answer such a question. "Beauty. The symmetry and the wildness of dancing and being a part of something so much bigger than myself. And after today . . . flying." I kept my eyes closed against the feel of his stare upon me, but I couldn't avoid the scent of him. If that scent were visible, it would be green—vibrant like fresh, growing things. It made me think of home and childhood, when I'd been so full of life myself. "I used to dream of flitting across the stage like a sylph, barely touching the boards. Almost as if I had wings, and I touched down enough to skim my toes on the water."

Silence reigned, and as the wagon rumbled on, I wondered if his attention had flitted elsewhere, but then he spoke, low and sincere. "I can imagine that. I can see you flying."

I opened my eyes, and immediately the radiance of the star-studded navy sky lay on my chest with the pressure of its beauty. Then Jack's eyes like two stars, closer and more direct, caught my vision and held it.

He shifted, propped on one elbow beside me. "So. Not a nun."

I shook my head and reined in a smile.

"But refusing all men." His blond hair flopped against his forehead to the beat of the wagon's rattle.

"Just certain ones. Well, most, actually."

His look was steady against the bumping vehicle, as if nothing could deter him from looking at me that way for three days straight, poking about the corners of my mind and unpacking all the crates I'd left there.

I forced my voice through the rich silence. "Well then, what's yours?"

"My what?"

"Your dream. You heard mine, about flying, so what's yours?"

He blinked. "*My* dream?"

I braced myself for some unsettling comment about women

or charms that would taint this luscious night. Perhaps I should not have asked.

At last he answered. "I wish to write my own ballet."

I had to study his face to see if he jested. He did not. Lines of longing etched themselves along the sides of his lips now firmly pressed together.

"I find it amusing to adapt the works of geniuses into ballets, but I cannot bear to be forever an echo. Reimagine, recast, rethink what other men have already created, over and over." He rolled onto his back, hands behind his head to shield it from the jostling. "Leaves one feeling rather like he isn't the hero of his own life."

I looked over his fresh face so full of its own life and suddenly couldn't imagine him doing anything less than creating. What splendor awaited the world when this man's creativity was unleashed upon the stage. "Have you any ideas? Perhaps you could try your hand."

"I've been writing the same one for ten years. Mostly in my head, mind you, but it's become larger than life to me and the players are as real as people. I worry about them at times, when I've left them alone for too long."

"Well, do you leave them in danger?"

"It's a terrible habit of mine. I do delight in leaving them in peril so they're begging me to return and continue working out their story. At the moment I've left a poor, misguided Vanessa in grave danger, near threat of death actually, and I've no idea who the villain is yet. You see, poor Vanessa has made herself quite a few enemies."

"She must be quite accomplished and lovely."

"Naturally. Yet I hardly know her. The villain, either. I feel as though I'm looking at them both through a veil of London fog, and I cannot see to look into their eyes. And now because of that, I've no notion of how to rescue her. She's gone willingly to a secluded place with an evil man I cannot see. The hero has no idea, of course, so he cannot save her."

I eyed him through the deluge of words. "Yet you've not written this story? Sounds quite written to me."

He shrugged. "I suppose I have a few scrawled pages here and there, but nothing firm. I've no idea who these people are."

"Well, the heroine, yes. But must you know the villain? Evil is evil."

He looked at her directly. "No one is truly a villain, you know. I only have to dig further into his heart and his life to understand what has brought him to this point. And I haven't the slightest idea what that is."

"Why not think about people you know already?"

"Splendid." He tipped his head my direction, leveling those bright eyes at me. "I could write you a flying part. Wouldn't that be something? I'd do that for you, in a flash, I would."

"As long as it doesn't include a flying machine. Maybe something near the ground. A sort of elegant grace, like a swan treading water." It was one thing to swing upon a trapeze in a forgotten old barn. It was quite another to attempt it before crowds of people glittering with jewels and expectations.

He offered a crooked grin. "I can do elegant, and not just in my ballet—the very next one you dance. We'll have you floating across the stage every performance, with your own spotlight solo to boot. An entire divertissement. What do you say? Keen to try?"

"Me, with an entire song to dance in the spotlight?" My lips turned up in a smile. "They'd never agree. After that last performance, I'd say it's an impossible challenge."

"I accept. And if I succeed . . . remember, I get my choice of reward. I have it in mind already." His lips curled into a playful smile.

"Don't grow fond of the notion."

We fell to silence as the horses rattled on, beating a rhythm on the rugged road that filled my head with music. I closed my eyes and imagined the lively ballet that would come from the heart of Jack Dorian, and I wished I could see it.

"Why Philippe?" He asked it as if the question had been gnawing at him.

My neck warmed. "He's the principal, is he not?" The straw behind my head began to itch. I shifted against the wagon bed.

"It's more than that—for Ella Blythe anyway. Her head isn't turned so easily. What's he done to you?"

"Nothing, really. It's just a silly thing . . ."

He stared right through those filmy layers of ambiguity I'd attempted to erect and demanded the truth with one quick jolt of his eyebrow.

"The truth . . . the truth is . . . well, I've long admired Philippe from afar. He makes a fine dancing partner." Which I knew from experience. I shivered against the rough wood under my back and breathed deeply of the scent of fields and rich dirt. "He'd make nearly any ballerina who danced opposite him appear charming."

"Ah yes, a fine partner. A wonderful dancer, and brilliant in nearly any role. Then of course there are the feelings."

"Which?"

"Yours, of course. For Philippe. Come now, you've the stealth of a child when it comes to him, and I mean that in the finest possible way."

My hands flew to my burning cheeks. "What's *fine* about being called a child?"

"There's not a bit of guile in your nature, and that's to your favor. It's . . . well, rather unusual."

I felt his eyes on me. Moisture cooled my neck.

"Philippe desperately needs such a woman. A sweet little confection of femininity and love who will come alongside him and make him take notice of the beauty in life. To pull him up from what his life has become. Perhaps our little nun will be just right for him."

I still couldn't look at him. I stared up at the sky and felt brave. "Why do I feel as though this is a trap? Do you aim to find out all my secrets and then ruin me?"

There was a pause. "Your hair is pretty this way."

My head tipped to the side, and there was his bright-eyed smile glowing out at me, those gold flecks in his eyes alight with sincerity. Admiration. Something loosened in me, weakened at my core, and I couldn't speak. He did that to me, and now it seemed I'd become like every other woman in Covent Garden—charmed by Jack Dorian.

The wagon jolted as it made a hard turn and entered the yard. Jack sat up and pulled me to sit beside him, leaving his warm hands on my back to steady me as we bumped over the field.

He was still studying my hair, the disarray of loose curls raining all about my shoulders and twisted with straw. "It always looks the same when you force it into that perfect little knob on the back of your head, but I prefer it down. It looks different every time you turn your head."

I glared, steeling myself against the delightful spell he cast. "It's a sorry mess."

"That finally has its own way. And it appears to know what it's doing." He fingered the end of one curl where it lay against my arm, and I tensed. A ripple of anxiousness passed over me.

He tipped his head as he looked at me in that quiet moment, as if filled with wonder at how I'd ever come to be.

The wagon bumped and jolted to a stop with a metallic clank as the brake was set, and we tumbled toward the driver's seat. I braced and rolled, but my head thudded against something soft—Jack's arm, extended to catch me.

He looked down at me with a most amused smile. "About time. I paid the sot to do that hours ago."

I dissolved into giggles against his arm, glad to be free of the tension, enjoying his smile. It was addictive, that grin of his. I pushed up and scooted across the wagon bed and jumped down. A dark-haired man that Jack had pointed out as Lizzie's older brother caught me and handed me down, but his manner was stiff. Unwelcoming.

I thanked him, searching his face for a moment to understand his reaction, until a cool breeze beside me signified Jack's absence. I squinted to see Jack in the dark but saw nothing until the barn door slid open and the orange glow of oil lamps inside spilled over the distant forms of Jack and Lizzie framed in the doorway.

"Known each other a long time, those two." Lizzie's brother Paul spoke beside me in the dark, clutching the horses' reins in giant paws.

"They seem close."

"We always thought one day they'd be wed. And they still might." He cleared his throat. "That is, unless someone stands between them." His look toward me was steady, and at last I understood.

"Your trouble is with Jack and enticing him to settle down." I wouldn't allow for guilt over what I hadn't done. I lived with enough as it was.

Paul turned back to the figures ahead as if he hadn't heard me. "That boy lives as one abandoned every day of his life. Wears it about as if it's sewn into his nature. Needs a solid woman—one he can trust."

I looked at Jack's face highlighted by the lights inside and all the fun of this night, of the day at the circus, solidified into a subtle kinship. Both of us, two fractured souls, always with a crack to fill. Who had abandoned him?

Paul's voice came in the chilly night along with a puff of breath. "Nobody knows how to drop a person like a dancer, I've heard. Only this time if anyone hurts him"—he shifted in the grass—"this time he's got us to right any wrongs."

I shivered at the hint, like a knife point resting against my arm in warning, and watched Jack more closely. It was shocking, the thought of him abandoned. Of all the stories I could have pinned on him, that never fit. "I have no romantic intentions toward Jack Dorian, so you have nothing to fear from me." I said it as if Fournier and Philippe could overhear. "Outside of the theater, we are truly nothing to one another."

But that only intensified his look. "Nothing, you say? Then why isn't he at Drury Lane today? His meeting with that Vestris bloke is, apparently, not as important as this, yet he is *nothing* to you. How glad I am to hear it."

I caught my breath. "He had a meeting with Vestris today? *Armand* Vestris?"

"He was fairly well singing about it. Not an easy connection to come by, from what I understand."

No, it wasn't. Nearly impossible, actually. The famed choreographer kept to himself and his work, shunning any potential protégés that happened along.

I looked the man square in the face. "I never would have let him do this if I'd known. And for what it's worth, I have come to see Jack Dorian as a remarkable and delightful man. I'd never do anything to hurt him, no matter how he vexes, nor would I stand in the way of sincere love."

With that, I separated from Paul and ran to catch Jack as he strode out to help with the horses. When I reached him in the path of lantern light just outside the stables, I simply stood, staring up at him like a little fool. How did one thank the man who'd quietly made such a sacrifice, especially after treating him to weeks of pure condescension?

"I could write you a flying part. Wouldn't that be something? I'd do that for you, in a flash, I would."

He smiled down at me and it was tender. Kind.

"Why today, Jack? Why not put me off when I asked for help?"

He shrugged, pulling a bit from the horse's mouth and lifting the reins over its head. "It was now, or let you kill yourself through the whole next show. Besides, you're as skittish as a colt. You'd have changed your mind."

The horse shook out its mane and Jack leaped astride her, bareback. He held out a hand with a most irresistible smile of challenge. "Care to join me?"

I smiled. That question, from Jack Dorian, always seemed to lead to something remarkable. I gave him my hand and he pulled me up before him, bracing me sidesaddle with his lean body. "Hold on tight."

He nudged the mount, and we flew, skimming over the dark wildflower fields and sending up a spray of fireflies into the night sky. He was showing me his world, this great moonlit expanse, and it inspired awe just like the sound of a full orchestra or the great gilded theater.

We galloped beside a stone fence, over hills, and along a creek, then he brought me back, slipping off the horse and turning to hand me down too. With one hand on the creature's neck, he led her into the barn with a natural magnetism that extended, apparently, to the animal world.

He passed the horse off and took my hand, bowing over it. "I shall see about your accommodations, my lady."

When he turned, I touched his arm with an overfull heart. "Jack." He pivoted to me. "My mother."

His eyebrows shot up.

I shrugged. "The answer to what you wanted to know, back in the cemetery. About how I was involved with . . ." I ducked my face. "She was my mother."

He took my hand as if thanking me for a most exquisite gift, tracing his thumb over every knuckle. Oh, how his face prismed! Tiny, expressive movements from his lips, those memorable eyes. "I shan't tell a soul."

"There's one other thing." I breathed long and deep. "She didn't die in the fire."

His hand paused. "What?"

"She was burned quite badly." Tears budded. "I shall never forget the feel of those scars on her hands . . . her face. Her career died, her romance died, her outer beauty died, but her body did not."

His face was frantic. "Why did you hide this from me? All that's needed to clear de Silva's name is for her to appear, alive. Scars or no, her presence will change—"

"Nothing. It'll change nothing, because now she truly is dead." The tears leaked out. "For several years. We cannot prove she lived beyond the fire."

"Surely people saw her who—"

"No one. After the fire, she never left our flat. Never saw anyone, save an old woman who'd never testify to any of it. My sister and I were the only ones who knew who she was, the only ones who ever saw her. Come to think of it, she had one friend—my sister Lily's real mother, but she's long dead as well. I'm afraid they won't take our word for it, two lowborn women."

He stared at me. Just stared.

"But now you have all the information I can give. There's nothing left but to find out who did this."

"We most certainly will. De Silva didn't kill her, and he shouldn't have to live under the weight of it a moment longer."

He was quiet after that, and the silence was potent. I looked long and hard into his face and found surprising things—deep worries and pains. Vulnerability. Raw, authentic beauty of soul. I had known his type, known what he was from the start. Yet this underlying passion for justice and honesty surprised me. Confused me. More than anything, after the night we'd had, I wanted a glimpse into who Jack Dorian truly was.

18

ack Dorian was restless. Even in the giant barn with everyone still asleep, his spirit felt caged. Nature's calming breath washed over his moist skin from an open window, and he sprang up to answer the summons. Despite the stiffness in his back after a restless night, he moved with quick steps and slipped out into the dark-pink hues of early dawn.

He exhaled, rubbing his hair and face to wake himself. Already he felt freer, calmer, simply being outside. Yet as he strode out toward the pond, wading through tall grass and bounding crickets, that heaviness returned. Not unpleasant, but impossible to ignore.

It had started when he'd jolted awake with a sudden awareness, a conviction. The ballet in his head—he *must* write it. Now. Somehow, it was significant.

He'd lain awake, the curve of his back aching against the unaccommodating wood floor, but the prodding wouldn't leave him. So he let his mind work on it, trying the new pieces this way and that. The hero and Vanessa, in love? That had never been part of the story. They'd always been at odds, forced to work together but never affectionate. His hero, it seemed, had been holding out on him.

That's what bothered him. Of all the characters playing about in his mind, the hero was the one he knew the best. The man had several shadowed corners, and he refused to reveal what he knew about the great fire where Vanessa had met her tragic end, but this was one twist he'd never expected. Had he actually been in love with her? Or had they merely produced a child together?

He adjusted and readjusted, but no position, no amount of heavy sighs, removed that undeniable pressure, so he rolled over and got up. Something wasn't right. And he was the one who had more pieces than anyone—the one who needed to figure it out. He'd meant to put the thing away, to leave well enough alone, but it wouldn't leave *him* alone.

Now as he stepped up on the rickety pier over the pond and looked across the pink-dappled surface, he acknowledged to himself what that sudden unquenchable urge might have been— and where it had come from. He recognized it. Try as he might to ignore the God his guardian Mrs. Hatchette had drilled him to know, to pretend denying him, Jack was encountering him once again. And it was *her* fault.

Wherever Ella Blythe went, there existed an aura of God, like a faint aroma. Despite her insecurities, her rote verse recital, all her preoccupation with perfection, God hovered nearby. Perhaps that's what had drawn him to her in the first place. Something deep at the core of him had immediately responded to her, that face full of character and pluck, her poise that did not demand respect but quietly inspired it.

He'd been disappointed to learn of her obsession with religion, but it had slowly begun to occur to him that it was a part of her charm and could not be divorced from her nature. It held her upright with a steadiness of character and strength that was not loud and showy like a fire, but more of the quiet brilliance of a raw gem. God had drawn near to her, and though she seemed to wrestle with how it all fit together in her life, God was part of who she was.

And now, after far too much time together, it was leaking onto him. He stared back across the field to the tall gray structure in the middle of it. He fully wished he could ignore the conviction threading through the loose places of his soul. Writing this ballet was a dream, but it would be incredibly difficult. He simply wasn't used to giving voice to sordid things, even in writing. She would be affected, too, if he went through with this. She would see the connection immediately, and the truth about her mother that came out in the ballet would crush her. This wasn't going to be pretty.

Ah! But it could be *put off*.

It wasn't as if Ella was standing in front of him this minute. They had the entire ride home to talk. He mentally shelved the discussion, but all too soon she was moving toward him in his peripheral vision, her gown displacing the tall stalks around her. He turned and let his gaze linger as he'd done so often. What was it about her? Jack loved the rush of danger, except when it came to women. And for all her innocence and quiet steadiness, Ella Blythe did not feel safe.

She stepped near with that unmistakable poise, and he welcomed her into his presence with a silent smile, chest tightening. Then that weight settled upon him again, that inescapable conviction, displacing the peace he'd come here to find. It was time to write that ballet, and time to tell her the truth.

19

The air had an odd mix of moist soil and plant aroma as I breathed deeply near the pond, and though it was strong, it was not unpleasant. "Early riser, are you?"

"I rarely sleep for long. I'm surprised to see you out here, though. Aren't you a bit nervous?"

I smiled, hugging my wrap around me. I didn't know if he spoke of catching my death in the early morning chill or the risk to my reputation, but my answer was the same. "I'm not afraid of much out here, it would seem." I perched on a large rock overlooking the pond. Bulrushes waved in the breeze from the fringes of the water. "Besides, you've so thoroughly done your job as a storyteller that I was compelled to find out what you've decided about that villain. And your heroine, Vanessa. Do you know either of them yet?"

"The villain will likely remain a murky mystery for a while." He sighed, weighted with the plight of his characters as if it truly mattered in the real world. "It's too much power for a man to have who isn't even the hero of the story." He stared down at the murky pond swirled with green. "Perhaps if I knew how the story ended, *why* the fire was set, I'd see the villain's face and . . ."

Fire? "I see." And at last, I did. I analyzed his face, his posture. "Why does Delphine Bessette's story fascinate you so? Why take such an interest in my mother's tragedy?"

"My interest lies with the suspect, because I thoroughly believe he's the true hero, and not the villain." His sigh was deep and steady. "Marcus de Silva was my foundation when I had none. My only semblance of something stable. I cannot give up on him."

I looked at his troubled face, vibrating just under the surface with all manner of nervous energy, and my displaced heart swelled with understanding. One was always restless until he knew what home was for him. Restless, and scrambling for any outcropping on which to place his feet. He'd found one in my father, it seemed. "How *did* you come to the circus?" The question was soft and gentle.

"My mother brought me when I was young, because of a silly obsession I had with tigers. I wanted to see one up close, and I begged and begged, so she took me. Snuck me out of the house and pumped me full of excitement, and it was everything I'd always hoped. And more."

I waited, my bones sore against the rock, but he merely threw pebble after pebble into the glassy water and watched it sink. Then a soft *whap-whap* above drew his attention, and he turned, expression once again flooding with life. "Shh. This is what I came to see. They're finally here."

I followed his gaze to a pair of pure-white swans gliding together against the bright pink morning sky, floating down with feathery grace. They circled and landed in the center of the pond, tucking their wings close and stretching their necks as gentle ripples formed around them. We sat in perfect silence for long moments, drinking in the sight of those beautiful creatures.

"That's you, right there. Your style as a dancer. You see? You needn't compare yourself to any other woman, when you dance as you were created to do. You, Ella Blythe, are a swan."

"That isn't my own style then, is it? It's the swan's."

He studied me, a smile playing on his lips. I was drawn to his presence, to the untroubled and easy way I felt around him. "Very well then, be a blend. One part swan, the other . . ." He leaned close to balance his chin on his fist, reading something in my face. "The other, Delphine Bessette."

My mind blanked. I forced my lips to part, pushing air in and out of them.

"There's an element of her legendary style inside you, but I see the swan as well. A sort of otherworldly aura—celestial, perhaps. Pure, lovely . . ." He tipped his head with a small smile. "Just out of reach for the common man."

I held my breath, allowing his words to both unsettle and calm me. I trusted him, I found, as far as dancing was concerned. His unbridled confidence had pulled me along, taking me to new depths and heights, new ways of understanding ballet. If Jack Dorian claimed I possessed an element of Delphine Bessette and swans, I'd embrace it as being so—with delight.

A hush of breeze swirled around us, tickling my exposed neck and cooling my warm cheeks. "Thank you, Mr. Dorian, for this trip. I've learned a great deal about myself as a dancer and my limitations—or lack of them, perhaps."

"We're not through yet, love. Once you've hired Jack Dorian, you're stuck until the work's completed."

"You truly want that payment."

His eyes glittered with danger. "Aye."

"You aim to keep me training out here in the country indefinitely, then? Breaking my contract?"

"Training is no more limited to one location than you yourself are. We'll pick up in London. Just wanted to ruffle your feathers a bit before we polished you up."

"You've done a grand job of it."

"Splendid." He winked. "Let's get you back to the barn. We'd best be on our way if we hope to reach London today."

Rising from the rock, I tromped through the tall grass, lifting my heavy skirt that was now hopelessly countrified—every wrinkled, wet, soiled inch.

"What if I wanted you to see de Silva? What if that's what I asked for as payment? Would you do it?"

I paused, considering his earnest face. Not a hint of amusement lit his features. "You truly don't let a thing go, do you, Mr. Dorian?"

"You're catching on."

"Well, I've already seen de Silva."

He stopped, blinking at me.

"I found him where you said he'd be—right under my nose. I followed him outside after a performance."

"And?"

I shrugged, unsure if I was able to say the words. It took a few moments. "He wanted nothing to do with me."

He stood rooted, a deep frown lining his face. "You're certain it was him? And that he knew who you were?"

"I made it clear. Who I am upset him even more."

Jack turned, still frowning. Disappointed. We continued on to the great barn.

When I stepped inside and pushed all my weight into shutting that door, the place was suddenly quite dark. I stood blinking, tempted to call out softly for Jack. I took cautious steps forward, thinking always of the tiger in the far corner.

I jumped when I felt his hand settle on my shoulder. "I've found some things for you to wear."

A puff of fabric and underskirts dropped at my feet. My eyes adjusted to the dark.

"Here we have . . . this." A taffeta overskirt wafted down. Then a puff of flounced fabric and boning. "A few of these for good measure, and that should do it."

For all his flirting and playfulness, he seemed so out of place around women's garments. I forced a stern voice to keep from laughing. "What's wrong with this?" I held up fistfuls of my own skirt. "It suited perfectly well for our journey *out* of London."

His eyes, two glowing marbles in the dark, met mine. "Precisely."

When he vanished into the shadows, I understood the nature of his gift. I smiled into the dimness at the notion that Jack Dorian was taking pains to protect my reputation. Sweeping the whole lot up in my arms, I made my way blindly back to where I'd slept and pulled the sheet across the rope to curtain me in. Pink now glowed in the window, a rosy light filling my little space and making it lovely.

I sorted through the garments and found three separate petticoat sets, the outdated bodice of a riding habit, and the gaudiest, most ridiculous taffeta overskirt I'd ever seen outside of a costuming room. With all the iridescent colors of a peacock feather, black fringe, and sewn-on beads, the skirt was a statement in itself. I couldn't bear the thought of handing the garments back, so I chose the petticoat and corset that seemed the nearest to my size, sucked in a breath to make it fit, and began dressing.

After nearly a half hour of fumbling with buttons and closures, I collected all my poise, emerged to a barn now subtly lit with the rising sun, and faced Jack—and, to my surprise, everyone else. Lizzie spat out her tea and Doc stifled a laugh with a cough into his sleeve. The others stared like deer about to dart.

I held my back straight, chin up, when Jack turned. His gaze took me in, head to toe, then with a smile tweaking his lips, he moved toward me in two bold steps with an offered arm. "Shall we, my lady?"

I dipped a curtsy and took his arm. "Of course." I smiled upon the others, still watching from their places. "Good day to you all, and thank you for a most remarkable visit. I shall remember it always."

Jack looked down at me as we left, and the smile on his face, the glow in those intense eyes, were unmistakably filled with admiration.

I clamped my hat to my head as the coach jostled us over the road toward London.

"You're quite a vision in . . . that." Jack had propped himself in the rear-facing seat where he merely stared from the shadows, left arm over the back of his seat. "I suppose I should have given some thought to coordinating colors."

"I've never felt lovelier."

He smiled. "It takes an exceptional woman to wear it well, and by heavens, you're first-rate."

A smile flickered about my lips. Somehow it was the most

romantic compliment I'd ever received. I tried not to shiver under the directness of his approving stare, but my heart pounded. I leaned one hand upon the cool window and watched the rolling countryside fly by, but I was ever aware of him. It was impossible not to be.

When I turned back to him, his gaze was still upon me, his arm braced against the seat.

"Why Philippe?" he asked again. His voice was soft this time.

"I've answered that already."

"I want the truth." His jaw angled left. "Tell me what it is, or I shall have to ask *him*."

Heat climbed my neck and I looked away. "He'll only think you mad. There's no understanding between us. At least, nothing firm."

"Why such an attachment to him, then? It all seems rather arbitrary."

I spun with a huff. "Why Marcus de Silva? Why stick your neck out for him so much if he's truly of no relation?"

"I've already told you."

"There's more. All this devotion merely because he gave you a hand up? What hold has he over you?"

A muscle flinched beneath his shirt. "That's none of your business."

"Likewise." I gave a prim smile.

He leaned forward with a hefty sigh and shoved hair off his forehead. "Very well then, your secrets for mine. Tell me what hold Philippe has on you, and I'll talk about de Silva."

Something fluttered in my chest at the name of my father, and standing here on the edge of knowledge where there'd been nothing but blackness for years, I couldn't turn away from it.

"And no half-truth—I'll know. You're a terrible liar."

I fidgeted with the folds of the frothy skirt. "It's rather silly, really. We danced together once, years ago, when I was but a girl." Memories sweet and tender tugged at me. "It was the first time I'd ever truly danced ballet. It was . . . incredible."

His eyes narrowed. "Go on."

"He happened upon me in the old materials room, the one off the—"

"I know it."

"Right, then. He discovered me there after I rescued him from a pair of drunken sots."

"Fight them off, did you?" He was amused.

"With a shoe. I threw it at them and they ran. I suppose he felt indebted to me. He came and found me and . . . well, he was my very first dancing partner. Led me in my first pas de deux."

How easily my mind drifted back to that night, as if it had just occurred. "It was lovely and innocent, yet so very unsettling, in a good way. I never knew it could feel that way. Then he showed me the ballet in the theater—it was my first glimpse—and he made me this promise that one day we'd dance together on that stage, that I would be a real dancer and . . ." And somehow the two had become the same thing. "It's always been my dream."

My thoughts drifted back to the present with one glimpse of Jack Dorian's face, contorted with some odd emotion in the shadows as he listened to me go on about Philippe and our surreal encounter so many years ago. His expression seemed to say the situation was more hopeless than he'd thought.

Good. Perhaps he'd give up on the bet, then.

I let my story dangle in the air between us and shifted back, the hard leather squeaking as it accepted my weight. I'd forgotten myself, and I suddenly felt as if I'd been discovered in nothing more than my shift.

"Why haven't you reminded him of your acquaintance? Surely a previous encounter with the principal of the theater would be advantageous for a woman in your position."

"I never thought to use it in such a way. I want to earn my place in the company. Besides"—I tipped my face away so he couldn't see it—"he doesn't remember it."

Those eyes. They were piercing on the soul level. I could feel them even though I had turned away. "You'll never know unless you bring it up. Perhaps he believes it is *you* who's forgotten. Or perhaps he's afraid you will not like what you see of him in the light of day."

My mind grasped at similar words from Mama, when she'd spoken of my father in that breathy voice of lost love. Nothing, it seemed, remained the same once the room quit whirling and the world came back into focus. But I made a hard turn, not allowing my mind to travel down the road of comparison.

I gripped the seat as another thought occurred to me. "How did you know I've not said anything to Philippe?"

"He'd have told me."

"You are friends?"

He shifted. "In a manner of speaking, yes. I suppose we are."

I watched Jack squirm in the shadows, recalling the night of silent sparring between him and Philippe. His look told me they'd *once* been friends, but that had changed. Along with so many other things in Philippe's life these past years. "If you are friends, I suppose you'll know what's happened to him."

His eyebrows shot up. "Happened?"

"He's burdened now. Heavy. Something's befallen him, and it's unsettling to always wonder what it could be."

"Then I suppose you'll have to remain unsettled. Those are his secrets, not mine."

"Speaking of secrets, you promised more about Marcus de Silva. I've revealed my connection to Philippe—now it's your turn."

He watched me, evaluating something. "How odd it's never occurred to me before, but their secrets and their stories . . . well, they're eerily similar."

I stiffened. It was as if a ghost I'd imagined I'd seen for quite a while was now pointed out by someone else.

"Let us hope Philippe turns a corner that Marcus de Silva did not. I'd like to see him find a happier end than the poor old *danseur* of years past."

"Of course."

He heaved a sigh, leaning back against the seat. "Now, Marcus de Silva. What would you like to know?"

"How are you connected to him?"

He considered my question for a moment before answering. "He sought me out. When I was a sorry twig of a boy, he saw something in me and offered to teach me about theater. I left the circus with all its troubles to go off and join the cavalry, until de Silva found me and held out his hand to help me. With his connections and training, I went on to adapt ballets and work with the Great Fournier. I had no hope, no family once. He changed the course of my life."

"No wonder you're so protective of him."

"He's a fine man, but with wounds, like everyone. Still, he stood there and pulled me up when I needed it most, and I'll never think ill of him."

I pressed my lips together and imagined Marcus de Silva, my father, reaching out to help some poor lad from the circus, from the cavalry, at his fine London residence with marble floors and jewel-crusted vases—at least, that's how I imagined his home—while his own daughter and wife scratched out their survival in a dirty little rookery mere streets away.

"Did he ask you to find me? To find out what had become of his child?"

"He wouldn't. He never asks those kinds of favors. In fact, he never told me he had a child. Those of us in the theater are often quite private."

I accepted this and sat back. "He was quite good then, years ago? As a dancer, I mean."

"One of the finest onstage. He came into his own at Craven and could have gone anywhere in the world. They say he only remained because he fell in love with someone at Craven. But then Delphine became angry and . . . well, it changed everything for him."

"Perhaps she had reason to be." I took a breath. "While they were partners on the stage, they secretly married. She was his wife."

His face steeled. "You're . . . certain?"

I nodded. "Eloped. Gretna Green."

He heaved a large sigh. "Even if they were involved in this manner—which I still cannot manage to understand—I still cannot see the justice in the way things have played out against him. He had to leave his entire life, the theater, everything, because he was accused of murdering someone who wasn't even killed, as it turns out. Part of me believes she . . ."

I pressed my lips together and stared at my folded hands. He might believe he knew, but he hadn't met Mama or heard her speak of her great love. Hadn't witnessed the sheer animosity on my father's face when I had mentioned her to him. All he knew was that the man who had been kind to him was suspected of murder, and he couldn't bear the disparity.

When I looked back up at Jack in the deeply shadowed coach, he was openly staring at me. "He's carried the weight of someone else's sins around with him for many years, and it's time he was free of it. If I accomplish one task with the rest of my life, it'll be finding out what truly happened, however I can . . . and releasing him at long last."

I clutched my hands in my lap, trying several times to swallow, and lowered my gaze from the man who had just spent the day pouring new life into my dreams. "I'm not certain I wish to be involved." Whether Marcus de Silva had set the fire or had merely lived tortured under the weight of suspicion, my heart twisted at the mere thought of him.

"I will find out—with or without your help. It's the truth I'm after, and truth is meant to be found."

The truth. Perhaps that would bring about my release as well.

It was raining lightly when he walked me home from the coach stop. A drizzly mist settled on our faces and dampened my odd clothing, and I sighed. "I may have one small idea to help your investigation."

20

Alone in the empty theater, I took out Mama's box of letters from her flat at Tavistock Place and traced the inlaid chips of stone and glass. I hadn't even read them all. I hadn't been able to bear the entire stack, but perhaps Jack, who had no attachment to my mum, could dig through and find something useful. It was the least I could do for him.

I made my way across Covent Garden and climbed the steps to Jack's top-floor flat. When he popped out in answer to my knock, I handed him the box and explained where I'd come across it. "Perhaps you'll find some interesting bit, a clue, or even a threat from someone. Do with the information what you will, but I would like it all returned to me when you are done."

He lingered against the doorframe, arms crossed. "So I have your permission? Your express permission to do *whatever* I wish with this information?"

Immediately I sensed the danger of agreeing. "Nothing public, no scandal. No newspaper or gossip column or anything like that."

He placed a hand on his chest. "You have my word of honor."

Then he exhaled and lowered his hand, face solemn. "Thank you . . . for this. It's terribly kind of you."

"You practically demanded my assistance."

"Yes, but you're not one to comply. Not easily, anyway."

A wry smile. "I do so love to prove you wrong."

"I see." A grin twitched over his face as he looked me over and set the box just inside. "Ready for the audition?"

"I'm never ready."

"Remember, though, you have a secret weapon this time. How is that Psalm coming?"

"Easier than I expected, actually." I'd spent hours already with my Psalm book and pencil, writing choreography in the margins. "We'll see how it works when it matters most."

"Ah, so the rare moment of proving me *right* this time."

"Don't become used to it."

He leaned against the doorframe again. "I've given some thought to my hero, actually. Because I know you were wildly curious about the ballet."

"Oh?"

"I've come to the decision that if Philippe is to play the lead, you must be the one to dance opposite him."

I laughed. "You'll have a fine time convincing Bellini and Fournier of that."

"No, truly. I think it must be that way, and you can have your dance with Philippe Rousseau at last. What do you say? You, dancing the part of Delphine Bessette, your father's legendary partner, and Philippe . . . well, Philippe would be dancing as the man she loves."

I caught my breath, smiled with concerted effort, and tried to appear unaffected. "That sounds rather nice."

"Quite fitting, don't you think?"

I sighed. "I don't suppose you could tweak the ending a bit, could you? A little less fire and a little more happy?"

He gave a gentle smile. "Fortunately, we have the right to our own endings—off the stage, at least."

When he appeared to want to ask me something, a question I knew would be uncomfortable, I gave a nod and turned. Leaving that unusual box in his hands, I backtracked down the stairs and through the street, sorting through Mama's story in my head. What would Jack Dorian think, after reading all those letters, of my mother? Of my parents' romance and its tragic ending? Would it solidify everything he believed Mum to be, or would he sense the same thing I had about their whole story?

It was not quite right. Something didn't make sense about their grand romance and the years of separation. All these letters, alongside the deep affection she'd felt for my father and the very truth of her nature.

I happened upon Philippe at the little café when I stopped for a bite, and he invited me to sit with him. "You look a bit peaked. Is everything all right?"

I released a long breath, looking into my deeply tangled heart. "A little excitement. Unexpected dramatics behind the scenes. Nothing out of the ordinary for a theater girl."

"Then I'm certain it's nothing you can't handle—with confidence."

I smiled, settling into the conversation like a warm cup of tea. Where Jack Dorian was the wild circus and tigers and free-falling on a trapeze, Philippe was all ballet and beauty and order with things as they should be. I felt at home with him.

Conversation drifted easily over lentil soup and centered on the upcoming production.

"He's chosen a Shakespeare for the next production, you know." Philippe stirred the broth and sipped.

"Oh." I straightened, pulling on my mask of sophistication. "*Midsummer Night's Dream*, I hope. I always thought it deserved a ballet." As if I'd actually read the thing.

"*The Winter's Tale*, actually."

"Well, then." I'd never even heard of that one. I edged a glance up at his face. "I don't suppose there's a North Wind role in that one, is there? It sounds the sort to have one . . . perhaps." My heart thudded nearly out of its cage at the hint that now lingered between us. How bold I'd grown.

"Thank heavens, no. That was the worst costume I ever donned, and it would please me to never wear it again. I was combing sparkle from my hair for over a week."

"Surely there was *something* you enjoyed about playing that part. Some trivial little . . ."

He bowed his head, a sudden blanket of awkwardness upon him. "Suppose we speak of *your* productions. I've told you most everything about mine."

I stepped back from the edge of the cliff and heaved a sigh—of both relief and disappointment. It truly must have meant very little to him. Obligation and gratitude, with nothing magical about it. "There's not much to tell for mine. I've never been principal."

"Then I suppose you'd best practice. Auditions are in a few days. Are you ready?"

I squared my shoulders. "Yes. Yes, I believe I am." All I needed was a loft and a trapeze. Well, and an empty theater. That would help.

"Splendid." His smile was intoxicating. "Perhaps I shall see more of you on the stage as you climb the ranks."

"I do hope so." I looked up into his face, trying to see even a trace of Marcus de Silva, but I did not. Where my father wore disinterest like a heavy cloak, Philippe was watchful. Alert and aware. Where my father was a turned back, Philippe was an offered arm.

He stood to escort me when we'd finished. Two blocks we walked in silence, then he cleared his throat. "About Jack Dorian. I assume you were . . ."

"Thrown into his presence. Quite unceremoniously, I might add." Well I remembered that walk through the cemetery, the exit that Philippe had observed. "Circumstances brought us together, time and again, and he's proven . . . helpful."

"Hmm." He studied me as we walked.

"He's been a fine friend."

He remained tense beside me, his face a mask of unease until we reached the boardinghouse. He turned to me at the door. "Forgive my intrusiveness, Miss Blythe. It's no business of mine if you've attached yourself to Jack Dorian or anyone else."

But it was.

"I'd just hate to see such a rare girl end up with the likes of him. Jack can charm nearly anyone."

I offered a prim smile to cover the churning inside. "You're in luck, because I'm not simply any woman." Why must he speak so of the man who'd been such fun, who'd trotted me about the circus and forced me past my fear of heights? He may not be the finest choice for a suitor, but he made a most amusing and sincere friend.

Philippe's face relaxed into a solemn smile, and he parted from me with a nod and a friendly "good day." But his words had tainted the beautiful memory of the last few days, the freedom and delight I'd found in Jack's presence, and I couldn't bear it. The little-girl part of me wished everyone could get along and my favorite people all liked one another as much as I did.

Yet that wasn't life. That wasn't drama and theater.

21

The violinist began, and I stood, grounded and strong. Poised. *The LORD is my rock, and my fortress.* How right, how very sweet, to weave these precious lines from childhood into my adult dream. How well they melded into one beautiful work of art.

Then on cue I swept up into a bold arabesque, chest lifted, the words of the Eighteenth Psalm threading through my mind. *And he rode upon a cherub, and did fly: yea, he did fly upon the wings of the wind.* Like the swans, I propelled myself across the stage with strength and precision, then slowed and opened my arms.

Several critical pairs of eyes were upon me, evaluating my every breath, but they felt almost distant. *Yea, thou liftest me up above those that rise up against me.*

I spun, arms in close, then burst up into an *assemblé dessus* with all the strength in me and landed in a soft *demi-plié*. It was the first time I'd carried peace into my audition like a garment, and it allowed me to dance with more control and grace than before. Fear had settled into a tame fizzle around my middle, and *that* could be got around.

For by thee I have run through a troop; and by my God have I leaped over a wall.

A pas de bourreé and a leap, landing neatly in fourth position, one foot tucked back. I rose alone on the stage and braved a glance out into the audience, toward the face of the Great Fournier. Only a thin curtain of smoke obscured his features, and no frown. Not even a small one. There was only mild surprise and, what, a bit of softening perhaps?

Claps split the silence and my gaze snapped toward Jack Dorian, who lounged in another theater seat, one leg crossed over his knee as he alone applauded my audition. It made me smile. He often did that. Bobbing a quick curtsy, I took my leave and let the next dancer on. My legs still trembled, but I felt lighter. Stronger. I'd done better this time—I could feel it.

Just past the drawn curtain hovered a cluster of dancers gathered to talk while they waited—but they stood silent, watching me. Some faces glowed with a little surprise, others with a skeptical sort of envy, and all I could think was, I did it. I showed them. Now I belonged among them.

But there was little welcome.

"You were stupendous." Tovah grabbed me by the shoulders backstage when the others had edged away. "You danced like you'd been at it forty years. All that extra practice has finally paid off, has it?"

"We'll see, once the casting list is up."

"You're sure to catch a decent role, with dancing like that. Chin up." She squeezed my arms again and hurried off to watch the next audition.

I turned and caught sight of Philippe Rousseau watching from the deep shadows of the backstage area, arms folded across his chest, and my heart jumped up into my throat. How fortunate that I had not noticed him there until after my audition. His expressive dark eyes sparkled with interest, admiration perhaps, but he said nothing. Not that he had to. Delight fluttered in my heart and leaked out in a smile. He returned it.

I finally took a long, deep breath and began to allow my dreams to unfurl.

After the others auditioned, I hurried back to the long, narrow cloakroom and twirled dreamily down the length of it, pausing to grasp the soft folds of my cloak and breathe in the hope of possibilities.

"Congratulations are in order for the lady." A low voice tinged warm with intimacy came from behind as I pulled my wrap from its hook.

I turned, air whooshing against the back of my bare neck. I glimpsed the face that was growing more familiar by the day. Jack Dorian. "Well, now." Heart pounding from the shock, I reached for my bag and hat. The room felt even more narrow than normal, more overstuffed with wraps. "I know why they named you Jack, like the kind in the box. Popping up at random, frightening the ever-loving—"

"Don't you want to know why I'm congratulating you?"

The edges of a playful smile curled my lips, though. "What have I won, another shove from a barn loft?"

His face brimmed with pleasure. "*Paulina.*"

I scrunched my nose and shoved my feet into a pair of too-big brown flats that blessedly did not pinch my sore feet. "What's a Paulina?"

He shoved hair off his forehead and leaned against the trim of the doorway. "Oh, just another solo part in the ballet."

I froze and my heart hit the floor—really and truly thudded on the long wood floor panels with the weight of shock.

"*That* Paulina? But how do you know? They've not posted the list yet, have they?" It was no lead, but it was the best part I'd managed so far.

"Posted, no. Decided on, well . . ." He shrugged. "It pays to be friends with Jack Dorian." He winked and urged me through the door. "Come, let's celebrate."

"What sort of part will you make Paulina?" We spun and giggled down the corridor as I searched his face for signs that this was all in jest. "Are her dances terribly complex? Will I have to learn a great deal of new combinations?"

His eyebrows rose in amusement as he guided me with light waltzing steps toward the door. "A wonderful one. Yes, and no." He took my hand and spun me, my feet shuffling in the dust. "She's Queen Hermione's lady-in-waiting. There are plenty of servants and shepherdess parts, but none is higher than dear Paulina when it comes to servant roles."

I laughed with glee, as if I were actually becoming a lady-in-waiting in the royal courts instead of just playing one. "Truly? And who is to play Hermione?"

The light in his eyes shuttered and he turned away, dance over, hand gripping the back of his neck.

I took a step toward him. "You didn't see?"

"I did."

"Well?"

"It's Minna."

I crossed my arms. "Indeed. Minna as queen, me as her underling."

"Ah, but this queen also dies." His eyebrows wiggled as he urged me out the alley door, draping my wrap around my shoulders.

"Does she, now?" I couldn't help but grin as my voice echoed in the empty alley. How evil I was. I didn't wish Minna dead, of course, but I didn't mind that her character would be. "This queen isn't the lead, then?"

"Princess Perdita carries most of the story for the female roles. Poor Queen Hermione has too many enemies to live through even the first act."

"How sad for her."

"Her name may be higher on the program, but this choreographer says she'll have slightly less impressive sequences than her most lovely lady-in-waiting."

"Also sad." I giggled. "Where are we going?"

"You know better than to ask." He slanted a daring look at me, offering his arm. "Will you come?"

"I will." I didn't even hesitate when we did not turn onto the Strand, but instead crossed it and continued north, a most unusual route that was nowhere near Mama Jo's boardinghouse. I nodded at the greengrocer packing up for the night and the woman sweeping up feather remnants in her milliner's shop. Then we left the market, and I ran my fingertips along the top of a black iron fence on a long street of homes, not once voicing the questions I had about our destination. Somewhere along the line, I'd come to take for granted that Jack Dorian ultimately wanted the best for me, that his purpose in this was to help me. I suppose that was the beginning of trust, whether or not it was deserved.

Well, he was about to prove one way or the other.

22

It was the smell that first caused me to hesitate—a foul mix of moist sewage and rodents. It hung in the air as we stepped into a large, open square with a pillar reaching to the sky, the odor swirling through my senses. I hardly noticed the chafing of the ill-fitting shoes against my feet.

"Where are we?"

Jack Dorian's jovial tone dampened as we paused in the square. "As Keats so famously put it, 'Where misery clings to misery for a little warmth, and want and disease lie down side-by-side, and groan together.'"

I turned a full circle, taking in the seven roads spidering out from the square, disappearing into an oblivion of smog and debris. Squalid tenements were stacked one upon the other in dubiously balanced rows and spilling forth with laundry lines and crowds of people who, for lack of any other option, called this place home. At the center of it all stood that pillar, lifting the faces of seven different sundials toward the smoggy sky, and I knew.

How many years had passed since that wretched night? Seven

or eight at least. Maybe more. He couldn't have known what this place was to me. I stepped over horse dung that clogged the overfull streets and peered at birds hanging by one foot from a long spit against a building where a boy stood, cap in hand, to sell his trappings. Across the square an ancient clock tower bonged out a wobbly announcement of the hour—five o'clock.

"Do you know the place?"

Even though I'd been in these streets only once, it was all too familiar. "Seven Dials." I breathed out the words, hardly more than a whisper.

"Ah, you are familiar with it." He stood, considering the buildings hemming us in.

"I've been before."

"Despite your great moral character."

I swallowed and held my ground, breathing only through my mouth. My stomach rolled over for so many reasons.

With a gentle tug, he led me through the square and down an eastern street bordered by noisy pubs and stores that sold items not quite secondhand—perhaps fourth or fifth. We turned where a street sign was embedded into the side of a nearly windowless pub and into an even narrower street, where the stench was mercifully halved by the tall buildings on either side, and he called a loud *halloo* into the emptiness.

It was chaos as soon as his voice sounded. Women of all sizes and shapes, some as young as seven or eight years old, appeared from doors and around corners, gathering in the alley. Then he turned to me with a sly look. "My lady, I give you training part two—the training of others."

"Training?" My voice barely came out.

"It's my weekly ritual. I come here to teach them."

How desperately I wanted to leave. To bathe. To forget. Nowhere on earth made me more uncomfortable. "Why Seven Dials? Why teach here?"

He straightened with a long inhale. "I grew up here."

I collected myself and gave a sidelong look. "With your mother, the silk heiress?"

"My mother is a silk heiress, but it's my father who sealed my fate. He was *her* father's esteemed estate manager. He was thirty-two and she seventeen the year of my birth, although they called my birth a 'summer abroad' and promptly left me here, with her scullery maid's elderly aunt. So yes, I grew up here."

"You've never even met your mother, then." A surge of pity warmed my heart.

"Oh, I've met her. I was her little plaything for a time, and she'd come visit me, then place me back up on the shelf of Seven Dials and hurry home to her townhouse in Belgravia."

"You said Chelsea."

"Well, now she's in Chelsea, where she lives with her husband—a duke. Always her aim, if I remember correctly."

Then the book of his past slammed shut and he turned to the gathering crowd, his voice lilting and full of charm. "Ladies, I promised you a special treat this week, and here she is. A true dancer, soloist at Craven Street Theatre, come to teach you. What do you say to that?"

Giddy chatter sounded and the shuffling of boots on the dusty road.

I glanced at Jack, wrestler of tigers and son of a silk heiress, who threw me the most beguiling grin I'd ever seen, and suddenly I realized every story he'd ever told me was true.

I stood before this tattered collection of London's poorest, likely burdened by no more than two shillings between the lot of them, whom I was now expected to teach—ballet, of all things. Which suddenly seemed utterly pointless as I looked into their gaunt faces.

One woman hovered in the shadows, back arched under the heavy load of her life. Sores trailed over her arms, which she didn't even bother to tuck into her skirts. I watched her in my peripheral vision, wondering if she'd join us. Humanly hoping she wouldn't, then feeling a surge of guilt. Mama would have welcomed her.

I stepped forward, moving my feet around in the shoes to keep them on, and nodded. "Ready, then?" After leading in a few awkward stretches, I swept into recovery and whispered to Jack. "Are they dancers?" They followed easily, as if the steps were familiar.

"Prostitutes, mostly. A few fortune-tellers, Irish immigrants, a handful of pickpockets."

I swallowed, hardly daring to breathe. I'd seen the likes of these women hovering about the fringes of Covent Garden when I'd wandered too far, but now up close, all I saw was hunger. The same hunger that existed in the petits rats, and in me, as I danced alone in that materials room, torturing my feet for the sake of earning my place there.

I scanned those faces again as I instructed them to twirl in place, surprised by their abilities and steadiness. And Jack—he was a surprise too. Spending time with prostitutes, but not, it now seemed, as a client. I worked past my welling heart, as we'd been taught in every training session, and forced poise into my spine. "We'll start with an arabesque, and I'll show you a trick for creating the perfect line."

I shed my cloak and lifted onto the ball of my right foot and into the familiar arch, tightening my spine and holding my arm long. "The secret is in the curve of my back. Do you see? I've pulled it into a strong line, and let everything else flow from . . ." My words vanished as I watched slender bodies in need of food lift delicately onto one foot, backs arched, bony arms lifted to follow my every move. "Yes," I croaked. "That's it."

I glanced about for the woman with sores hovering near the back, but Jack Dorian blocked my vision to the right, striding with purpose toward an old Gypsy woman seated on a crate. I watched in horror, then awe, as he bowed at the waist, extended his hand, and accepted her crusty, gnarled one in his, all his charm now shining out upon her withered self.

With imaginary music playing, he pulled the old woman up, spinning her around with a clinking of little gold coins on her headscarf, and dipping her crooked old body back. She cackled as he righted her, toothless face aglow, giving her a unique charm I never would have noticed if Jack hadn't lit the flame in her.

She bobbed and spun along with his smooth, even strides, making quick circles in the alleyway behind the rows of others. It was both ridiculous and enchanting, this uneven pair. Jack was smiling at her with all the lively playfulness he flashed toward the well-dressed dancers at Craven. It brimmed over upon the lovely and the unlovely, the wealthy and the poor.

How sadly different he and I were.

I turned fully back to my unusual class. After directing them to lift into one last demi-pointe spin, I moved back toward Jack with a lump in my throat that refused to be swallowed. "They were quite good. I can tell you've worked with them."

He shrugged. "They have time, and so do I. They have a need, I have a solution."

"Do they not work?"

"Not during the day."

"Oh." A furnace of heat eclipsed my face. "Right." How trivial it seemed to teach these women about arabesques and pointed toes. What good was ballet to a starving, desperate world?

"Well, then. I suppose you'll want to hurry back to the theater and practice. I've kept you long enough."

I glanced down the squalid street to the left as we crossed it, at the gray linens swinging on lines under a sunless sky, the little soot-darkened children dodging rats as they hurried home from climbing chimneys. I felt the burden of "not enough" coming down on my shoulders again, but for different reasons.

"No, I don't believe so," I said. I had the painful sense that I'd wasted my life. My heart. My second chance from God.

I could feel Jack eyeing me. "It was too much bringing you here, I suppose. I've taxed your delicate constitution."

I looked down at my feet, which I'd spent years torturing. For show. For vanity. I couldn't see the exact place from here, but somewhere among these streets was the place I'd stumbled and fallen all those years ago, frantic with regret and fear after what I'd done, at my ugliest inside, and that's exactly where God had found me. Where he'd made himself known to my conflicted heart, and rather than judgment, it was a hand of mercy reaching out to me. The hand of a Father. I'd been granted forgiveness and a chance, and I'd gone and spent that life . . . on theater. "I just don't see the point." I said it quietly, but he heard. He always did.

Only this time, he didn't truly hear. "The *point* is infusing beauty where it's lacking. Bringing hope to despair. Taking bodies that are regularly degraded and drawing out something of beauty—making cheap merchandise into art. Proving to them what could be." His voice was firm but gentle, lacking condemnation. "I train them, then bring some into the corps at Craven. The pay is worse, but the work slightly more dignified. Some are quite eager for the chance."

"You bring these women . . . into Craven?" I was stunned. Touched. Convicted.

"Half the corps at least, and a few of the sujet." He sighed. "This is why I could never sign on for any sort of religion. Call me a heathen, my dear nun, but I could never feel righteous by sidestepping places and people like this to keep myself 'wholesome.'"

I cringed at the silly name I'd somehow earned at Craven. All at once I was weary—of struggling to rise, of working harder, of trying to prove myself. Of covering up how very human I actually was.

We didn't speak for a few streets, and we descended into our own thoughts as we crossed back into the gaslit streets of Covent Gardens bordered by parks and columned theaters. "Jack?"

"Yes?"

"I don't think I care so much for that name anymore."

His long stride slowed in the orange air of sunset as it prismed in the fog. "Fair enough. Perhaps I'll simply call you Ella."

I gave him a crooked smile. "I'd like that." We ambled around a lamppost on a corner and continued east, crossing over to Bow Street to head north. "Have you been to church before, when you were younger?"

He shrugged. "Years ago, but not lately. I've mostly kept away." A rotund lamplighter just up the street paused to lift his flame to the gaslight on a long gold stick, pausing in the descending night until light glowed behind the glass. "There's no single version of me they find acceptable. To the pious, every orphan is a thief, every scruffy lad looking for trouble, and every circus man incurably immoral. I don't have to tell you what they think of the theater."

Moments later we slowed before the Bow Street entrance of the Theatre Royal and looked up at the thirty-foot Grecian columns supporting a triangular vestibule leading into the grandest of atriums.

"As I said, I simply never saw the point in a weekly torment. My logical mind could not make sense of it all, and my heart could not abide any moral system too twisted and clogged for human decency to pass through."

"Please. Don't write off God because of mere people who are too shortsighted to love as they should." Including myself. Outward purity had been my priority, but not God's. Not the main one, anyway—he had far bigger things in mind. "It *does* make sense, if you give it a chance, and it has everything to do with acceptance—not by people, but by—"

"You will not change my mind, Miss Blythe."

Miss Blythe? "What happened to Ella?"

He huffed a sigh. "How should I know? It seems she's turned back into the nun."

I recoiled, drawing into my cape.

He deflated at the shoulders, expelling breath. "My apologies. That was wretched of me, and I'll not use the name again. On my honor as a gentleman." He turned me to face him. "Now, if I may be so bold as to invite you to the *real* outing of the night . . . Lady Ella?"

I straightened, lifting a small smile. "You may."

He led me around the theater to the piazza, and through a dark door off to the side.

"Where are we going?"

"Let us forevermore strike that question from our acquaintance, shall we? I'll never answer it." He gave me a wicked grin in the dark and led me up a rounding narrow staircase flanked with candles set into recesses along the walls. Muffled orchestra music thrummed somewhere nearby, every crash of a cymbal making my heart skitter.

"Isn't this a private entrance? Are we allowed to be here?"

"So many questions," he whispered. "Perhaps we should strike them altogether."

"Will we be in trouble?"

"Only if we're caught. Come, now. This is lesson number three." We exited the stairwell, and he led me through a long anteroom beset with tall white statues of Greek mythology and laid with soft blue carpeting. Chandeliers dripped crystals high above our heads, and Jack Dorian walked as one quite at home in such surroundings.

All this beauty, this fabled, remarkable building with the generous fireplace, plush cushioned benches, and abundant lighting, struck my weary eyes with the harsh brightness of the sun. So gaudy, so excessive. I tugged on his arm. "Perhaps I don't want lessons anymore." In a world of hurt and need, what good was ballet? If I spent my life on it, what good was I?

"Nonsense. I'll have you dancing better than you've ever dreamed."

When I'd been a very young maid to the Cavendish family, I'd once bit down on a brass candlestick after I'd seen the housekeeper do it to test the authenticity of a piece. The unpleasant taste of that metal in my mouth came back to me now on the sound of Jack's confident words. When had my dreams soured so? Or perhaps they were merely changing.

He tucked my hand back into the crook of his arm, bowed at

an attendant who passed on the way to stoke one of the recessed stoves on the south side, and ushered me toward the fifth red-velvet curtain. "How fortunate, once again, that you are friends with Jack Dorian." He grinned and lifted the curtain back to reveal a small private box amply appointed with two light-blue brocade chairs and fringed curtains framing its view of the renowned Theatre Royal stage. I inhaled as I stepped inside, and the music boomed from the pit. The well-lit stage swarmed with dancers leaping across its expanse in perfect formation.

"You've brought me to a ballet? *Here?*" Jack was ever full of surprises.

He shrugged. "You taught those behind you earlier today and now you learn from those ahead. It is the logical next step in your lessons."

The undeniable magnificence struck me full on, as it had that first night from the peep at Craven, and I descended into the moment as one sinks into a familiar chair by the warm fire at home. Gaudy as it had suddenly seemed, I belonged to ballet and ballet to me, for I'd loved it and desired it before experience had told me it was evil. There was a raw, unfiltered beauty on the stage before me, and my God-created heart was magnetized to it.

"Does belonging to God mean I have to give up my dreams?" I'd asked this once of Mama when I was small—maybe seven or eight—and it had nearly broken my heart to even voice it. *"No, little one,"* she'd answered. *"But it means you'd best be wholly willing to."*

There was a silent shattering in my chest at the memory. Perhaps that was why the trip to Seven Dials had happened, to prepare me to let go. To bring that bitter metallic taste into my mouth for what I should not want. I owed *God* my life— not ballet.

I turned away. The theater was full of immorality and evil. Vanity and uselessness. How could I ask God to come into this place—to help me succeed in it? *I will follow you anywhere, Lord. Even out of the theater.* Tears leaked from the corners of my eyes as I looked straight ahead, absorbing the sight of the dancers twirling in tandem arabesques.

Then came the female lead, a dark-haired beauty with vibrant skin and lively steps, measured control in every lift of her arms.

"There now, see what she's doing?" Jack pointed out toward the stage. "This is what I wanted you to see. She's known for this. It reminded me of the dancer who wished to fly . . . but not too high."

I caught my breath as she popped up onto the very tips of her toes several times, landing down again with acrobatic precision and bouncing back up. I leaned over the bannister, drinking in the sight of every movement, every pointed toe, every graceful leap and lunge on that stage. I merely tried to breathe as the ballet spun on, with chiffon scarves floating, ribbons swirling, and strength pulsating.

I would, God. I would leave the theater . . . if you made it clear that's what you wanted. I closed my eyes. *Do you?*

I opened them again and waited, breath shallow and vision spinning. Only the orchestra filled my senses. What had I expected, a voice? A bolt of lightning?

Jack's voice jarred me. "Look, look over there. Did you see the prince regent is in his box tonight? How wonderful." He pointed across the way toward a lavish second-story box with a rounded balcony that extended from the rear of the auditorium. Several figures could barely be seen from our angle, but one wore a startling red coat with yellow fringe at the shoulders and a white sash. The skirt of an ice-blue dress hovered near the man's black-clad legs.

"How odd it is that the royal family will come to watch the dancers who aren't deemed fit to step inside a church."

"Nonsense. Ballet is as royal as the prince himself."

I stilled, my hands laid limply together on my lap. "What do you mean?"

"Precisely what I said. Ballet is many things, some of them less than savory, but it was always meant to be a most noble dance in the royal courts, ever and only for the pleasure of its primary admirer—the king. Why, some royals even took part, dancing along with the principal."

I grasped the edge of the chair, feeling the carved flowers below the cushion against my palm. "Is that so?"

"Others have always been allowed to look on, but it was always, from the start, meant primarily for the king." His fingertips brushed my skirt searching for my hand, then rested across my fingers. "A great many things that were originally noble and beautiful have been tarnished by this world, but that doesn't change what they were originally created to be."

Shaking, I looked back out to that exquisite dancer as she again popped up on her toes—up, up, up. Up toward heaven.

Praise him with the timbrel and dance: praise him with stringed instruments and organs. Praise him upon the loud cymbals: praise him upon the high sounding cymbals. Let every thing that hath breath praise the Lord. *Praise ye the* Lord.

God hadn't been taken out of the theater. Oh no, we were not big enough for that. At last, my wandering gaze had found the correct focal point. I turned to my companion and rested my hand on his. "Thank you, Jack. Thank you."

His lips parted, revealing white teeth against tanned skin. "You're welcome. Lady Ella."

I smiled, tempted to tell this playful rogue exactly how many times he'd been used of God in my life lately. *Thank you, Father.* In that opulent theater surrounded by orchestra music and pieces of my own heritage, my heart brimmed over with gratitude, with awareness of God. And a completely fresh view of myself as a dancer.

The curtain to our box whipped back, and the narrow, reddish face of an usher broke into our moment. "You're not Lord Favelroy. Have you any right to be in here?"

"Much as you do. This is a private box."

"Let's just fetch the manager and see what he says." The curtain fringe whipped down over his face and the man disappeared.

Then Jack leaned down and whispered, "*Run!*"

With Jack, every moment became an adventure. One never knew.

23

We laughed most of the way down a flight of narrow stone steps that were not plushly carpeted, and certainly not lit. It released all the tension that had built like a band around my chest, and it was as wonderfully freeing as the night air.

"Many pardons for the hasty exit, my lady. I'm quite certain ole Favelroy wouldn't mind a bit, my sitting in his unoccupied seat. He has paid for it, after all, and he's a fine chap. He's offered me the box once or twice, but I wouldn't care to convince the manager of that. We've had run-ins before."

"Shocking."

"I came here once when I was in the circus to do an act with Lizzie, and he decided he disliked me to the extreme."

"Did you do something to deserve it?"

"Of course." We reached the bottom, a tiny circular landing with only one way out. He shoved his shoulder into the door to open it. "I broke his nose."

My gloved hand flew to my mouth. "Over what?"

"What do you think?"

He took long strides into the night and I ran to catch up. "A woman."

His steps slowed to match mine, and he tucked my hand into the crook of his arm, but he didn't speak as we rounded the theater to Bow Street again and continued south. Those ill-fitting slippers rubbed my heels raw, but I couldn't bear to stop now. Jack Dorian was a box full of surprises, and I never tired of opening it. I tucked my wrap tighter around me with my free hand and tried to hold the flats in place by curling my toes inside them.

When we came in sight of the arches of the Waterloo Bridge, looking about for a possible destination, I had to stuff down the temptation to ask the forbidden question. The heady smell of the water greeted me, and it was all very familiar. Where *were* we going, though? We took the stone walkway across, watching horses trot past pulling carriages, then walked uphill to another section of town that still glowed with life.

Muffled orchestra music floated out into the slightly chilly night, and Jack's footsteps slowed. "I've not made friends in this theater yet, so . . ." He made a hard turn onto the lawn of the great stone building and went around to an empty courtyard in the back. "Would you care for lawn seating, my lady?"

I smiled and he removed his coat, draping it across the grass for me and lying beside it. Uncertain, yet tickled with the unusual nature of our outing, I descended onto his overcoat, skirt ballooning around my legs, and lay back. He tucked his hands behind his head and closed his eyes, as if absorbing the feel of the music through the ground. I could see why—the ground below trembled with every low note and the air seized up with the high ones.

In this private moment, with Jack's eyes closed and darkness curtaining us, I dared to force off the aching shoes with the toes of my other foot—just for a short while. I'd slip them back on before I caught my death, of course. I tucked my throbbing soles beneath my skirt, nearly gasping at the loveliness of the cool grass on them through my torn stockings.

"It was over Lizzie, actually." Jack's voice surprised me. "The broken nose, that is. It was because of her."

"He made you jealous."

"Angry. Thought his money gave him more rights to Lizzie than merely her performance onstage. I made sure he knew different."

I shivered. "I once thought all your stories of heroism absurd. But you are a hero in your own way, aren't you?"

He didn't answer.

"For all the women you pursue, it somehow doesn't surprise me that you'd go to such lengths to protect the honor of one. You confuse me sometimes, Jack Dorian. I cannot make sense of you."

"Part of my charm."

"Indeed." I ran my hand along the carpet of grass and wiggled my toes in it. "Have you worked any further on that ballet of yours?"

"Those main characters haven't spoken to me lately. Especially the hero. Stubborn bloke, that one."

"And the heroine?"

A pause. "I've discovered only what I did not wish to know. What makes her less a heroine every day." His voice was hushed. "It seems she has a desperate need for affection, giving and receiving it, and is not content to let the hero alone fill it. I simply cannot imagine why they were in love—if they truly were."

"Perhaps you merely don't understand her yet. Why don't

you begin by giving *her* a noble gesture? An interesting twist—she can even rescue the hero."

"By throwing a shoe, I suppose." There was a smile in his tone.

"What a silly thing for a heroine to do. But then you'd have a reason to love her, of course, her being so brave and resourceful."

"Then I suppose you'd suggest they dance together in a forgotten old room."

"Yes, and beautifully so. But then he disappears." I sighed. How easy it was to fall back into the memory of that unusual night.

"Well then, they must find one another again." His voice was quiet. Undefinable.

"Of course. But he doesn't recognize her, because it's been so many years. Then finally, when they are dancing together again at a sumptuous party, with her in a most stunning gown, she reveals it to him." I closed my eyes, feeling the romance on the breeze about me. "'Hero,' she says. 'Dear hero, I have a secret to tell you. We've danced this way before. You don't recognize me, but I've never forgotten you. I once saved your life. Now I want to offer you mine.'"

"That's some speech."

"I may have rehearsed it a few times." I heaved a sigh. The muffled strains of violins softened the quiet of the night, and I drank in the moment, the daydream whose sweetness dissolved in my heart over time like hard candy enjoyed for hours.

Jack's voice jarred me back. "I still don't see what she loves about this hero. He was saved. They danced. Any man can do those things."

"Most wouldn't. Not with a ragged little child who didn't

belong there. He was gallant and kind, showing her how pure and sacred ballet could be, and it was all so *perfect*." My chest rose and fell twice. "Of course it seems absurdly silly to a trifler like yourself, but to the rest of us . . ." My trailing voice mingled with the rise of orchestra music.

"She did belong there. That girl." His simple words dropped into the night, then Jack didn't speak for a moment, and I sank unquestioningly into the silence.

I closed my eyes to picture the dancers in the climactic moment, feeling the gentle pressure of Philippe's hands at my waist, seeing the vibrancy of his face once again as we danced, the overflowing kindness. There was simply no way to express what I knew about that night—about Philippe.

"Show me."

I rolled over to look at him. "What?"

He sat up, offering me a hand. "I said, 'Show me.' Come now, I know you can dance at least tolerably well."

I shifted and felt the chill of grass on my bare feet. I rooted around under my skirt for the terrible brown shoes, but my feet only found more grass. I sat up and looked about, but the world around the blue-green grass had grown surprisingly dark. Insufferable man, dragging me into this. "I dance every day, Jack Dorian. What makes you think I'd want to do it now?"

"Because this time it's with me." His smile was so enchanting, so very inviting, that I took his hand.

"Perhaps you should dance, and I can watch."

"Nonsense." He gave a gentle tug. "This is an opportunity for me too, dancing with the soon-famous ballerina Ella Blythe."

"I'd much rather watch."

He released my hand and frowned. "What's this about?" Again, his eyes gently demanded the truth. I looked down. He lowered himself until his bright gaze was right before mine, head tipped just so. "Well?"

I leaned up to whisper into his ear. "I've lost my shoes."

He considered me with an amused half smile, then without a word, he kicked off his own shoes and offered his hand again. "Better?"

Smiling, unable to resist this gallant gentleman standing before me in his stocking feet, I took his hand and allowed myself to be framed in his arms. We stood there for a moment in the throng of crickets and night music as the violins died away to silence. He never once took his eyes off me. Then the music began anew, and he swept me along, turning me into a ballet-waltz through the grass, moving faster and faster, spinning and dipping until the music had worked into the fibers of my muscles and I too was committed.

We moved this way through the darkening lawn of the grand theater, stealing their muffled music and creating our own performance, dancing for no one but ourselves. Lifting my arms, I arched back with his arm holding my waist and felt the night cool and wild against my skin in a moment of glorious abandon. Then he pulled me to him and we moved together through the paces he'd written for the last performance. When the instruments dimmed and the world again fell quiet, we slowed our steps as the dance seemed to continue. We came to a stop, but my mind didn't quit whirling, and I found myself powerfully drawn to Jack Dorian.

I shook it off, backing away and looking up at the theater. "They certainly have a lovely orchestra."

"You've not yet told Philippe your secret?"

I shook my head. "I haven't your bravery in such matters, you know. I'm still a bit intimidated by the whole idea—by him."

"Ella, not every hero of a story is truly heroic and no one's real life is a stage performance. Do not think him more perfect than he is."

I looked into Jack's face and thought of everything I knew about him. "Yes, I know."

By the time Jack hailed a cab to take us back across the bridge, for my shoes were never found in the dark, we'd fallen silent again. Most of London was at home, but the streets were alive with scavengers hollering to each other, cabbies and their horses winging by, and a few lean-looking costermongers calling out their wares. He handed me into the hackney and tucked a lap rug over my legs, even though there was only a slight chill in the air from the river.

I rested comfortably against the seats, and as my limbs buzzed with excitement under the warm blanket, the pull of sleepiness washed over me like a great ocean wave. Jack leaned my head against his shoulder, and I didn't have the energy to resist. In fact, I closed my eyes.

I felt the rumble of his voice through his coat. "You truly think me a trifler still?"

I blinked open my eyes and looked up into his face, which looked far too concerned for such a beautiful night. "I consider you one of my very favorite friends." With a happy smile, I rested again, allowing the slow-moving carriage to lull me. It was such a long trip back to the boardinghouse when one was hemmed into traffic, but after a full evening it was so much nicer than walking.

"Shall I tell you my big secret?" His low voice barely pierced the lovely cocoon of drowsiness, but I managed a small sound of assent and he went on. "It's an act. All an act. Life is one big stage, and that's the part that fits me best, so I wear it."

"Well, you carry it off splendidly."

The noisy streets—rattling carriages, loud voices, and distant boat horns—slid into the background as we rolled through the congested neighborhoods. I roused at the light "whoa" as our vehicle creaked to a stop. We'd returned to the boardinghouse and the night was over. I rubbed my face and only then did I realize how silent Jack had been. I looked up into his face, which was unabashedly tilted down toward me, watching. Examining. Knowing. Didn't he tire of looking at the same plain face?

He smiled, but without the usual brightness.

"Thank you for a most wonderful lesson." I hadn't said it before, even once, had I? Perhaps that was what bothered him into silence. Yet Jack didn't seem the type to be sore over that kind of oversight.

"You are most welcome, my lady." He folded the lap rug and helped me alight, handing me down to the walk after springing out himself. "I hope you now feel sufficiently prepared for your new part."

A smile tipped my lips up. Ah, yes. I *hadn't* dreamed it. I was to dance Paulina in the new production. "If I am, I have only you to thank."

"Which means I'm entitled to my reward."

The kiss. The bet. Now I was fully awake. I looked at him solemnly. "You did accomplish the impossible."

"That I did." He stepped closer, daring to brush a stray lock from my cheek. How mussed my hair must be.

I stood rooted to the walk, arms folded. Suddenly they were trembling. And bet or no bet, the intoxicating moonlight nearly had me willing to give him what he was about to ask. My voice came out soft and nervous. "Well? What is it you want?"

"What I want . . ." His voice was soft against the muffled

noise of the market two streets away, his look a sort of caress that I wished, in that moonlit moment, would materialize into reality. What would it be like for the charmer to come that close? His gaze lingered on each feature of my face. Then, while he still watched me, I felt something slide into my right hand. "What I want . . . is for you to *fly*."

With a playful smile, he tipped his hat and bounded back into the carriage, taking an essential piece of me with him. When had I become so attached to this man? When had the famed trifler become my dearest friend?

I looked down into my hands and saw a luscious pair of ivory satin slippers. I ran my fingers over their smooth shell, across the leather soles. The toes—that's what was different. They were slightly stiff, and it was more than extra darning. I swept my fingers around inside. A leather pad and casing of some sort held the toe firm—so I could dance on them. I clutched them to me, blinking at the pair of swinging lanterns muted by fog in the distance. Tomorrow I would become a soloist in a Shakespearean ballet—and I would fly.

I stared after that surprising character, wondering what his role in my ballet would turn out to be. I had thought him a villain, then a friend. Yet he was threatening to break the cardinal rule of storytelling—after a night of theater and starlit dancing, he was beginning to outshine the hero. I heaved a deep sigh and tried to think of Philippe, but I couldn't picture his face just then. Not beyond the memory of bright eyes and smiling lips.

"*Marco*." The nearby whisper startled me.

"Polo." Eyes wide, I looked around. It was a game we'd played in a crowded marketplace in that horrible year when we were too young to find work and we'd had to filch our food. There'd been some ancient Italian explorer by the name, and his team had used this method to find each other again. I suppose I'd loved it so much because Mama had first used it with my father when they'd had their secret courtship. Lily and I thought it quite clever and adopted it as our own. And now, once again it was put to use.

My parcel-laden sister emerged from a shadowed bush, smiling in the worst way. "You've better taste than I thought. But I don't know why you let him walk away without a kiss."

My skin heated against the chilly air. "I don't know what you mean."

She stepped closer, her face aglow with sisterly knowing.

I groaned. "Oh, Lily, I haven't any idea what to do. He isn't who I meant to like."

Her smile was fox-like. "Sometimes it cannot be helped, now can it? Love is a wonderful, terrible thing. Just don't let it knock you off your feet when you aren't looking."

I noticed just then the shadows beneath her eyes, the ironic look on her face. "What's got you so down in the mouth, Lil? That captain of yours stop coming around?"

She grimaced and shifted her load to the other hip. "Oh, he's been around—just not alone. He won't even look at me when she's on his arm, as if he had sudden memory loss."

"He's under pressure to marry well, no doubt."

She wrinkled her nose. "Oh, he married quite well. But they've never been in love, and she's a greedy little thing, and he's—"

"*What?*" White stars of panic flashed before my eyes. "What sort of man do you have designs on, Lily?"

"It's only on paper between them, and he never meant any of it. If only—"

"You'll check a man's socks, but not his *ring*? Lily, how *could you*? If he's willing to betray his wife, there's no telling what he'll do to you, the woman to whom he owes nothing. Do you have any idea what might have happened?"

Her scowl turned dark. "I should have known I'd hear nothing but a lecture from you. They're right, you being a nun. You know nothing of reality. Marriage has little to do with love, and everyone deserves a slice of happiness. Even him. Even *me*." She stood taller. "I came to ask your advice, but I see I won't be granted any sympathy here." She whirled around in her billowing cape and disappeared into the darkness, footfalls echoing through the night.

"Lily!" But she didn't return. "*Lily!*" Only crickets responded, and my thudding heart. "Marco!"

Only silence. She was in one of her moods again, and I knew there was no catching her. Like a cat, everything was on her terms and advice would only be taken when she was ready for it.

I slipped inside and up the stairs weak and heavyhearted, almost tripping over a parcel leaning against my door. My pulse pounded as I lifted the thing by its string, but it bore Minna's name. I tossed it on her bed, and when she climbed through the window an hour later, I pointed at it. "Came while you were out."

She pounced on the little package to tear off the strings and paper, and drew out a crystal figurine, which she held to the light and admired with a giggle. "My, how he indulges."

"He seems kind, at least."

She turned, crossing her legs on the bed. "He took a fair bit of training."

I stared.

"Come, don't look at me that way. It isn't uncommon."

"He's married, and I'll never feel right about that."

She walked further into the room, no hint of apology on her bright face. "I've not told you much about him, have I? I suppose

228

I cannot expect you to like a man you don't know." She yanked off her hat and tossed it onto the table, then came to sit across from me on her bed. "He's a battered old cavalry man who's seen a lot in his lifetime, and he wears all the scars of it. They never heal. He sailed in to help the fights at Waterloo twenty or so years ago and was injured twice in battle. Fought so hard they made him Major General."

"His family let him stay away that long?"

"He had no choice, you know." Her voice grew soft, her eyes oddly tender. "He fled England after his wife died, out of sheer desperation. He couldn't bear it here without her, in her house with all her little touches about. Came back to claim his title when his uncle passed on, and according to his servants he'd become a stiffly bitter man with iron for a heart. His children were cold, his siblings all turned against him because of hard feelings about the war, and no woman would ever have him for a husband again. I am the only indulgence he has in life. A small taste of warmth in a world that's otherwise been quite punishing to him." Her voice was soft. "He's a decent man who deserves for someone to see him as such once in a while."

I looked anew at this woman who had both intimidated and provoked me. I saw Mama in her, in the softness she turned toward this broken man everyone else scorned. Choices had to be made in real life, and many in the murky gray areas.

I couldn't help but think of Jack. Jack, who had also surprised me. In the end, he'd earned his reward and it hadn't been a kiss. I glanced at the white shoes strung over my mirror. His eyes always burned with such visible intensity that it should be easy to grasp what he was thinking, everything that lay beneath, but I suddenly realized as I stared at those white shoes how little I truly understood this man. And that I rather wished to.

24

Sometimes loving a person meant giving them up. Jack Dorian knew that well, but he'd never expected to feel it so intensely. He stared at the cemetery of St. Paul's the following morning, recalling their walk, the way she'd crumpled before her mother's grave. The slight weight of her head on his shoulder in the carriage. Had an entire night truly passed since then?

In the afterglow of their time together, everything felt magnified. The rainbow of colors spread out before him, the voices of people calling out, the aroma of sausages and bread. The great, aching need for her. He'd never found anything so purely beautiful through and through in his entire life.

He arrived at the tall gray building he knew almost as well as his own and forced himself to ring the front to be admitted upstairs to the second-story flat. At the top he found Philippe Rousseau, slumped in a small horsehair sofa before a solitary game of cards, elbows propped, and three—*three*—mugs spread over the surface, leaving rings on the wood table.

Yet the man's face looked oddly sober. Long and morose, but most definitely sober. Jack slid into the opposite seat and took a whiff of the mugs as he passed over them—cream was the only scent his nose detected. He looked at the man's face hanging over the fourth mug of the half-drunk concoction of buttermilk and corn flour, salt, and pepper, the famous Scottish remedy for a night in one's cups. Never had Philippe reached this point of the circle—the clear-your-head stage—without Jack even knowing he'd begun another round. "This one was short-lived."

"I'm doing better, Jack. Far better." Philippe lifted his countenance still heavy with evidence of a wretched headache. "It's been years."

He stiffened. "Yes, but here you are again."

"I know you won't believe me." He toyed with an empty mug, idly smudging drips. "I've grown too old for this nonsense. Hurts worse than it used to and doesn't clear away the problems half as well as it once did. Besides, I've a reason to become healthy."

"Your 'reason' wouldn't happen to be a woman, would it?" His stomach turned even as he voiced the question. He knew her feelings on the matter, but what were his?

Philippe's brooding gaze leveled on Jack's face, eyes snapping. "What business is it of yours?"

It was worse than he'd thought—he was as far gone as she was. "I suppose she knows about all your secrets and shadows."

He straightened on the sofa, locking gazes with Jack. "You won't go and ruin this one for me too, will you? I'm that determined she'll never have to know most of it. Oh, I'll tell her about it eventually, but I'm hoping it will all be in past tense." His eyes pleaded. "It's been *years*, Jack. I had one bad day, one slipup. The pain was terrible."

Jack tried to swallow a hard lump in his throat. He remembered the night that injury had occurred, leaving Philippe scrambling for a quick fix that landed him in his cups. It was only the right foot, but the pain had been so intense that it had to be dulled by something.

Even when it had healed, the pain came again at times, shooting up his foot as if he'd been stabbed, and no doctor could explain or fix these "phantom pains" that often left him too crippled to dance for a few days. But, no matter. The deeper damage had already been done. The road of addiction was like a spiral staircase, round and round it went, a constant circling back to all the same places.

Once Jack had made a stand to keep Philippe from being fired from the theater when he'd fallen especially hard into his cups. He'd agreed to help Philippe from then on out, with the condition that Philippe agreed to do likewise for someone else—just as Marcus de Silva had done for Jack when he'd rescued him from the transient life of the circus and the cavalry, and brought him into a more solid life in the theater. That was the agreement—one favor, granted to another undeserving soul—and Philippe had been his favor, but Philippe had yet to pass his on.

I wish to invoke my favor. It would be so easy to say. *Stay away from Ella Blythe. Let me have her.* Yet he didn't. Couldn't. Philippe was who she wanted, and Philippe, from what he saw, wanted her. Perhaps they were a good match, for she was unique enough to overlook his flaws and draw out the immense talent, the abilities Jack had always known Philippe possessed.

He almost wished, selfishly, that he'd left well enough alone and let Philippe fall however he would. He studied that whiskered face, ruggedly handsome even now. He did seem remarkably improved of late, missing work only when his phantom pains returned or his mistreated liver made him too sick. The spiral staircase had gone round and round, yet it circled up with each turnabout, Jack realized. There was progress. Still, Jack had a hard time passing Ella Blythe over to him. "What do you even like about the lady?"

"She's nothing sensational to you, perhaps, but she's . . . well, quite unusual. I knew it the first moment I saw her, and there was something about her—something I'd seen before. The way she dances, she reminds me of Craven's legendary ghost dancer, and I suppose that made her all the more interesting to me at first. But after that, I saw other things about her that quite set her apart."

Indeed.

Philippe's features softened. "She's so true and lovely, intelligent and kind to the extreme. Like no one I ever thought I'd meet in a theater. She's a loyal one, she is. And . . . you know how it has been with me."

Ah, yes. Florentine Georgescu. Jack shuddered. How close she'd come to kicking out the delicate ladder of Philippe's new life, of ruining everything he'd built up. Not that Philippe would have believed what Jack had witnessed, if he'd told him. No matter—she was gone now, and Philippe, although never quite forgiving Jack for running her off, was at least sensible enough to realize he needed Jack desperately. Their peculiar friendship had come around.

"Jack." Philippe leaned forward, face twitching. "You have to help me with her. Help me do this right. There's no one else I can trust."

He stiffened against the emotional assault. "I don't think you need my help with her."

Philippe rose on trembling legs. "I'm ready, Jack. Ready for my new life. One with her in it. You may not think much of her, but she's perfect. Precisely what I need."

Jack fingered the handle of an empty mug. "No one's perfect."

Before nine that morning, Jack strode with purpose that burned up his frustration until he left Covent Garden. Stopping at Philippe's had been foolish. It had accomplished nothing, aside from checking in on him, and he already had another mission he should be on. He paused to look at the little missive and remind his distracted brain of the address he was supposed to be finding. Number 57 Cheapside.

It had become a secret love offering, this ballet he was writing, and all the research that went with it. He could do little else for her, especially with Philippe so firmly entering her life, but he could offer her closure. Truth about her parents, and what had happened to them. Perhaps it would sting a little, but the conviction to pursue the truth, to write this ballet, had hovered ever near until he'd begun to relent. And in the end, he desperately wanted her to have her father, a most worthy man who could love her if ever Philippe failed her.

He'd visited several of the addresses from the letters in that box Ella had given him, but there was one more he knew he needed to call upon. The short letter he now held had been at the very bottom of the velvet-lined box, and it was the one he'd most dreaded visiting.

For her. All for her.

It was from Delphine's sister, who seemed a less than pleasant woman. She'd written mostly to shame the famous ballerina into sending her money, claiming neglect and abandonment, which was probably true. Jack approached the rookery labeled number 57 with some loathing. Not so much for the squalor and stench as for the woman who'd let her sister wallow here. He dodged a bolting pig and a handful of dirty children, whipping gray sheets out of the way.

He knocked and asked for Etta Mae Fawley, and in a moment a gaunt, sharp-eyed woman appeared at the door, hands balled up in her apron, and spoke exactly one angry sentence. "I've got no business with the likes of you."

He stood firm. "Actually, I'm here to enquire after your sister."

She turned, fixing those rat-like eyes on him. "Which one?"

He lowered his voice self-consciously. "Delphine Bessette."

Those beady eyes lit in her plain face at the sound of that name, and she stepped into the doorway. "Jane Fawley. That's her real name, you know. She's no more French than the prime minister. What about her?"

"I'm quite plagued by what happened to her, and I've taken a personal interest."

"You an inspector?"

"Merely an interested party."

"I keeps my mouth shut, I do. I won't be talking to no interested parties. You have no business in my family's affairs."

She backed into the door, but Jack slapped his palm onto it. "I'm here on behalf of her daughter. Who most definitely deserves to know the truth."

She stopped, blinking. "A babe? Jane had a child?"

"She's grown now, and desperately missing her mum. Any help you can provide would be most welcome."

"Well, then. If it's for family." She cracked the door a bit further and waited, hand on hip. "I don't suppose you have proof."

He held up the little box, opening it so she could see the letters. "Her daughter gave me this. It's how I found you."

She poked one dirty finger through the pages. "Did she, now?"

"What can you tell me about Jane? What was she like?"

Her mouth worked, chin jutting as she retracted her hand from the box. "Determined. Broken by life like the rest of us, just a mite prettier. She had her windfall, she did, and never let a one of us forget it."

Jack probed further, and Etta told the story of Jane Fawley, an unusually pretty girl who used to take injured animals and sick children into their home even when they hardly had enough to eat. "She always wanted better, that 'un. For her, and for everyone. Wanted more than anything to leave town, go out into the country. Have a quiet life in a great big house with a garden and a few pets. Perhaps a husband, if he didn't get in the way too much."

"There was actually a secret marriage. I'm not sure if you're aware. It is said that she was quietly wed to her dancing partner, Marcus de Silva."

At this, her mouth went slack, hand to her chest. She took two steps back.

"I'm sorry you had to find out this way, but—"

"No, it isn't that. It's just . . . well, it seems he ain't the only bloke she married."

25

I did it to myself, really—ruined my chances of dancing Paulina. It was raining, and important events often seem to happen on rainy days, when we're trapped inside and gloom leads to deep thoughts. I was terribly nervous too, having been summoned to the Great Fournier's mansion to meet with investors and subscribers, and nerves always made me brave. Or brash, perhaps, depending on one's outlook. I straightened, in that gown that held my every curve captive, and strode into the parlor when beckoned by a liveried servant. "They're ready for you, miss."

Fournier's parlor was quite a French affair, with terra-cotta floors, striped parlor chairs standing at attention, and ornately carved wood edging the room. Five men in dark suits clustered near a piano. Coral-colored couches with walnut feet surrounded the lot of us, with matching tassels hanging from long curtains. I hovered near the fringes, invisible to them. Then I heard a nearby whisper on a familiar voice: "Well, if it isn't Paulina herself."

Well, *almost* invisible. I turned with a smile toward Jack. "Why are you here?"

"Why not?"

After a few moments of listening, I gathered they were talking about a visiting king, and how to entice him to the theater—specifically, to Craven. It was a long shot, most seemed to believe.

"Who are they talking about?" I whispered to Jack, leaning close enough to smell some sort of cream on his skin.

"The king of Belgium. He plans to take a tour in Great Britain this summer. And where he goes, throngs of the art world follow. It would mean everything if he came."

"Is it William?" The slender Prince of Orange, with nervous eyes and a balding head, had been one option to lead the fledgling little nation, but not a good one. Perhaps I held it against him that the late Princess Charlotte, Mama's most ardent fan, had refused to marry him. Anyone she despised I could not help but do likewise.

"No." His breathy voice relieved me. "No, it is Leopold."

I gasped. "Leopold? As in . . ."

"The German prince. He reluctantly accepted the Belgian throne in '31."

King Leopold. What sweet irony that this royal, dashing, and darkly handsome Leopold, who'd fought in the Imperial Russian army, had dethroned that odious Prince of Orange both as Belgium's potential ruler . . . and Princess Charlotte's suitor.

"But . . . I cannot dance before a *prince*." The room tilted as if I were staring down from a high balcony. I dared a look at Jack. "You put them up to it, didn't you? You convinced them to give me that part." I hadn't improved *that* much.

"I figured you just needed a little . . . shove. I know you wouldn't go out and grasp it for yourself, so I did it for you. Rather like shoving you off that loft."

My fingers trembled. I couldn't breathe. I felt as if Jack Dorian had thrown me onto the tracks of an approaching train.

"Listen, these are the investors, Craven's business partners. They make decisions, give money, and take a share of everything the theater does—both losses and profits. It's important that they like you."

Fournier's bold voice cut through my fear. "He's been to Craven before, so it's not out of the question."

"What makes you think he'd ever visit the smallest theater in London on such an important tour?" said one of the men. "We're not Drury Lane, nor King's."

"We must give him something truly special, then. Something personal that he cannot resist. A character named for his late wife, perhaps."

Jack's smile was smug and I knew his thoughts already. He saw *me* cast as Princess Charlotte. Fournier would never stand for it, though. I held to that little security. I simply wasn't good enough for that.

"Theatre Royal is having a special box built for him."

"Wood and nails," Fournier grumbled. "Let them have their old box. We'll find something better."

I straightened, turned to the men. "What about a new ballet?"

A metallic silence lay across the room. They turned to look at me—the visitor, the mere woman, who had deigned to enter their conversation.

Fournier recovered the moment with his gruff voice. "Gentlemen, I'd like to introduce Miss Ella Blythe of London, the other matter of business. She's something of an experiment—a scholarship program I believe will make our theater solvent within the year."

Experiment. Like a potion to cast a spell of good fortune over the hardscrabble seasons at Craven.

"I wanted you to at least meet her, and I'll provide you with the business details later. For now, merely observe her poise and bearing, her dramatic appearance."

They did. I stiffened. "How do you do."

"That is all, Miss Blythe. Stay and enjoy, or depart, as you wish."

"What's this about a new ballet, Fournier?" A mousy little man with well-oiled hair looked at me as he asked the question. "What's special about it?"

I stepped forward, pushing through the tingle of fear. I stood taller than I ought to. "I believe he could be enticed with a brilliant, sensational new ballet no one has ever seen before."

The Great Fournier turned his massive frame, looming over me in a way that prompted flight in my heart.

Yet I remained, feet planted on the edge of that precarious platform as I looked up at the man.

"Plenty of new ballets are written every day."

"This one is quite modern, with a flair of romanticism and the fantastic, which is all they're speaking of in France these days."

A pockmarked old man turned up his fleshy lips in a frown. "Who does this little—"

"But most important of all, it features a story he won't be able to resist." I dared not glance at this unwritten ballet's author, whose tension I could feel beside me as an open flame radiating heat. *I can play too, Mr. Dorian.* "The great mystery of his wife's most favored ballerina, one of Craven's own—Delphine—"

"That's quite enough." Jack brushed through, shuffling me

away. "I'm sure these men don't wish to be bothered with absurd suggestions and fanciful ideas. Please excuse yourself and come along, Miss Blythe. These men have a great deal to discuss."

"But—"

"*Now.*" His guiding hand was firm against my back.

"Hold on a moment, there." Fournier's voice ground our escape to a halt.

Jack stiffened, waiting.

I couldn't help but smile. I'd always remember this as the day I'd bested the charmer.

"Delphine Bessette." A tall investor in spectacles spoke up. "It's quite bold. A real-life tragedy."

"What's on the docket now?" another said.

Bellini paced, throwing about his arms. "Shakespeare. Blasted Shakespeare. Everyone's seen it a hundred times."

Jack released me and took three slow steps away, his tanned face ashy gray.

"We might be interested in backing this new ballet *if*," said the mousy man, "it's as remarkable as the girl claims. If it's worth our time, I for one could be convinced to raise my contributions by one hundred pounds. Provided the prince does, in fact, consider visiting."

"Aye," piped up another. "I'd wager on it too."

Other murmurs like grumbles came from the other men. "How much will this *brilliant* ballet cost us?"

Jack's voice cut through with saucy irritation. "Ten thousan—"

"It might be had for quite a bargain. Its author is already writing ballets for Craven."

All those stiff necks swiveled toward Jack Dorian, and the thunking of the clock again filled the silence.

His eyes flashed, chin jutting as he attempted to formulate a response.

"Indeed." Fournier rose, a tower of pressurized emotion, and turned his heavy gaze on Jack—poor Jack. "Have something for me to look at by next week. If it's decent, we'll have three, maybe four weeks to prepare the dancers. We'll have to use familiar variations. Standard scores. It isn't ideal, but neither is it impossible."

"The dancers can wear costumes we have lying about, rather than sewing new, yes?" This came from a tall man in the back who'd been silent until now. "Shall we put it to the others?"

"Of course we should, but there will be *new* costumes." Fournier was nearly growling. "New and spectacular. We can do that much in short order, at least. I want sensational sights, stunning dancers, everywhere he looks."

"What if he does not come? We'll have invested all this—"

"Then we'll give London the most brilliant show it has ever seen." He spun, punctuating the conversation with a firm period.

That was my cue to leave, it seemed. I slipped toward the tall double doors and lingered, looking back toward Jack—but he had disappeared. Clinging to the knob, I searched each corner of the room for him once more.

Then I was pummeled from behind, Jack's whisper assaulting me. "Do you realize what you've done?"

I spun on the man and lifted a demure smile. "Why, of course I do. You're quite welcome, Mr. Dorian."

"Jack. It's *Jack*, for all that is holy. As in, Jack, the one you lately threw to the lions. Placed between the two iron jaws of a vice."

"It wasn't easy to speak out that way."

"Congratulations on finding your voice at so opportune a moment. Now if you'd kindly undo what you have done . . ."

"Jack." I placed my hand upon his chest, where it looked surprisingly tiny. "I knew you wouldn't go out and grasp it for yourself, so I merely did it for you. A little shove off the barn loft, if you will." I gave a wry smile. "Now, if you'll excuse me, I need to return home."

"Oh no you don't, your ladyship. You'll stay right here." He spun and slid like a panther between me and the exit. "You've delivered me into a heap of trouble, and you can make up for it right now with a little favor to me." He propelled me forward, one hand on the small of my back, and I braced myself, clutching a chair.

"What is this favor?"

"You shall see. Look, the subscribers have begun sneaking in the back. They're the annual box seat holders, so you'll want to impress them too. One most especially. I imagine you're bright enough to figure out who."

My smile faded. He guided me toward Bellini, who was speaking to a cluster of new arrivals in top hats and tails—including one who was the very image of the portrait hanging in the theater. Even from a distance, Marcus de Silva swept me with an accusing glare that made me want to shrink away.

26

A thudding pounded in my head, filling my ears. My steps slowed as we neared the small gathering of subscribers, a repelling fear pushing me back. They were discussing the royal visit, being caught up on all that had taken place, and Jack's ballet.

Jack cleared his throat, and Bellini turned. "Ah, here she is. One of our dancers this season, and a little experiment of Fournier's. One we hope you will consider backing in the future."

I took two small steps forward, back straight, and tipped my head in a small greeting.

"She's one of London's own. If all goes well, Fournier is convinced that scholarships like hers may cost a small fortune, but they shall keep us from paying any more dancers from the continent outrageous sums to dance for us. A regular investment in London girls such as this one could save the theater's financial state and boost the profit margin by nearly thirty percent."

I blushed at the mention of money, and the heat deepened at the continued stares of these dour-faced men standing about in the Great Fournier's parlor.

There was a powdery smell to the air in this corner, or perhaps that was merely the scent of my fear. I tried to glance at everything and everyone except Marcus de Silva, but the edges of my vision always seemed to catch on his striking face, that gaze narrowed on me. He was so silent he might have gone unnoticed by everyone, except for how his presence filled the room—at least for me. That quiet steadiness pulsed in waves perhaps only I could hear, thrumming like a heartbeat in my awareness.

"Can she be trusted?" This from a gent in striped gray with a carnation in his buttonhole.

"She's not missed a single day of training." Bellini's voice carried with ease through the group. "In the end, she's proven more dedicated than dancers raised up in the normal fashion."

But not more talented, apparently.

"Many days she can be found staying late to rehearse, making up for lost time."

"Where does she come from? We've no idea if she's a respectable sort. Who are her parents?"

A hard intensity rippled through me. I averted my gaze out of sheer necessity as silence reverberated again through that crystal-and-gold-crusted room, whirring in my ears. I shivered. Seconds ticked on as a tea cart rattled in somewhere down the hall. Someone forced a discreet cough into his arm.

Breathe. In and out, breathe.

"This is the theater, for pity's sake," cried one man at last. "Not parliament."

"Does her background matter if she can dance?" Fournier's voice boomed behind me with the confidence of one whose questions never required a response.

Then Marcus de Silva spoke. "How old is the girl, Fournier?"

It was rich and velvety, soft enough to miss if the room hadn't been so wretchedly silent.

It was Bellini, that infernal ballet instructor, who spoke up. "She has the look of a famished waif, I know, but she is, in fact, twenty-one years of age."

Another man spoke. "Perhaps we should have her dance for us and see what sort of training our money would afford these little street waifs."

I attempted to swallow.

Bellini gave two jarring claps in my direction. "Come, come. Give us a show."

"She's not your *monkey*, Bellini." Fournier's heavy voice blanketed that alarming suggestion. Then to me, with an edge of gentle pity—"Thank you, Miss Blythe. You may go."

I hurried out of the room, not caring that I hadn't anywhere to go *to*. It was dark outside, and I'd no idea how to summon a hackney cab to this neighborhood without the aid of a servant.

Was a theater woman, as a guest, even allowed to address the servants?

I retraced my steps to the ghostly hall and stood in the lovely blue-black darkness, shadows of bald trees casting gray fingers over the tile through the windows. It was pleasantly eerie, and I felt much more at ease here in the cool quiet. Moonlight filtered down and I stepped toward it, drawn to the glow. This room felt most like my theater, with its two-story expanse above and exquisite trim and décor.

Footsteps on marble made my shoulders tense into my neck, but I remained fixed at the window. It felt necessary. I fisted the edge of the curtain and remained still.

"Miss Blythe?"

I turned with pounding heart to face the man who was,

willingly or not, my father. He walked toward me with wonder playing across his masculine features. He'd silvered gracefully, wearing the same lean elegance that had earned him a name in the ballet world, and I couldn't help but stare. In an instant, that quiet moment, I caught a surprising strain of aloneness beneath the mask of calm. Every dancer wore a mask, I supposed, even when not onstage.

The creak of his boots cut the eerie silence, and I remained rooted, eyes focused on the lighter streaks of gray at his temples as if it were my anchor to sanity and control. I couldn't bear to look any longer at his eyes—those gold-flecked orbs with intensity at which the painter had only been able to hint. Up close, anger glinted off their steely depths. My breath caught.

"What is it you want from me?" His smooth voice wrapped around my being—calm, but dangerously so. "You can tell Jack Dorian that if he wishes to hire some woman off the street to play a part, to ease my conscience, he might at least have—"

"I only wished to speak with you that night. To meet you." Although I hadn't any idea what I would have said—what I even *could* say. "I don't want a thing."

His voice was quiet. "Please. I'm an old man. Leave me in peace. Whatever compensation you're receiving from Jack, it isn't worth the agony you cause me." It was confusing—all so confusing. He hadn't stolen my red shoes—he couldn't have. With all the shock and confusion . . . whoever had stolen them knew who I was. He seemed not to believe it. Yet how desperately I wished him to.

He spun to leave and only one word sprang to mind. "Marco." My little voice echoed in the empty chamber and stopped him cold, seeming to vibrate through his body.

"How dare you?" His low voice cut like blades. "How dare you even pretend to know her?"

I understood then why Jack was so convinced of his innocence. The man was broken, but not by shame. The quiver in his voice, the strained passion in his eyes . . . I felt the first twinge of wondering as I looked at this man my mother had left behind, and I was sick with the unfairness of it all. He loved her, that much was clear. Possibly as much as she'd loved him.

Did she realize how utterly her "death" had broken him? For a fleeting moment, I longed to go to the man and put my hand on his arm. "You truly loved my mother, didn't you?"

His eyes narrowed. "Who did you say was your mother?"

"As I told you. Delphine Bessette."

He paced toward me again, his gaze tunneling into mine, trying to read something hidden in its depths. He was evaluating something. Evaluating me. "The woman you speak of . . . she had this lovely little habit when she was nervous. I don't suppose you recall . . ."

It was a test. "That little birthmark on the back of her neck, almost on her shoulder. She walked her fingers over to it and touched it while she was talking and it calmed her. Somehow."

His rock-carved face melted into wonder, shock, and he stepped toward me, standing in the path of a long beam of moonlight that highlighted every perfect cut of his figure. How lost he suddenly looked—helpless and vulnerable. "How can this be? How can you . . . *Who are you?*"

I allowed myself a deep breath. "I am Elodie Blythe. They call me Ella." I looked at the ground. Why was I even sharing such details with him? Why was I opening myself up so? I knew why. "You, I am told, are my father."

His jaw firmed. Eyes flashed. Fingers raked silver hair. He

paled and sparked in rapid turns. A door clicked shut behind him and he spun. Of all people, Fournier stepped from the shadows. I held my breath.

"All is well, I trust?" Fournier paused, looking from one to the other. "I'm not interrupting anything?"

"No." We said it together, quick and sharp.

I suddenly saw this shadowed tryst through Fournier's eyes, and the creases across his face made sense. My face flamed with heat. Fournier looked the hardest at me, steady gaze boring holes in me, and I wondered what he saw. A theater girl, like the rest? I felt the prick of embarrassment, the moisture at the tightest places of my costume, despite my innocence. It was that stare—never pleased, always searching for that pinhole of error in the women at Craven. Especially, it seemed, in his scholarship dancer.

"I should rejoin the meeting." De Silva's tone didn't waver from that gunmetal smoothness, even in the presence of the Great Fournier. With a poised bow, he turned and left us, but his demeanor had changed and he was shaking.

I sagged against the window frame, heedless of the curtains smashed between me and the glass. *Father, what on earth do I do now?* He'd seemed so affected by everything I said, my words assaulting him with each sentence. Mama's warning rang like gongs in my head, her fear tightening in me as well. I'd vowed to keep away from him. All this time, I'd borne her secret, honored her request to keep hidden, but now . . . Well, I no longer saw the point. She was gone and out of danger. A bridge had been roughed out and I wished to cross it. If ever I had the chance.

Fournier stood staring at me, heaved a breath. "You are all right?"

"Much as ever, thank you." Which lately, was not at all.

27

*H*e always came. No matter what other catastrophes or celebrations went on in the world, no matter how many times I betrayed him by shifting my focus to some shiny thing or failing to notice him, my Creator came to every rehearsal in that old materials room. No father on earth could compare.

Practices had transformed into something new. It wasn't about the art itself, I found, but the creation of it. All those daily tasks like tiny brushstrokes that blended into the grand whole, that's where the color and flair was. Each brushstroke was offered up in thanksgiving, every small rehearsal a sacred act of worship, no matter the outcome.

I put on the ivory shoes from Jack and lifted onto my toes, reaching toward heaven. It took effort, but I could hold myself up on the tips of my toes. Instead of the heavy feats of acrobatics we'd seen at the Theatre Royal, I danced on my toes in a slow spin, feeling the stretch across my calves, through my arms and upper back, bringing my own swan-like style into the move. My feet held the arch in these wonderful new slippers as I moved sideways in a pas de bourreé, then I spun round and round with my arms stretched heavenward and my toes barely touching earth.

Dancing was different now, or at least springing from a different place inside me and, though my toes still blistered and my muscles ached, those private moments with God were refreshing to the core. Turn after turn, dance after dance, I found myself unwinding from the constraints of this world, muffling its beat as my heart matched the rhythm of its Creator. Simple and useless as practice might be, there was something sacred in the monotony.

I will praise thee, O LORD, with my whole heart; I will shew forth all thy marvelous works.

I had no choreography chart to follow, but I wasn't here to prepare for a performance. I was merely here to dance, and I danced the Psalms.

The LORD is the portion of mine inheritance and of my cup: thou maintainest my lot.

Others may look on from the audience, from around me in the greenroom, but this was for the King, an offering that overflowed from a grateful heart.

I have set the LORD always before me: because he is at my right hand, I shall not be moved.

There had come a new strength at the core of me, anchoring me and yet somehow giving me flight. We'd been living in limbo as a company, waiting to hear what we'd dance, if anyone would be cut, if the theater would go broke preparing for a possible royal visit, but I was more centered than I'd ever been. I'd forgotten, and God had, through Jack, reminded me.

My heart shall rejoice in thy salvation. I will sing unto the LORD, because he hath dealt bountifully with me.

"You should dance this way." A familiar voice echoed in the room. "Always."

I pulled myself from the dance as if forcing wakefulness to leave a dream. Lily stood framed in the doorway, gloved hands clutched before her. It had been more than a week of silence, a full eight days since our disagreement outside of my boardinghouse. This was her version of a truce, a temporary sort of cease-fire that occurred when necessary between sisters who often walked the line between rivals and close friends. I lowered myself to the ground, still feeling the weight of unusual grace, hearing the silent music that had fueled my dance.

"You remind me of your mum." Her face was oddly tender.

"That's the highest praise I could imagine." I offered a genuine smile. "And she was *our* mum." I removed the white shoes, gingerly touching the raw places on my feet.

"I've come to look in on you, make certain you're doing well." She eyed me. "Are you?"

I smiled. Her, checking on me? "Quite well."

"You'll also be pleased to know of a new development in my personal affairs."

I sucked in my breath at those words. There was no telling what might come after them.

"I've met someone."

"And?"

"He's an adorable little clerk at James and Rowe on Bow Street, but he hopes to have a booth in the new market when it opens next year. He's completely unattached and quite taken with a certain someone who happened to pass by his shop. He calls me a *lady.*"

I clasped my hands. My words, like little seeds, had taken root in her heart, watered with time.

"It isn't official," she hastened to add, "and I cannot promise anything—there's no understanding between us."

"*Yet.*" With a smile that grew by the second, I stood and wrapped my arms around Lily—dear, wandering Lily who was finally making her way back to the path. "I'm so happy for you, Lil. So happy." I pushed her back to study her face, remembering what I'd done for her so long ago. Remembering Seven Dials. "You're happy, aren't you? Life is good for you, yes?" It would all be worth it if she was.

She merely squeezed my hand. "I'll bring him by if you like."

I studied her face. "Yes, I would like."

I parted from her with a smile in my heart and a lightness I hadn't felt in months.

My lighter steps carried me toward home, then veered in the direction of Westminster and the big brick mansion with green doors. I climbed the narrow stairs on the side, no veil over my face this time, and knocked. Jack threw open the door, his shirt unbuttoned at the top, face lined, and took me in at a glance. "I hope you aren't expecting another lesson today. Some fiery lass decided to offer up a ballet that hasn't yet been written."

He looked horrid. "Have you slept?"

His fingers moved through the deep grooves already running through his mussed hair. "Well. Last week, I suppose."

I slipped past him into the flat. "It's fortunate I came, then. I hope you have some good, strong tea."

He dropped his forehead onto the doorframe. "By all means, do come in."

I stepped in and unpinned my hat, hit immediately with

the warmth of the place—and the scarcity. I stood in a single-room flat with one narrow dormer overlooking the street, and the most threadbare furnishings I'd ever seen. A fire popped under a dented kettle, highlighting the room that seemed clean, but thrown together with castoffs. "You don't keep much of anything, do you?"

"No need. It's just me. And I don't like things—they make it hard to move about."

I set my hat on the crooked table and tipped my head to the side. "Now, about that tea."

Jack leaped across the room to rescue his pot before it boiled over. "Of course, my lady." His personality flooded the tiny space, alive and vibrant even now, and suddenly it made sense. He would be too much for a lavish flat with large, showy furniture. The combination would simply knock a person out. Here he turned a dull flat lively and made a small space rich with atmosphere.

"Where do you work?" I couldn't help but stare around me. Two cups rested on a top shelf, a stack of books waited on the table to be read, and a plain quilt covered a bed in the corner. Even the diamond-patterned wallpaper clinging to the walls paled into the background of Jack Dorian as he swept around the room.

"Here and there." Freshly inked pages lay on every surface to dry, in no discernable order, and he hopped over them to bring me the tea. Some pages were scrawled narration, the rest were filled with lines and x's showing the dancers' movements with all manner of scribbles in the margins. "Come, I'll clear you a spot." He swept a few dried pages to the side and pushed them off one of the chairs, as if preparing it for royalty. The place spoke of a master who was something between frenzied genius and miserly vagrant.

"Have you perfected the opening at least?"

"Why don't you read it and tell me? It's here. Somewhere." He lifted a page and skimmed, then discarded it for another. "This. No, this is the night scene with the moon . . . Ah, here. Yes! Here's the opening." He shot about the flat like bottled energy. Hopefully he came uncorked near these pages so they might be filled with everything inside him. "Now, then. Tell me how bad it is and be on your way so I may finish before Monday."

"Why do you assume it will be bad? And isn't this what you wanted, for your work to see the light of the stage?"

"Yes, but . . . of course not!" He couldn't cease pacing. He covered the floor in three squeaking strides, but I was certain he could easily have crossed the Thames already, had he set off in that direction.

"Why ever not?"

"Because then people would actually *see* it! And the king . . . oh, the *king*. Uuuuugh." Both hands raked through his hair. It stood straight up, his face gaunt with tension at the idea of his work actually succeeding. Of fame and recognition.

My lips pursed into a smile. "Now who's afraid of heights, Mr. Dorian?"

He glared. "Jack. In my own house at least, call me *Jack*."

I removed my gloves finger by finger and looked up at him as I settled into the tiny space cleared for me. "Well then, *Jack*. We've a lot of work to do. I hope you have plenty of candles." I steeled myself to dive headlong into my parents' story, into the mystery of the fire that had changed everything. To the rest of the world, it was merely a fascinating mystery. To me, it was my history—and quite possibly a mirror to my future.

He grabbed a box from a top shelf and froze, the candle

nubs tinking together. One golden eyebrow shot up. "What's this *we*?"

"We, as in the brilliant composer and the woman who got him into this mess. We, as in the two friends who always come to one another's rescue." I smiled. "You didn't think I'd leave it all to you, did you?"

His fingers sliced up the back of his scalp. "Well . . . yes, actually."

"Come, catch me up and we'll sort it out together."

He stared at me with red-rimmed eyes, cocked a grin, and collapsed upon a paper-strewn chair beside me. "Aye, captain." He threw back the remainder of his very black tea and looked at me. "How did it go with de Silva? Do you yet see him as the hero of the story? Or at least, an unwitting victim of blame?"

Stiffness crept up my shoulders. "It's hard to think the man a hero when he hardly says two words to me."

He frowned, then a light shone through his features. "There may be a reason for that. Here, look at this—I've done some digging." He rose to point to a wall of newspaper articles, all about the fire and Delphine Bessette. "Notice the date."

I walked over to it and looked, willing my eyes not to latch onto his name anywhere in the articles. "Here it is."

"And when, exactly, were you born?"

I blinked at the faded date in the corner again. "Why, the fire happened before I was born. Many months before."

He gave a solemn nod. "You see why he'd be shocked then, to have you approach him. By telling him who you were, you also revealed to him one other startling fact."

"That my mother survived."

Another nod.

My stomach churned. What a complicated mess—especially

if he believed, as a remarried man, that she was still alive now. It wasn't exactly good news, discovering one's daughter under such circumstances. He must have been thinking of that. Of course, it was that. He hadn't rejected me—not truly.

I shook off the building emotions. "Right, then. So what about your villain? Have you come any closer to a possible motivation?"

He studied the pages, jaw jutting out to the side, then looked at me with a steady gaze. "I have. I simply haven't had time to follow up on it."

I rose, shocked. "You mean, you found a real lead?"

"Possibly. A decently sized surprise, at least, that may explain many things. Or it may make the story far more complicated than we'd imagined."

I clung to the chair, trembling.

"I want to untangle it, believe me I do, but it requires a trip outside of London, and I simply haven't the time to do it until I've finished this."

"Horsefeathers, as you say. Take a day, uncover the motivation, and watch it unlock the rest of this entire story." I trembled with the desire to know, and the sheer dread of it.

He stared at me, wavering. "I cannot afford the time."

"No, Jack. You cannot afford *not* to take the time, if you want to do this properly. Come, let's go."

28

It was morning before we set out, as there were no coaches to be had at that time of night, and midday by the time we arrived. He had come for me at the boardinghouse first thing and escorted me to the coach, which seemed a much shorter ride than the journey to his winter circus. From the coaching station, we hired a hackney to take us out to Balthorp House, the family seat of Lord Gower. And only then did Jack Dorian, that fiend, reveal to me what connection this man had to my mother. "He was her husband."

I blinked, gripping the edge of the bouncing leather seat. "Her what?" Apparently he hadn't gotten up the courage to reveal this to me on the long ride out of town.

I rather expected a cocky grin or a laugh, but he seemed almost pained to say it. "Her *other* husband. I'm not certain which came first, or if they were perhaps at the same time."

My face went warm, then my whole body. What manner of foolishness was this? What woman had two living husbands? It wasn't logical, especially for my mother. Her heart had been entirely full of one. As the driver handed us down from the carriage, I couldn't speak. What could I say that would make any sense? None of this did.

I stared blankly up at the large brick Georgian with white columns at the end of a tree-lined lane. "Where on earth did you hear such a thing?"

"I met your mother's sister in Cheapside—"

"She has a *sister*?"

"—and she told me about this man Delphine—well, Jane Fawley—had married years ago. I found the man's London address on the envelope of a letter he'd written to her, from that box you gave me, and I paid a call. His footman informed me that his master makes frequent visits to London, but now resides almost entirely here, at his country estate." Jack turned to me with a grim smile, holding one hand out toward the manor house. "Thusly, here we are."

"*Thusly?*" This was ridiculous. Everything was ridiculous. Surely there was no credibility to anything Jack dragged up. "You cannot seriously expect me to call upon this man."

He leveled a look at me. "I thought you wanted to know."

I looked down at the rocky lane. "I suppose there are some things I don't wish to know." My voice was small. Insignificant.

"I have a feeling about this, Ella. The truth is just beyond those walls, if only we can find it. What if this man, in some jealous fit, is the one who set out to destroy your mother? What if I can prove your father is innocent?"

I did not acquiesce, but I followed him through the open gate and up the lane. The noonday sun shone down at us through the trees, blinding me with every break in the canopy of leaves. "Other husband," I mumbled, shaking my head.

"Perhaps there's an explanation."

"I know what you're thinking, but it isn't money. Mum wouldn't have married someone else for that reason, no matter how desperate she was." Yet there was the niggling little truth that my parents' fairy-tale romance and their marriage had always remained a secret.

"You cannot know that for certain. People are surprising."

"I *do* know. We lived in near poverty all my life. A rookery south of St. James Street. And she seemed quite content with it too."

He said nothing. But then there was a woman up ahead, kneeling before a flower bed, pressing new little plants with gold blooms into the earth.

"I cannot, Jack. I cannot do this," I whispered desperately.

"Just listen. Let me talk, and you keep your eyes open."

The woman stood with some hesitation and turned to greet us as we disembarked the hackney, her lovely face both aloof yet quietly welcoming. "Forgive my stiffness," she said pleasantly. "Age has snuck up on me, I'm afraid." Although her fair skin hardly looked a day over forty and her figure was slender. "Welcome to Balthorp House. This is a delightful surprise, having strangers happen upon us. May I ask who you are, and how you've found your way to our home?"

Jack extended his hand. "Please forgive the unsolicited call, but we were hoping to have a word with Lord Gower." She offered her hand and he bowed over it.

"He isn't home at present, but perhaps I can help you. I am Lady Gower."

Jack flashed me a look of uncertainty. Dared we risk revealing what her husband may have kept from her?

She broke through his hesitation. "Come, let us take tea on

the veranda. You've had quite a journey, I'm sure. There isn't much within a comfortable distance of Balthorp House."

We followed her to the well-appointed side veranda laid out with white metal benches and tables and took our seats as Lady Gower rang for refreshments. I stared out at the fountain to our right with water cascading down two levels. What would it have been like to grow up here? To have these gardens as my escape every day, this house protecting me every night? Perhaps it had once been the intention.

In the shade of the veranda, I looked at Lady Gower up close, peering under the brim of her straw hat, and she was quite lovely. Pure of skin and self-possessed, the way a lady of the house ought to be. And she did look like Mama. Startlingly so. Blonde hair waved back from a heart-shaped face and wide smile. There was no comparison to Mama's homespun sweetness in her, but the woman's poise spoke of good breeding and the serenity of one who did not worry about money, or much of anything at all. Perhaps she truly didn't know. "Now, how may I help you?"

"We're here from London tracking down some information." Jack dove right in. "We're wondering what you could tell us about Delphine Bessette."

She blinked with a tiny frown. "Why would my husband be concerned with a dancer?" She looked at us both, then stared at me, her gaze lingering upon my face.

"We heard that he may have been acquainted with her." Jack, always the diplomat.

"I see." She looked back and forth between us, as if assessing how much to tell us.

"It has even been said that she was once . . . romantically involved with him."

Her eyebrows rose, and she looked a mite offended. Somehow we had to urge her past the strict social code that told her one never spoke of such things, even if she knew of them. Her silence was all the answer she afforded this question.

Jack rushed on, unplagued by social rules. "We were wondering if, perhaps, your husband has mentioned anything about her. Anything of her nature, or her friends. Something to give us a small picture of what she was like."

"What interest have you in the personal affairs of a theater woman?" She seemed to be deciding still if she approved of us, with our involvement in something she was meant to find distasteful.

"We're working on a ballet about her life. She's become something of a sensation in London, the ghost of Craven, yet no one truly knew anything about her as a dancer. A woman."

She fingered the design on the table. A tea cart rattled out then, with two maids coming to set up the service. Lady Gower paused to make an elegant show of pouring tea for us. "Thank you, Glenna. You may go." After she'd poured three cups and taken a leisurely sip from her gold-rimmed one, she looked at us. "I'm afraid I cannot be of much help to you. I knew the name of course, but . . ." She waved away the rest of that sentence.

"Surely your husband has mentioned something about her, or you—"

She sat and rested her forehead on her fingertips. "If you please, I don't wish to speak of my husband's previous conquests. It leaves me rather faint."

Her directness gave me hope. At last, we were breaking through.

Jack leaned forward. "Can you simply tell us, then, how long they were married?"

"*Married*? Delphine Bessette and my husband? Certainly not. I am his first and only wife, Mr. . . . ."

"Dorian. Jack Dorian."

"Where have you come upon your information?"

"A relation of Delphine's, actually."

"From what I understood, Delphine had no relations."

"Perhaps not, but her true-life counterpart Jane Fawley certainly did. A sister, to be precise. Apparently Delphine was merely a stage name."

She stared between the two of us, a slight frown marring her perfect face. "You know a great deal about this woman."

"As I've told you, I'm writing a ballet about her life."

She turned that ivory face toward me. "And you? What is your interest in a dead ballerina?"

I pushed back my shoulders, chin up. "I'm helping him write his ballet."

Her gaze passed over me thoroughly. "Unfortunately, most of what you think you know is simply not true. Delphine Bessette was little more than a fleeting thought in any man's mind, not a permanent part of his home. No respectable man would have taken her as a wife."

Two secret marriages. That was almost more than any woman would tolerate.

Then in a cloud of dust, a carriage rolled up the long drive behind four matched horses, rumbling closer as we watched and coming to a stop under the portico.

The lady leaned forward in her chair with a hostess smile, as if to rise and show us out, but Jack, the consummate actor, ignored the hint and pressed on. "Lady Gower, did you ever have the pleasure of meeting Miss Bessette?"

She wavered under Jack Dorian's oblivious charm, and I

couldn't help but think that if any of these questions had come from me, they'd have been snubbed at best. "A time or two perhaps. Nothing of any real substance."

"Did you speak to her?"

"She was a rather elusive creature. It isn't as if we associated with her often." She stirred her tea and looked out at the man being handed out of the coach. "Remarkable, but rather lonely, I believe. Now if you'll excuse me, it seems my husband has returned." She rose again to attempt to show us out.

"Impeccable timing!" Jack's grin pivoted her attempted dismissal as an inner door slammed in the house. "I should like to meet the man. Perhaps he'll have a bit more insight to offer on Delphine."

"I'm quite certain he wouldn't."

"Won't hurt to ask, now that he's arrived."

"I'm afraid he'll be rather tired, and won't welcome—"

"Who do we have here?" A heavily bearded older man came out the patio doors with anything but welcome on his face. "Guests, is it, even here?"

Her white face grew paler. "Harry, these people are here to ask about Delphine Bessette. Can you imagine, after all this time?"

Something flashed in the man's eyes, and he looked not at us, but at his wife, as if assessing her reaction—what she knew, maybe.

"They heard you were once married to her, but I assured them that wasn't the case." She stirred her tea rapidly. "You don't recall much about her now, do you? It's been so many years."

He turned his attention back to his wife, studying her face for long moments, as if deciding what to say. "One does not forget the extraordinary. I remember what she was on the stage, how astonishing . . ."

Her hands stilled, lowering to her lap. By the look of her pale face, she did not like what he was saying. Not at all.

"I'll never forget the sensation she made of every ballet, lighting up the whole of London with her energy. Nothing like it." He exhaled with the exertion of so many words.

Lady Gower rose, teacups clattering. "Harry, we shouldn't bore our guests. You do like to go on so. Perhaps we should excuse ourselves and let them take their leave."

He shed his overcoat and loosened his cravat in the heat as he turned back to us. "Leave. Yes. They should leave."

Jack rose, extending his hand. "Thank you kindly for your gracious hospitality, and the conversation. It was a delight, and I do hope we may call again, if it isn't too much trouble."

Lady Gower's smile spread across her rice-powder face without a bit of sincerity. "But of course."

Her sober-faced husband offered nothing.

The coach rumbled away from the station, pulling us toward London and the rest of that ballet waiting to be written. "I do believe you've found your villain." I dropped the fact in the cool darkness of the carriage, and Jack looked up at me.

"I'm not convinced. It's clear they're hiding something, but I simply don't see such a man setting a fire across the room and running away, if he was angry enough to kill someone. And the way he spoke of Delphine . . . No, he simply doesn't scream 'villain' to me."

"No. But *she* does."

"Lady Gower? Why?" He crossed his arms.

"She concocted the lies smooth as silk. Her husband looked to her for cues. It's her secret, her lie. Maybe not the fire, but something. She's responsible for something."

"Or she's the more practiced deceiver and he knows it. Why would she give two bits about some dancer? She clearly isn't in love with her husband—not enough to kill for him. And there have always been an abundance of older monied men who desire a pretty wife, if that's all she was after."

"You don't have to believe me."

"Oh, I do, actually. But I simply can't understand why it happened."

I drummed my fingers against my jaw. "I cannot say. Money, perhaps? Or Lady Gower is right and my mother never actually married him, but there was something between them—something scandalous that needed to be covered . . ."

"Horsefeathers. Your mother was married to Gower—her sister witnessed it—and for some reason, they don't wish the connection to be known."

I gripped the seat, trying to wrap my tired brain around Mum agreeing to marry that overstuffed grouch. It seemed ridiculous, the way she'd gone on so about my father. Not to mention the secret marriage that had occurred between my parents . . . at some point. I slouched against the buttoned leather seat. "Well, you have a villain, at least. You can write your ballet."

He shook his head. "There are too many holes yet."

I sighed, wrestling my emotions into place. "So then we must write what we know and make up the pieces we don't. Enough so Fournier can hold auditions and begin rehearsal. Unless you have other leads."

"Very well, we'll do it like this." He sat back. "Delphine Bessette, the famous ballerina, catches the eye of Lord Gower, and he convinces her of the benefits of wedding him, so they become engaged. Meanwhile, his longtime childhood acquaintance has become destitute after bad investments, and she's afraid for her future—no, her very life. She's near starvation. She placed all her hopes in being rescued in marriage by Lord Gower, who had once loved her, but this ballerina has danced onto the path between them. Delphine and the woman fight over his hand, and Gower elopes with the dancer but realizes his mistake soon after, and one of them decides to fix the matter. So . . ." He lifted his hands like an explosive fire.

I eyed him. "And Marcus de Silva? What of him? What of their marriage?"

He shook his head. "That's the part that makes no sense. De Silva couldn't have married her. He wouldn't touch another man's wife, and besides, from what he's told me, they were little more than civil with each other. Romance with her was the furthest thing from his mind."

I cringed at my father's side of the story, shuddering through my being. "You should have heard *her* tell it, then. She'd have convinced you of their love. There was nothing like it outside of storybooks." Yes, it was a fairy tale. A true one, though.

We lapsed into silence, then he smiled. "I shall enjoy casting this one."

I could sense his veiled attempt to steer us out of murky waters for my sake, and I played along. "Why is that?"

He leaned back, tipping his head to the side. "I never really could envision this uniquely magnificent heroine . . . until I was suddenly sitting across from her." His knowing smile glinted in the dark. Surely he wasn't hinting that I might take the lead. It was preposterous. "You have your Psalms mapped out? I cannot wait to see what you will do in the auditions."

I sucked in a breath and let it out. Quite frankly, neither could I.

29

A lone figure moved into the golden glow of gas-lights over the stage, tall and slender, and anticipation tightened in Jack Dorian's chest. They'd watched a great many dancers wing their way through various dances, but they all bore the rhythmic sameness he'd come to expect in ballet. He'd mentally placed them each in appropriate roles, scratching his thoughts onto the paper in his lap.

But now it was her turn. Jack could sense what was coming—what he hoped was coming. The lone violin cued up. Fournier and Bellini sat beside him, with four other investors in the rows behind. A pause, then the violin sang out. She lifted along with the music, as if the instrument's strings moved her, and pushed the song-filled air about with her arms. Every movement lifted upward, drifting across the stage, spinning on the very tips of her toes with delicate swishes of fabric. Casting off the classical style for a wholly expressive and show-stealing solo, she absorbed all attention and the male lead would have been strangely overshadowed.

The footwork was incredible. He could barely stop watching,

but it was her entire body—the whole of her—that arrested one's attention. Innocence mingled with confidence for the first time in Jack's entire experience with ballet. She danced through all the common variations—but *en pointe*, on the very tips of her toes, taking center stage rather than merely embroidering beauty onto her male counterpart. Few others had dared it. She excelled at it.

"What is she doing?" Bellini hissed.

"This is . . . unexpected." Fournier spoke with a frown as he watched her swan across the stage.

Ella whipped into an arabesque, using every inch of that stage. Rather than meekly tipping side to side, pointing her toes with little jumps and turns, she had become a full-bodied picture of music, lifting and spinning as high as she pleased. A series of movements connected with liquid grace and freshness.

He longed to cheer for her. Who had ever before dared to dance nearly an entire variation, light as thistledown, on the tips of her toes? There was something so very real about her dance, as if she was finally at home in her own body and merely sharing a piece of herself with them.

The song unfolded and so did her confidence, her impressive strength. When she lifted again to her toes and whipped through a *fouetté*, kick after kick, he could only stare, helpless and entranced. After ten long years of being locked in his mind, the energy and color of his ballet was unfurling before him in glorious reality, shining in quiet strength and femininity.

He was not falling in love with her through this dance—oh no, he'd already tumbled hard down that slope—but this was the moment he sensed the vast difference between their worlds, and knew that he desperately wished her to reach down and pull him up into hers.

The finale came, and she bowed and rose before utter silence.

One investor shifted, another coughed, and the spell broke. "What on earth does she think she's doing?"

Tension rolled across Jack's shoulders. "Dancing. Remarkably so."

"She's ruining the art of ballet," Bellini hissed from his right. "*Ruining.*"

The investor nearest the aisle shook his head. "We cannot have her performing a solo. The newspapers will go wild. She'll shock them all."

"Exactly." Jack braced himself between seat backs. "She has something fresh and exciting, yet it's a combination of everything we know—the old-world restraint and modesty of French ballet blended with the stunning modern techniques of the colorful Italian theater."

Bellini glared at him. "She's everything that's wrong with our modern world, nothing like the dancers—"

"Who are hampered by classical styles and heavy dresses? The entire rest of the art world has moved on to something new, and she's the best of both worlds—woodland sprites and nature, the romantic and the fantastical. She'll be a sensation."

"Sensations offer something of beauty to look at—which neither her dancing nor her person accomplishes. For all her wildness, she has not one speck of sensuality or allure. Look at the way she dances—she's like a child, flinging herself about with abandon. No one will pay to see that."

"I have to agree, I'm afraid," another said, shifting their direction. "I will not support a theater that has lost sight of what our patrons desire."

"*Hang* sensuality. She's offering something far higher and better. People don't encounter art to gawk, they come to *feel* something, and that's exactly what she accomplishes. She excites all the senses as well as the heart and mind."

"I *won't* have it." Bellini slapped the seat back, the few wispy hairs atop his head whipping about with his anger. "She'll be an abomination to this theater, and I *refuse* to be a part of it. I want her out of this performance entirely, or I'll be out of this theater."

Jack leveled his face before Bellini's red one. "You can't fire her, even for one performance. She's contracted by Craven and she'll be paid one way or another, so you might as well have her on the stage."

"I'll never allow her near it if she dances in this wild, Bohemian manner—"

"Very well, very well." Jack raised his hands, ready to paint a picture. "Not a lead then, if it's too risky, but another part. A role I haven't even written yet, but it can be done in a heartbeat. Picture this—a sylph, a little fairy who's the voice of reason for the hero, drawing him toward something higher and better than this tarnished world can offer. She'll be sensational."

The second investor adjusted his spectacles. "It does sound rather like the paintings in modern galleries. All fields and trees . . ."

"Yes. Forget the castle backdrops and the manicured gardens. Let us paint dark, shadowy wooded glens and gauze curtains that will rise one at a time to give a sense of mist pouring over the scene. Atmospheric and mystical. It'll be perfect. *She* will be perfect."

Fournier looked up at her and spoke across the great expanse. "Very good, Miss Blythe, you may go."

She swept into a bow, accepting their looks with her usual charming dignity, and moved to the side.

The investor directly behind Jack leaned forward. "You mean to say, Dorian, that you'd reimagine your entire play just to include this girl?"

"I'm saying I'd draw in the character who perfectly completes the entire story—the one who should have been there all along—*her*."

"But how will you manage it? You'd have to change nearly every character's dynamic and reaction throughout the entire piece."

His gaze focused in on her lithe figure standing alone near the drawn-back curtains while all the other dancers milled about in groups. "Perhaps she's invisible to everyone but the hero." His voice was low. "Yes, I think she is."

Together the watching dancers all hurried off the stage as the next one peeled off her calico gaiters and prepared to dance.

"A star who cannot see its own glow." This came from Fournier, the rocky old hill of a man who'd been mostly silent through the performance. His face mirrored everything Jack had felt in the dance, as if Ella Blythe had invited them all to experience the music along with her and only the two of them had accepted.

They filed out, still seeming unconvinced, but Fournier remained. He leveled a steady gaze at Jack that seemed to say, *You see it too, don't you?*

"What do you say? May I write the extra part, Fournier?"

The owner's face remained impassive as he turned to stare at that stage for endless moments. "I'll fire you if you don't."

Jack suppressed a wry grin. "I'll make you proud."

Fournier shook his head and looked at the now-empty stage. "Other dancers love to perform. This one . . . she merely loves to dance. And at long last, she's begun to figure out how to get out of her own way." He hesitated, leaning on the seat back. "It seems you finally managed it. You've more than won the bet. You shall have your reward, as promised."

Jack gave one firm nod. "I'll hold you to that, sir."

Fournier straightened his jacket, checked his pocket watch. "I haven't seen the rest of the ballet yet, Dorian."

"And neither shall you—until the opening night. It's to be a complete surprise how the mystery is resolved." To the audience . . . and also to him.

Fournier's brows lowered dangerously, and a rumbling growl came from his chest.

"Very well, very well. I'll have it for you soon enough. I have a lead I must follow up on today—right now, if you'll permit me. Even when we do have the answer, it shall remain a secret outside of this theater. Give the public a tease of what's coming, but let them wonder and speculate until the highly anticipated opening night."

His pointed beard twitched, but he gave a single nod. "See that you get it written within forty-eight hours."

Jack tipped his hat. He'd make his stop at a certain records office in Gretna Green to look over a few marriage certificates, if they existed, then there should be time enough to scratch out the rest of the ballet. He'd use one of his made-up scenarios if he couldn't find the truth.

But he'd find it. They were close.

30

I perched on the edge of a flowered damask chair later that day in Balthorp House, watching the drawing room doors for her willowy form. The maid had promised Lady Gower would be down to meet me shortly, but it had already been—I glanced up at the clock—ten whole minutes? They felt like an hour each.

Perhaps I should have told Jack about Lady Gower's invitation to tea, but he wouldn't have let me go alone. The man felt the need to manage and protect through every minute of the day, and right now I wanted neither. She would speak differently with only me present, I was certain, and I was hungry for whatever she wished to reveal to me.

The darkness between the slightly open doors beckoned me. After fidgeting for another minute and a half, I sprang up and went to them, slipping through and peering around in the vast tiled emptiness. There was a flutter and clink of distant activity in the kitchen and footsteps echoing on wood overhead. My heart beat out of my chest as I moved step after step into the great hall and toward another corridor. At the end, a door opened to a music parlor, with a harp on a rug and a shining ebony piano. I moved through it to another door on the opposite end and walked into a gallery, two stories high with walnut railings on the second floor. A winding staircase led up to the balcony.

In awe I made a slow turn, scanning the pictures for anything familiar. Then my eyes locked on a bit of red on the wall, my chest tight. There, hanging from their knotted ribbons, were Mama's famous scarlet ballet slippers. Hardly daring to breathe, I approached in the dimness and ran a finger over their satiny sides, touching the familiar leather soles, the darned toes. Yes, it was them.

A door slammed, echoing through the house. I spun and hurried back, heart racing my thoughts, and stopped short in the great hall. Lady Gower stood there in the deepening shadows, a column of poise in the midst of the great openness. Just past her, a man's green hat perched on a hook in the entryway. It caught my eye and I couldn't look away.

"Begging your pardon, Lady Gower. I was lost."

"In a drawing room?"

I stood, bearing the weight of her glare in silence.

She took two steps closer. "You didn't ask a single question in the garden the other day, yet you seemed intensely curious. I thought perhaps we ought to have our own conversation."

"We told you already of my involvement." My voice croaked. "The ballet."

"I want to know why *you* are interested. Enough to go traipsing uninvited through my home. The true reason, Miss Blythe."

I hadn't given my name before, had I? Holding her stare, I backed into the shadows, feeling every bit out of my element. Trapped. "I knew her once. Before she died."

Her brow rose. "You'll have to do better than that. You

hardly look older than the fire that took her life. I will ask one more time, Miss Blythe. Why?"

I kept my gaze steady on her. "What was she like? Was she as wonderful as everyone says?"

Her narrow little lips pinched further in.

"Was she a rival, perhaps?"

Her jewel-eyes flashed.

"Anyone would be jealous. She was remarkable, from what I've heard."

She hesitated. "Harry did make quite a fool of himself over her, before he met me."

"They *were* married then, weren't they?"

She leveled her unblinking gaze on me for several ticks of the clock before answering. "Yes."

Yet somehow, even though it was what I'd expected to hear, the answer seemed a deception.

"Come, sit down in the parlor. I'll tell you everything." We took our seats in the hushed floral room where she neatly arranged her skirt and lifted her gaze to me. "Delphine Bessette was a mystery, even before her death. Thus, she was greatly misunderstood. It's time to set things straight, if her story is to be told."

"Who set the fire, Lady Gower? Who disliked her so greatly?" I studied her face for signs of guilt, of knowing.

"This may surprise you." She took a breath. "It was Napoleon's men."

I blinked. "Napoleon Bonaparte?"

"She was a spy against them." She straightened. "Everyone believes dancers to be silly creatures, but Delphine was quite intelligent. She was also quite good at befriending French officers and wheedling information from them. That's how Harry came to know her, in fact. They worked together in the underground resistance, helping to bring the great army down."

"Why ever would she care about that?"

"Don't you know? She had grown up in Sweden and she didn't want her home country attacked. They were Napoleon's next goal. Everyone loved Delphine, and she could walk into nearly any room and command any man to do her bidding. She used that to her benefit and saved many lives on the continent."

I clasped my hands in my lap, thinking before I spoke. "What a resourceful woman. She must have been quite magnificent, even in everyday life."

"No woman can ever live up to her, on or off the stage. Her charms were known through the world, her beauty unrivalled. But not even her beauty could stop those men from being rid of her. She was simply too smart, too powerful against their cause. So one night when she practiced late, all they had to do was slip unnoticed into the theater with a kerosene lamp . . ."

"It's all so remarkable."

"Such a woman would have to go out in a blaze of glory." She inhaled, eyes fluttering closed. "The world would believe no less for her final curtain call."

The room was quiet, save the echoing footsteps of distant servants and muffled voices.

"So what do you think of Delphine Bessette now, Miss Blythe?"

"It was a most brilliant story." I grasped the chair arms and leveled my gaze at her. "Unfortunately I don't believe a word of it."

She leaned forward like a crouching tiger, eyes narrowing. "Who are you?"

I hardly knew how to answer. And with the sudden change in her expression, I felt an urgent desire to leave, even before the tea. I stood, brushing out my skirts. "I should return to London before dark. Thank you for the offer of tea, and I'm sorry I could not stay long enough to accept. Good day, Lady Gower." It was the most ill-mannered exit I'd ever made, but relief washed over me as I neared the drawing room doors. I focused on the open space beyond, and the double doors that led outside, to freedom. Which I desperately felt I needed then. I paced toward those doors quickly. With intention.

A hand clamped down on my arm. I cried out and spun to face her dangerously calm expression. Her eyes were like steel, her voice low. "Where is she?"

I swallowed. "Out of reach." I jerked away and ran into the hall, nearly colliding with a shocked-looking manservant holding an empty salver to his chest.

After a long coach ride back to London, I hurried to Jack's flat and flew into his arms the moment he admitted me. I spoke into his chest, giving my account in rapid little sentences that probably made no sense.

He embraced me, smoothing one hand down my back while my words continued to erupt until I was breathless. "Come, sit and have something to drink."

He settled me in a chair, but I popped up the minute he went to fetch me a warm drink, and I paced before the old newsprint clippings tacked up on his far wall. "They're guilty. They have to be. If I ever doubted it before, I don't anymore. She talked about the kerosene lamp, but every single article talks about a *candle* being knocked over."

Jack stood before me with a steaming cup, which I did not take. "Why didn't you tell me you were going there? You shouldn't have gone alone."

I rushed on, right over his admonishment. "It's true, about the lamp—Mama told me she heard it smash just before she saw the flames, but no one knew that's how it started except for her. And, curiously, Lady Gower. Either she was told, or she was there."

His face glowed. He was growing excited along with me. He dropped into a chair, rocking back and resting a notebook on one bent leg. "An astute observation. Yes, that does fit with what I've found." He started writing.

"It still doesn't add up, though. Lady Gower was jealous enough to rid the world of my mother, or cover up for her murderer, yet she has displayed Mama's scarlet ballet slippers on her wall. It makes no sense for the scarlet slippers—*those* slippers—to be hanging in the woman's own house. Or for her husband to go to the trouble of stealing them from me." I thought of that green hat hanging in the hall of their house.

"Of course it does." He dropped his chair forward on all fours again, his face solemn. He rose and dropped his notebook, taking hold of my shoulders as if to steady me. "Because the woman you just met with *is* Delphine Bessette."

My mouth opened and closed, then opened again. "How . . . how . . . ." My brain spun. I stood, agitated, palms on the table. "You're calling my mother a fraud."

"A backup. But not the only Delphine Bessette. After what you told me, and what I found in Gretna Green, it's the only answer that makes sense. I've been turning it over in my head all day. Lord Gower has only *one* certificate of marriage, and it's to a Miss Jane Fawley, age twenty-eight years, dated two days *after* the fire. A different woman named Viola, age twenty-two, is listed as the wife of Marcus de Silva, also married in Gretna Green two years prior. It seems they are not the same woman although they oddly shared the same wedding location."

I braced my throbbing head with my hands, trying to sort it all out. "You're saying she's a fraud . . . *and* the mysterious other woman who stole him away."

"I don't believe Marcus de Silva was ever in love with the real Delphine. That's why he spoke of her with such disdain."

I shuddered as I recalled the look on his face when I'd told him I was Delphine Bessette's daughter. He believed I belonged to this woman, Lady Gower—and had no connection to him.

"So that means the fire merely gave her an opportunity to fake Delphine's death. Then she lit out of town and married one of her many admirers and lived out her life rather comfortably in seclusion."

"She loved being Delphine, though. The way she spoke of her today . . . Why would she have allowed all of that to come to an end?" The minute I asked, though, I knew the answer.

"Forced retirement. She must have been nearing the end of her prime, and this allowed her to fade away into memories."

"But why the elaborate hiding? What was she trying to escape?"

He sighed and shrugged. "There's a good chance your mother, since she also claimed to be Delphine, was a stand-in for the real one. A sort of last-minute back-up for emergencies. The good news is that the love letters, the sister, the many admirers, the terrible temper . . . those all belonged to Jane Fawley, the true Delphine—not your mother."

"A small consolation." She was a fraud. *I* was a fraud, and I felt again my utter smallness.

His hands stayed steady on my shoulders. "I didn't want to tell you all of this, but I felt I must warn you. I've no idea what Jane Fawley—Lady Gower—intends if she feels threatened by you. By us. There's a good chance she herself set the fire, and she believes she's guilty of murder. I'm writing a different ending to the ballet so she doesn't know we're onto her."

I sank back into the chair, keeping my eyes on him. "This cannot be true." All this time I'd known that Jack Dorian was many things, but I'd never considered him a liar.

Yet he must be. Because if he wasn't, it meant Mum was. The notion left me feeling lost, and quite adrift. I'd always been Delphine Bessette's daughter, even if I was the only one who knew it. I may be poor and less talented and less amusing than the others, but I had that secret in my pocket, like an anchor for my identity. I'd wanted to be more, to prove myself—to God and others—but I was truly nothing. No one. Just some poor wretch brought here on charity.

He urged me toward the table. "Come now, have a cup. I'll let you pick the ending we use." His voice was gentle. Almost apologetic.

I couldn't do anything but perch on the edge of a chair opposite him and blink back tears over my untouched cup of tea. There was a sordid ring of truth to his conclusion. I recalled Lady Gower's stiffness—almost a limp—the day she'd first greeted us in her garden. I recognized that gait. It came from extreme overuse.

Of *course* she was a dancer.

"It is the great paradox of art, ma petite. Ballet is all delicacy and grace, yet it brings out the barbaric side of every woman who dances it."

"Please. Trust me, will you?" His hand slid over mine. "There's more to the story. I'm certain of it. I just have to find out what it is."

I wasn't certain I wanted him to. After a moment I straightened my spine, spun toward the table, and began to pile completed pages. "Right, then. Where were we?"

He sighed. "An alternate conclusion to the mystery, I suppose. What about this? She's rehearsing. It's the night of the fire. Someone sneaks in. Maybe . . . several someones."

I frowned.

"That's the big secret. It wasn't just one dancer. It was several, who all joined forces to rid the theater of her and then provide each other alibis. That's how they managed to get away with it all this time. It works, yes?" He looked haggard.

I blew the hair off my face and tapped my teacup. "No. We need to do the real ending."

"Out of the question."

"I thought that's what you wanted from the start."

"I did." He stared down at his page. "Until I thought it through. She knows we're writing this ballet about Delphine's murder. She's done a mountain of work to keep her secret safe all these years. You think she'd just allow us to display her guilt on the stage?" He shook his head. "We cannot let her know what we've discovered."

I closed my eyes, breathed out. "I think she knows." Why had I ever opened my mouth? I could have walked out of there letting her think I'd swallowed her entire ridiculous story.

He eyed me.

"Mum deserves justice. No matter who she truly was, someone tried to kill her in a most violent way and went on to live as if nothing had occurred. The world should know what happened. What *really* happened."

He hesitated. "You're certain this is what you want?"

I gave a single nod. "When you have the world's ear . . . the truth, Jack. Always the truth."

31

It was June, and casting lists had been posted and choreography outlined. Philippe danced as the male lead, of course, but I did not, in fact, dance opposite him in the role Jack had envisioned for me—the part of my mother—and for that I was relieved. I should never be able to concentrate under such strain, and dancing as her might be my undoing on the stage. Instead, I slipped easily into a role Jack had written precisely for me. It was obvious even without him stating it was so, for the role seemed the very extension of who I was as a dancer.

We began learning combinations and bridges, with the notion that we'd put the whole ballet together into one show when Jack finished it. It was a most haphazard way to do it, but excitement buzzed in what had once been mundane rehearsals.

Jack Dorian reached his zenith as the ballet took shape. Pressure drove him, it seemed, for he came alive just as I'd seen him do at the wintering circus barn. "No no, arch in midair, for heaven's sake. Throw your head back. This is meant to be *dramatic*." He cleared the four steps in a single bound and exploded onto the stage with his characteristic energy, arching his back and *grand jeté*-ing before us all, and ending in a dainty pirouette. With a look of feminine affectation, he threw back his head, one hand upon his brow, and swirled into a faint with one prolonged twirl of his masculine body.

Applause sounded and chittering laughter popped across the stage while men scurried across with pieces of set design. The place was always an anthill of activity, swarming with people and props and pieces of costumes. We approached the twenty-third of June like a locomotive headed toward a cliff, and I held on for dear life.

Fournier had somehow managed to hire artist Clarkson Stanfield to paint a lusciously shadowed forest for the backdrop, and the walkers-on and stagehands had been cutting strips of tulle in various shades of green to hang from the ceiling as murky willow fronds and mist. To further the feel of romanticism and nature, we had created many forest scenes for the lovers' trysts, and only the fire and a few small scenes occurred within a theater.

For the most dramatic scene, gas jets had been concealed in wooden boxes hooked to flies for a moonlight effect. The world of Jack's imaginings was taking shape on the stage, and it was glorious.

Minna grumbled and stalked across the stage, ever dramatic as she rose in the ranks. She had earned herself the lead role of Delphine, the tragic dancer, and she'd never been more elated—or on edge.

I turned to Tovah with a smile. "You are stunning in your divertissement. It shows your every strength to full advantage."

"Which is ironic, seeing as how Jack Dorian has never noticed before what those were."

I pinched my lips and gave a shrug. Jack had received more

help from me over the weeks since the ballet had been accepted, especially in the choreography sketches. Our imaginations had fueled each other, and the ballet had sprung forth from our combined minds. It was Jack's story that had blossomed and taken shape, but I still felt a sliver of ownership when my mere presence sparked his ideas in rapid-fire succession. Perhaps I was becoming his muse—or we were becoming partners.

Jack, in all his sensationalism, had decided to make an unprecedented move to raise the needed funds. Our boxholders and investors would be allowed to attend an opening night preview—of all but the third act. It was meant to whet the appetite of theatergoers and press, and perhaps even King Leopold, before the official opening. If all went well, London would appear in droves the following night to discover what had happened to Craven's famed dancer.

The night before our preview performance, the first before an audience, I forced myself to bed early, and I intended to sleep at least eight hours. Truly, I did. But once my bleary mind faded from the real world, it fell down one dark hole and into another.

I was fourteen again, running toward the little church outside of Seven Dials in the dark and without the warmth of my cloak. I pushed through the broken fence, dodged the tombstones, and approached the weathered door. I stared at that building, knowing it was a place of God, knowing the parish minister to be a good man, yet I sensed God pushing me away from it. I raised my hand to knock, but my fist wouldn't cooperate. It merely hovered, then something overcame me. More than chills from the biting wind. Cloak wadded up in my arms, I turned and ran, fleeing that churchyard with my secret.

Instead, I ran to a house. It was a small brick cottage with black shutters, three neat little steps leading up to the front door. Several candles were lit, glowing underneath the closed shutters, and that's why I chose it. How homey and warm it seemed.

I paused around the corner after sprinting away, letting reality catch up to me, the immensity of what I'd done knocking me off balance. It was done now, though. I couldn't go back. I stood there staring up at the house, into the neat little windows, when suddenly a man appeared at the door. A tall man with stooped shoulders and a long face. He looked down at my cloak on his stoop, then out into the dark, in my direction, stunned confusion on his face.

I ran. Ran with all my might, feet pounding the brick street as I hurtled through the shadows. I slipped into the narrowest, most unappealing of streets until I found myself staring down the blocks at the tall centerpiece sundial of Seven Dials, the heart of the slum. I caught my reflection in the panes of glass guarding an old curiosity shop, and I was quite blue—my lips, my poor hands. How I longed for that cloak now. Another chill convulsed me, then I turned a second corner and ran harder. My foot clipped a broken stoop, my head banged the door with a shuddering thud, and I fell, a miserable, shivering wretch in the piles of refuse lining the grubby street.

As I lay there, noxious odors invading my senses, God began to overwhelm me with an awareness of his presence. I was afraid in the face of it, sensing the magnitude of him immediately, but it was a surprisingly welcoming hand reaching out for me, not a punishing one. I never forgot that moment. That encounter.

The very feel of God's pursuit, his awareness of one invisible girl. A strange sensation of warmth filled my limbs again despite the winter wind, down to the tips of my fingers. It was a sacred encounter, and my gratefulness immense.

Yet what had I done to show it?

My mind lifted from the memory, rising from sleep into my darkened room at the boardinghouse, but I still felt the weight of it, the weight of all I had to prove to God. I blinked my eyes open and stared at the dressing table mirror in the dark room.

I felt it again. *Not enough.*

As Minna snored, I rose and dressed, stealing down the stairs in a long cape with the hood concealing my face. The night was warm and wet, with summer finally beginning to gain solid footing through London, and I didn't fear the chill or the aloneness. I waved for a hackney and sped toward that tall brick house and banged on the green door that was three stories up. After a moment, it flew open.

A flickering candle lit the haggard face of Jack Dorian, and it struck me that this was the night before *his* big day too. These were *his* dreams hanging in the balance as much as mine.

I gulped and my words rushed forth. "I'm sorry, Jack. I can't do it. I can't dance tomorrow. Can you possibly take the sylph part out of the ballet?"

His face was grim. With a quick puff, he blew out the stubby candle, grabbed his coat, and waved me along. "Come with me." He jammed his feet into boots on the landing and draped his coat over the bedraggled white shirt and brown trousers he wore.

He took my hand and down the stairs and off we went, where we strode toward the gaslit streets with all the noises and smells of a city thick with people and their wares. I didn't ask where we were going and he offered no hints. We moved through darkened streets and turned before a multi-wing brick building framed by budding gardens. "What is this place?"

"This is lesson number four." He jumped up to the first step. "My lady, I welcome you to the great hall of Middle Temple."

"Are we allowed here?"

He draped a protective arm about me without answering and hurried me up the stairs to a set of doors on the upper level. With a tug, they yawned open to a wide wooden indoor balcony overlooking unlit lights strung from every beam and hook. A cavernous, dark-wood room lay empty below us, but as my eyes focused, I saw something hanging from the rafters that both excited and terrified me—a trapeze.

"The circus is set to perform here for another two weeks. Lucky for us."

"There will be an elephant in here? A tiger?"

"*Part* of the circus, at least. It's to be a trapeze and high-wire act."

I shivered at the word *high*. "What are *we* doing here?"

He pulled the trapeze bar over with a twiny rope and handed it to me. "Relearning how to fly."

"It's so dark." I tried to blink away the inky blackness.

"All the better. You won't be able to see anything below us."

I took hold of that bar and looked into his face that always held a welcome for me, even in the middle of the night. "Jack, how did you go from Seven Dials . . . to the circus?"

He sighed, running fingers through his mussed hair. "I begged her to take me for years. My mother, that is. The great lady. Every time she snuck away to visit me in Seven Dials, I asked again. Finally she took me for my birthday, and it was more than I'd dreamed. Larger than life, every moment spectacular."

"So you grew up and returned to it?"

He fumbled with the knot tying the trapeze up, allowing several long seconds to pass. "Yes. All on the same day I arrived."

"How old—"

"Eight."

"Oh."

He bent to set a candle stub upright in a brass holder and flicked a match. "After the elephant act, she spotted a man she knew across the way. She couldn't speak to him with me in tow, of course. It was our 'special secret' that we were related, and I thought that was truly something. She was so lovely and perfect. Lace and earbobs, little hats perched on blonde hair. 'You'll be good, won't you, Jackie boy, and stay here while I speak to him?' I promised, and there I sat, a dutiful man-child, willing to do anything for her—wrestle tigers, jump about to make her laugh, fetch a star from the sky. So I sat there waiting for her to come back."

"And?"

He tugged the trapeze. "Still waiting." That familiar face turned to me, and it suddenly occurred to me how very closed off the charmer actually was. "There's no space made in this world for illegitimate children. They've got to carve out their own."

I watched his masculine profile in the flickering glow, seeing him in light of his story. *That boy lives as one abandoned every day of his life.* Suddenly the friendship he'd always offered me, the endless help, seemed far more valuable than it had before.

He pulled the bar one last time and held it out for me. "Come, take hold."

Shivering, I shed my cloak and gripped the bar. Then he disappeared in a whish of cool air. It looked as though he'd grabbed another bar and swung into the air himself, but his voice sounded from somewhere in the dark emptiness below. "Now start flying."

I climbed up on the rail and tugged on the bar he'd given me, testing its security. A dizzy fear took hold, and I closed my eyes, bracing myself. Then I pushed off the railing and sailed into the cool, open air with a whoosh. The trapeze arced down and up, my feet swimming in nothingness, then it sailed back, the air against my back. My heels struck the railing and I swung toward the openness again. I blinked looking down, then back. Lonely candle stubs now flickered on the opposite balcony where I'd stood, but I couldn't see Jack in the glow. Panic fizzled in my chest. "How do I stop this thing? I can't see to get hold of anything."

Then his voice echoed off every wall and surface of the room, making it sound near yet distant. "Let go." Wind whistled past my ears. "Don't be afraid."

Do not be afraid. That was in the Bible somewhere. Not in Psalms. My panicked mind grasped for the verse. But my eyes looked down. "What's below?"

"I said, *let go*."

Panic seized me. "I can't do it. Just help me find the railing again."

Silence. *God is in the midst of her; she shall not be moved: God shall help her.*

I inhaled. He'd found me once in Seven Dials, and I hadn't even been looking for him. He had a special love for me, it seemed, and he was always there. Simply there.

Even in the theater, Lord? Are you truly with me there too?

I struck the blank wall and careened back through the air. My hold tightened, but my hands ached. Moisture slicked my grip. I braced myself to keep from whimpering up there suspended above who knew what. I looked down, tried to force my vision to clarify whether or not there was a net below. I didn't see one. I looked up as my body collided again with the railing and lurched back into its downward arc.

My left hand slipped. I shifted my weight up to grip with my right, but that only made it slip further. I clung with naught but my fingers as pain knotted each knuckle.

Jack's voice echoed. "I said . . . *let go.*"

Fear thou not; for I am with thee.

I gulped.

Let go.

With a shiver, my throbbing fingers slipped further. When I could not hold on any longer, I let go. I hung in dark, musty air for an eternity, then a muscular arm clamped about my waist, hurtling me through the cool darkness. I held on to nothing, limbs flailing, as Jack Dorian swung us both from one side to the other with a speed that would have frightened a pair of racehorses.

Air whooshed in my ears, the line went slack as we reached the top, then we twirled, blindingly rapid spins in the air that left me fearfully, delightfully dizzy. A laugh of sheer relief bubbled up from somewhere inside my trembling body, echoing in the open room. We reached the other side and his boot connected with the wall with a *thud* before we flew back the other way again, arcing around the entire room in one great circle, then spinning to the middle.

I heard the zip of rope against rope and we lowered to blessedly solid ground. He set me on my feet and disappeared again. All I heard was the whip of disturbed air as the trapeze took off. "That was rather a dangerous stunt. There wasn't any net."

"You were never in danger of falling." His voice arced through the room. "I was beside you on a second trapeze."

"I didn't see you."

His foot thunked against the balcony as he landed. "You were too busy looking for a way to land on your own."

"Then why did you let me dangle for so long? I was slipping!"

"I wanted you to experience what it is to let go. There's nothing like it."

I stood in the center of that great expanse and looked up into the dusty rafters. Was he swinging somewhere up there? It was impossible to see clearly. "Unless there's no mad trainer there to catch you."

"If you believe in God as you say you do, there is always someone."

The shuffle of my boots echoed through the hall as I turned in a slow circle, a smile tipping up one corner of my mouth. "You've such a way with words, Jack Dorian." I stared up at the darkness, catching a flying glimpse of his boot above. "It's no wonder you've charmed all the theater girls."

The *thwip* of a rope sounded somewhere above. "Not all of them."

You're closer than you think. "Are all those rumors true of you, Jack?" Suddenly I wished he'd say no, in the way one wishes for a happy ending to a novel already known to be a tragedy.

Another swish high above. "I can see your eyes from here. Have they always been so stunning, or is it merely the angle?"

"How many times have you used that gem?"

"Gems! Yes, they're like gems."

I crossed my arms, pinched my lips. "Has any woman yet believed such a line?"

"You're lovely when you're pleased. Stunning when you're not. Like now."

"I'm far too sensible for such nonsense." I stood in the center of that great room, turning in a slow circle as my puny girlish voice bounced off the walls.

Then he dropped right in front of me, boots striking the floor, his warm breath fanning over my face. "I've never had a home. Never anything sure. Yet there's something sure in you. Something aglow and so very . . . real. Sometimes I wish I had it too."

His gaze held me captive even as my mind ran haywire. He moved nearer, his hands taking mine, drawing me close, past the point of no return.

"I saw it in your eyes the moment we met, and it creeps back out when you dance sometimes. Especially when you think no one's watching. From that first glimpse, I wanted to know what it was. To touch it. To . . . taste it."

I ran my tongue across my lips. There was a bet. And he was about to win it.

The windows rattled in their loose panes. Wind howled, and a chill crept around the room. He brushed his thumb over my lips first, and when I did not push away, he leaned down and he had his taste, drinking deeply. My eyelids fluttered.

Everything I thought I knew fell away in a shocking instant. That kiss was unspoiled and tender, silkily vulnerable with a tang of fear. That rogue, the world-weary lady's man, lingered in that simple intimacy, framing my face with gentleness and savoring the moment as if he couldn't get enough of the sweetness he'd discovered.

I reached up and put my arms around his neck, pulling him closer. Had kisses always been like this? I should have

tried one sooner. It was so good. So honest. A natural extension of everything lovely and delightful that had occurred
between us.

He stepped back, stroking my cheek with his thumb, and I
hardly recognized that face—it was almost youthful in its raw
vulnerability. Hopeful. The glow of his features had turned
to burnished affection that shone like copper, and it made me
shiver. I could still taste his lips, a heady deliciousness that
lingered. But as he released me and the unwelcome cool air
swirled up between us, my senses returned.

This was Jack Dorian. I had kissed Jack Dorian, and betrayed Mama, Philippe, and the God in whom Jack had no
interest.

I looked to the floor that was too dark to see. "I do feel
better now."

This is exactly what it had been for them, hadn't it? Secret
kisses, encounters veiled in the romantic darkness, swelling
doubts in the face of so much disapproval. My heart pounded
with the awareness of their tragedy threading through my entire
life—inescapable, potent.

But this was different. I was not choosing the principal
dancer but the theater trifler. The flirt. The known scoundrel.
If Mama's story with a fine man ended in fiery tragedy, what
would become of mine with a man like Jack? I gripped a post
on my left, nails digging into wood. "Perhaps we should make
our way back. It must be late."

Jack paused, something flickering across his face, then he
disappeared into the dark. He clunked up a ladder and back
down, then returned with my cloak. "As you wish."

As he stood there holding out my wrap in the long shadows,
I faced the realization that Jack wasn't the trifler everyone

imagined him to be. He simply wasn't. No trifler spent half the night and much of his free time teaching a stubborn, plain-looking dancer. No trifler swept an old beggar woman into an enthusiastic dance. No trifler kissed with such exquisite restraint.

32

I managed to keep myself together in the solitude of my room that night, but the moment I arrived at the theater in the morning the unraveling began. Dancers whirled about the long dressing room, a dovecote of flurried activity and excitement, and I sat before the long dressing table with my hair trailing wildly about my back and shoulders, and not one hairpin lay about. Not one.

I blinked. How could this be? I looked around to all the other coiffed heads and estimated the number of pins holding each set of tresses in place—and none were left for me. This is what came of remaining in my room until the final moments. Every last set of paste jewels were firmly secured around the necks and heads of other dancers, with only a handful of broken strands lying abandoned on the marble dressing surface. A thumping panic set in. All those spins—how would I carry them out with long, wild hair whipping across my face?

And I was plain. So very plain. Didn't they know that? Those jewels gave me all the color I ever had.

I put on my costume, ran out into the wings, and headed for the stairs to the cellar, hoping to find a few rusty pins in the old abandoned dressing rooms below. I collided with a solid body, and something tore.

"Watch where you're going!" It was a stagehand. A delicate frond for the scenery had ripped in his hands. I leaped back and apologized, my scattered brain trying to think of hairpins and jewels and calmness and self-forgetfulness, then Jack was there, reaching me in two long strides and putting his hands on my shoulders with that deep gaze that mined through the fear and trembling to reach the core of me. "You are well?"

Nothing about how late I was, bless him.

"I need pins and jewels and so many things . . ." I was stammering. Like a fool—stammering.

His firm grip on my shoulder turned me toward the wings and the shared dressing room just beyond the greenroom. "We'll make do. There must be something left." He grabbed a bunch of silk flowers and twisted their stems into my hair with a bit of thin wire lying about from the set design. "You'll have to accept my attempts at hairdressing."

Relief cooled my body in long, quick sweeps. "Of course. Will that be enough?"

"Seeing as it's all we have . . ."

I sat obediently before the long mirror and watched his face. He frowned, the tip of his tongue protruding as he worked with my mane of hair, twisting and shaping it into something manageable and quite elegant. The warmth of his fingertips against my scalp calmed me deeply, and I gave myself over to his ministrations. I smiled. "You're also a hairdresser?"

"I've been a lot of things. Including a monkey." He straightened, and each twist lay securely against my head, wrapped around the wire and stems and decorated with lovely white flowers.

"A monkey?"

He jumped, kicking his heels together. "Every circus needs one. There, now." He bent and twisted together a quick belt of white flowers to match, securing it around my waist. "One needn't be extravagantly costumed, only exceedingly talented. These look more natural with your face anyway."

"And jewels? I've nothing."

"You have two stunning pieces here." His fingers brushed my cheek just below my eye. "And here. They will dazzle." He winked.

I looked at him, searching his face for more solid reassurance.

He dug in his pocket. "There is also this. A little thank-you for the past weeks." He draped a delicate vine-like necklace around my neck, its single topaz stone resting securely in the little dip at the base of my throat. "You don't need a thing more." His fingers lingered on my bare collarbone until I shivered, and he withdrew them. "You're more than ready."

"Is it . . . real?"

"Real as you are, my lady." His deep voice rumbled in the quiet as he knelt before me. He touched the stone, turning it in his fingertips. "See now—see the inclusion there? Only real gems have flaws. It's what sets them apart." His stunning gaze locked onto mine, as if lifting the layers of fear so his meaning would sink in. "Do not be afraid of imperfection, my lady. Even tonight."

I inhaled and gave a brave nod.

He walked me to the stage, his tall presence hovering just behind me in the shadows as muffled voices carried on around us. Violins and oboes and cellos all stretched out long notes to bring the instruments into tune, and footsteps sounded up and down the aisles.

"There you are." Tovah touched my arm as she whirled past. "Are you ready?"

I smiled and moved to follow her, but a hand in the dark wings took my arm in a gentle grasp and Jack's breath was warm on the back of my neck, frantic. Eager. His words rushed forth, bursting through a wall of fear. "Ella, I've waited for this day my whole life. So have you. This is the culmination of both of our dreams, and I want to share it with you." He turned me toward him. "Face it by my side. Please." His fingers slid down my arm and fumbled for my hand, but I moved away.

"No, Jack. I can't. It's . . ." I cast about for some escape.

"Philippe still, is it?" His voice was quick bursts of air in the dark. "You still want Philippe because of that one night years ago. No, you want a fairy tale. A perfect ballet in three acts, but that only happens on the stage, and that's a good thing. Real life has its own sort of beauty, and it's pulsing with color and dimension, the warmth of another person beside you—a real one, flaws and all. You *know* me, Ella. You know exactly the sort of man I am, but Philippe . . ."

I wanted to close my ears. Every word unsettled my mind and scattered my logic into a prism of thoughts. "It's not about fairy tales, Jack. I'm not the sort of woman you'd want—believe me."

"You know me so well, do you?" Those eyes flashed with such force. Dangerous—he was dangerous. Unsettling. But he'd always been that. "Then what happened last night—"

I put a hand on his chest. "That was very new for me. Very unusual. Yet you . . . how many women have you kissed in your lifetime?"

His chest tightened under my hand. His mouth parted, but he did not speak. Instead, he stepped back. I had the odd sensation that I'd hurt him deeply. I couldn't see his face anymore in the shadows. Dancers hurried past, orchestra music sounded beyond the curtain. The opening strains of Jack's ballet came to us.

"My scene comes up so quickly. I need to . . ." I tipped my head toward the stairs down to the old dressing rooms.

"Go. I'll guard the steps."

Yet I knew this wasn't over. Not for someone like Jack Dorian. It was only coming closer to an explosion, a moment of truth.

I nodded and hurried off, flying down the stairs to the chilly sanctuary where I could meet alone with God—balance myself and reset my focal point. I knelt on the floor of an old cellar dressing room while the orchestra boomed above, opening the first scene, and quieted my soul. I felt a loosening grasp on that insatiable need to prove myself. In its place rose a brilliant gratefulness, an awareness of God's presence, of our connection and his continued pursuit of me. Of *me*.

I offer up to you my body as a living sacrifice.

Then I rose, strong from the core and ready to dance.

There was a sacred moment just before the music began, that silence when I closed my eyes and forced the world to drop away like the lowering gauzy tree fronds, and my being filled with such unexplainable peace and delight. All I had to do was be still, cease striving, and know. Know, as I knew breathing and gravity and Mama's love.

The lights were blinding—wonderfully so. They'd hooked them to bars overhead to give the impression of rising mist and ghosts about the stage, but it served to blind me as well, which did wonders for my focus. I latched my gaze onto my focal point and spun, upward and open, arching back to lift my fingertips high. The right focal point made all the difference in the dance.

Be Thou my Vision, O Lord of my heart;
Naught be all else to me, save that Thou art.

I remembered familiar words on Aunt Lucy's smiling lips as she sang the old Irish hymn in English for me, her voice riding up the minor notes with a pleasurable Celtic lilt. I danced in the glow of childhood memories, in the rich awareness of God's presence.

Be Thou my Wisdom, and Thou my true Word;
I ever with Thee and Thou with me, Lord.

The ballet slipped by with surprising speed, each scene drawing out more beauty and ease in the steps.

The heroine could not see my character of course, but it didn't stop the little sylph I played from beseeching the heroine to turn from the villain, to come away to the true hero. I held out my arms in longing as if toward my sister, my dear Lily, and begged with my very being for her to come toward me, toward safety. Then I danced a short variation of lament when she did not come, acting out the anguish of realizing my greatest fears.

The music rose and tightened, crashing into crescendo after crescendo as Minna leaped and swept across the stage, then she sprang up into a sixteen-point fouetté with astonishing precision—kick after kick executed beautifully, ending in a lovely demi-pointe run and a dramatic faint at the end of the second act.

Bows stretched long over instrument strings and drew to a hushed close, and there were tears in my eyes as I lifted into position. I stood breathless and poised, my heart pounding in my ears. Then the cheering roared from some distant place, rolling over us from the shadowed auditorium.

All at once I became aware of the immense size of this unseen audience. I scrambled from the stage and leaned on a wall in the wings, hand to my racing heart. What had I expected, an empty house? Yet there they were, all those people with eyes and ears and minds forming opinions. Thank heavens for those lights, which had helped me forget about the lot of them.

Jack had insisted on those hideous lights and the mirrors to magnify them, despite my arguments for more subdued lighting. No dancer wished her every flaw noticed and commented upon by the press, yet here they were, bright as ten suns—and just as blinding. Dear Jack. Sometimes he knew what I needed even more than I.

The curtain rolled closed, groaning along its metal rods, then reopened by the strength of two men with pulleys on either side. I was nearly run over by the great throng of corps dancers in tulle and silk rushing out to take their places for the closing bow. Applause rang through the auditorium. The *coryphée* dancers swept out next, four on each side. Minna and Philippe stepped forward and the applause rose with hearty approval.

It was then I realized, clinging to the velvet curtain, that I had no place. We'd barely rehearsed this ballet, let alone the curtain call, and with my odd role, I had no idea where I should appear. So I did not.

Until Jack, that is. He marched by in a long coat with tails, and in one deft move he took my hand, compelling me forward with easy spins and maneuvers until I found myself near the front of the stage with him.

Then applause rolled from the great belly of that auditorium like thunder, echoing up to the gilded ceiling and drawing people up out of their seats. All across the theater they rose with a flash of jewels and flutter of programs, their approval loud and enthusiastic as we stood there, the writer of this remarkable ballet and the novel sylph creature written in at the last minute. Flowers rained upon the stage at our feet and I blinked.

Through his stage smile, Jack whispered, "Minna may have the lead, but make no mistake—you are the Delphine Bessette of this performance."

I swayed on my feet. *Delphine*. He was right, I was her. I'd lifted out of my body and was looking down upon Delphine Bessette. Yes, it was Delphine now bowing before them, accepting their praise. Delphine looking down the row at a deeply shadowed lead dancer she did not know. Jack's words echoed: *"You know exactly the sort of man I am, but Philippe . . ."* Her story had merged with mine so completely that I'd begun to take her spotlight. Her fame. Her glorious existence. Even her love story.

Yet the flames came in the next act. The final act wouldn't be played until tomorrow, the official opening night, but as I thought of it I could barely breathe. I had to make a turn—but in what direction?

Three bows I took with Jack before I wrestled my hand away and darted from the stage on shaky legs. It was all the attention, wasn't it? The lights, the applause . . . it was dizzying.

Jack caught up with me in the narrow passage on the way to the greenroom. He did not touch me, but his eyes were arresting. "You are not well."

"I need a rest." I stumbled toward a straight-backed chair and sat, hand to my moist forehead. There was so much I wanted to say to Jack about truly knowing and being known, about the heady reality of authentic love, which I had begun to feel for the first time in my life. I looked up at Jack, dear Jack, with eyes as blinding as those stage lights. "I know Philippe isn't perfect, Jack. I know that."

He took my hand, studying my face, brushing the hair away. "You need a doctor."

"I have my own flaws, you know—a terrible secret I've kept for years." There was something giant between us, standing in the way, just as there must have been for my parents. A large, hard ball of ugliness that could not be gotten around. My ears pulsed with the utter sameness of our stories, the inevitability of a shared tragedy.

But now, I would make a pointed turn away from their story, no longer allowing them to parallel. Instead of running away from whatever it was and from him, I would yank off the curtain and let him see. Then he could decide for himself if he truly wanted me.

Regret over the past came fast and hard. I began to cry, tiny pinprick tears leaking out. "I shouldn't have kept the secret."

He waved it off. "I already know it, and it isn't even your secret. It's your mother's."

"No, Jack." I forced myself not to wilt, and whispered, "Not that secret." Warmth flooded my face, my neck. I took a breath, then I told him. I told him everything about the night I'd ended up in Seven Dials, and about what I'd done with the cloak and its precious contents.

He was shocked. His shock turned to white-hot anger, then he left. It was the kind of leaving that wasn't temporary.

I braced myself against the chill of his rejection and shivered hard. Why should it matter, anyway? It didn't. Truly. All I'd done was rid myself of a rake. Not even a friend, as it turned out, for what friend blanched at a person's admitted mistakes and ran away? Good riddance.

Yet there it sat, the hard ball of guilt that was magnified by Jack's reaction. For years I'd minimized it, but now I felt the full weight of what I'd done, seen finally through someone else's eyes, and couldn't dislodge it.

God . . . Father . . .

I didn't even know what to ask. All I felt was the echoing clang of *not enough.*

With three long breaths, I rose and forced myself to walk back to the stage with the other dancers—but all was chaos. Press men in bowler hats and cheap suits formed a tight circle around Bellini, who looked both shocked and pleased. "Congratulations" flew around. They were, it seemed, congratulating the ballet master for creating a unique sort of a dancer who broke the mold. *Me.* Forward thinking, they called him, and brilliant. I was his crowning achievement.

The poor man. He looked rather helpless.

Then they spotted me, and they shifted as one, ants piling from one crumb to another.

"Miss Blythe, where did you train?"

"What are your plans for the future?"

"How were you compelled to divorce yourself so from classical style?"

I answered a few questions as vaguely as possible, and as I made to leave, a bespectacled man in a wool suit stepped into my path to ask if he could have a word privately. He was Mr. Meechum, he told me, from the *London Illustrated*.

Yes, I supposed he could. I'd dreamed of speaking with *Illustrated* for longer than I could remember. He put the usual questions to me that I'd always imagined them asking, the ones

Mama had told us she answered after important performances. Yet in the wake of Jack's leaving, I felt sullen. Dirty. Undeserving of their special attention.

Then he straightened, placing his pencil in an inner jacket pocket. "Miss Blythe, I hope you will indulge our readers with a hint of your secret. We've seen you dance tonight, the way you nearly scoff at gravity, yet Fournier insists that no flying contraption was used."

I laced my sash through my fingers. "Well, it's actually a very wonderful pair of shoes that—"

"No no, Miss Blythe. Forgive me, but that isn't what I mean." His kindly face melted into a smile behind his spectacles. His voice was easy and welcoming. "When you began dancing, it seemed you were saturated with . . . something. A thing not sullied by the gritty world to which I'm accustomed, and I cannot help wondering . . . I've come away from this ballet feeling as though I've tasted something of a divine nature."

I smiled, a growing pleasure inside at his bumbling explanation that struck closer to the truth than he realized. Yes, it *had* been a divine experience, a pas de deux to remember.

"How have you managed to create that illusion of floating, that bewitching sense of inner music that has breathed *life* into the marble of the old classical form? I've never seen the like. Who has trained you to dance this way?"

Why God had chosen to dance with me, knowing everything, still made little sense, but I grasped at that knowledge, holding it tight. I had found my true focal point and I mustn't let it go. "Mr. Meechum, it isn't always about the steps or who has done the training, but what compels us to move that makes us unique."

His notebook inched down toward his middle and he frowned. "I'm not certain I understand."

Warmth flooded my voice and the words came easily. With gratitude. "We all have a focal point in the theater. For a dancer, what she looks at she reflects." I closed my eyes, remembering Mama's warm voice and thinking it was all right if this part of our stories aligned. "We can talk about me if you wish, but I'd much rather speak of the God for whom I dance." My heart thrilled. *Out of Zion, the perfection of beauty, God hath shined.*

"I . . . see." He blinked in wonder. Intrigue. "So you are religious. And it is your religious zeal that has gifted you this extraordinary . . ."

"No, it's God. He himself is extraordinary. So of course, anything that is born out of his strength will also be extraordinary."

"How curious." Fascination glinted in his gaze. "I should like to hear more, if you'd be so inclined."

"I'd be happy to oblige you."

Ballet was a fleeting art, its dancers so quickly forgotten once they left the stage. All that effort, the tiny, endless stitches of rehearsals and stretches and many repeated tasks sewn into the larger tapestry of a performance, seemed a waste in the end. A futile way to spend one's life. Yet for Mama, all those minuscule, repetitive stitches blended together into a larger tapestry that showed the glory of the Almighty to everyone who looked at her.

Now the tapestry had been handed to me, those loose threads ready for me to continue the legacy she had begun. If people had glimpsed a bit of God through my work, if I could honor his name . . . My despair began to lift, and a light cut through the shadow of my *not enough.* I had, after all, something to offer the world, and it was God. A glimpse of what he could do.

"Would you be willing to meet with me—perhaps at a more

convenient time—to talk at length? I could arrange an exclusivity fee, if it helps. I admit, you've enchanted me into wanting to know more."

My voice was soft. "I'll be here tomorrow. Come by if you like. No fee is necessary."

Mr. Meechum's face beamed his gratitude as he tipped his hat. When he moved, I saw the faint outline of Jack in the shadows, watching. But he turned instantly and disappeared down the corridor.

It was the sight of rejection, that turned back, but my heart felt peace, delighting in the surprising door that had opened. I still had God, and he had given me back ballet. Any work one did, it seemed, could be intertwined with God and point onlookers to him. *I will praise thee, O LORD, with my whole heart; I will shew forth all thy marvelous works.*

There. That was my story. No romance or tragedy, only ballet, colored with the presence of God.

When I'd changed out of my costume, most everyone else had gone. The theater rang with voices as dancers left in droves, and I would soon be alone. I moved through the dimness toward the greenroom in hopes of finding the one person to whom I needed to talk.

Tovah hurried by with hat in hand and paused for a quick hug. "What are you still doing here?"

"I was hoping to find Jack."

She blinked, stepping back to study me.

"To walk me home, I mean. Since Philippe is already at the inn for the celebration."

She grabbed my arms. "Come with us this time, won't you? Then Philippe can walk you home from the Lamb and Flag."

"Thank you, but I should get home." I was drained beyond all reason and had to perform an even longer ballet tomorrow. Perhaps before royalty.

"You will be all right? There may be someone up at the front offices to see you safely."

I gave her a nod, a gentle squeeze, and a sendoff. When she hurried away, still intoxicated by the thrill of the night, the sudden loneliness of my life settled over me.

Then there was a small whoosh of warm air behind me, a few footsteps, and a voice. "Will I do? For an escort home, that is."

I spun and there he was, stepped down from the portrait. "Mr. de Silva." Hot and cold whooshed through me at the sight of my father so close.

He strode into the greenroom with a quiet sense of ownership and came to stand before me, looking me over with unsettling thoroughness. "It occurred to me after our last meeting that I hadn't any idea about your circumstances. It was all rather sudden and . . . perhaps it's best if we talk. Come, I'll walk you home."

I simply stared at his elegant figure, trying to wrap my mind around this image of my father. He held out his arm and I accepted it, my legs trembling as we crossed through both sets of corridors and out the alley door toward the boardinghouse.

33

*F*orgive me for behaving so abominably before." We had been silent for the first street and a half, but now the dark timbre of his voice interrupted the night. "When you tried to tell me who you were, I'm afraid I misunderstood. But then at the meeting at Fournier's when I realized . . . well, it was quite a shock."

I let the moment go by without forgiveness or question.

"I never cared for Delphine—that is, Jane Fawley—even though every other living person seemed to adore her. She was devious. A schemer. When you approached me and indicated that you were her daughter, I couldn't help but see Jane Fawley in that moment, with her coy smile, hand outstretched to receive whatever bauble she'd elicited from some poor sap."

"But . . . my mother." I gulped. This was important. "You loved *her,* at least, yes?"

"More than my own life." His voice shuddered and I felt the tension in his arm. "Our lives were stitched together, and something in me ripped irreparably when she was torn away."

My head spun. I hadn't expected this. I hadn't any idea what

I wanted to know at this point, or what I dared ask. Many parts of the story made sense . . . except the ending.

He kept his gaze down. "What became of my Viola after the fire? How did she . . . ?"

"It's true, Mum escaped the fire, but not without harm. She had burns on her arms, face, and neck for the rest of her life. Yet nothing dimmed what was inside her."

He gave a quiet "hmm," as if the last part pleased him, but his sadness ran deep.

"She died three years ago of cholera. She was weak after the fire, and never left the house. Never had fresh air, save what came through the window. She simply couldn't recover when it hit."

He paused on the busy walk, letting throngs of people pour around us from either side. "Why wasn't I told?"

I shuddered as he voiced my own question. "She wouldn't let us tell anyone that she'd survived that fire. She kept herself a secret from the world, for as long as I can remember." That, and some other reason. Something between them that could not be moved. I had no idea what. I could only settle in my heart that she knew more about it than I did. She alone had lived in her shoes. I looked up at him, at that lightly lined face. "Did you set the fire?"

His arm flinched under my hand, but his face remained the same. "I suppose you don't know me, do you?" A pause, a deep sigh. "We did argue that night, and she stayed to learn the new flying contraption, refusing to come home with me. She had a soft voice, but she knew how to use it, that one." His voice was tender, as if we'd broached a sacred subject.

I swallowed.

"I left after the argument, quite put out with her. It wasn't until I reached home that I received the dreadful news . . . of the fire . . ." His voice began to break. "Many were quick to accuse me. And I . . . well, considering my final parting words to her, the weight of guilt settled, and I could not refute it. Couldn't help but feel equally responsible."

"But you weren't even there."

He shrugged. "I told them, but I had no proof about the timing. I came home to an empty flat and lay by myself until the knock on the door."

"Everyone assumed it was Delphine who was in the fire—Jane Fawley—but it wasn't. It was Mum, and she was only the stand-in, wasn't she? Not the real Delphine."

He spun on me in the street, grasping my shoulders. "You mustn't think that. She was no fraud. She was a magnificent dancer, beyond compare, and I'll not have you look down on her."

I nodded, and we continued walking. "Why did she tell me, then, that she had been Delphine?"

"Because she *was*. She was no stand-in." We turned onto Bow Street, taking the long way around, and the London air grew thick with noise and smells. "Years ago, Jane Fawley coined the stage name Delphine Bessette and created quite a stir with her dancing. When she was injured, a tendon in her heel, I believe it was, it was rather a shock, and a blow to Craven. We had no idea if she'd dance again. Tickets had been sold at exorbitant rates for the entire season, hinging on Delphine Bessette dancing there. Craven had already arranged a tour afterwards too, all around England and on the continent, and they'd be bankrupt if they refunded all those contracts and tickets, so they scrambled to find a stand-in. A slightly younger rising dancer not yet known in the theater who was highly trainable and moldable. One who looked passably like the original, at least from the stage.

"They pulled her in, slathered in cosmetics so the other dancers wouldn't know under the stage lights, but I saw the difference immediately. I was Jane's partner." His voice quieted, his steps slowing. "The moment I spotted your mother dancing on that stage late one night, I sensed a beauty that radiated from her core. A deep kindness and a purity that she could not help displaying in her every movement. This was not Jane Fawley, I said to myself, but someone rare and beautiful and interesting.

"They told the other dancers she would be practicing and training separately, only onstage for the performance, because of the risk of another injury. Most believed it, I think. But I, her partner, knew the truth from that first night. And I fell deeply in love with the replacement."

So that was it—two complete Delphines, one picking up the threads as the other had to lay them down. Emotion shuddered through my frame. "So that's why you kept your marriage a secret. Everyone thought you hated Delphine, and you had to keep her secret. Craven's secret."

He gave a single nod. "Yes, but more so because your mother detested public intrusion. She was a quiet woman and embraced her privacy even in stardom. She wanted her private life to remain private. When she finished out her season at Craven and prepared to go abroad for Delphine's tour, we married on her condition that our affairs remain private. She wished it that way always and lived every moment humbly."

"That is how I knew her too." It relieved me to say these words, to know she was truly as I'd always believed her to be after all.

"Viola quickly earned that famed title, and in time even outshone the original. It was as if she was born to be magnificent and only needed a fluke like that to prove herself. There was nothing false about her talent—not at all. Even if she was not the original Delphine, she was the *true* Delphine. When we got word that Jane Fawley would never dance again, we talked it over, the few of us at Craven who knew that Viola was standing in, and it was decided that she would take the name of Delphine Bessette and continue the role indefinitely. She worked harder than anyone I know, earning that name and dancing the part with such devotion—until the fire."

Before I knew it, we stood before the boardinghouse door, but the story felt terribly unfinished. "Won't you come inside? There's a parlor where we can talk."

"We won't be disturbed?"

"No one ever uses it."

He hesitated, looking me over, glancing behind us. "I suppose, for a moment."

I unlocked the door and led him with a small oil lamp toward the parlor. I set it on a table and perched on the couch facing him, expectant. Nervous.

He sat, his face alight in the shadows as he processed various emotions, waging his own internal battles. He stared at my face until it grew warm, and I was thankful for the dimness. "I should have known. From the moment you approached me outside the theater, I should have seen her likeness in your very bearing, that unmistakable quiet grace, and known who you were. It's . . . remarkable. The fact that you even exist, that I have a *daughter* . . ." He touched my cheek hesitantly and with a quizzical frown, as if ensuring I was real.

My throat swelled, and I hardly knew what to say. All the

secret cracks of my fatherless heart rose to the surface, eager to be filled.

"I shall be a father to you, if you wish it. We can meet sometimes, in a quiet little shop or an empty park. Your needs will always be met, provided they're not extravagant. My wife must not question . . ."

"Of course." I forced a smile even as my heart sank. I'd heard what he said about Mama's need for privacy, but I felt a faint wondering if he had other reasons for keeping their marriage a secret. Perhaps the thing between them that Mama couldn't live with had been the same that had dogged my steps too—*not enough*.

"It wouldn't do to have you appear at my home, of course. We must keep all this quiet. I'm sure you feel the same."

I forced my heart to buoy with the truth. He had a new marriage to protect, plenty of secrets already, and a delicate reputation. He wasn't Marcus de Silva anymore, and he had no way of reasonably explaining who I was—especially since no one had even known of his first marriage.

Still, I felt the slice of a knife through the thin cord that connected us.

He moved an inch closer. "You must tell me what you need, though. I've no idea about these things. I want to free you from having to depend on any other man to give you independence."

I straightened. "I've never depended on a man." Not even a father.

"I've heard someone has been watching out for you."

"I have no abonné, and I've not fallen under the spell of Jack Dorian, if that's what you've heard. Everyone may think what they like, but I'm smart enough to see what he truly is." My words smarted against my lips. I couldn't stop the guilt—the grief—from swelling whenever I thought of him, and the way he'd looked at me when I'd told him my secret. Another turned back, another dismissal.

He looked me over, that steel-gray gaze passing over me entirely, missing nothing. "Pray, tell me what it is about Jack Dorian that offends you so? Perhaps I shall change my mind. Or yours. When he spoke to me of his interest, I rather liked him as a suitor for you."

"Surely you're aware of his reputation. How could anyone want such a man for one of his own?"

"Have you anything other than hearsay to base this . . . *reputation* on?"

"His very manner. Why, he cannot help himself. His charm overflows onto every female in his vicinity." Including an old beggar woman in Seven Dials. And an overlooked dancer who needed his help. But I glossed over those, pushed them aside with growing angst.

"You underestimate his affection for you."

"Do I?" My fingers trembled where they clutched the wood frame of my seat. In reality my father *over*estimated it.

"What other proof have you?"

My mind scrambled, latching to a small niggling memory. "Ask him about the bet. See what you think of his affection for me then."

"Ah, the bet." He leaned back on the horsehair sofa, folding his arms. "Yes, I've heard something of it."

"He . . . told you?" Heat climbed from my gown up my neck and face to think my father knew of the kiss.

"Actually it was Fournier who mentioned it to me the night we were at his house. Months ago, Jack Dorian bet Bellini, who had attempted several times to cut you from the company, that

318

he could make you into the most show-stopping dancer ever to grace Craven's stage if they left you in. He stood his ground and convinced them you had it in you."

"And in return?"

"In return, if his hunch proved right, he received the pleasure of seeing you entrusted with a leading role, as befitting your talent. Fournier guaranteed it."

What I want . . . is for you to fly. I swallowed. Trembled. Regret punctured me, sharp and sour. That foolish, foolish decision—it had happened so long ago. It hadn't anything to do with Jack, yet telling him my Seven Dials secret had cost everything between us. Just like the unseen rock-like thing that stood between my mother and father, keeping two people apart, it had fractured something precious. But why? Why did they all have to end this way? I gripped the chair, suddenly needing freedom from this trap, this track my life could not escape no matter how I turned.

I raised my gaze to his face. "Why *did* Mama keep away from you? What was the real reason she didn't come to you after the fire?"

His tanned face paled, as if caught unawares by an oncoming carriage, then he looked down. "She wanted her own way in certain matters. I was not prepared to let her have it. Some women are born with iron-clad opinions, and marriage simply doesn't suit them. There now, that's all I can say without speaking her mind for her. You know yourself that she did what she wanted—she defied her own parents to wed me, did she not?"

"What was it?" My voice was a whisper, but he did not answer.

He rose with regret darkening his face and bid me good

night. He would be in touch, he said, about when we could next meet.

I remained in that dim parlor alone, staring into the flickering flame in the oil lamp. I had gained a father this night, yet I still felt utterly fatherless. Disconnected from everyone. As displaced as Jack Dorian, and as misguided as Lily.

There was a soft rustling of petticoats as a serene figure entered and sat beside me. "He won't tell you the truth, but I will." Mama Jo made no apologies for interrupting my private grief.

I turned and looked at her lined face, wisdom etched in every crease.

"I hadn't planned on telling you, but it sounds as though you have important decisions to make regarding a future connection with Marcus de Silva, and you should know what he isn't telling you."

"I'm ready to hear it."

She gave a nod. "I do not know your mother. I'm not even certain who she is exactly, or where she came from, but I can tell you what I know about her reasons for disappearing from him. You see, I was at the theater the night of the fire, cleaning up. I overheard their argument, and I think you need to know what it was about."

34

It was not Josefina Herrera's habit to spy, but the sound of soft crying, of a sweet voice speaking in low, pained tones, drew her toward that old materials room.

"How can this be?" Marcus de Silva's unmistakable voice came from inside the room, terse and low. "You're certain?"

An unseen woman's soft voice responded meekly with something in the affirmative.

"Well then, you must deal with the situation. Immediately." He sighed and his voice melted into a soft, caressing tone. "Not to worry, I'll be by your side. I'll look about for a surgeon."

"No!" The suddenly emphatic voice drew Josephine closer, hand upon her heart. "I will *not* allow it, Marcus."

"Your future will be over. Ruined. I've seen what you can do on that stage, darling, what has become of your career. And it's only just begun. I will not let you throw it away because of a simple accident. We will fix this."

The silence quivered. So she was a dancer—someone from Craven?

The woman's voice came again, low and firm. "I mean to stop. To quit the theater."

A bang sounded. "*Quit?* Be serious, Vi! This isn't finishing school, it's your *life*. Nothing will ever be the same."

"Is that such a terrible thing?"

"And what of your dreams? Do you truly want to let them go, just like that?"

Her voice was soft, but steady. "What if *this* is my dream?" A brief silence. "I do love the ballet, but I want this new chapter in my life even more."

"Then you'd simply be a wife and mother, absolutely no different than any other woman. I'd be ashamed to be your husband, and we'd both be ruined besides—all our years of work, everything we planned. Is it really worth all that?"

"What you want me to do . . . it is *monstrous*, Marcus. Utterly despicable."

"So now you've set out to prove you truly could have both. Is that why you're here, practicing so late?"

"Yes." Her voice was soft, her eyes bright. "As it turns out, I merely proved that I couldn't. I'm already exhausted, Marcus. So tired of dancing, but I push myself, because you want it. You and my parents. The only thing I truly want is what you're asking me to destroy, and I simply *will not do it*."

"We have no choice—I will not sit back and let you destroy your career, your very dreams. Our future."

Her voice grew dangerously steady. "And I will not let you destroy our *child*."

"It's not a child, it's a leech. A problem. You'll not be able to dance when it grows bigger—why, you'll barely be able to walk!"

"A leech?"

He was silent. There was pacing. "Listen, Vi—"

"No, *you* listen, Marcus. You may be my husband, but you have no right, under God, to force me to end a life that the Almighty has created." A soft rustling as she moved close. "Created between us, out of our love. Don't you see how precious it is?"

"If it came in another five years, yes. I could see the beauty in it. But now, when everything is just beginning for us? I'm sorry, but it simply isn't possible. Nor will you convince me to want it. I'll send a surgeon by your rooms and we'll speak no more of this."

"*Marcus!*" Her voice was frantic.

"That's my final word, Vi. As your husband. As head of this family. I will not accept any refusal from you. I give into your whims whenever I can, but on this, *I will not be moved.*"

Something slammed, then the footsteps stalked away, and it was over.

I clutched the arm of that couch so hard my fingers ached.

So that was the big secret. That was the reason for the end of their epic love story—the end of Mama's stage career. He'd been the love of her life, she his prop. And I—an unwanted mistake. I could barely breathe around the shattered pieces of my heart. Never before had I felt the intense burden of my existence, and such a disconnect from humanity and purpose. I had ruined everything—simply by existing.

I climbed to my bedchamber and stared at my face in the mirror, the plain features offset by vivid eyes—the eyes of my father who wasn't truly a father at all. He was merely a man accidentally saddled with a child. I took that hurt to bed with me, huddled up around it, and tried to sleep before the big performance.

When I woke in the morning, the sense of loss felt heavier. There was only one thing I could do with myself, one place I could take all my thoughts.

35

*J*ack had followed her out of habit. He'd been watching over her for so long that he couldn't seem to cut himself off. He'd spotted Ella Blythe striding across the market square in Covent Garden, obviously on a mission, so he'd followed her all the way to a little church just off Cheapside.

She stood now with another woman—her sister, most likely—huddled together in the hilly cemetery before a new stone that had been placed on a grave that had already been patted firm with time. He sensed that the stone, that neatly carved slab, bore the name *Viola de Silva*, and that knowledge made him ache for poor Ella in spite of everything. At last she had a real name to put on it—and closure. He'd done that much for her, even if he couldn't see his way clear to doing more.

The taller woman leaned onto Ella, wrapping her arms around her. How interesting that it was Ella's true mother lying there, yet Ella was the one holding up her rather distraught sister. But then again, her sister was the one completely alone in the world.

Well, almost alone.

Did Lily have any notion of it? Any idea of the precious child somewhere out in the world who belonged to her, was a part of her being—but now lived with strangers? No, of course not. Ella had chosen to purge her sister's life of that "troublesome complication" so that her sister might appear righteous. Enough for a respectable husband, at least. In reality, though, how could any sort of moral purity be achieved by removing the purest being to exist in that house?

Then she had gone home and lied about it—lied to her mother and sister, breaking their hearts with the news that the baby had died on the way to the free hospital. Even with the deception, she seemed to think now that her choice was not so very terrible—she'd been young, acting out of love, making what she could of a terrible situation—but that only made it more repugnant.

Hands buried deep in his pockets, he slipped up the stone steps and into the modest little Methodist church to offer them privacy—and to escape. He paused just inside the entrance, enveloped in silence, standing small and still at the back of the empty nave lit by high windows and glowing candles above. He hadn't been inside one of these in many years, and the solemn atmosphere invaded his calm.

It was a simple church erected in a poorer parish, a stone structure with a wood-beamed ceiling and unadorned stone pulpit up front, but the magnitude of the place, the vast openness above, the pillars along the aisle all the way to the chancel, culled an inescapable sense of awe.

He didn't like being overwhelmed in this way. It unsettled him. Especially when he was aware of his own smallness. Jackie Dorian, the circus monkey. The adapter of other people's creativity. The disposable plaything of his mother.

He walked up the aisle, the sunlit stained-glass windows casting colorful shadows over his clothing as he passed each biblical scene, and he was a boy of seven again, staring high up into the rafters beside his reluctant guardian, fully aware of the great God whose silent presence seemed to occupy this space so completely.

There was a permanency to the great stone structure, a place strong enough to weather any storm without and shelter the most vile of wretches within, all their scars, their mountains of doubt and cynicism.

Ella Blythe always did this to him—throwing him accidentally into the presence of the Divine and forcing him to face that which had always been so easy to ignore. He'd known a great many churchgoers in his life, those people who made him ever aware of his gross inadequacies before they even spoke a word, but Ella . . . well, Ella had scars of her own. Deep ones, with a surprising wretchedness that still disturbed him.

He *should* forgive her, overlook the decision she likely made with good intentions, but he could not. Another man, perhaps, but not him. As far as he was concerned, the cracks she'd covered up for so long reached down to the foundation, and she was irreparably broken.

Yet God was with her. It was undeniable. Pervasive, reaching into every part of life and weaving evenly through the good and the bad, carried about like a mantle with every step and breath and pulsing heartbeat. It made no sense.

It isn't supposed to. The notion whispered through his heart, clear as day, awakening his mind.

He tensed, gripping a pew back. He'd never had a father, never cared for the heavenly variety, yet the way Ella now lifted her tear-streaked face to God, as if seeking comfort and finding it, was like the scent of warm bread as his stomach growled. He closed his eyes, grasping the back of that wood pew like a lifeline, standing strong against whatever was threatening to sweep over him.

When he opened his eyes, they had left the cemetery, but Ella's sister lingered at the outer gate, looking back to the stones within. The desire was huge to approach Lily and have a conversation—he hadn't promised not to tell her—but the notion of Ella walking home alone after this quiet graveside remembrance wouldn't release him. He bowed his head and strode out of the church, eager to feel the weight of it lift when he left this place.

Yet it did not, not on the entire walk home. God, it seemed, was not ready to let go of him. He threw his hands in the air and yelled, "What? What do you want with me?" His voice sent a pack of pigeons flapping up and away between crowded buildings. A few people walking on St. Charles Street glanced his way, but he wasn't interested in them. None of them. Only one person mattered in the moment, and her memorable little face wasn't anywhere to be found.

Yet when he found her at last, standing outside Craven with her back to him, she clung to the arm of Philippe Rousseau. The man looked down at her with tender devotion that made Jack step away, the intruder. The outsider.

She'd once leaned on Jack that way. The memory caused a physical ache. At least he could verify with his eyes that she was safe—and that she no longer had need of him. He turned, head bowed, and left her to the life she'd always dreamed of.

He shook away the images and turned on his heel, pretending to inspect a rack of cooling candles hanging in pairs. Suddenly he felt as foolish as the small boy sitting in the stands, awaiting his mother's return. She didn't need him. No one really *needed* him. Not even Philippe would need him for long. Jack stared at the back of Ella's trim figure, trying to recast her in his mind, to put her in a new, more distant role in his heart. She was no longer his concern, and that's the way he wanted it. The way he needed it to be.

He'd been drawn to her from the start, and for once he'd become attached. Painfully so. God had folded back the layers of his soul around her, bit by bit, until he now lay exposed—and alone. What was the point?

Well, the *point* was opening his eyes, of course. The answer came to him almost automatically. Nothing else would have shaken up his world quite so much as encountering Ella Blythe, and it was the only way God could have gotten his attention. Beyond that . . . perhaps he'd been a conduit. Someone used of the Almighty to bring this woman's dreams to her, and to prepare Philippe to be the man she needed. The one she believed him to be, and the one Jack sincerely hoped he was now capable of becoming.

36

carried the weight of everything I had learned onto that stage. There was such a significance now to my performances, for they meant far more. Success was not optional. Not with all that I had cost this theater—and even more so, my mother.

There was nothing for it but to pour everything into the performance and make it count. So pour I did. Every lift, every turn, every raise of a pointed toe was infused with the intensity of my angst over Mama, indebtedness toward Fournier, and a passionate desire to be worth the expense to them all.

"There's no space in this world for illegitimate children when they come into it. They've got to carve out their own." Jack's words came back to haunt me, and the ache to speak with him deepened.

Up until today, I'd felt equal to the task of earning my place eventually, of proving myself. Today, I felt I was a child pretending at life.

I looked over the audience before we began the first full night of Jack's ballet. Not one blue-velvet chair back was visible in the whole place and the rear walls were packed too.

Aisles were jammed and balconies overflowed. My gaze drifted as always to the peep, reconnecting with a memory. I smiled sadly as my hazy mind imagined a face there, looking out at me. Mum's face, a white porcelain profile framed by delicate tendrils. And she was smiling—always smiling. Philippe's face, watching as I once had watched him, delightfully shocked at what I could do on the dance floor.

I moved with ease through all the scenes but felt my heart pounding as we began the third act, the lover's argument and the fire. The revelation of a murderer.

The scene opened as two dancers moved in tandem, one directly behind the other—the two Delphines. Then they divided, each dancer mirroring the other, and there was an audible gasp from the audience. The paces grew impassioned, fervent. One would spin, then the other, competing for the same position. Then one ran behind a sheer curtain. Philippe as de Silva twirled behind it and the pantomimed argument ensued. I turned away, sick with the knowledge of what they were saying.

Then he left, and I held my breath. It was coming. The big reveal. How would the audience react? From the wings of the stage where I waited, I looked up into the high ceiling of this fabled old theater that was about to relive a most horrific night of its history. Would it allow such secrets to be released after keeping them in close for so long?

A cymbal clash, a flash of light, and the theatrical fire flared. The audience gasped. I spun back onto the stage for my part, but something was wrong. Minna had frozen in her dance. All the dancers ground to a halt, even though the music continued. Minna screamed and darted offstage as one tulle frond went up in an instant *poof* of flames and disappeared. Smoke poured around the set design from backstage, and shrieks came from the audience. "*Fire!*"

I tasted metal in my mouth as realization struck me. The theater had not forgotten that night. And we had only stirred its memory, re-creating the cataclysmic blaze that had changed everything.

I stood frozen in place, acutely aware of past and present converging in a single moment. All along I'd been marching toward this. Living her life within a mirror, one of those stage props to give a ghost effect. And now we'd reached the tragic ending that I never could have avoided. Smoke poured over the stage. It was coming for me, marching me toward my fate, the theater ready to swallow me whole too.

I will not let the theater ruin you as it did me.

Heart thudding, I broke away and scrambled backstage with the rest. Flames ate up a discarded curtain on the floor, raced up a dangling pulley. "Drop the fire curtain!" The call came from somewhere, and Jack the circus performer scrambled up the ladder at stage right, swinging from the harnesses to yank a cord that dropped a heavy curtain. Men surged past with buckets and blankets, dancers fleeing through the side door to the alley.

I hurried toward them, but bodies clogged the narrow steps down. I looked back and the flames leaped toward us, as if searching me out. Then I saw Tovah scrambling in the other direction, toward the cellar stairs. Maybe she knew of an exit. Perhaps she was heading for certain death. Lifting the overlayer of skirt to cover my face, I bolted after her. I coughed as the smoke thickened quickly, flailing about to find the doorway down. I saw a cape moving not far away and ran for it, reaching out for my friend. "Tovah!"

The figure turned and grabbed my arm, the strength of it

biting into my flesh. She yanked me toward her and a white face appeared between the folds of the hood. "*You.*" It was Lady Gower. Jane Fawley. Delphine. Crazed and frantic, she pulled my face to hers and I felt the moisture of it. The heat. "You stole my name. Everything I am. You . . . *replaced* me!" She grabbed a fistful of my costume in her other hand, staring into my face and seeing my mother. Seeing the story my life inescapably resembled.

"What did you do to her?" I was paralyzed, in the grasp of this woman's fear that had destroyed my mother. Another tragic end of a story that began with *not enough*.

"Delphine must end." Her breath fanned my face, her spit landing on my chin. "There can only be one."

With a savage growl I tore away, stumbling toward the stairs. Then she clutched me with a vice grip. For a flash, I felt immense pity. Then her face contorted as one possessed and she shoved me back toward the stairs. I grabbed her arm in fear as I pitched back into emptiness, but she faltered, her body colliding into mine and we were falling together. I flailed, nails desperately scratching at the wall, but her weight sent us hurtling down into darkness. Stone steps battered my body, knocking my head and jamming my shoulder and hip. Sickening thunks and blows that knocked the wind from me.

At last I struck the cool floor at an odd angle and lay still, denying the blinding pain coursing up my leg and through my pelvis. It wasn't serious. It couldn't be. I'd escaped the tragic ending I had been dreading.

Hadn't I?

I struggled to roll over, to orient myself in the dark, feeling every place the steps had struck my flesh. I merely had to keep hidden from Jane Fawley, and I'd be all right. Where was she?

I rolled the heavy weight off my torso, and realized the weight was her. She lay slumped and crooked in the dark, and the dull thud of truth struck me—she was dead.

I scrambled to stand, fumbling about the chilly walls for a doorway, a window. Anything that led out.

It was this place, wasn't it? Something about this theater. Jane Fawley and I both found and lost ourselves in the pursuit of significance, allowed it to destroy us.

I turned a corner and light gleamed through a dirty window high up in the distant wall. I clawed my way up toward it and hoisted myself, pushing up off crates as dull aches and sharp pains made themselves known all along the side of my chest and my right leg.

I forced myself up those crates and yanked that window open, grasping the frame to climb up and pull myself through to my waist. I pulled and strained, but my skirts were a bulk and a weight, refusing to go through the small opening. With a strangled cry, I forced my body further, then collapsed onto the ground and shook. Rain pelted my upturned cheek like little pebbles, and I lay there, accepting it for what seemed like forever. I was too heavy, or my arms too weak.

Then there were voices. "I've found her!" Boots pounded on the street, then Philippe was there, guiding my body from the window and scooping me up like a pile of sodden rags on the street, asking a hundred questions as he carried me.

"Tovah. We must find Tovah." My words were jumbled, but he understood. "And Jane."

"Jane? Tovah's with the others. Came out the back way. Where are you hurt? How much did you inhale?"

"I'm all right. I just need to get home. Is the fire—"

"It's controlled." He wiped hair off my wet face.

"But is everyone safe?"

"Two stagehands were injured—they'll recover. The audience stampeded the exits, but the fire didn't move past the stage. And you?" He searched me frantically. "You're hurt?"

"I told you, I'll be fine." My story had reached its dreaded scene, and I was still here. I had survived the fire—and been rescued by my principal dancer, not abandoned. He shifted me closer, bringing a severe jolt of pain in my leg, but I forced myself to relax into his arms, sinking against his chest in a way I'd only dreamed of. Rescue for rescue. We were even.

But he still owed me that dance.

37

We both wore an air of ruin, the theater and I. Sagging defeat that went deep. That was my thought the following week as I stood in the doorway of the now-forsaken auditorium. There had been a buzz among the dancers at Mama Jo's that Craven would rise again, and that we'd all be dancing just as soon as the stage could be cleaned up and made ready for use.

Yet I knew in my bones that everything was different now. I knew it with every limping step I took up the aisle, felt it in the hush of ruin. For a week I'd attempted to stretch out the pain, to ease myself back into dancing, but the pain had only swelled and stiffened. I'd visited a surgeon to see about it, and he'd told me plainly my right knee might not fully recover, and I'd be unable to dance for at least six months. I'd set aside his pessimism—he wasn't a dancer, after all—but now his words haunted me. Strangled me.

A door slammed, the bang echoing from the main entrance. Someone was at the offices. With a backward glance at the stage, at the tragic Craven auditorium, I limped back down the aisle and through the doors toward the offices and paused in the grand theater entrance.

Bellini emerged from his office, blinking away his shock at seeing me. His dislike was still evident in his posture toward me. "I suppose you know they're counting on you now. The entire stage area needs to be rebuilt, and with no theater this season we must take the company abroad and make a sensation out of Minna . . . and you."

"Me?"

"You created quite a stir with the press at the preview. They're all talking about what you'll do next, and they'll buy tickets just to find out. Wretched as it is, it may just be all we have left. You can bring ticket sales, and that's what Craven needs more than anything right now. I hope you're prepared to work harder than you have in your entire life. Fournier already has it laid out and has negotiated several appearances on the continent. Jack must approve the choreography of course, to make certain it plays to what strengths you have and disguises your weaknesses."

If only he knew how extensive my weaknesses had become.

"We must make something sensational on the stage, and—"

"I cannot." I clung to the doorframe. "I'm sorry sir, but I cannot do any of this."

"I beg your pardon?"

"I've come here to give my notice. I won't be dancing anymore this season."

"Your *notice*?" His eyebrows descended low over narrowed eyes. "You've signed a contract. You cannot simply walk away."

"The season's almost over as it is." My last shreds of confidence melted under his hard stare. I fumbled about for my purse, which of course was not with me. "And I'll repay the theater. For everything. The scholarship, all the training. It'll take time, but—"

"Repay?" His face was red.

I straightened my shoulders against the weight settling upon them. "As I said, it'll take time, but I have every intention of making it up to you all. I hope this most recent performance has proved—"

He banged the doorframe. "You *foolish* girl! Have you any idea what instruction in Paris costs? Respectable boarding near the opera house? Private training with one of the most renowned tutors on the continent? More money than you'll ever see, and plenty of favors called in besides. No, you'll never be able to *repay* it."

I stiffened. "Then I suppose you'll merely have to accept what I can give. I realize curiosity will have worn off by the time I can return, but I do hope you accept me back so I may continue to carry out what I owe you. It may take years, but I *will* make it all worth your while."

I turned on my heel, sincerely hoping my words would prove true. I nearly doubled over at the pain in my knee, along my hip, and limped as fast as I could down the corridor, past the ruined stage, and on to the materials room and privacy. The theater had ruined me, in a way, for no respectable place—even a washhouse—would have me now.

He was right, I couldn't simply walk away from the contract. I had given my word. Besides, what would become of me? Of Lily? I'd paid her way quite a bit lately. I'd sent a boy to fetch her on my way here to see exactly what her current situation was, and meanwhile I forced myself to stretch.

I'd accomplished a great deal in my life by sheer determination, and I wouldn't stop now. Injuries healed. Pain lessened. It would only take time and dedication—if not this season, then next. Giving in now was simply not an option. Finally with my muscles warm, I braved a simple *relevé* and pain seared through my leg in both directions, dropping me to the floor.

"A star, you say?" she'd overheard an investor say of her. Some star. A shooting star, perhaps. A bright flash, followed by a quick plummet to earth. But how could this be? I cried out into the silence of my mind, and despair was all that returned. God was utterly silent. I began to wonder if I'd imagined everything concerning him. I certainly felt no measure of peace now, no sense of his presence.

I set out candle stubs on ladder rungs, on weathered tables, a circle of light for my dancing floor, and gently worked on the injured knee, forcing myself to relax through the pain. I inhaled deeply in the subtle candle glow and wound Mama's music box with a hairpin. Dancing was all the value left in my life. In me. I'd been forced to release my mother—I wasn't ready to let go of ballet too.

I stilled in the chilly room when I sensed another presence behind me. The door had swung open—I could feel the slight breeze of it. I forced myself up to standing and turned.

"Lily! Oh, am I relieved to see you. I've so much to—"

"I've only come to say goodbye." Lily looked older somehow. Resolute. Perhaps it was the dainty hat perched at a becoming angle on her head. Her garments even made her look more a lady than a walker-on at a second-rate theater, which was her latest bid for work. "I've decided to accept a governess position at a country estate."

Governess. That sounded moral—reasonable. Lily was neither of those things. I straightened and swallowed, waiting for, dreading, the rest.

It came. "He's promised to take care of me."

The captain. I could tell by the armed way she stood before me, shield up and ready to do battle. "But, Lily, you've a fine young man from—"

"That isn't love. Nothing close to it." Her full lip quivered. "You cannot go back, you know. Once you've tasted the real thing, everything else is vinegar in one's mouth."

I glared, turned away, and cranked Mama's music box until that hairpin broke. Then I swept into second position, my arched back facing her. *He* was the vinegar, that wretched man. She'd soon taste it when the sweetness had worn away. The music I'd so loved in childhood pinged through the empty room, hitting a few odd notes. It sounded rusty and old. Outdated. Slightly off. Yet familiar and homey.

"I've no reason to stay any longer. Mama's gone, and you never needed me. I want to have real love in my life. I won't settle. I won't."

I pointed my toes and spun on my good leg, welcoming the dull ache. Shards of pain shot through the bad leg. My spins grew tighter and faster.

So did her voice. "For pity's sake, Ella, answer me!"

The pain in my lifted knee was muffled by whatever was now piercing my heart. One of the candle stubs sputtered out.

"I've been offered something beautiful, and I want to take hold of it while I can. I won't stand on some antiquated principles and watch love pass me by. I want to seize it. Can you understand? Can you, even a little?"

I swept my arms overhead, refusing to allow her words to penetrate. To settle in as reality. I'd had too much of that lately.

The music jarred suddenly—a whirring sound. I spun as Lily

heaved that delicate box against the wall with an animalistic grunt. "*Listen* to me, will you?"

The box splintered, springs rolling across the floor, the ballerina spinning on her side. I froze. A line had been crossed. Trampled. The precious pieces of my childhood lay scattered among the rubble on the floor. It had been a gift to Mama from her parents so many years ago, one of the only trinkets she brought with her, and then she'd given it to me. It was a sacred moment of my childhood I'd never forget.

Two more candles flicked out. My childhood was dying a very sudden death in every way, piece by piece ripped away. Consumed by flames.

I crouched, fingering a splintered box piece as my heart pounded in my ears. Every muscle throbbed. Tensed and released. "You're better than this, Lily. Respectable. You'd found a good man, were on your way to a happy life, and—"

"No! This was *your* idea, living with all this virtue and pointless restraint. I never wanted to be respectable—only loved."

I looked up at her delicate face contorted with anger, lost and helpless. I should speak, attempt to undo what was about to happen, but my tongue had hardened to the roof of my mouth.

"Goodbye, Ella." Her voice was softer, her shadowed face a mix of vulnerability and childlike determination that I hadn't seen since her mother had died years ago. "I hope you understand." She turned in a whirl of white lawn skirts and showed me her back for the very last time. At last I knew—I had done the right thing. Not for Lily, but for the child, once bundled against the winter night in my cloak, whom she never could have properly loved.

38

*t*ánd. *Get up. Go after her.* My leg—it wouldn't even straighten. It was as locked as my words. I should cry out for her—or for help. I should call upon God. Should, should, should. So much I *should* do. But couldn't. Stony and wretched inside, I swept together all the broken pieces of that music box and bowed my head.

I will make thy name to be remembered in all generations: therefore shall the people praise thee for ever and ever.

Another fire, and so much had been lost. Ruined. My heart ached with unquenchable pain when I thought of Jane Fawley, Lady Gower, who had died wrapped up in the bitterness that had plagued her.

Yet somehow I had been spared. All this twisting and re-shaping of my heart, all God had brought me through, was in vain. *No, you'll never be able to repay it.* I could do nothing for God. For the theater. Nothing for anyone. *What good am I to you now, Lord? Why rescue me at all? What on earth do you want from me?*

It never had made sense, God's personal pursuit of me. The longer the pain wore on, and my dim future stretched before me, the less I believed it had ever truly happened. And that thought made life seem bleak.

As I lay there trembling, distant pops of footfall echoed through the heart of the building. A man's long stride, somewhere deep within the theater. The structure around me creaked and groaned under life's heavy weight, shifting on its foundation as wind pushed and pulled on its walls. Another of the candle stubs—now a puddle of wax—sputtered and died, turning to a long curl of smoke, and the room grew even dimmer.

I lifted my gaze as a massive figure blacked out the light from the passageway. It was Fournier, the Great Fournier, whose name meant "oven" and whose standards I'd nearly ruined myself attempting to reach. "You're leaving." It was a statement rather than a question, and he looked more uncomfortable than I'd ever seen him. He wouldn't step inside.

"I am, I'm afraid." I swallowed, forcing myself to hold his gaze so he could see my sincerity. "I'm ever so grateful for the chance—truly, more than you could know. I'll do anything I can to repay the investment. I know it was quite a lot and—"

"A lot. Yes."

"I'll give everything I can, however possible, until you are satisfied that I have repaid the contract."

"Don't bother. You can't."

A fresh wave of *not enough* passed over me.

He crossed his arms over his broad chest. "Why?"

I owed him the truth. "I cannot dance anymore." I wanted to cry. "At least, not right now. In time I may heal, but I've been injured, and I . . . well, I won't be of much use to you." I took a deep breath. "I never did belong here, did I?"

He stiffened, backing into the corridor, as if his body was suddenly compelling him to leave. He looked hurt, as though

I were personally rejecting him. "I didn't bring you here to be of *use* to me. What do I care about any of that?" With that, he spun on his heel and left the room.

I sat in shock for a moment, then I pushed up onto my feet and went limping through the darkened corridors to find him. He had vanished though, and I saw only Mama Jo in the green-room.

She turned from balling up strewn silks and fabric and came to stand before me. "What has happened, Miss Blythe? What have you said to Fournier?"

"I've just given my notice and the man seems unwilling to accept it. I'm afraid I've cost him a great deal. And now I will cost him this theater since I cannot dance. The money he could be using now to save the theater was spent on years of training and . . . Oh, it's all such a mess."

"He's asked me to have your things sent to his house. If you agree, that is. He does not wish you cast out in the street."

I blinked. She couldn't be serious. "But whatever for?"

She shrugged. "Perhaps he's lonely, wishing for a ward to keep him company. Or perhaps you remind him of someone. He lost his only daughter years ago, you know, and he's not been the same. They say she was a dancer too, and he was quite hard on her. She left her father's house on bad terms with him."

I gripped the chair nearest me, digging in my nails. "Indeed."

"You don't look much like her—at least, the few times I met her as a child—but he did say something about your having similar shoes when you auditioned for the scholarship. I came to believe that was the reason for his unusual favor toward you."

"Favor?" I breathed out the word.

She patted my arm. "Believe it or not, he thought a great

deal of you. He took extra time with you because he saw what you could become. Just like he did once with his daughter."

I could hardly breathe as the truth of everything settled into my mind.

"Give him a chance, ma petite. He may be gruff, but he's been hurt badly. He misses his little Viola. He could use a bit of sweetness in his house, I suspect. If you've no other plans, that is."

"No." I quivered inside. "No other plans." I paced back to the materials room and fetched the little ballerina still attached to her mechanism from the box, turning it over in my hands. I limped slowly past the stage where my mother had seen her rise and fall, where my parents had fallen in love, and out the auditorium doors toward the one man who still truly loved her.

Who truly loved me.

It was impossible. Unbelievable. Shocking in its unexpected beauty. All the bound-up tension of striving dropped away with each step down the center of that auditorium, the clanging echoes of *not enough* falling silent in the opulent place that had yet one more surprise to unfurl for me. I belonged here, more than I could have ever imagined, and it had known all along, drawing me in, embracing me until I fully understood. And it was all tied together by those scarlet slippers.

Enchanted, indeed.

Fournier stood with his back to me just inside his office, and I approached quietly, with the gentleness of knowing. Yet I had to be certain. Turning the little dancer and her broken mechanism about in my hand, I held it out and spoke. "I don't suppose you recognize this, do you, sir?"

He turned, looking at me and then the little ballerina. He paled as his fingers pulled on the narrow beard, all the way down to its point, then he scooped her in his palm as if she were the actual person to whom he'd given her. Lowering with much squeaking into his leather chair, he rummaged about in a narrow desk drawer and drew out a key, fitting it neatly into the mechanism where we'd always jammed the hairpin. With a firm flick of his fingers, the dancer I thought forever ruined sparked into motion and familiar strains emanated from it, even without the beautiful box around her. So much brokenness, but so much was being set to rights too.

He looked up to me, and in that moment everything came into sharp focus, a warmth pouring through my soul as I finally believed it. "You belonged here before you ever tried. You still belong." He looked down at that dancer turning on his palm, and tears began an awkward journey down the many crevices of his old face. "She only did it for me—taking Delphine's place—to save the theater I loved so much. She was a far superior being in every way. Inside and out, she . . . was . . . *magnificent*." His great chest shuddered.

I could only nod in humble agreement, full to the brim to know Mama had been loved and appreciated as thoroughly as she'd always deserved.

"She never told me she had a child. We hardly spoke after she married, but you must be . . . I can see her in you. And the shoes." He rose and walked around the desk to stand beside me. "Please stay, Miss Blythe. Ella. Whoever you are. You have a place at my home, if you wish it."

His deep-set eyes begged me to say yes, but I hesitated, picturing the overwhelming London home where I'd met with investors.

"Perhaps your mother has told you awful things about her old father and you don't care to be around me, but . . ."

"I shouldn't like to impose." My voice was scratchy when I found it, but my resistance fell away in layers. How pointless it all had been—that striving and worrying, forcing my way into a place I already had free admittance. The absurd freedom of that made me want to laugh.

His face fell. "There's no one at my house to be put out. My wife was lost to me some years ago, and my little girl . . ." His expression crumpled. "Well, there's no one."

"Not 'no one.'" I braved a smile and reached out to touch his arm, overflowing with affection for the man who had so loved my mother. "You *do* have a granddaughter."

The old man squeezed my hand, an involuntary flicker, a steeling against the emotions surfacing in his features. He lifted my hand, first holding it to his chest, then dipped his head to kiss it. He spoke with a broken voice. "I always regretted how I pushed her. How my ambitions drove her to that practice room late at night . . . especially *that* night. And I promised myself when I heard about the girl in the red shoes that I would do better this time. Have I ruined everything?"

Thank goodness for those shoes, and for a sister who all but forced me to wear them to the scholarship audition for luck. I smiled, squeezing his hand, revelling in the beauty of belonging. "You've nothing to fear. Whatever you do or fail to do, you are, after all, my grandfather. And as I've no one else, I'm afraid you're quite stuck with me."

39

Grandfather strode into the room where a fire popped and crackled, and I set my book on my lap to look up at him. He said only four words. "They're beginning to talk."

It had been months since I'd come to live with him, and I'd become used to his proclivity for walking into a room and dropping a few spare words that made no sense on their own. "Are they? And what are they saying?"

"That Jack's ballet should be run again, the ending completed. We've whetted their appetite, and they want to know what happened. And they'd come back to *her* theater to see the performance too."

I tucked my feet under me and looked at his face shadowed by the bouncing flames. Life had become comfortable, filled with tender moments and blessed quiet in this generous old house, and we'd worked together to keep Craven's ballet company performing across the continent. It was a balm to my soul, and it made me long for the heady rush of being part of a performance. More so as time passed, although I hadn't admitted it.

"Jack has been working on a new production of it—smoothing out the rushed pieces, making it even better."

I frowned. "That last one had plenty of merit as it was." There was something precious and sacred about that creation. Would someone else play my woodland sprite role? Would they use the same choreography that had sprung from that deep well inside Jack and me together?

He settled into the chair across from me and looked into my face. There had been a time that he'd asked all about my mother, about what had happened to her and what she'd been like in the years of her marriage that they hadn't spoken. Then, once he'd felt a sense of completion about it, he'd simply stopped asking, like a spigot turned off. His face held that curious glow again, though. "Would it set well with you to have her story told? It wouldn't trouble you, would it?"

"It would please me."

He gave one firm nod. "You will, of course, dance as her." The words were spoken so simply, as if he were merely requesting that I shut the garden door behind me.

"Dance . . . the lead?"

"It'll be the story on display, of course, not the dancers. You needn't worry about mistakes. Stiffness. No one would notice, as long as the climax came this time. And no matter what happens, how many times you fall . . ." One corner of his mouth lifted in that quiet smile I'd come to recognize. "You still have a place to sleep."

I smiled, ducking my head. "Aren't you forgetting something? I don't dance anymore."

"Not when anyone's watching, anyway."

My neck warmed. "You've seen—?"

"You cannot keep away, and you never will. We'll have that knee examined if you wish it, but it does seem to be quite healed . . . and put into use already."

The heat rose to my cheeks. "I assume you've discussed the matter with Jack Dorian? He might have a fair bit to say on who plays the lead." And who doesn't. "Besides that, I wouldn't care to work with him." Being around Jack felt like nearing the edge of a balcony and looking down. He stretched me and poked at my comfort. And when he was near, all I could think about was the last time I'd spoken to him. What I'd told him, and his response.

He heaved himself up against the arm of the chair. "And why is it that Jack Dorian seems so intolerable to you of late? For the past year you've flinched at every mention of his name."

The man truly did notice everything. Every last thing. I may have left the stage, but my life was still on display a bit.

"Has he done something to you?"

"No, it's simply that he's arrogant, he's impetuous and utterly wild, untamable and flirtatious, with such grandiose notions that he will always bring trouble. You should see the way he is around the other dancers, Grandfather. He makes me even more thankful to know someone like Philippe, who is so utterly different." I swallowed, hoping he wouldn't see this for the wretched excuse it was. "I shouldn't work on his ballet. Truly, it's best if I don't."

"We might be able to arrange private practices for you, just as we did for my Viola. It isn't unheard of. You wouldn't have to work with any of them for very long."

My voice grew soft as temptation played at the fringes of my heart. "Perhaps someday, if . . . things change . . . at Craven." Like the hiring of a new choreographer.

"If you're waiting for Craven to be rebuilt, it won't happen. Not without this ballet, at least. The insurance money did help a little, but I cannot afford a total rebuild of the stage area if no one will come, and nothing short of *Le Fantome de Craven* will make them."

"The Ghost of Craven. A fitting name." I sighed. "I cannot do it, though. You know I'd do anything to help you, Grandfather. Especially after all you've done—"

He stepped closer and drew out a tissue-wrapped parcel, placing it on my lap. "Think it over and we'll talk again." He turned and walked toward the door. Conversations always ended when he decided that they should, his cane the period that punctuated it.

Had he not heard my refusal? "My answer will be the same."

"One cannot escape who she is." He paused, one hand on the door. "By the way, you'd be dancing opposite Philippe Rousseau. I assumed that would be a welcome treat."

I caught my breath, melting from somewhere deep inside. *Dancing opposite Philippe Rousseau.* "What makes you think—"

"Jack told me." He hesitated, fingers resting on the edge of the door. "You know, if you desire something as deeply as all that, you have only to tell me. I delight in giving you these things."

I smiled. How strange it was to be loved this way—and by him, the Great Fournier. When he rose to go, I untied the string and folded back the paper and there they were—a new pair of scarlet slippers, all my own. I clutched them with wonder, running my fingers over the red satin and remembering the day I'd laid similar ones on *her* lap.

I looked up at the doorway, and Fournier stood there watching me.

"How did you—"

"Where do you think they came from in the first place? I gave both Jane and your mother those red shoes myself, before every glorious performance."

They were exquisite. Timeless. Just like my mother. The sight of them brought me back to myself, stirring my desire for beauty, for being a part of it all, once again.

I lifted my book as he slipped out, but my heart pounded and my mind wandered back to that old forgotten materials room on a starry night a million years ago, when a girl with these red satin shoes danced the most brilliant pas de deux of her life with a most perfect partner. Philippe had been by a few times over the months, but he disappeared often still. I had not allowed my heart to pursue anything with him, or to even hope.

Yet with the warmth of the fireplace, I felt myself melting into his steady arms once again, following his movements as if our very souls shared a rhythm. How deeply I still felt that dance, how ardently. I could have that again. It was being offered to me if only I would accept it. I looked down at the shoes again, my fingers still running over their surface, along the length of the ribbons. Then before I knew it, quite against my will, the dancer's heart in me was awakening, sparking with life, and answering yes against the silence of the room.

The adventure began a mere three days after my reluctant acceptance, and nothing went as I'd imagined. Dancing with Philippe in rehearsals had been harder than I had anticipated. With everyone watching, the pressure of a grand performance, there was none of the smooth magic of that first midnight dance in the materials room years ago. My own heightened awareness of the situation, the magnitude of a dream now reached, infused my limbs with a terrible awkwardness that was at times hard to press through. He was patient always, working through the paces over and over again, but I often left frustrated with myself.

We saw each other only in the theater in those days, which was for the best. I couldn't fathom how my parents had carried on a love affair off the stage while dancing as partners on it. I was simply too rattled.

It was manageable until the night before we were to perform, and suddenly after the final dress rehearsal, I couldn't stop shaking. I ran down the empty corridor, past the glowing sconces on the wall, and released my breath in the dusty old materials room that continued to be my sanctuary. Yet it wasn't sanctuary I needed. I had once again become afraid of heights—afraid of dancing the lead before the wild expectations of a packed audience, afraid of grasping my years-long dream that had been at star height for so long—and I desperately needed someone to remind me how to fly.

Philippe, kind and attentive, had his feet too firmly planted on the ground for such things, and there was no one else who understood. No one who compared. Once I'd experienced a night lit with vibrant stars, every other light seemed dim and inconsequential.

I'd hardly spoken to Jack since returning for his ballet. He flitted from this complication to that, attending everything at once as he'd done before, and he didn't stand in place long enough to have a conversation. Perhaps he intended it that way.

I caught him looking at me a handful of times throughout the rehearsals, but I couldn't read his bright-eyed look. I had hoped in time the scars his rejection left on my heart would heal, but they only intensified every time I watched his vibrant energy and remembered what it was to be touched by it.

Still shaking, and growing desperate, I returned to the backstage area that had emptied so quickly, but Jack was gone. In the familiar hush of the place, I walked across the great space illuminated only by two high covered gaslights and frowned at the emptiness—but his coat was still there. That gray wool thing with large black buttons in place of brass, because Jack had enough shine for his entire person.

I walked over to it and picked it up, holding it close and drinking deeply of the trapped scent of him. It was all life and vitality mingled with strong black tea and warm sunshine. I closed my eyes and was back in that barn looking at the trapeze in the loft, that smile radiating nearby. I could *feel* it, much as one felt the sun.

A tiny sound shuddered through the empty space and I spun to look. A small gust of wind curled over my skin. No one was visible, but I could sense someone there. I waited for several heart-pounding seconds, but no one appeared. The past would always haunt this old theater, it seemed—all the tragic love stories played out on the stage and behind it, all the passion released here vibrating through the emptiness with an air of tragedy.

Mine included.

I slipped that coat around me and held it close like an embrace and remembered him holding me firmly as we flew through the darkness on the trapeze, my panic ebbing away in his solid hold on me. In that coat I smelled freedom from fear, freedom from rules, freedom to be wholly myself as I had never been with any other human. Even Mama had held unspoken expectations for me, but Jack—and only Jack—embraced me fully, then pulled me up with a sense of adventure into more.

I buried my face into the oversized sleeves, hugging it tighter about me, and let the tears fall on it, allowing myself at long last to acknowledge the deep pain of his rejection—and my desperate desire to be in his arms once again. A light swish of air drew me upright, had me looking about. I clung to the coat and walked around, but again there was no one. No one but me, Craven, and all its collective tragedies.

40

*L*ights blinded me. The curtain swept back with a whoosh of cooling air. Every seat, every balcony, even the aisles were filled to capacity as we opened Jack's ballet for a second time. The stage had been rebuilt over long months, with a loan against this performance's profits.

Smooth and steady, the music from the orchestra pit climbed in volume and intensity. I rose in a slow spin, unfolding my body and stretching heavenward. It felt magnificent to dance onstage again, to offer my body as a living sacrifice in worship. *Hello, Father.* I swept up first one arm, then the other, feeling the music of Fournier's orchestra sink into my marrow and animate my limbs, inviting me into spins and lifts.

I'd promised myself I'd go easy now that I was back, and I had at rehearsals, but once the music flooded my being, I couldn't help it—passion came out in full measure and I danced with it. The cellos wound me up like the key in Mama's music box, and I flew through my turns, whipping about with my eyes on that peep, thinking of Mama, thinking of Jack.

I breathed in. A double fouetté, then an arabesque. I pushed myself, giving my mind over to the music.

The end of the first act came quickly, and I grand jeté'd to stage left and collapsed into the curtain with all my spent passion, huffing and holding my head, cooled by the moisture trailing down every crevice.

The Great Fournier hovered over me, his shadow stretching across most of the backstage area. "Not terrible, for your first attempt."

I lifted my head to smile at him. "Not my first."

"First in a while."

It was then, as my racing heart steadied itself, that I noticed the twinkle in his quiet face—that knowing glimmer in his eye. Lily used to wear it too, and I knew what it meant. "What? What have you done? Who's in the audience?"

He lifted an eyebrow. "It's never about who's watching—you should know that."

"What is it, then?"

He heaved a deep sigh, clasping hands behind his back. "He's the one who made the promise. I'm merely making sure he keeps it."

Philippe. "You've told him then, have you? About how I've wished to dance with him again." This is one outcome I'd never have guessed from telling Jack my story so long ago. Served me right for opening my mouth.

"We had quite the talk. You've no idea what you've done to him."

My breath came in gasps.

"Well, it's too late now. It's been a long time coming, and you owe it to the both of you to see this vow through."

Then the callboy came for me, his urgent whisper beckoning me back to my position. It would start with a lengthy divertissement before the hero's entrance, so I posed alone behind that curtain, feet in second, the cool hush centering me, allowing me to regain my footing with God. With a long inhale, I reached my fingers and my soul up to him, wrapping myself in the Psalms.

Bless the Lord, *O my soul: and all that is within me, bless his holy name.*

It was my favorite time, that moment just before the music began and the curtain opened—a sacred rest where my soul settled back in place and the nerves fell away in the presence of something far greater. Then my heart turned to the familiar, soul-centering words.

Be Thou my Vision, O Lord of my heart.

My vision. The only right focal point. I poured myself into that opening movement, and as more dancers joined me on the stage, my thoughts turned to the hero. The principal dancer who would soon be joining me. It was a perfect bookend to my theater life—for I'd decided this would be my last public performance—this dance with Philippe. So much had changed in me since then, and I found it was no longer my dream. Perhaps because I'd discovered what it was to dance a pas de deux with my heavenly Father, and that was plenty.

Orchestra music began and the curtain swept open. Unfurling my limbs, I twirled out before a hushed audience and once again wrapped myself up in the music of the theater, alive under the lights and invigorated by the dance. I twirled between the wooden trees and swept down to brush the floor and sweep up again.

Then even though I closed my eyes, I felt him join me on the stage, all the way on the opposite end. It was time. Memories flooded my being, taking me back to that night, then to the star-filled dreams and prepared speeches that followed. How much had occurred in all those years.

Then he came, bounding across the floor to a burst of applause, the hero who used to haunt my dreams and alight my heart with hope. He whooshed by in a cool breeze, and finally I dared lift my head for a glance—but oh! There was no Philippe with his dark hair and darker aura slicing dramatically through space. It was Jack Dorian, vivid and alive, commanding attention with contagious delight, his every buoyant leap an invitation to join his high spirits. How powerful—how very dramatic he was.

Shards of pain mingled with inescapable magnetism. Despite everything, I was drawn to him. I lifted my arms, rising onto my toes, and in three beats he had swept me up into his dance, his heady rhythm, and we flew about the stage together, our energy mingling and multiplying. He looked at me as we danced close, searching deeply as he always did, likely seeing my entire heart on my face. In the end, it was Jack Dorian I'd not been able to forget. On and on we danced, apart, then together, our bodies circling. "Where is Philippe? Fournier told me—"

He leaned close, and I caught the fresh scent of him again. "I have a secret to tell you." His deeply familiar voice lighted sparks in me—a flame I'd hoped was put to rest. He was breathless as he led me. "We've danced this way before." A breath. It was *my speech*. The one I meant to give Philippe. I spun out, then he pulled me close again. "You may not recognize me, but I've never forgotten you."

I caught my breath, stared directly into that sharply handsome face that glowed so vibrantly. I couldn't speak. We moved apart and I focused on my turns, my gaze locking onto that peep.

Then in two leaps and a turn he was again before me, his face inches from mine, his body poised in the dramatic pantomime of his character. "I promised you we'd dance together on this stage one day. I don't keep a lot of things, but I keep my promises, love."

Then he captured my hand, and we were spinning, spinning, blurring the world into a haze of muted colors, with only his presence, those incredible eyes shining out at me. That was the moment, caught up in the pas de deux, the heady delight of it, I realized that I'd danced with Jack Dorian before. The perfect harmony of our movements, the infectious delight spilling forth, the inescapable draw of his heart on display in every move—with a sudden rush it felt *familiar*, and I knew.

All this time I'd danced at Craven, I'd had, as usual, the wrong focal point. It wasn't Philippe—it had *never* been Philippe. I could merely stare as we danced opposite each other, our bodies circling back and forth, round and round under our clasped hands held overhead, our gazes mingling and catching.

"Lesson five. Always look beyond the greasepaint." At the sight of my shock, he offered a most unsettling, roguish smile. "What, you think this is the first time I've stood in for that poor sot?" He winked.

He twirled me out, then I spun back in close, and he anchored me to him for a brief stolen moment together.

I spun away, letting the music carry me once again, winging my way about the stage as I had in that cramped old materials room so many years ago. It was the same—orchestra music sinking into marrow, the greatness of the theater billowing around me, and a most unusual man watching me with unguarded admiration.

In a moment, the corps and the sujet dancers swarmed out

around us, taking over the stage. I sailed with one final lift, grand jeté'ing into the wings where I clung to the curtains, trying to catch my breath, my runaway thoughts, as reality circled and refused to completely settle. Jack. Jack Dorian. He had been the cause of that magical pas de deux.

Then he was there, slipping into the folds of the heavy curtain with me, holding me up as he always did, emboldening me with a mere look. I could see it as I looked into that familiar countenance—that vibrant North Wind with the glowing blue face alive with delight and energy, buoyant of spirit and eager of heart, inviting me to dance, seeing the ballerina I could not even see in myself, daring to draw it out of me.

"That Philippe," he whispered, breathless. "He has no idea what he missed, all for the sake of drowning those sorrows in his cups. And I, with a wig and a few spare hours, got it all."

Dear Jack. I touched his face, his cheek. "You should have told me."

"What, and have you fall in love with some romantic ideal?" His face sobered, that deeply vulnerable look coming through his handsome features. "I tried. I tried to tell you, in all those little outings. All the silly gestures that mimicked that night, hoping you'd remember. In the end, I couldn't bear to tell you outright. I had it in my head to wait for the perfect moment— the one in which you fell in love with me in the light of day, without the fairy tale, but . . ."

I dropped my hand. "That took a terrible amount of waiting."

He lifted my hand back to his cheek and held it there. It was smooth and strong. "I wanted nothing less than the real thing from you, Ella Blythe. Not a fanciful ballet that would end in two hours' time."

"What's that supposed to mean?" My voice was soft, my senses full of him.

A smile flickered against my hand. "I'm envisioning a much longer pas de deux between us." He dropped my hand and touched my hair, somehow drawing me closer. "We'll stumble, we'll collide a time or two, but then we'll hold each other up, lift the other closer to the heavens. It'll be you and me, always partners, always moving together." He closed his eyes and leaned in close, kissing my forehead as if bestowing a blessing. "There's simply no one quite like you."

I blinked away tears. "I thought you hated me. The look on your face . . ."

He ran his thumb along my jawline, then dipped it toward the topaz he'd once given me hanging in the little hollow of my throat. "It's the flaws that tell us when something's real. And what's real . . . well, that's quite valuable indeed." He placed a solemn kiss on my temple. "Do you know, I believe it is your flaw that has saved me."

"Oh?" I smiled from my heart, clear through to my lips.

"You'd just as well have saved your breath trying to convince me about God in all your little speeches. For all your talking and prattling on, it was what you refused to tell me for so long that finally rescued me. I'm so very broken, you know, and God so unfathomably *good*. Yet . . . yet if he could pursue and abide with a girl who'd done the worst possible thing I could imagine—what was once done to me—well then, just maybe he could tolerate a wretched man like myself." He rested his forehead on mine. "The question is . . . can you?"

A bubble of delight bobbed in my heart and I smiled up at him. "It was never about what you do or don't do." *I just love you. Just love who you are.* My breath shuddered as I acknowledged the truth I'd held so close. It was too much—too much to voice just yet.

"Fournier tried to convince me months ago when we started this ballet, but I wouldn't believe it. You were so gone on Philippe Rousseau before, that all I could do was try to help you reach him. Until . . . well, until last night."

"Oh?"

A smile tipped the corner of his mouth. "I've never seen anyone . . . *smell* my coat."

I buried my laughter into his chest and clung to him, feeling the heat rise in my face. I *had* heard someone last night.

Then he pushed me back, holding me by the shoulders as he always did before saying something vital. "I've nothing to offer. My mother the silk heiress has officially disowned me—legally and otherwise. It seems she has quite the passel of legitimate children among whom to divide the pieces of the pie, so I'll not see a farthing."

I leaned close, resting my head on his chest, feeling his heartbeat, absorbing his presence. "As I said, it was never about what you do or what you have. You are enough, Jack. An adventure and a half by yourself."

His expression melted into gladness. Relief. His arms tightened around me, then released and tightened again as if he could not get enough. He lifted his smiling countenance, leaving a trail of kisses along the side of my face. "You called me Jack."

"I've done it before."

"Yes . . . but this time you meant it." He brushed the loose strands from my face as he leaned close, and he sought my lips with his and kissed me with all the passion and wonder and heady vulnerability that had swept me up the last time. I pressed into him, feeling the extent of my devotion to him, and the same in return from him. When I moved back, he did not release me from his hold, as if afraid I'd dart, so I looked straight up into the most dangerously handsome face I'd ever seen—the golden-haired trifler I'd been warned against, troublemaker . . . abandoned little boy.

"How's about this, love? If your answer is no, spin off stage left and be done with it after the third dance. But if you'll have me, go stage right and then come back to join me for the final sequence." He looked me over as if he couldn't get enough of the sight. "Finish this story standing beside me, as I'd always dreamed you would."

My heart pounded so hard I couldn't speak. I could barely breathe as the music cued up and everything was before us.

He pulled me close again and laid his cheek on my head. "I suppose we'd best go finish. We've a theater full of people dying to know how it ends."

I knew how it ended, though, at least in part. It ran parallel in some ways to the complex story of Delphine Bessette, but here is where it diverged forever. Jack had taught me how to dance as one who already belongs, as one set utterly free, and we'd learned together how to live that way too.

As the music began, I turned back toward the man who'd once pushed me, opened me up to the freedom I'd always possessed, and tugged him along with me. "Come. It's time."

My heart pounded as we danced together on that stage, the perfect symmetry of our movements sweeping us through the song. But it wasn't the audience that made my heart pound so much. It was the last little sequence, the one that hadn't been in this rewritten script. In a moment I'd spin off stage right then burst back upon the scene for the final pas de deux that I had been prepared to dance for all these years, and Jack would sweep me up once again, guiding me along to the end of the performance.

But of course, it wouldn't stop there.

Author Note

There's a huge difference between slaves and children in our standing with God. A slave's worth is primarily in his performance—what he can accomplish that's of value to his master. A child has immense, permanent value no matter what he accomplishes, simply because of who he is—who he is to God.

The root of perfectionism like Ella's is fear—the scarcity mindset of "not enough." And fear is what drives us when we forget who we are and exactly why we belong to God. We act as though we're servants, purposed only with serving God, winning souls, doing good, proving our salvation, even if we know better. Yet we've got it all backward, haven't we? I know I did for many years.

What's your story? How did God connect with you? More than anything, my personal story of being pursued is what solidifies in my mind the truth of why I'm rescued. I did nothing—I wasn't even searching for him at the time. I thought I had him already back then, serving in the church and being connected to the Christian life, but God mercifully decided to get my attention in a personal way, to throw off the scales from my eyes, and show me what he actually wanted from me. You know what it was? Me. Not writing, not being a good enough person, not any kind of ministry or service—just me. Intimacy. Relationship. Father-and-daughter closeness that isn't some small thing orbiting about my life with all the other things I have going on, but something all of life orbits around.

For a long time when he drew near, I couldn't grasp it. I couldn't wrap my head around why an astounding God of such breadth and depth and magnitude would really care to reach out to a broken, messed-up girl who'd fumbled so much in life. He could have anybody, create anybody—why me? Why pursue *any* of broken humanity? It made no sense.

The answer was vivid in my heart within minutes of asking that question—it *doesn't* make sense, and that's the rich definition of grace. It makes about as much sense as a parent's love for a newborn who takes every last shred of its parents' resources, emotionally and physically, and receives its parents' unconditional love, yet it hasn't been able to offer anything in return.

Speaking of children . . .

Little E, sweet girl of my heart to whom this story is dedicated, you're sitting beside me as I write this story—and this note, even—the gentle pressure of your little arm against mine as we both type our "stories." That sort of connection will always be open to you, no matter what. You are my daughter, which is all that's required.

You have the same welcome with your heavenly Father—not related to anything you do or fail to do, but simply by virtue of who you are. Treasure it. Embrace it and lean into it the way you now lean almost unconsciously on my arm. If you ever become wrapped up in striving for love, hoping to gain someone's attention, just know you already have God's full heart (and mine) without doing a thing. You had God's sacrificial love before you were even born, and he paid everything to have you close. Keep that in mind if the world makes you feel neglected, unwanted, or invisible. You aren't. Where it matters, you aren't.

You're his. And that's enough.

Notes on the Era

$\mathcal{M}$uch has changed in ballet since the burgeoning romantic period when Ella's story takes place, and those of you with a dance background may notice the differences.

Most female dancers were required to have a "sponsor" for their rise in theater, as most ballerinas did not earn a living wage. It's much like actors today who must work a side job while trying out for bit parts as they wait to catch their big break.

The greenroom became a marketplace for mistresses with the highest-paying subscribers allowed in for practice, and in some theaters even onto the fringes of the stage during a performance. The dancers vied for the most established, well-to-do abonnés, as these sponsors were called, as much as they did for the lead roles. A dancer's time on the stage ended by her midthirties at best, and she was seldom qualified for respectable work that would earn a living wage, so she depended upon being "set up" by a wealthy benefactor.

Also different from modern ballet, male dancers were the focal point with the women "embroidering their dances" with beauty. Their movements were much more restrained than what we see now too.

As Marie Taglioni brought "en pointe" into popularity, and proved to be the glow of the stage, the focus shifted to female leads for complicated dances and technical feats. Ella Blythe is loosely based on Taglioni's reputation and personality, as well as her fascination with dancing on the very tips of her toes. Much of what we enjoy about ballet today can be traced back to her influence in the earliest years of the Romantic Period.

I have taken some literary license, but for the most part, I tried to remain true to the atmosphere of the theater in Victorian England. I hope you enjoyed this visit to the past.

Visit my YouTube channel for a deeper look at my Victorian theater research and specifically how ballet was different then. I'll be discussing Degas, pointe shoes, and more. Search for my channel "JDpolitano_historical adventurer" on YouTube or find it here: https://www.youtube.com/channel/UCq-3lpb 2rVDXsOqMJX4hA_g.

Discussion Questions

1. Ella is a staunch rule follower. Why do you think she became so dismissive of "the rules" for the little corps de ballet girl who stole her sash? What other times does she break from this character trait in the story, and what brought her to it?

2. Along with that, Ella and her sister see rules very differently. To Ella they are safeguards. To her sister they are restrictions that prevent her from finding real happiness. Yet both let their extreme views ruin things for them. Who do you think is closer to the truth? Why?

3. How does Jack signify the circus and everything wild, while Philippe stands for ballet and all the rules and precision to which Ella is drawn? Which one drew you more?

4. Do you think Jack wanted Ella to lower her standards as she progressed in dance or raise them—or perhaps a bit of both?

5. What was the spiritual significance of Fournier's revelation at the end? Why did it matter to whom Ella belonged, and how do you think that impacted her heart?

6. What is the difference between perfection and excellence, and why does it matter for what we, as humans, create and do?

7. Do you agree with what Ella did years ago to help her sister? What do you see as her truest motivation?

8. What do you consider the defining moment for Ella as a woman and as a dancer? Did it have a positive or negative impact?

9. Ella's mother called ballet a "fleeting art" because dancers and their art are forgotten as soon as they leave the stage. In what ways is that true, and in what ways do you think the impact remains?

10. Throughout the story, which characters lived in freedom? Which didn't?

Turn the Page for an Exclusive Look at

JOANNA DAVIDSON POLITANO'S NEXT RELEASE!

COMING FALL 2022

First Movement

CASTLETON, ENGLAND, 1879

I was playing Berlioz the night my father died, Symphonie in C flat major, with arpeggios smooth as a horse's gallop that left me breathless. I did not smile when I got the news of his death, for that would have been wicked, but I did relax, more than I had allowed myself to in many years. After a moment and several deep breaths to acknowledge the passing of a soul, I lifted my fingers to the ivories and played again from the beginning.

The song was the perfect end to our tumultuous years together, powerful dissonance brimming with deeply textured tones that climbed to a deep, heady climax, then suddenly stopped at the obvious point of conclusion, and the room was empty. Quiet. There was only me, my music, and the grand piano shop downstairs that had filled my home—and my very marrow—with music.

There was a breezy emptiness in my soul at the sudden silence. A sense of unfettered spring air blowing through hollow places. Gone was his company and his uncanny business sense, but so were the sting of fresh lashes across my fingers as I practiced, the silent fight always knotted up in my belly, that menacing voice bellowing through the halls. I grieved the man, but I couldn't say I was unhappy.

In the weeks after, the house became a sort of Beethoven sonata, calm and predictable with frequent trills of beauty, and though I'd always been bored by Beethoven, I came to appreciate boring. I reveled in my freedom, opening like a slow-building minuet that moved from shy flower to strong and richly imagined climax, and it felt life would always go on this way, with this splendid freedom—plenty of air to breathe.

And the chance to do what I'd always meant to do. My entire childhood here had prepared me for the work, this immense rescue mission that was the only thing into which my life could funnel after living with Father, and I was ready, come what may.

My aim was so contrary to London society, to the world's expectations of a lady, that most of my friends would be shocked at what this concert pianist secretly chose to do with her life outside of music. Few people actually knew me, as it turned out. I was a Chopin nocturne, surprising, complex, and impossible to master.

Many tried. I'm happy to report that they all failed.

Well, nearly.

1

Symphonie Fantastique, fourth movement

And those who were seen dancing were thought to be insane
by those who did not hear the music.

~Friedrich Nietzsche

One day in late May of the year 1886, I found myself wrong-
fully imprisoned in the Hurstwell Pauper Lunatic Asylum,
which was unconscionable. I had *never* been a pauper.

I woke in an unfamiliar, damp room, and the music was
entirely wrong. I'd fallen asleep at home in a Beethoven sonata, white and airy wrapped up with pleasant delight and
silky reality and after a few hazy days woken in the dark heart
of Berlioz's Symphonie Fantastique, my head thudding with
deep bassoon, the echoing rhythm of moisture on stone, and
the vague memory of pain. As my mind surfaced from sleep,
collected the memories of my arrival, the bassoon solidified
into a voice—one quite near the foot of my bed. "Don't go too
near. She's moving."

"Waking?"

"Not for several hours. Involuntary muscle spasms, most likely."

Indeed. Either they'd overestimated whatever drug they'd injected into me when I arrived or, as people were wont to do, they underestimated me.

"Will we keep her?" A light timpani voice contrasted with the first.

"I'm not sure yet. It's a rather odd case. Not much background on this one, but she's already proved volatile."

I had fought, hadn't I? My mind swirled with the angst of it, recalling the need to escape. The failure to do so.

"Hysteria?"

"Delusions. She hears music."

"That's rather a pleasant affliction to have—hearing music."

"Not when there isn't any playing."

"Oh. Quite right."

I let the voices lull me into stillness, my body melting into the unforgiving cot that wouldn't suffer a dent from me lying on it. My body was heavy. I didn't fight it. I breathed deeply, but a stench—stale and dry—nearly made me ill.

"Has she a name?"

"Vivienne . . . Vivienne . . . something. I've forgotten. Her last name is of no consequence. She doesn't belong to anyone."

Ouch. Like a pin into a live pincushion.

Scribbles on paper. "Epileptic?"

A frantic rapping on the door interrupted the meeting occurring near my feet, and the door squeaked open. A breathy female voice inserted itself. "Pardon, Doctor. It's the man in the male long-stay ward—he's fainted."

After a blustery exhale, footsteps shuffled, then the door slammed shut.

But it did not lock.

My heart pounded, three beats for every second that swept silently on, drawing those men further from my cell and its unlocked door. My skin grew clammy, a line of moisture gathering along my upper lip and my legs where they lay cemented together. No one came. No one.

I slowly activated my stiff muscles and pushed up on the bed, head to my chest, swinging my heavy legs down and feeling about the cold floor for shoes as I fought the oddest sense of imbalance and weightiness. I could feel the blood recirculating, as if I'd lain comatose for a week. Maybe I had.

Whiteness closed in around the edges of my vision as I lifted my head, and I tried to look around the room, to edge noiselessly off the bed. I saw two of everything, then four, back to two, then only one again, and the air felt thick. My whole body pulsed as I forced myself to stand, holding out my arms for balance.

I could do this. I could. The woman who played an entire piano concerto without a scrap of music, who drew more listeners than her male counterparts, who survived her father, could certainly stand up and walk out the front door of a rotten asylum.

Stretching my neck, my legs, I eased into movement, preparing for whatever would come.

"You're getting on quite well."

The voice to my right slid under my skin and chilled my bones. I turned on wooden legs to see the bassoon-voiced doctor, who had apparently sent his partner on, observing me from against the closed door. "Where . . . ? Who . . . ?" I worked my mouth, but there wasn't enough voice to come out. It was so dry. A cotton-lined tube.

"The Hurstwell Pauper Lunatic Asylum, and your father."

"My . . . *father*?" I clutched the back of a wooden chair. Even from the grave, he controlled my every move. My parched throat could hardly eke out the sounds.

"He brought you in a few days ago, and placed you under our care."

My eyelid twitched hard. "No." Muscles in my neck jerked. I began to shake. Impossible. *Impossible.* I croaked out, "Dead."

"He's dead, you say?" The asylum doctor, a bulldog of a man with a heavy face resting upon the cushion of his neck, availed himself of my bed now that I'd vacated it, perching on the edge and sinking it quite low. "Well, then. Perhaps it was another man." He lifted page after page on his clipboard, scanning for the answer. "I just assumed. I was not here to meet him, of course. It was rather late when you arrived. Ah yes, here—Oh." He blinked, as if absorbing the information he read on my form. He looked up at me, frowning, then back at the paper. "Well, now."

I expelled the aura of perspiration and old moisture clinging to the room. The stench would strangle me. Choke out every bit of breath. "Mistake." I forced out the word from the thickness of my throat as my knees buckled and I collapsed onto an old chair against the wall. "It . . . is . . . a mistake." I coughed, scratching the dry walls of my throat.

He moved me to the bed and scribbled on his paper, not even allowing me the dignity of eye contact. Then came the instruments from his brown leather satchel. First, the listening device, its cold metal horn shoved down the top of my dress. "Hold still."

I cleared my throat. He handed me a small cup of water from the side table, which helped considerably. It cooled going down. "Why am I here?" My voice was scratchy and tight, but functional.

"To get well." He recited the line with unconscious ease.

"What is my affliction?"

"Delusions."

Ah right, he'd said that. It sounded even more ridiculous the second time. "I don't need to be here."

The cold metal found a new spot. "Wouldn't you like to be well again? To stop hearing music and be like everyone else?"

I pinched my lips and lowered my gaze, not answering. His question didn't invite one—the answer seemed obvious to him. "If I stop hearing music, you'll let me out?"

He blinked, as if the notion of my leaving had never occurred to him. "Perhaps." His calm smile had a numbing effect on me. Not the pleasant sort, but the way one's leg feels after its owner has been lost in a book too long and forgotten it has been tucked under the body. "We'll just wait and see, shall we? I'm Superintendent Allen, head doctor here. You can call me simply Dr. Allen. We'll start with the routine information and get you admitted."

He worked through a series of questions—name, sex, age, hair color—as if I'd be an inmate here long enough to need a record.

"Living conditions?"

I looked about the place with a grimace. "Deplorable."

"At home, that is."

"Lovely." My voice took on a tone as distant as my normal life.

"Parents' mental state?"

"Quite at peace in their graves."

Something twitched on the lips beneath his beard.

"Siblings similarly afflicted with—?"

"None."

"Other relatives?"

"Deceased."

He jotted. It didn't take long, for the entirety of my family could be summed up in one word: *dead*.

He blinked at me. "Forgive me, but who *did* you stay with, then?"

"A friend of the family." How did one sum up Marcel Beauchene in a word? Mad scientist? No, that was two. Perhaps just mad. Erratic. Busy.

No . . . Guardian.

Guardian.

Hope lit inside me. "Actually, if you would send word to—"

"Your presence here is of no concern to anyone outside the asylum. It's a private matter."

"Let me write him, then. He'll—"

"Out of the question. We don't allow contact with friends or relations—it's bound to excite, and we can't have that, can we?"

No letters. No contact. He scribbled a bit more as I began to sense the quicksand onto which I'd stepped, drawing me into a pit I would not escape without a fight.

Very well, then. I knew how to do battle.

"Occupation—none, I assume?"

I edged my chin up. "I am a concert pianist."

He sat back with a steady gaze upon me. "I'll warn you, we don't indulge delusions at this institution."

"I'm not delusional."

His look of pity soured my belly. "Then let's talk about your true occupation, shall we?"

"How, pray, can you possibly know that I'm not what I say?"

He took my hand and I snatched it away, holding it close. With a firm look he took it again, pulling it away from my body with gentle tugs and turning it, palm up, to touch indents on my fingertips. "Calluses. Signs of hard, physical work. If I were to guess, I'd say you work at a loom. I've seen similar indentations on other patients. And there has been a girl missing from the looms over Menston way."

My upper lip trembled as I stared at my empty hand, clouds of drugged confusion clogging my brain. Yet I remembered playing the *pianoforte*. Remembered the music that had gently worked its way into the fibers of my muscles and lay like silk upon my skin. It belonged to me, the one and only gift my father gave me. It had burrowed in too deep, and this Dr. Allen could not take it. No, I was a pianist and I could hum nearly thirty pieces in my head, note by note, after playing them so many times.

Or . . . had I merely *heard* them? I'd always had such vivid dreams. My skin chilled with sweat. I stared at the red indents on my fingers and remembered the beautiful sounds, pausing to listen, especially at night when I had trouble sleeping. It always had an arresting effect, drowning out whatever troubled me. The melodies would come from distant parts of the house, balming my heart. Someone else had been playing. My father—he had played, and his students, too. And me—did I play? The questions tortured my foggy mind.

The doctor set my limp hand back on my thigh and his face folded in gentle pity. "We're here to help you, Miss Mourdant. Institutions aren't what they used to be, and I'm not your enemy. Just remember that."

I tucked my cold hand against my body.

He put down his paper and peered into my eyes with another

tool, his fingers so close I caught their metallic scent, but his touch was a hair kinder, more tender. "Now. Had your mother any mental afflictions?"

"I don't know." A powerful weakness swept through my middle at the mention of her, leaving me breathless. I knew hardly anything about my mother, other than the very sacredness of her name. *Helena Garley Mourdant.* It was that way whenever anyone spoke of her around me, except Father. He never spoke of her at all. I shivered.

"What name was given—the person who brought me?"

He edged his papers closer to his chest and snapped his bag shut. "I'm afraid that's confidential. Surely there are several people in your life who are aware of your . . . afflictions."

Or who despise me enough to send me here. Lately there had been plenty. I felt the weight of fear. Tension. I closed my eyes and allowed my mind to drift, collecting the scattered images of everything that had happened just before coming here. There had been a sophisticated gathering, a glittering parlor, a glorious mahogany Erard with keys like matched pearls and a sound like liquid glass. But who . . . ?

"Well, now that you've given up your hope of escape . . ."

I lifted my gaze to the doctor. Had I? Would I ever?

"Perhaps I can have a nurse show you to your new ward." He rose on stiff legs with a grimace and shifted to relieve some unseen pain.

"I won't be staying." My voice was tight.

His was sickeningly placid. "I'm afraid that's not up to you. But you will receive the treatment you need here. Unlike the medieval methods of the past, we employ Tuke's Moral Treatment here—plain food, hard work, a clean atmosphere."

"When will you evaluate me again, then?"

He straightened the cravat straining to encircle his neck, his face pained. "There are hundreds of patients in this institution, Miss Mourdant, and we are painfully understaffed at the moment. You cannot expect me to personally attend you on a regular basis."

My eyes were dry. Fixed. "*When?*"

He adjusted his suit jacket with his free hand. "I always aim for an annual consult with each patient."

A whole year. I swallowed the bitter news, shaky hand shoving hair off my face, and tried not to weep. I had a calendar at home with the twenty-fourth circled in red. *Vienna*, it said, and it was important. The specifics escaped me, but I could picture that date and knew I had to be released by then. Had to resume my life. Hundreds of desperate women—I could see their faces—depended on me. For what, I couldn't say exactly. But I had to go, had to keep their secret, had to help them. Vienna on the twenty-fourth, all those women.

Why wouldn't my heart stop racing? It was outpacing my thoughts. My lungs felt hollow. Breathless. My life had been interrupted, stolen from me, so many strings left hanging, but it deserved to continue. *Needed* to. It was a good life—happy and purposeful. Freedom was still a sweet taste on my tongue and I wasn't ready to give it up.

"Ready?"

My gaze shot to him. I rose, demeanor eerily calm. "Yes. Quite." I smoothed the rumpled blanket over the cot where I'd lain.

He clutched his bag and papers, but paused as he reached for the door. "There's always the possibility of a checkout, I suppose, too. That would be the only other way you could leave."

"Yes, please. I'll do that, please." I clutched the oversized garment around me. All my nervous energy swirled and gathered into one sharp point.

He gave a soft chuckle, a vaguely condescending look. "Not by you, Miss Mourdant. By the person who checked you in."

Panic clawed at my throat, urged me to lunge for those papers against his chest. Whose name was on them? Who held such control over my life? I had enemies—faint memories soured my stomach even as the names and faces feathered into oblivion in my brain.

He pulled me out into the hall where the air flowed free and clean by comparison, pouring into my lungs and disturbing the fog around my mind. I felt stronger. More clear.

The doctor waved over a nurse in a long gray uniform and white apron as I continued to drink in lungfuls of air. The woman's face as she approached resembled the worn-out blankets on my cot—thin and discolored, with every inch put to use until it was threadbare. "Nurse Duffy, prepare this woman for her stay, if you would. Dresses and the like, whatever she'll need."

"Of course, Doctor." She dipped a curtsy as the doctor disappeared into the dimness, and I glanced about, mind and limb pulsing with awareness. Long dark hall, rows of wooden doors, and open stairs descending behind us.

Stairs! Wide, inviting stairs led down into some well-lit area below. I had no idea who had done this, or if I even belonged here, but one thing was certain—I'd never learn the truth in here.

"You heard what he said. Now start moving, will you?" She poked me in the back. "Down the hall and to the left."

Moving forward on limbs of jelly, I reluctantly walked away from those stairs. Distant cooing sounds echoed about the walls.

Birds? No, voices. Residents. Humans. Short little screeches followed, and those echoed.

I shivered, and looked about. I must be ready to sprint back to those stairs at the first opportunity so I noticed things—the arched doors with heavy metal locks, the raftered ceiling, two high barred windows at the end. A longer hall stretched off to the right with angel statues recessed into thick stone walls and hanging chandeliers that were only half lit. As we paced through the corridors, each step cleared my head as if I were emerging from a dense fog.

The woman paused at a narrow linen closet and rummaged about inside, and in the quiet I was seized with a sudden urgency. A free-falling sense of needing to escape.

I'd done this before. Escaped, that is. I couldn't place my finger on when, but I had. I could again. Heart thudding, I took one silent step back, laying my foot down toes first and rolling onto my heel.

"Don't even try it."

I froze and she spun back to me with a wary look. She looked only about thirty, but judging by her pallor, she'd been a prisoner in this place far too long. She tossed me a faded gray gown of the same coarse material I already wore, but with more yellowed stains on it. "There's underthings tucked inside. Now, this way."

I followed obediently, but my rebel eyes cast about, judging the height of the small windows set way up in the wall, the possible value of a little statue as a weapon. Was it attached to its stand?

Down a narrow, squared staircase, the constrictive passageway suddenly released into a wide, pillared area with heavy red rugs over tile floors. We approached a tall window and it was dark—too dark to see outside, as if nothing beyond this dungeon of a place existed. Then I caught sight of a woman's sodden face and limp hair reflected in the windowpane, eyes wild and hollow. Her dark auburn hair was the very same as mine and her features similar, only this woman—well, she looked quite mad.

Until now, I'd been floating above the experience with disbelief, waiting for someone to spring out from behind a crate and announce his joke. Waiting for the rescue to come. Waiting to realize the obvious explanation for all of this. Waiting to wake from this odd dream that was surely happening to someone else. That wan face in the window—that wasn't mine. *You poor dear.*

But with each step through the cool openness, I realized it was *my* face that looked so crazed, and it matched my stomach folding in half with hunger. "When will I be able to eat?"

"Breakfast is at six."

"How . . . how many . . ." I took a breath. "How long have I been here?"

"About four days."

"And I've had nothing to—"

She spun on me. "See here, you're in a charity place, and you'd best be grateful. I've no time to fetch you dinner, unless you'd like to be the one to clean up the vomit on the third floor and the chamber pots in the infirmary. That's what you're keeping me from now." She sunk her fingers into the flesh of my arm and propelled me forward with a longsuffering sigh. "The absurdity."

We paused before a cluttered, oversized kitchen and she released my arm. "This is likely where they'll put you, unless you don't behave. Then it'll be the slop work or cleaning the slaughterhouse."

"They have one of those?"

"Hurstwell takes care of itself. Everything done right here on the grounds, from the meat to the dairy and the farming. Even the graves are dug by the men in the west wing."

"*Graves?*" Perhaps they simply dug them for a local cemetery. A parish service to earn their keep.

In answer, she grabbed me by both arms and led me down another hall and jabbed one long finger at the window. In the bleak lantern light of the barn, stones rose and fell like crooked teeth protruding from the rolling green hills that stretched forever. Absolutely forever. There must have been hundreds. "Got to have somewhere to put the bodies, don't we?" Every breath of her voice strained with annoyance.

I put a hand to my pounding head as a memory surfaced, sharp and fresh. It was a man's voice making a joke—I hadn't understood it at the time. "You know what they say about the asylum—anyone who leaves hasn't far to go." Laughter. Had I joined in? Blood pounded through my skull.

My gaze connected to that window as we moved on and refused to budge. My heart drummed out a rhythm of fear, a desperate sonata, and I closed my eyes, fingers naturally curving into position. Yes, I played. I played the piano, and I did it well.

I didn't belong here. They were wrong. That date on the calendar, it was for a concert. Mine. I had to rehearse and focus and prepare, with only a handful of days left. I'd lost four to this place, which meant. . . .

The twenty-second. It was already the twenty-second, and I must be on a train by morning—early tomorrow morning—if I had any hope of Vienna. I *had* to reach the station. I had to play, had to be paid. People were depending on me, on the wages

I brought in. On this performance. Yet I was stuck, worthless and alone, in this place where I couldn't even help myself.

We stepped back into that opulent front hall obviously meant to receive guests, and all I saw was one front door standing open. A man—a liveried hand of some sort—frowned in the doorway as he looked out into the night where tiny stars pricked the sky and a man struggled toward the door under the burden of several crates. Lanterns hung along the drive like arrows lighting the path to freedom, but the rest of the world was dark. I didn't mind. Let the dark swallow me, for it couldn't be worse than this place.

Silently I clutched a heavy candlestick, the only object around that would make a nice distracting clunk when I threw it down the opposite hall, and let it hang in the folds of my gown. I gripped it tight, watching that door, that oblivious footman. There were ten paces between me and the outside world. Eight steps. Now six. Time slowed, focus narrowed on that door. I held that candlestick tighter and wondered, in a tilt of vertigo, if I'd be desperate enough to use it as a weapon.

With only two steps between me and freedom, my fear lifted and I saw only hope and necessity.

Acknowledgments

*L*eave it to God to make something out of nothing—which is what he does with every book I write. I thoroughly enjoy the time spent together on these projects.

With each book, I grow increasingly thankful for readers too. It still astounds me that people I've never met want to read the stories I come up with in my little rocking chair. I've loved getting to know many of you, praying for you and connecting through a love of books and God. Thank you, thank you, for taking time to read the stories authors enjoy writing!

I owe a lot of the heart behind this story to the brilliant dance company Ballet Magnificat! My daughter and I attended a show in Chicago while I researched this book, and that night was a breakthrough and a heart refreshment. I finally understood what it meant to praise God through ballet by experiencing their performance. The dancers, producers, and everyone behind this company—your combined artistry inspired me more than you'll ever know. Please continue ushering audiences into worship.

I'm always in awe of my publishers and the way they come

around a book—before it's even turned in to them. Their support is priceless to me.

My dad truly comes up with some of the best plot twists, and I'm so grateful for his insights into my books. He always gets me thinking when I'm at a brick wall, and I love talking stories with him.

Susan Tuttle is my ever-gracious sounding board as well, who reads my books when they're terrible and somehow still makes me feel excited about them. Thank you for helping me make this story better, and reading it when it was a terrible first draft.

There are several local friends who have become unabashed cheerleaders and encouragers, and I don't know how I'd manage without them. Olivia, your insights and help were invaluable! Rachel and Angie, your enthusiasm kept me going, especially in this book. It was hard to write, but your excitement for this hero and story kept me on track and meant so much to me. Thank you for reading so many rough drafts and being excited about every last one.

I also sent a terrible first draft to Allen Arnold, who brought out hidden nuances I hadn't even noticed, helping me reshape the messy draft into something worth reading. Thank you for investing in this project.

I'm also grateful to the late dance historian Ivor Guest for his intelligent, exhaustive books on romantic-era ballet and all the dancers involved. His work was invaluable in my understanding of Victorian ballet.

Joanna Davidson Politano is the award-winning author of *Lady Jayne Disappears*, *A Rumored Fortune*, and *Finding Lady Enderly*. She loves tales that capture the colorful, exquisite details in ordinary lives and is eager to hear anyone's story. She lives with her husband and their children in a house in the woods near Lake Michigan. You can find her at *www.JDPStories.com*.

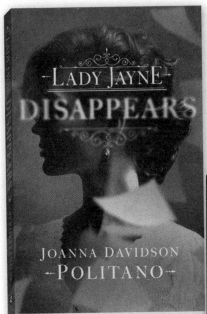
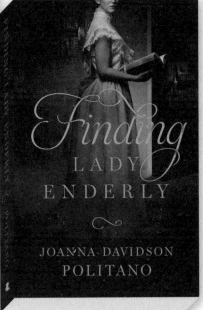

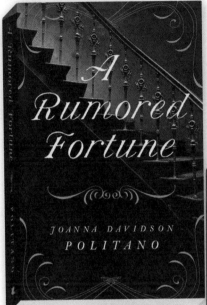
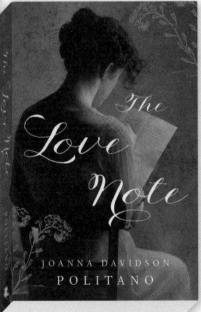

— MEET —
JOANNA

JDPStories.com

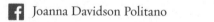 Joanna Davidson Politano    @politano_joanna